The Killing Flower

The

Killing Flower

W.K. Dwyer

Published by Jannicke Blomst
P.O. Box 2044, Springfield, VA 22152
© 2016 W.K. Dwyer

ISBN 978-0-9977383-0-8

Editing: Katherine Pickett, Christina M. Frey
Proofreading: Lori Paximadis
Cover art: Carlton Tomlin
Book design: Amber Morena

http://www.killingflower.com/

To the John Humes of this world, who get it: listen to the Bloody Sundays and respond only with Good Fridays

The Killing Flower

Prologue

F unny. Of all the times in my life I'd asked God to turn back the clock, the one time I didn't was right after 9/11, and that was what put it all in motion. That's what led me to the little girl, and she set the stage for it to happen.

Of course I could have asked him, easily. Sitting in the horror and desperation, I could have cried out as I had so many times, praying and pleading: *Please, make it all go away, go back and erase the past. And not just for me this time, for all of us.* But he wouldn't have listened. He never had. All my life I'd lived that delusion: I was special. Precious in his sight. Precious enough to be saved, rescued, even raised from the dead if needed. We were *all* special, entitled, exceptional. In our darkest hours, we could use our own personal God hotline, and he would actually answer the phone and get on it, take care of things.

But it didn't happen. He never protected me. And he didn't protect us that day. So that September morning, something finally snapped inside me. I stopped asking him for anything and just started doing it myself. I threw away my plans for college. I set my sights on joining up. I was going to change the world. I was going to fix things he obviously didn't care about; I was going to prevent the next one. And that is just what happened. I don't know exactly how, because it involved some bizarre relativity shit I will never understand, but it happened, believe me. My friend and I saw proof.

T he first time I asked God to erase the past, I was thirteen. My best friend, Joshua, had talked me into joining his church missions group, and we spent a summer in Brazil, trying to sell Jesus to some of the poorest people in the Amazon region. "You're Episcopalian," he said, smiling, "but that's okay, we won't tell anyone," and he gave me a wink. The only reason I had even been interested was that I thought the word *missionary* meant something like Indiana Jones—exploring, hacking through jungles with a machete, stumbling upon ancient ruins, discovering the Ark of the Covenant. Instead, all we did was lay bricks in unbearable heat and humidity, go to prayer rallies, and pile into buses, clapping and singing songs on our way to tiny villages so we could "witness," which made me feel weird and uncomfortable.

It was my third week there. The airline had lost my duffel bag with all my clothes and supplies, so I had spent most of my money replacing them. One of the counselors had put me on toilet detail for sleeping during devotionals (I swear I was praying). Then I'd caught a horrible stomach virus. Plus, I'd just gotten into a huge fight with Joshua after he warned me to stay clear of my uncle because it was scientifically proven that all gays were pedophiles. That was the day I decided I wanted to leave, the same day my mom dropped the nuke on me in the form of a letter.

I lay in my hammock, opening the handmade paper envelope, and began to read. I could practically hear her sweet, lilting voice as she told me how proud she was of me for going to Brazil to help others, how she admired my courage, how amazed she was I was "so grown-up already," reminding me for the millionth time I was the best Mother's Day gift she could have ever, ever, ever asked for. But as I read on, I realized she had begun to talk about something else, something about our family, about me not worrying, keeping my chin up, even remembering that "God will take care of you no matter what happens, isn't that right, son?" She talked about how my sisters and I would all be okay, and "Aren't we such survivors, son?" I knew at once things must have gotten even worse at home. Whenever she talked to us about how firm and imperishable our family was, all I heard was a low, disquieting rumble.

I knew what was coming, but at the same time, I didn't. There was no way to imagine it, no way to prepare myself. When I got to the word *divorce*, something collapsed inside of me. I went numb, motionless, staring at the paper and Mom's cursive handwriting, noticing where she'd traced over certain words, made black smudges with the felt tip. My eyes skipped down toward the bottom of the page. The phrase "your father and I"—I sat and stared at that phrase.

It was the end of God caring about me. It was the end of the blessing of our wonderfully perfect, loving family. Gone was the last bit of security my parents could offer me. Gone was the sweet, lilting voice, buried beneath the roar of things crashing. I took her letter and ran out toward the revival center, knelt, and prayed: *Dear God, make it not true. Reverse everything; let me go back and do this over. I won't go to Brazil. I'll say no to Joshua. I'll tell him it's wrong to go to poor countries and preach to them like they are bad people, try to save them when they didn't ask to be rescued. I'll tell him it's wrong for us to think we are better, more Christian, the superior, enlightened ones who can force our beliefs on others. I won't go, I promise. Please, please, God, send me back.*

And I prayed like that. Every day. For weeks. I even went to Joshua in desperation, and he reassured me, said the Lord was omnipotent. So I kept praying, kept praying: *God, dear God, all-powerful God, turn back the clock.*

Well, of course I got no response, and the worst thing that *could* happen actually went on happening, tra-la-la. God's in his heaven, as they say. And it was no different from the other times in my life I asked him to make it all go away.

But 9/11, that's when everything changed. That's when I finally said no, I'm done with this shit. To hell with praying, to hell with begging, asking for mercy. In fact, fuck that nonsense—believing someone's out there listening, requesting shit and getting no answer whatsoever. I'm done knocking on doors when the house is empty. I'm not a kid anymore, I don't need Mommy or Daddy or anyone. I can do this myself.

And that's what happened. Well, kind of. See, it's not that this story is about how things were so different. It's about how they were so very much the same. In fact, the following story is a reprise.

Iraq, 2006

When we were in Anbar we used to call it "doing crack"—going on patrols into the city to draw out insurgent attacks, roaring down streets in our Humvees, laying down some serious fire on bad guys lurking in buildings or crouched behind walls, wielding RPGs. It was an incredible rush just knowing a firefight could happen at any moment. And when it did happen, fuck. It was like the coolest video game you could imagine—looking down the thumping barrel of a .50-caliber M2 machine gun, red and black smoke, dust and shit flying everywhere. Calling in for fire support and watching one of those A-10 Warthogs whoosh across forty feet off the deck and blow the ever-loving shit out of a building. Oh my God, it was just fucking bizarre how cool it made you feel.

When I was five I loved to play Transformers: Autobots battling the evil, weaker, kinda stupid Decepticons. I'd spend hours building up some ridiculously humongous base of operations for the bad guys, using all my old crap left over from Microman, and then assemble the Autobots' forces about ten times as big, with all the cool vehicles with laser cannons, ion shields, nuclear warheads. And after all that elaborate setup, I'd have this mondo epic battle scene, and it took about two minutes to completely obliterate the Decepticons and their whole operation.

Yeah, Iraq was pretty much like that. We had all the cool toys. Bad guys had nothing. They drove around in their busted-out Toyotas—"jingle trucks," we called 'em—scurried around in bathrobes, holding antique AK-47s. Behind walls, on rooftops, crouched in some shop doorway, who knows. You couldn't see 'em half the time. They were just some amorphous, undefined . . . *thing*. And as long as you couldn't actually *see* anyone get waxed, and of course as long as none of them actually took out any of us, blowing the shit out of cars and buildings where the little fuckers were hiding made you feel giddy as hell. Giggle factor was way off the charts.

That's how it began, the first real day of the war for me. Tearing through city streets in a Humvee, everybody in the squad all pumped up, me sitting up in the turret, firing off rounds like I had lost my fucking mind. Radio chatter, the constant clamor of orders being yelled, external loudspeakers blaring that song by Drowning Pool: "Let the bodies hit the floor, let the bodies hit the floor . . ." It was three weeks into my first tour; we were finally, actually *doing* something.

My main man was Ethan, my best friend from high school, who'd joined up with me. Smart as hell, read quantum physics in his spare time, eidetic memory—one of those guys who are not so much nerdy as just unassumingly brilliant. But he was a total anomaly: grew up in the sticks of southeast Tennessee, home of the quintessential hayseed, yet he went to an all-boys private prep school, where we met in eighth grade, and scored a fuckin' genius on the Mensa test. Then again, you would have no idea by looking at him. He wasn't exactly Ed Grimley, with the greasy hair and pants up to his chest. He actually looked remarkably like Nicolas Cage: rugged features, solid jawline, lean, muscular frame. Did free-climbing and parkour for the hell of it and was pretty damn good. He could also rattle off NASCAR stats and knew all about deep-frying candy bars. So the idiots in the platoon, the guys with barely two rocks in their fuckin' skulls, might normally try to say, "All you gots is book learnin'," but not to Ethan. They couldn't touch Ethan.

Our rifle squad was kind of small. Two fire teams plus Staff Sergeant Huey, our squad leader. He was awesome. An older guy on his third tour in OIF/OEF, he knew what made a good soldier, and he totally believed in us. He set a great example, pushed us to excel, and spent a lot of time with us individually, honing our skills. He was also extremely funny, pulling pranks and shit, which kind of threw me at first, but I soon realized it was intentional. He did it for morale, to keep our sanity.

I didn't know the other guys in the unit, really. Except PFC Ma-

seth. He was by far the craziest motherfucker we had. He had this total country-boy southern drawl, talked slowly, with sarcasm in every
word. He clowned around constantly. From the very first mission I
was on with him, he'd do this stand-up thing, trying to crack everybody up. He had gotten the dead lowest score on the marksman test,
didn't give a shit, and was also known for sleeping when he should
have been out on missions. We met him on our first bivouac in basic
training, where we were supposed to be all roughing it, surviving off
dirt and rainwater for days on end. The first morning, we look over,
and there is Bryan Maseth in his tent with a frickin' box of Cookie
Crisp cereal. From then on we painted this caricature of him in this
plush family-sized tent with a sixties-style waterbed and a beer cooler,
watching HDTV. It was funny as hell. We were so brutal, even with
the commanding officers.

There was Specialist Christopher Thiessen, a tall second-generation
Greek guy who seemed to talk about money a lot, and there was a
Hispanic dude, Barco, who was in the same team as Christopher.
Then there was Terrell Walker. He was the grunt Maseth seemed to
hang out with most. Short, stocky, jet-black skin, a big, wide nose and
"what the fuck you lookin' at" eyes. Reminded me of that actor Ving
Rhames from *Pulp Fiction*. He listened to a lot of Public Enemy and
rap metal. My first impression: thug. Seemed like he was just itching
for a reason to start some shit with other soldiers, especially if you was
whitey.

Then there was me, Mr. Higher Purpose. They'd already started
tagging me as the spoiled rich kid just 'cause I had a few T-shirts from
Diesel and an Alessi espresso maker. I was hoping that didn't stick. I
needed to blend in, to go kind of unnoticed for now. I had reasons to
be there others didn't, ideas I had to keep to myself. They wouldn't get
it. Not like some secret plot or anything; I just knew I'd be playing a
lead role. Which part exactly, what lines, I wasn't sure. But I had the
big poster taped up over my bunk, the one with the graphic of 9/11,
The Falling Man. The one Sergeant Huey said was a little disturbing.
"Yeah . . . ," I said, wanting to explain. But it would have been too
soon. First I had to show them I wasn't just some sheltered, oversen-
sitive, fragile motherfucker who couldn't handle war. *Fuck that. I got*

through my nightmare childhood; I doubt any of these punks could survive the shit I've seen. But that was actually a good thing; it was exactly what made me stronger. Because when things got bad, the guys would need someone to bolster them, to show them how to deal with emotional trauma, to survive mentally, not just physically. No one ever protected me—not God, and definitely not my parents . . . hell, if anything, *they* were the ones bleeding out. Well, I wasn't my dad and I wasn't my mom. And I sure as hell wasn't going to repeat their mistakes. I was better than that.

M ost times Ethan and I would be in the same Humvee, bumping down back alleyways on some routine daytime mission, in full battle gear and sweating our asses off. It was so hot, so incredibly hot. Together with all the palm trees and sand, it reminded me of days at the beach in midsummer, when the air just sat and stuck to you, the blistering sun made it impossible to see, and you couldn't walk five steps without burning the shit out of your bare feet. Every day in Iraq was like that, as far as I could tell—the beach, plus mortar rounds and IEDs.

But a lot of times Ethan seemed to be the guru. Like the cool older brother—reserved, yet comfortable sharing his knowledge. Guys in the squad were always asking him about shit they should have known from their OPSEC training, or daring him to do some jackass stunt. He'd usually do it, too. It seemed like he obliged them more for the sake of their education than anything else. One time we were stopped on the road, getting some chow, and one of the guys found this vicious-looking scorpion crawling next to the Humvee. Ethan went over and started messing with it. Whoever was on security detail yelled down from the top, "Coffelt, that's a fucking scorpion. Cease and desist the hell away from that fucker!"

Ethan bent down to look closer. We started to gather around, getting all excited and goofy. Walker peered in to see, lifting his shades. "Oh snap, you mean *dass* the kind o' shit crawling around this muhfucker?"

Ethan grabbed a stick and bent the curled tail down until it was straight, and the guys seemed to go nuts. Sergeant Huey heard the yelling and came over. I thought he'd bark out some order, but before he could say anything, Ethan had picked the damn thing up by the back with his two fingers.

"You fools," he said, holding it up with a deadpan look on his face, "no telson! It can't sting without a telson," and he pointed at its tail end.

I looked closer at it, just as amused and curious as the other guys, and sure enough, it looked like the stinger had been cut off by something. *How the hell does he know what a telson looks like? Jesus.* Ethan was like a walking Wikipedia.

Cookie Crisp was taking a bite of his burrito rations and giggling so hard he was almost choking. "Holy shit, Cockfelt, you are fuckin' *insane!*" he said in his wry southern drawl. I was just about to ask Ethan if he was some kind of damn arachnid expert, when the scorpion all of a sudden clamped the shit out of his finger.

"Fuck me running!" Ethan shouted, flipping his hand wildly to shake it loose.

Everyone just about wet themselves, they were laughing so hard. Maseth spit a mouthful of burrito onto the sand and ran up to Sergeant Huey to slap him high five. *"Jackass: Iraq,* baby! . . . now in theaters!" he said in hysterics.

There was one day, though, that stood out amid all the ridiculousness. It was my first exposure to a casualty, at least one close enough to touch. I woke that morning to thundering classical music coming from Ethan's iPod. I rolled over to see him standing next to his bunk, wearing only his ACU shorts, waving his right arm like a conductor.

"Dear *Gott im Himmel!*" I moaned, rolling over to check the time. "It's fuckin' seven o'clock, and it's our day off."

"Oh, come on," he said. "All the more reason for 'Ride of the Valkyries'!"

I dragged myself up, walked to our makeshift kitchenette, and started some espresso, then grabbed a towel and walked next door to the showers. When I got back, Ethan had put on some camo pants and his favorite T-shirt: "Operation Iraqi Liberation." He was pouring a cup and had lit up a cigarette.

"I can't wait to see you try and explain that shirt to the colonel," I said.

He feigned seriousness. "Sir, I apologize. I honestly never noticed it spelled out O.I.L."

"Cute," I said, pulling on some shorts. "That's really gonna help morale around here."

We shot back our espressos, then swung by the PO at the plaza, and they said I had something from stateside. It was a letter from my grandmother. Ethan stood outside and waited for me, checking out a memorial plaque they'd put up recently. I put the letter in my ruck, and we walked down to the DFAC tent to get some chow. We sat at the same spot as always, directly to the left as you walked through the huge tent flaps, all the way down in the corner. Fewer dickheads making noise around you, and near enough to the exit but without the traffic. Ethan had gotten quiet since the PO. Just sat and ate his scrambled liquid eggs and slurped down his soda. Must have said two words, except for this Nobel Prize–winning burp that sounded like you could sing "The Star-Spangled Banner" to it. We looked at each other and laughed, which gave me the go-ahead. I mustered up my best Russian accent. "Vot is on mind, Comrade Koffeltski?"

He looked up at me, squeezed out a smile. "'Nother damn day in the suck," he said.

I thought his tone sounded fatalistic. "Yep. Gotta git them terrists!" I said, mocking Dubya. "No, but seriously, isn't it weird, everybody's so fucking gung-ho—they get here itching to jump into major combat, kill some hajjis, all that—then we sit around half the time doing absolutely nothing? It's like, 'Congrats on your combat training, loser. Now take this can of kerosene and go burn another fifty-five-gallon drum full of shit.' And then one day, out of the fuckin' blue, 'Ready up, Joes! Shitstorm of insurgent activity. Time to go do some more crack!'"

Ethan gave me a yeah and kept eating. Suddenly I felt like a presumptive jerk for going on about something that probably wasn't even on his radar. Something *was* on his mind, though. I thought maybe I should ask him. *Gotta keep the morale up, keep everyone focused.* That's what Sergeant Huey would do.

I swear, the exact second that thought came into my mind, the table jumped up about three feet as a huge explosion blew us against the side of the tent.

"Holy fuck!" I heard Ethan shout. Coke had spilled on his face and all down the front of his T-shirt.

I looked to my left, and there was a wall of gray-and-black smoke filling up the back of the tent. It was billowing up and flowing over the chow line from the kitchen. I heard a couple of muffled voices shouting something, but for the first thirty seconds it seemed strangely quiet. Chairs were turned over near us, food was spilled everywhere, and guys were standing up and looking around. A soldier walked into the entrance and shouted, "Mortar round!" and began guiding everyone out. Ethan and I walked toward the main aisle to make our way to the blast area as several contractors ran past us, almost knocking us over. Goddamn, it was as if they were in a sniper's crosshairs or something. These were the type of idiots we laughed at, always running from these mortar rounds, like it did any damn good—panicking, pushing their way through, possibly causing a stampede, as opposed to actually helping the situation. Essentially they were trying to run away from lightning. So annoying.

"Running does nothing," Ethan said loudly, scolding a guy in a suit stumbling his way through the exit of the tent, with his tie all crooked. Outside I could hear the siren begin blaring over the loudspeakers, signaling everyone to get to concrete shelters.

As we entered the kitchen area, we could see a little more as the smoke moved above us: trays all over the ground, soup pots spilled onto a pile of knives. First person I saw was a third-party national—looked Pakistani—squished in the middle of the doorway with his head turned sideways against the frame. Blood was all over his apron, and he was moaning things in Arabic. It looked like he had a piece of a saucepan or some kind of shrapnel stuck in his chest. One PFC was leaning over him, yelling out for a dressing. Ethan and I dumped out our packs and handed him what we had, then helped pull the guy out of the doorway while holding his neck stable. I sat down cross-legged and started applying pressure where I could. "*Lah za,*" I said—"just a minute"—and then "It will be okay."

Ethan looked at me. "Jesus, you sound fluent already."

"I wish," I said.

Ethan went to check the rest of the kitchen for more injured. Smoke was everywhere, and shit was just all over the fucking place. The floor looked like the edge of a city dump, where you can barely see through to the ground. I think I was even sitting on top of some plastic lids. I might have done something about it, but I was too busy noticing that my hands had been completely drenched in blood and thinking, *Damn, where else is this dude bleeding from?* It seemed like it took ten minutes for Ethan to get back, and he had this robotic expression on his face.

"Only one other guy in there. Very dead."

So that was Sunday. They had an announcement on Monday afternoon. Pakistani guy didn't make it. Massive internal bleeding. There wasn't even a ceremony, as far as we could tell. When we walked over to west FOB to do our PT, we noticed a game of football going on in the field beside the plaza. Ethan was pretty annoyed by the whole thing.

"Oh, that is just crazy fucked up," he said, motioning to the game. "If an infantryman loses his life in the line of duty, he gets a big, huge four-star general visit, twenty-one guns, speeches, medals, the works. Oh, but Habib the cook gets blown up stirring the beans? He gets a flyer. But is the game still on? Hell yeah!"

I thought of the cook's poor family back home, probably in some small village somewhere in the mountains, maybe an apartment in the city. "Yeah, and you think his wife will get the respectful knock on the door from an officer or chaplain?"

Ethan shook his head. "Exactly. Probably won't get jack shit. A letter at best, or a phone call, maybe. I can hear them now: 'Hello? Yes, Mrs. . . . uh . . . Ahmed . . . Mush-Take Butt-Karr?'"

I felt bad cracking up. "Jesus, dude, that is horrible." But I tried not to take what Ethan was saying too seriously. I mean, he *was* kidding. Goddamn. The army has some messed-up shit, but they wouldn't forget to honor the fallen.

I was exhausted from the trauma of the day before, so I tried to turn in early, but I couldn't sleep. I finally dozed off but woke at midnight, realizing I had forgotten about the letter from my grandmother Dottie. I pulled the envelope out of my bag and grabbed a mini Maglite, then sat against the cabinet and read.

> Hey Kiddo! Just thought I'd drop ya a line, let you know I'm thinkin about cha. Your mom drove me up to Chattanooga today for lunch, and I saw a recruitment office. I stopped an army Captain and told him about you, proudly. And the whole drive back to Dalton I kept thinking about you. As you know I'm not too happy with our President for this war—more like "invasion"—but I do support you all the way.

It struck me how meticulously she wrote: the neat cursive handwriting, with her *f*'s so ornate I could hardly decipher them. She was definitely old school. World War II era. I'd always respected her and Paw-Paw's views about war; they'd lived through a ton of them. I kept reading—damn thing was five pages—and was impressed how much she was following the action in Iraq: removing the Ba'ath party, reconstruction, some guy named Chalabi I'd never heard of. "Here is one absolutely horrible idea," she wrote. "Let the men forming the new government of an Arab nation all have names like Perle, Feith, Wurmser, and Wolfowitz . . . it's like a bar mitzvah! Is Bush *trying* to make these people angry?!" She talked about the history of the Mideast, President Carter, and Israel and Ariel Sharon unconditionally pulling out of the Gaza Strip; "God bless that man," she wrote. I read the rest of the letter, really amazed by how much she knew.

> As you know, kiddo, Granny Fricket's never shy about speaking up. So let me tell you something, Bush says all this stuff about freedom for the

Iraqi people. I can tell you that is a bald-faced lie, what they want is the opposite: more control. All they are doing with this war is smacking the Mid East around to get them to do what they want. It's that simple. Iraq had something America wanted, but Iraq wouldn't give it to us. So finally those architects devised a plan to get it, and now they're over there to take it by force. I know this is confusing. I tell you they are lying, but other people will tell you it is me who is being lied to. Well, you have to decide, and you are a smart cookie. So you take care of yourself, kiddo. I know your dad always wanted you to join, and I'm sure he's proud of you now. But take care of yourself, okay? Love ya bunches. Dottie.

She was right, my dad had always wanted me to join. Wouldn't shut up about it sometimes. And yes, he was happy I did, but not so much proud happy as self-satisfied happy. 'Cause I had done it on his terms. When *I* wanted to enlist my junior year, that was being "emotional" and "irresponsible." And when I forged the consent form and was going to do it anyway, he found out about it and stopped me. My reasons didn't impress him; so no, he wasn't proud. Ever since he and Mom divorced, it seemed like I was just one big disappointment to him. Like when he looked at me, all he saw was my mother, and she represented all that was wrong with America; if she was a spineless, head-in-the-clouds, sandal-wearin' liberal, then I must be too. The military was what I needed, but it was to straighten my ass out.

So Dottie was way off about that one. I sure as fuck didn't join up 'cause Dad wanted me to. It had nothing to do with straightening myself out—in fact, had nothing to do with me at all. The opposite. I was there to help others. To serve. It's called patriotism, Dad.

I woke up later than usual the next morning, only to discover I had a plastic bottle cap filled with sand stuck in my mouth. Huey, Maseth, and Walker must have decided it would be hilarious to sneak in and fuck with me just to see what I'd do. I guess I had been completely out, probably snoring with frickin' drool dripping off my lip, who knows. I kind of remember hearing snickers just as I was coming out of deep sleep, and some kind of disturbance of my body. I pulled the damn thing out of my mouth and sat up in my bed, sand going all over my chest. Ethan wasn't there. He must have been at the internet hut.

"Yeah, very funny, you f-tards. Hilarious," I said, spitting on the floor and wiping my mouth. As I did so, I noticed it was coming out green. *Fuck me, they put some kind of food coloring in my mouth.* Of course, this caused roaring laughter from everyone. I looked up to see Walker and Sergeant Huey standing above me in their boxers, giggling. Bryan was behind them, holding up his phone and taking a video. "You just got punk'd, bitch!" he said playfully.

But Walker was different. He stood there glaring at me with a subtle, disdainful smirk. *What's with the stupid gangsta look?* I thought. I'd come across a few of these guys. They joined up for no reason other than they were bored out of their fucking minds growing up in their pathetic hometowns, the type of place with like one and a half traffic lights and those sad little malls with the Tower Records and a Shakey's Pizza. Where everyone goes to either the one and only redneck bar or, if you're in the hood, the one and only seedy dance club, with their dumbass trucks or their stupid blinged-out rides and their bitches and hos. And they start fights. People like Walker are scary. They're the type who need to fuck with somebody once a day just to keep themselves breathing.

Walker didn't say one word to me, just turned to leave, shaking his head and laughing. Bryan put his phone down, and he and Huey grabbed me a few towels before slapping me on the back. "We make fine joke with you, yes? Ver' nice!" Bryan yelled with a rising and falling Borat accent, and they left.

A few days after that I saw exactly what I had known I'd be seeing sooner or later with Walker. We were on our way out of the main city, coming back to the FOB after a patrol, and just as we passed the very last intersection, this insurgent with a colored turban started firing at our vehicles from a building behind a food stand. Of course we were supposed to pursue these little shits, so we slammed on the brakes and started to turn down the street. Meanwhile, the gunner in the lead vehicle took the guy down with a quick, controlled burst. Mission accomplished? Oh, no. Next thing you know, Walker, who was in the bucket that day, swung the 240 around and started just fucking unloading on the entire area. I'm talking food stand, shops, cars, anyone and anything that were anywhere close to where that guy in the turban lay. Walker went completely Rambo for about twenty seconds. We sped off—I assume we didn't have intel on anything and had no idea what else might have been down that alley—and as we drove away I looked back through the palm trees and could see bodies lying in the dirt, bearded figures in those man-dresses bending over them, and one of those busted-out old red Corollas or something, totally cut to Swiss cheese from all the rounds, rolling slowly into one of the shop fronts, its driver slumped over the wheel.

N o one ever talked about that day. I don't know if it was because Walker was such a freak or what, or maybe it was just too fucked up or sick, what we had witnessed, but no one mentioned it. The CO didn't chew him out—nothing. It was like it never happened. But I kept thinking about Walker.

I heard from Maseth that he used to be in a platoon that was filled with hooah baby killers and had been on one mission that ended up being a huge bloodbath firefight, and Walker, for whatever reason, had not gotten a kill that day. Supposedly they never let him hear the end of it. So now I wondered if his entire goal in life was to get a high body count so nobody could call Terrell Walker a punk ass. I guess if you're the smallest black dude in the platoon and joined up maybe 'cause Momma didn't have no money fo' college . . . yeah, who knows. Hell, maybe he'd dealt with dumbass racist Iowa pricks all his life. But still. Walker was scary.

Ethan said he reminded him of a guy on our wrestling team at McCallie, Charles Key. Skinny little dude in a one-piece Lycra outfit. Ninety-nine percent muscle. "Remember how he'd glower at you through the two holes in that freaky medieval headgear?" he said. "All you could see were those deep-black eyes behind that little cage. Charley didn't just pin his opponents, he punished them."

The week after Walker's freak-out, Ethan and I got put on cordon and search, helping out with a different platoon. Sergeant Huey said Higher had relayed a FRAGO, so don't ask questions, 'cause they didn't explain shit to him. The first night, we were sent out at three in the morning to a house in the middle of nowhere, outside of Fallujah. The owner was supposedly running a little operation with his son, storing weapons. They told us it was a pretty sure thing. Ethan and I stayed up and played cards outside the trailer, waiting until we got the call to go out. He didn't seem too enthused.

"So you know about this little mission we're about to do, right?" he asked, laying a card down in the dim light.

"Uh, yeah. So?" I said, like, was there some kind of catch I was supposed to know about? I wasn't concerned, in fact was in kind of a goofy mood, so I didn't give a fuck.

"From what Dewango tells me, what happens is one of these local Sunni dudes gets pissed off at one of his neighbors, maybe he gets stiffed out of a goat, who knows."

Dewango—birth name, Brandon Delaney—was in one of our brother platoons. We knew him from basic. For some reason his last name was bastardized to "De-lame-o," "Debrainey," and about twelve other stupid renditions before "Deweenie" or "Dewango" stuck. For God's sake, I swear they spent more time trying to turn every guy's name into something phallic than they did worrying about getting shot or blown up.

"So the guy decides he's gonna get even, the asshole goes and tells our intel guys some elaborate story about how the other dude with the goat has a hidden room full of AKs or stolen cash, and bada bing, bada boom, we happily go and fuck the guy's place up."

Ethan then waxed into his Chris Rock accent. "Excep' fuh one leeeetle bitty detail . . . they ain't no damn guns!" He put down another card and took a puff off his Dunhill, then blew the smoke up above his head, keeping a straight face. I had to laugh. He had this look about him—very well aware he was funny, but enlightening you at the same time. Aloofness. A nonchalant wisdom about the world. Ask him anything, he seemed to just *get it*.

"Yeah, but any idea how many of these leads actually turn up anything?" I asked.

"No way to know. There are no numbers on it. But from what they say in Echo, maybe one in one hundred, one in two hundred if they're lucky."

I thought about the overall mission, what effect we were trying to have on these communities, our objectives. We hadn't been told anything about such things, simply that we'd raid this house or that. I could tell we were more than policing the area. We *were* the police . . . and the detective, the judge, the jury, and the executioner if need be. I didn't know if there was some bigger plan the military had that they weren't sharing with us, but I wished I knew, wished we'd been briefed, been trained. Because in my mind these were the kinds of missions we were here for.

"What's with the box of padlocks?" I asked.

Ethan gave me this raised-eyebrow glance. "Well, as I understand it, after we bust down their door, ransack their house, and find nothing, we'll turn to them and say, 'Oops, sorry about that,' and give them a padlock to lock their house to quote-unquote protect from thieves." He laughed sarcastically. "Or maybe from guys coming to take their goat back."

We played a few more hands, then I had him quiz me in Arabic phrases. An hour later we got the call to saddle up. About a dozen guys gathered at the motor pool. We loaded up into seven Humvees, activated our night vision goggles, and headed across town. The platoon leader was Lieutenant Gafni. I recognized him from somewhere but couldn't place it.

It was always an adjustment, switching to NVGs. The green, glowing images of the streets, the bright white of the lights, reflections off the eyes of dogs. Turned the experience into a surreal YouTube video: grainy, distorted. I felt like I needed to take them off to see the real world, the world where someone could be shooting at me. But way worse than that were the IEDs. Just knowing they were hidden all over the place—on the side of the road, in trash bags, inside dead animals, even buried under the pavement. Damn near impossible to find them in daylight, and no way in hell through fuzzy NVGs. I had a hard time making sense of the concept—how I supposedly could die any second yet kept living through each one. I stared through the windshield and focused on anything that looked out of place, turning my head to follow as it passed by, then turning back to scan for the next one.

At zero three thirty we arrived at the location, a small one-story concrete house with a tiny porch, which was just a cement slab with a wall around it, and an iron gate. Vehicles split off along different streets to set up a security perimeter. We stopped down the street and dismounted as all the dogs in the area began barking. We waited for the order, then moved quickly to offer at least some element of surprise; a couple guys took cover in front of the wall, while the rest of us pushed the gate open and gathered on the porch. Ethan and I were tasked to knock the door in. After two or three kicks the doorjamb broke around the lock, and we entered the main room of the house. Several of us switched on infrared headlamps, and circles of glow-in-the-dark green scanned the walls like searchlights: a painting of women at the market, a cheap tapestry above the couch, an open doorway to the back room. For the first few milliseconds the place seemed completely silent, completely empty, like a grayish-green cave.

We cleared the house quickly, mechanically splitting into groups of two, pointing our M4 rifles into doorways, peering into the empty kitchen, an empty room with a mat and a small lamp, and a tiny bathroom. I had just called out, "Kitchen clear!" when I heard Lieutenant Gafni yell something from the back door.

"Roof! On the roof!"

Ethan met up with me as I walked down the hall. A makeshift wooden stairway went along the back wall of the house. Soon as it was cleared, there must have been a half-dozen soldiers up the stairs, all of them with Maglites. When I got to the top I saw the family standing facing Gafni, their backs against the edge of the roof. Slim man in boxer shorts, dark beard. His wife right beside him, wearing nothing but a bedsheet, apparently, desperately adjusting it to make sure every inch of her skin was covered. A little boy about six and a tiny little girl clinging to her dad's leg. They looked fucking petrified. Gafni held at the top of the stairs, waving his arms frantically, yelling for us to stay back, and asking where the fuck was the terp. He had this ridiculous scowl. The other guys had already started snickering and getting all crude.

"Looks like Habib's got him some pussy tonight!" Dewango said.

"Damn, son. She a hot-ji, straight up," Walker said, smiling.

I kept my weapon on the father and switched off my night vision. We could see plenty now, with all the Maglites and the moon right above us.

Gafni was under orders to interrogate the guy, even though it was pretty clear to all of us there was nothing there. But Gafni didn't give a shit. When the terp arrived he barked out, motioning to the father, "Tell this motherfucker to come here."

The man took two careful steps forward, arms raised, and it was then I noticed a small bag hanging from his shoulder. From what I could tell it was a camera case, but why would he grab something like that at three in the morning? *No time to grab a robe for his wife, yet he just had to have his Nikon?* I kept the barrel pointed at his face as he moved slowly forward.

"Good enough!" Gafni yelled, and put his hand out like a traffic cop.

The guy took another step forward.

"Halt, motherfucker!" Gafni screamed at the top of his lungs.

He was a microsecond away from shooting this guy in the head. Luckily the interpreter stepped in and told the guy to stop, explaining quickly to Gafni that the hand signals are not the same in Iraq. "This means 'keep going' in Arabic."

"Do I look fucking Arabic? These fuckers should know our hand signals by now. Ask him what's in the bag," he barked at the interpreter.

The interpreter had a brief exchange with the man, who appeared to be getting more nervous and seemed reluctant to say. From what I could tell, he had asked several questions. Gafni didn't like it. We were told nothing about our interpreters. All we knew was they could be completely on our side, or then again, they could secretly wish death to America. We watched them like hawks.

"What the fuck did he say? . . . Why didn't he answer immediately?" Gafni had a look of fury on his face.

"He said he doesn't want to show it right here. He said it was personal."

Gafni yanked the bag off the guy's shoulder. "I'll show you fucking personal, you fucking hajji." He unzipped the main compartment and turned the bag upside down. Just as the contents poured out I saw a movement behind the man. I looked toward the mother just in time to see the little boy jump up on the wall and jump off the roof. I heard a thud and a scream of pain.

"Nobody fucking move!" Gafni yelled, looking around, then bending down to riffle through the stuff.

He pointed at Ethan and me. "You two get down there, make sure the kid doesn't leave."

We made our way down the steps and through the house and found the boy sitting near the front gate. He was moaning, holding his leg, which looked like it had a serious fracture. Ethan called in for a medic, and we waited. I tried to communicate with the kid, who looked like he thought I was going to break his other leg. I was able to get him to lie down and not move, saying, "It's okay" and "What's your name?" in Arabic to try to soothe him. I held his hand for a few minutes until Gafni and the others came downstairs. I didn't want that maniac to see me aiding Al-Qaida.

Gafni came stomping outside, pausing at the gate to look down at the boy. "Hajji Junior break his leg?" he asked, looking only at me.

"Probably a tibia, Lieutenant. Swelled up like a balloon."

Gafni paused for a moment and looked up at the interpreter, who was rushing out with the parents to check on the boy. "Tell them he'll be fine, medic's on the way, we'll take him to the hospital."

I moved out of the way as the mother burst into hysterics over her son. I glanced at the father, who stepped behind her and glared at me with eyelids half closed.

Lieutenant Gafni opened the gate and stormed out, letting it slam behind him. I took it this mission was being wrapped up, but I guess

Officer A-hole was just going to let us figure that out for ourselves. I stopped one of the NCOs walking out. "So what was in the guy's bag?"

"Photos of his wife, half naked." The guy laughed and rolled his eyes.

Un-fucking-believable.

On the drive back to the base, Ethan and I smoked cigarettes and stared at the darkness passing by. I wasn't paying much attention to the road, just following the lead truck in front of us, tuning out the radio chatter, processing what had just happened. It pissed me off; it was fucking embarrassing. *This is what cordon and searches are like? I* thought. *No way they're all like this. We're better than this. Gafni is just a bad apple.*

"Well, dude, another mission accomplished," Ethan said wryly, turning to look at the idiots in the backseat sleeping.

"Come on, man," I said.

"Dude, are you high? That was a complete disaster. Deweenie is gonna upload the After Action Report to the MFD—Mission Fuckup Database."

"Look, let's just hope these Iraqis understand we're trying to help them."

Ethan let out a laugh. "Pfft, oh, I'm sure with shitbags like Gafni, we'll be getting a dozen fuckin' roses delivered to us!"

I looked at Ethan and smiled. I couldn't help it. The way he said shit always tickled me. Didn't matter how serious, he just kept this deadpan look on his face, rattling off some sarcastic quip.

I didn't agree with him, but I didn't want to make more out of it than it was. Situations could get ridiculous. I knew that. But it was rare. And sometimes you gotta break some eggs, as they say. I think they even told us that in training. Sergeant Huey would agree.

But I thought about it and remembered where I'd seen Gafni. "Dude, tonight wasn't exactly my first time seeing Lieutenant Gafni in action."

"Oh really," Ethan said. "Do tell."

"A few weeks ago I was getting coffee at Joe-to-Go's, right?"

"Uh-huh, Joe-to-Blows—shittiest coffee ever. Continue."

"Right." I chuckled again. "So I pick up my espresso, walk over to get cream and sugar, and there's Gafni, standing, scowl on his face, waiting behind this dark-skinned dude who's doctoring his latte or something."

"Oh, this ought to be good," Ethan said.

"So two seconds later the guy for some reason backs out from the creamer station holding his super vente grande or whatever—huge cup—plus, the thing is like filled to the brim."

"No lid, I take it?" Ethan said.

"Right, he's got this damn supersize-me bucket o' coffee, no lid, and he either backs into Gafni, or Gafni moves forward, or something—a little of both, maybe—and they bump into each other."

I look over at Ethan lighting up another Dunhill.

"So next thing you know, Gafni lifts his arms up in the air with this aggressive 'what the fuck's *yer* problem' thing, and I look at the guy with the coffee. And Jesus, wouldn't you know, he's one of these TPNs working on base, looks *totally* muj."

"Oh God, here we go!" Ethan giggled, then launched into his famous deep-fried-in-sarcasm staccato voice. "Mister Goldstein, meet Mister Hussein!"

"Ha ha, exactly," I said, laughing. "So, dude, Gafni had this look on his face of pure fury, looked like he was going to drop-kick the guy into next Monday. He was fuckin' pissssed off."

"Damn, did they throw down?"

"God, almost. They exchanged some choice words. Gafni was like, '*I* bumped into *you*?' with his New York 'I shot the clerk?' inflection like in *My Cousin Vinny*. The TPN was like, 'I only take small step, you move also. And coffee spills only to me.' Well, they glared at each other for a minute, and then the TPN went to clean his shirt."

"Damn."

"But can you fucking believe that, dude? The Middle Eastern guy's coffee spilled only on *him*, not Gafni! Gafni didn't have a damned drop spilled on him."

Ethan shook his head and let out a puff. "Fucker's got issues."

"Oh! Plus, when the dude walked away? Gafni mumbles, 'Fucking Arab.'"

The Humvee in front of me slowed to turn right into the main gate. I could see sunlight starting to come over the Conexes behind the guard station as the soldier waved us on.

Just a bad apple, I thought. *No big deal.*

O n humid, sweltering days, when a breeze flowed over the sand and rustled the palm trees, an F-18 would swoosh over our heads, reminding me of the trips to Pensacola when I was young. Every summer we'd rent this three-level beach house on Santa Rosa Island. Right on the Gulf, it was the very last house built on the dunes. I have these sharp, lucid memories of the moments after we'd first arrive, pulling our Volvo station wagon into the carport underneath the house. The breeze would hit us as we opened the doors—that wonderful warmth and smell of salt and sand—and Dad and I would untie the ropes from the luggage rack as my sisters ran squealing up the spiral staircase to rediscover the rooms. "Oh, the suitcases can wait," Mom would tell Dad. Within minutes my older sister, Karen, would be out on the deck sunbathing, Alanis Morissette's *Jagged Little Pill* blaring through her headphones. I would take my first look out over the tall grass onto the bright white sand and hear the waves coming in, and soon I'd be out there with a skim board or building sand castles with my little sisters. I'd hear a roaring sound and jump up to watch five or six Blue Angels in formation streaking toward us, flying just above the water alongside the beach. I'd wave my arms in excitement.

We'd always plan to stay one week, but then Mom would guilt Dad into staying longer; it was almost an annual tradition with her. We could all miss the first week of school. No worries. Dad would have to ask Dr. Fletcher to cover his surgery cases again. Didn't matter. "Where's your joie de vivre?" Mom would say. With Mom, the sweetest moments in life somehow only came through thumbing your nose at being responsible and boring.

But the best part of those trips was when the Geislers would come—Mercer, his wife, Dreda, and their two kids, who were a year apart and the exact same ages as me and my younger sister Kelly. Old friends of my parents' from Dad's med school days, they had met up with us on summer vacations ever since I could remember. They'd always fly down from Memphis and stay with us. Had tons of money, but they absolutely could not have cared less. They'd bring us cool gifts they found in Switzerland. Dr. Geisler would take all seven kids—the five of us and two of his own—to the water park. He'd pick up a case of some weird imported beer, and the adults would plot ways to sneak it out to the beach. "You know the Netherlands is one of the happiest countries in the world?" he'd say. "And they work like twenty-five hours a week." Dr. Geisler was so fun. He'd be sitting at the table and would start twitching his face. Then Dad would join in; they'd groan and snarl at us, "Zombie need brains!" and chase us around the beach house. They were like family to us, like our very favorite aunt and uncle.

But Dr. Geisler was more than that; he was really good for my mom and dad. He seemed to transform them, to turn them into a couple again—not just parents—like I pictured they might have been long ago. He'd smile and ask them, "Well, so how are my favorite newlyweds?" and listen intently. Mom and Dad would hold hands, laugh, and tell a story about driving back from Dot and Paw-Paw's in their old Austin-Healey convertible and getting caught in a downpour. They'd look in each other's eyes and smile. Mercer would put on some eighties song like "Games Without Frontiers," and we'd laugh at the adults dancing. They'd let us stay up late while they mixed piña coladas and did tequila shots.

These were the images I most remembered, or tried to, for years. They were the ones that would correct the record, would someday be vindicated. They were an assurance. We were happy together and always would be. This was what we really were, the few rare glimpses of our perfect family. Evidence I should hold on to—and shred the rest—because it fit the fairy tale. I could rely on them—they lied to me.

The next few weeks after the Gafni incident we spent doing nighttime convoys from Ramadi to Fallujah and setting up flash checkpoints. We'd roll down dirt highways doing like Mach 3 in a Humvee in front of about six or seven KBR trucks full of toilet paper and plastic plates, and run through stop signs and intersections, firing warning shots at taxis or buses that didn't clear the way. Standing on the horn to tell these people, "Move, or we *will* run over your ass." Ethan and I would sit in the front and smoke like ten packs of cigarettes between the two of us, me behind the wheel with my rifle across my lap, eyes glued to the dimly lit road, him moving his head back and forth like the damn Terminator, scanning, tracking every single eyeball that lit up in the headlights, every movement, every vehicle. These mangy-looking dogs would cross every once in a while, looking to the side as we came roaring onto them. Skinny, droopy ears, looked like all their hair had fallen out except for on their backs. *Weird*, I thought, *even the dogs look different here.* Like they knew more about how the world worked or something. Never startling or scurrying away like the stray dogs back home, often they'd see the vehicle coming and calculate the exact pace they needed to get safely to the other side of the road just as we roared past, the front grille almost smacking their tails.

But we'd see all sorts of strangeness. We'd be out on patrol during a perfectly clear day, and a huge, billowing, tsunami-sized cloud of dust would roll in over us. In the city a boy walking next to a donkey would look back at us as we approached and give us the devil horns with both hands. We saw a woman with a baby in a cardboard box—no blanket, just a fucking cardboard box. Didn't matter if it was the crack of dawn, noon, oh-dark-thirty, we saw the weirdest shit. A lot of them would get really startled by the sound of our convoy coming around a corner, lose their footing and go into a ditch, drop their figs or whatever. I tried not to laugh, but the shit was funny. And Ethan cracked me up once when he leaned out the window at this one old grandpa-looking guy who looked all in a panic, and yelled sarcastically in a snooty British accent, "Terribly sorry, old boy. We're late for the Warwickshire Hunt." I know the humor was probably totally lost on the dumb fucks in the Humvee, but it put me completely in stitches. I mean, first of all, how is some old Iraqi guy going to understand a single word of English, much less pick up a British accent coming from a dude from Soddy-Daisy, Tennessee. It was so off the wall. I started giggling and kept looking over at Ethan's face, and he had this deadpan look with just a hint of a smirk that said "yeah, dass right, I'm one funny sumbitch." And after years of watching Monty Python, he really had the accent down.

But it was during those missions that I knew for sure Walker was going to be a problem. One day we were driving out early in the evening on our way to a checkpoint. The road was deserted, and it was one of the cooler days, so we had the windows down. With no Sergeant Huey around, the guys were in a crazy mood, acting like they were on spring break. Our iPod speakers were blaring the song "7" by Prince. Ethan was driving, munching on a PowerBar or something, singing with his mouth full. I was sitting up top in the turret; Walker and Maseth were in the back, fucking around with the fire extinguisher. I wasn't paying much attention to them, just nodding my head to the rhythm, enjoying the scenery. It wasn't too often you got to sightsee, but that evening I could relax a little; we were on a long, straight dirt road, no cars to look out for, little chance of IEDs, just every once in a while a food stand or someone on a bicycle heading for town. I could hear lots of muffled laughter and shouting coming from the cab. I was glad they were able to blow off some steam. But for me, this was it. I wanted to just kick back to some jams, try to figure out what the hell Prince was referring to.

I heard a loud voice out of the temple,
saying to the seven angels,
"Go and pour out the seven bowls
of the wrath of God on the earth!"

A few minutes later I saw a sheepherder coming up ahead of us on the side of the road. About a dozen sheep were walking neatly behind him along the shoulder. It was awesome. I had never seen anything like that; it seemed so ancient. Just as we passed, I started to stick my head down into the cab to ask Maseth to throw me his camera, when I heard a loud pop. I looked back behind us and saw a cloud of smoke right next to the herd. I barely was able to see one of the sheep stumbling toward the road, trying to get its footing, then hopping, holding up one of its rear legs. I leaned back in the cab to ask what the fuck had happened, and Maseth and Walker were laughing their asses off, leaning out the window with the camera.

"High five!" Bryan yelled with his Borat accent.

"Hey, what the fuck was that?" I demanded, looking at Walker.

"*That*, muthafuckah," he said, laughing hysterically, "was the funniest shit you is gonna see on YouTube!"

"Was that a flash bang? Did you assholes throw a fucking M84 at that guy's sheep?" I glared at Maseth.

"Look, holmes, I'm just the film crew. He worked demolition."

"Jesus fucking . . ." I paused, totally stunned. I glanced back at the road, but by then the sheepherder was out of sight. "You fuckers."

Walker stuck his head underneath the turret. "What, you don't like lamb kebab, white boy? You prejudice?"

With that I just sat back in the turret and left them alone. *I can NOT believe what I just witnessed*, I thought. *I just saw two soldiers throw a grenade at some poor guy and his sheep, and for absolutely no goddamned reason, and those poor animals could be seriously burned or injured. The man didn't do fuck-all to any of us. Jesus fucking Christ.*

I thought about it for the next thirty minutes, and when we got to the checkpoint, I decided I just had to say something to Walker. I caught him while he was alone—one leg propped up against a barrier, his M4 across his knee—watching cars coming down the off-ramp.

"Look, man, we need to go talk to that hajji."

Walker burst into incredulous laughter. "Are you for real?"

"Hey, I know it sounds stupid, but that old man could have friends. He could have friends with IEDs, man. If one of our guys gets blown up by a—"

Walker cut me off. "Them sand niggas *already* gonna blow us up, fool!"

"Sand whats?" I said, smiling involuntarily. What he said was so insanely fucked up, my only reaction was to smile.

"Sand nig-ger-z," he said, overenunciating. "Oh, I'm sorry, hajjis. Is that better?"

I didn't know what to do with that. "Terrell, this guy was a fucking sheepherder. He wasn't doing shit to our men," I said, trying all I could to reason with him.

"Whatever, man, they all the fuckin' same. 'Death to Ahmedika!' One day walkin' sheep, next day plantin' muhfuckin' roadside bombs."

"Oh, so we piss 'em off for no reason," I said.

"They as pissed off as they gonna get," he said, taking his foot off the cement.

A car was coming down the road. I walked back to Maseth and Ethan to wait for the vehicle. I helped check the guy out, then kept to myself as much as I could; I couldn't believe Bryan. Why would he be in on something like that? I sat on the cement barrier and pulled out my smokes. Maseth was trying to talk to Ethan, but Ethan was giving short, polite answers—for my sake, I was guessing. The scene played back in my mind as I stared into the sand. I pressed into my temples with my fingers as hard as I could, then took a deep breath to try to shake it off.

I felt I had done what I was supposed to, done my part. And Walker would probably come around, stop being such a shitbag. At least I told myself that. I remember thinking I was just one of many who would say something to Walker; even Bryan. We'd all play a part. Lessons learned. We'd be the best squad ever. Make a difference.

The following Saturday I got a chance to call my mom. I did some PT with Ethan, studied Arabic for a few hours, and straightened my side of the hooch. I waited 'til the late afternoon to make sure she'd be up. The phone trailer smelled horrible, and another guy was in there working on a laptop, so no privacy, but I didn't care. It was just nice to hear my mom's voice for a few minutes. In letters I had tried to give her a clear picture of what it was like to be there, the modified trailers we called hooches, the importance of the missions, the Iraqis, good and bad, the scorching weather. But as much as I told her, she still asked the weirdest things.

"Are you making time to do something fun too?"

"Uh, fun?"

"I know what you're doing is mostly serious, son." She tried to clarify in a flowery voice. "Gosh, it's the most serious job a man can do on this earth." She paused for effect. "Right, honey?" More sweetness, but just a tad patronizing. Her referring to me as a man sounded like she was trying to make her little boy *feel* older.

"Yeah, Mom. Pretty serious," I said.

"So try to . . . is there some kind of play area . . . I mean . . ." She burst into laughter. "Oh, listen to your mother. 'Play area'—as if you were five years old! What I mean is, is there a recreation place or something?"

"Yeah, Mom. We've got chess, poker, Boggle. Lots of stuff mailed to us from the US." *From moms who actually care to look into it*, I thought briefly.

"Oh gosh, all these *thinking* games! Well, okay, but try to just unplug every once in a while. We all need some good old mindless fun sometimes, okay, son?"

Typical Mom. Always acting like life's the middle part of the Boston Marathon, and for God's sake, pace yourself or you'll have an embolism and collapse on the ground and die. Usually I'd be annoyed, but today I let it slide. All I wanted was to be as close to home as I could. I imagined sitting in my mom's cluttered den, with yapper dogs running around peeing on Oriental rugs and chaise longues, while she washed my clothes or fixed me a bowl of her famous gumbo. She'd send Glenn out to rent a video like *Shawshank* or *Rabbit-Proof Fence*. Had to be something gut-wrenching and tragic, but supposedly overcoming adversity. That was Mom.

"I wish I could be there, Mom. We could plan a trip to Pensacola. Glenn's never been, has he?"

"Oh, Glenn's not a Gulf person. He prefers Hilton Head."

"What? With the muddy gray sand?"

"Well, yeah, but that's okay. I'm getting used to it. No other choice, right?"

I knew what she was getting at. "No, no. You guys should go."

"Well, that's your father's territory. Last thing I want to do is run into him and his sweet young thing."

I rolled my eyes. That familiar jab: "your father," expressed in a pejorative tone, like how dare I even have a father.

"Oh, come on, it's every bit as much yours, and what are the chances you'll—"

"I don't care. It's just not worth the risk," she said. I hesitated. *Should I go down this road again?* But she added something I couldn't leave alone: "Son, you wouldn't know, not having lived through what I did with that man."

"Oh God, Mom. Really? I wasn't there? Gee, where was I?" I glanced over at the guy on his laptop. He had put his ear buds in, so he hadn't heard me.

"Let's drop it," she said after a long pause.

"What happened to Ms. . . ." I started to say, but stopped. I had been through it a fucking million times with my mom, my post-divorce, post-traumatic, Chicken-Little-let's-all-run-screaming-hysterically-for-our-lives mom.

"Ms. what?" she said, challenging me. "You might as well say it now."

I paused, thinking of how to phrase it just right, which got me choked up. "You were always so gutsy, Mom. Freethinker, independent . . . never afraid of Dad. Never!"

"Yeah, son, and where did that get me? Almost killed."

Oh God, how melodramatic. "It's not like he's going to walk up to you and Glenn strolling on the beach and shoot you."

"Well, gee, son, I guess you're just too logical for your mother! You've got it all figured out, don't you?"

"Oh, that's a fucking cop-out, Mom, and you know it," I said, immediately feeling that familiar sense of dread.

And right on cue she screamed, "You didn't get the hell beat out of you for nineteen years!"

"Okay, Mom. I know."

I always had to back off at that point. Fucking guilt. It always won over logic. She was in my head now, her imaginary voice and my thoughts all one garbled mess: *Were you there, son? Behind those closed doors? No. So how do you know I'm being melodramatic? Exaggerating? How can you be sure? You only heard things, you never actually saw anything. So have some empathy, son. Believe your mother. Stop being so rational. Stop acting like your dad.*

Fuck you, Mom.

"Oh, look at us," she finally said, "how'd we get off on the wrong foot like this?"

It was as if all was forgotten. She was a master at switching emotions a hundred and eighty degrees on a dime.

"I don't know," I said.

"Well, look, I love you very much, and Glenn loves you."

"Love you too, Mom," I said, looking up. The one guy on the laptop had gotten up and left, and the attendant was walking around shutting down laptops.

"Oh, and Glenn found a store that carries those yellow . . ."

Her voice started sounding emotional. *Great, now she's fucking crying.*

"The yellow stickers that go on the car . . . the, um . . ."

"Support the Troops bumper stickers?" I said.

"Yes." She seemed to recover momentarily. "I've been looking for one in particular. It says 'Keep our . . . keep our son safe.'"

"Oh, that's cool." I tried to sound upbeat to make her stop crying. I felt bad, but what immediately popped into my head was when we were in Kuwait and everyone was making fun of those ribbons and just about writing a thesis on how useless they were.

"I'll tell the guys. It'll help keep their morale up."

She paused for a second. "Okay, son, well, I love you. We *both* love you . . . very much."

"You too," I said as the attendant skipped me and got the laptop next to mine. "Gotta go now, Mom."

"You take care of yourself, okay, son?"

"I will, Mom. Bye."

"And remember, son. J-Jesus is with you, whether you believe he's there or not. He'll keep you safe. All you have to do is ask, okay?"

I took a deep breath. *Fuck me, now the religious shit?* "Sure, Mom."

"Love you."

There it was again. She threw 'I love you' around so much, Ethan and I used to joke she used it like southern cooking called for sticks of butter. Used to be so endearing. Now it was just annoying. And in this case she only said it to get an okay from me for her throwing in that religious plug.

"Love you too," I said, even more annoyed I had no choice, and disconnected. As I walked back from the call-home trailer, I had every emotion imaginable swirling around my head, battling it out for control. *Fuck her, I'm not my dad. Why is she always so fucking helpless? I feel so sorry for her. No, goddamn it, I'm not ashamed of my own mother; I just want to help her. Why was I so mean to her? No, I refuse to feel guilty. Keep your stupid Jesus comments to yourself, Mom.*

It felt like someone was poking at me, reminding me who my mom used to be—cool, hip, so cosmopolitan. Gone were the days when she and I would sit outside in the secret garden and she'd let me have some wine. No more of her opening up, telling me she was a virgin bride and would warn guys on the first date, "I'm an intellectual lay." No more swearing, no more having raunchy gay friends over for dinner. I used to brag about her doing volunteer work in Chattanooga with the LGBT support group. Nope. Not anymore. Ever since 9/11. Might as well put her photo on a milk carton, 'cause she's nowhere to be found. Gone, along with all my sisters. Abducted by evangelicals. *Whatever. I'm so over all that. Ancient history.*

When I got back to the trailers, the guys were hanging out in front of Thiessen and Barco's hooch. Ethan and Christopher sat at the rickety plastic table playing chess. Barco and a couple of rookies from the other squad stood around watching.

"Um, you sure you wanna do that?" Ethan asked. I stopped for a moment and looked down at the board, propping myself against the sandbags that reinforced the trailer. Ethan was crushing him. He had almost all of his pieces left, while Thiessen had like two pawns and a bishop or something protecting his king.

"Oh my fucking God!" I said sarcastically. "Coffelt, I don't know much about chess, but you may wanna just give up at this point. I mean . . ."

"Yeah." Ethan smiled. "I'd better do the honorable thing, be a gentleman, save some of my dignity."

The rooks laughed. Christopher didn't seem too amused, trying to concentrate. His bald head was dark pink from the sun, and his hand propped his head up under his chin. A couple of guys walked past us, talking about going to get chow.

A few seconds later our poor victim took a drag off his cigarette. "Okay, how about I agree to concede and give you twenty instead of twenty-five."

Everyone burst out laughing.

"Ahh, nice try, but Momma ain't raised no fool," Ethan said. Thiessen managed a half smile; he knew what was up. Smackdowns were just part of Iraq. Everyone was used to it.

I went inside to clean my weapons and check my gear. Batteries had to be tested, lenses had to be wiped off and checked for scratches, water in the CamelBak had to be changed. I used my days off to get all my shit tiptop. Ethan played a few more games of chess, and after a while I heard obnoxious banging on the trailer door. He poked his head inside. "Dude! Chow!"

"Okay, hang on a second." I checked off an item and laid the pad and pencil on top of the cabinet.

Thiessen, Walker, and Maseth joined Ethan and me, and we walked through the sand and dirt to the DFAC. "Oh my God! Again?" Maseth said, seeing the huge chow line. "I'm too hungry for this bullshit." We stood in the hot sun as the line inched along. I could see Ethan was getting pretty annoyed. After about thirty minutes people were making remarks and peering out to see what was going on ahead of them. Finally someone behind us yelled out, "Okay, now, everyone huddle up so they can take us out with one mortar. Perfect."

Amid the laughter, Ethan took a few steps away from the line and addressed the guy. "And we can thank our good friends at FUBAR, who could *easily* do multiple shifts, but they don't, 'cause they get paid per soldier fed."

The guy in front of us turned around to Ethan, grinning. "FUBAR. That's awesome."

Finally we got to the entrance. They'd finished the repairs and replaced the tables damaged in the explosion. The only obvious thing was a poster tacked to the wooden support with a picture of the Pakistani cook and two others. The line was moving now, so I couldn't stop to read it. Thiessen and Walker strolled right past it, talking about life after their tours in Iraq. Of course Walker was spouting shit about makin' some serious coin, movin' to Cali, bein' a baller. "Yeah, son. Bugattis in the driveway, parties, drinkin' XO, bitches . . ."

"Wow," Thiessen said, "all that with a background in military service and no four-year degree, oookay." The way he said it struck me as sarcastic and deriding yet trying to sound indifferent.

"Man, don't be hatin'. You can come work for me."

"Okay, man, well, good luck," Thiessen said, walking way ahead to grab a tray and silverware. His body language was so obvious it was ridiculous.

Walker didn't give a shit. He saw one of his buddies from Echo walking into the tent and waved him over, all animated. "What up, holmes?" They fist-bumped and started talking and ended up sitting by themselves near the chow line. *Good.* The rest of us went in and lined up, filled up our plates with mashed potatoes and roast beef, and sat down near the tent doors.

"What about you, man?" I asked Thiessen, trying to make conversation. "What are your plans when you get back?"

"College in Norfolk. I'll be getting a degree in intel and counterterrorism, then I'll work for DoD contractors around Washington, DC." He rattled this off so quickly, with no hesitation, as if he had memorized it for an interview. "I already have a contact with Halliburton."

He raised his eyebrows at me, like I was supposed to be all impressed. "Cool. Good for you," I said.

"You can make over a hundred dollars an hour, and northern Virginia has six of the twenty highest-income counties in the nation," he said. *Who is this guy, my damn career adviser?*

Maseth got all excited. "Holy shit, that is some serious bank, bro!"

"What about you?" Thiessen asked me. "What are your career plans?"

I was taken off guard, not expecting the attention to be turned on me. "No plans yet."

"Oh, come on," he said.

"Honestly? Careers, making money aren't exactly that important to me right now."

Thiessen smirked and made this exaggerated frown, like who in the world would say such a thing? He seemed almost personally offended. "What d'you mean? So after the war you're gonna go back, and they're just going to hand you a good job?" he asked sarcastically.

"No, of course not," I said, trying to figure out where he was going.

"What were you doing before? Were you in college?"

I was sure he'd find my next answer unacceptable, but I didn't care. I said it anyway. *Like it's any of his fucking business.*

"Yeah, well, I'd planned to go to NYU, but . . . let's just say 9/11 changed all that." I was trying to just end it there. I glanced at the other guys. I seriously doubted they gave a shit anyway.

"What, did you lose somebody?" Thiessen asked.

"No, no . . . well, yeah. I mean, who *didn't* know someone who . . . you know. But that's not why I joined up," I lied.

At this point Thiessen really poured on the sarcastic laughter. "Oh, right, after 9/11 you just tossed your entire plans for college, but 9/11 had nothing to do with you joining up. Gotcha."

I scooped up some potatoes, keeping my eyes on the spoon. It felt like everyone at the table was listening, staring at me. I suddenly thought about the tat on my biceps. *Shit. Okay, my sleeve is probably covering it.*

"Whatever, man," I said. "Let's just say, after that day *my* needs became way less important. I guess things got a lot more serious."

Maseth made a goofy sound like he was choking on a bite of

food. "Fuck yeah, more serious! Serious like Shock and Awe serious, motherfuckahs!" He stuck up his hand to slap a quick five with Ethan.

"Funny guy," I said, looking at Maseth. "No, really. When you're young everything's about yourself—you're all selfish, self-centered, whatever. But when you grow up and realize shit like 9/11 happens in the world, you have to see outside of yourself and think about other people."

"Uh-oh," Thiessen said with a half smile, "I smell mommy party!"

"Shut the fuck up. I'm not from the mommy *or* the daddy party," I said. *Jesus, this guy is unbelievable.*

"Know what I was thinking about after 9/11?" Ethan asked, pausing for effect.

"What?" Thiessen finally said.

"Maybe it's just my father's influence talkin' here, but I must confess my initial response to the attacks of 9/11 was something like 'Hmm, how about a tactical nuke right in the middle of Mecca during the hajj?'"

He said this calmly but held his hand up nonchalantly to fist-bump with Maseth, who yelled, "Yeeea, boyeee!"

Ethan nodded, smirking. "Take *dat*, beaaaches!"

I knew Ethan was joking, but I just had to respond to that. "What, so they can greet us with flowers again?" I said, doing the quote fingers. "Come on, guys, think." *They know I'm right,* I thought.

Thiessen burst out in mocking laughter, addressing the others. "Oh, but he's not from the mommy party, everybody got that?"

I looked around the table. Everyone looked like they were so goddamned amused. "Whatever, dude," I said, trying to play it off, and continued eating.

"Anyway, so when'd you join up?" Thiessen said, sounding conciliatory.

"'04, after I graduated. Would have joined junior year but had to wait 'til I turned eighteen."

"Oh, right, couldn't get your parents' consent?"

"No, just my dad's. Couldn't get his," I said. *Let's be real fucking clear about that.*

"Oookay, I won't ask," he said, turning to Ethan. "What about you, Coffelt?"

Ethan motioned to me. "Same time as him. He roped me into this shit," he said dryly.

"Really? How'd you get the same duty station?"

"My cousin's a recruiter. We got it written into the contract."

We finished up and left the DFAC. Maseth ran into an LT buddy of his who started walking with us. A few minutes later Ethan and I were ahead of the others, and I heard Thiessen calling out to me. I turned around to see him trotting up to us.

"I forgot to mention I've been promoted . . . to sergeant. Still some paperwork to do, but should be soon." He seemed to say this as if I gave a shit, like we were buds.

"Oh, cool," I said.

"Yeah, I know, right?" He paused when I didn't follow up with anything. "So anyway, I thought you'd want to know. I mean, anyone could do it. Not saying it's easy, but with the proper training, talking to the right people . . ."

"Hey. Congratulations. Good for you," I said, patting his shoulder. He seemed to get the hint.

"Okay," he said with that stupid admonitory tone.

Later that evening I made an espresso, grabbed my spiral notebook, and stepped outside. There was a little hidden spot on the side of our hooch, a gap between the two units that had a stack of sandbags in the back. I could sit there and look out across the field, smoke, write. If anyone walked by, they probably wouldn't notice me. The sun was setting, and I could hear the droning from the nearby mosque. I took a drag and flipped to a blank page.

Dear Dottie,

Thank you so much for your letter! I don't hear much from anyone else in the family, not sure why. Ethan says Americans are all too busy shopping to be bothered. Haha. Except in my parents and siblings' case more like they're all in church. Maybe they just don't get this whole war thing I'm doing, I got the feeling when I left they just didn't want to think about it. One of my sisters actually said she thought the war was over. Wow. I am so glad to have you to talk to, you DO seem like you get it.

Things are good here. Sergeant Huey is awesome, my squad is okay. They need to grow up a little, maybe, stop thinking of their service here as a career booster or one big party, but I'm sure they'll get there. Hate to say it but it may take traumatic events to show them it's not about the individual, it is about the team, fellow soldiers. Dottie, I feel good that I had the proper focus when I joined up. I joined to serve, to give back. To me that is what patriotism is, sacrificing something for the country. Am I idealistic? Maybe, but to be honest it's better than what my parents did. As you said one time, Mom gets all emotional about stuff like earthquakes in Afghanistan but never gets out her checkbook. And my dad? I honestly think he despises that idea. And Mom hates what he stands for too, thinks all he cares about is himself and making money. Before Paw-Paw died I heard him say the day they got divorced Mom and Dad lost their minds and became walking contradictions of each other. How perfectly stated was that?

Remember the time I came over after that big fight with my dad, when my teacher had graded my exam wrong and Mom and I wanted to fight it? I never told you this, because of the swearing, but you know what he said to me? "That's just another fucked-up idea you got from your mother." I'm so glad I had such awesome grandparents like you guys to go and talk to. Otherwise I'd probably be schizophrenic. I never thanked you for that. Anyway, I guess I've rambled on enough. I love you and miss you very much. When I get back I'll come over and help you plant roses or fix that damned sink again!

Keep writing!

Your favorite grandson! Haha ☺

The next morning Ethan and I woke up early to do a run. We put on our gray army tees, black shorts, and sneakers, stepped out of the trailer, and did a few minutes of stretching while our eyes adjusted to the predawn light. The phone call from the day before was on my mind, but people would still be sleeping, and I had to wait until we'd gotten away from the trailers.

"I talked to the moms yesterday," I said as we crunched through the gravel, heading toward the DFAC.

"How's she doing?"

"Okay, I guess." My voice must have sounded slightly off.

"Uh-oh, Glenn getting dicked over at his job again?"

I gave a short laugh. "And then staying another five years? Yeah, probably. But that didn't come up." We rounded the PX and ran along the outer perimeter security wall at an easy pace. The parallel lines of the straighter-than-straight wall and the evenly spaced storage Conexes adjacent to it created a vanishing point effect that seemed to stretch out forever. "No, it's my mom. She's just so . . . dude, what the fuck happened to my mother?" I gave him a quick recap of the phone call. "My mom, she is just unrecognizable now. Ever since she found Jesus."

"Yeah, it is kinda weird, considering she used to be the queen of calling out the pious crowd on Lookout Mountain."

"I know, right? All those hypocrites from Joshua's church. She used to call Lookout *Dead Poets Society* meets *700 Club*. Old money southern folk, with their frickin' stone mansions and country clubs, naming their kids Fluff or Precious and shit." I switched to a posh British accent. "The Kruesis, the Luptons, the Friersons . . ."

Ethan laughed. "Muffy, be a dear and hand me my driving gloves."

"Exactly. Meanwhile, kids are starving in Africa. If there was a God, how could he allow such suffering? She talked about that all the time."

"Yeah, she was quite the bleeding heart."

"I know, but in a good way, Ethan. She was empathetic but passionate too, assertive. She was so cool. Read all the classics, read poetry. Kerouac, Truman Capote, Alice Walker. And she totally got those guys, spoke the same language. It was almost like she belonged in the same—"

"And like them, drank a lot," he said, "don't forget."

"I know, but hello? She's from New Orleans! They like to party. And it's not like she sat around the house with a bottle of vodka."

"The *social* alcoholic," he said.

"Well, she had an abusive husband. Who wouldn't drink? But see, I think right after the divorce was her best moment—freed herself from Dad, got away from the *Stepford Wives* crowd on Lookout Mountain, met some real people, did all that social work, met Glenn—and then *poof*, out of nowhere she fuckin' disappeared."

"Okay, but dude, how long's it been?" he said.

"My sisters too . . . ever since 9/11."

"Well, you need to put it behind you."

"I'm over it, Ethan. It's just hard being constantly reminded of the family I used to have. We used to be so close."

"Look, the way I see it, you had a nightmare childhood. Domestic violence, parents got divorced, but instead of making peace, it started the fucking intifada."

"Ha, yeah, pretty much . . . except they found their bomb shelters, remarried just as fast as they fucking could. Found total polar opposites of one another, dug in, left us kids to fend for ourselves, decide which extreme camp to belong to."

Ethan chuckled. "And you're wondering why everyone's a little cuckoo?!"

"Well, I feel like I'm the only sane one," I said.

"Or not. Dude, maybe you didn't spin wildly off to the left or right, but you stayed in the middle, where there's ten to the shit-ton Newtons of opposing force!"

"Yep, thanks, Mom and Dad . . . why even have kids if your marriage is that volatile? How'd they even get together in the first place? Hell, how'd they even get through the first date? Mom wanted to fix the world, Dad wanted to capitalize on it. Miss Idealistic and Mr. Authoritarian!"

"Yeah, it's hard for me to imagine them together. Seems like each of them thinks the other is the prince of darkness. When's the last time they actually had a civil conversation?"

"9/11," I said.

"Oh, right, Dr. Geisler. The tragic phone call."

"Uh, which we will *not* be talking about."

"Roger that, understood," Ethan said. There was a long pause. We turned the corner behind the last Conex and started down the service road toward the main gate.

I wouldn't let myself think about what happened to Mercer, but one thing did pop into my head: *I wonder if I ever thanked him.* He was pretty much my parents' last hope, the only one who seemed to pacify them. He and his wife would come visit when we lived on the mountain. Dad would totally loosen up. He'd quit bitching about Clinton and doctors being in a huge tax bracket. No snarky comments about malpractice insurance, the "poor" nursing staff at Parkridge, or socialized medicine. Mom quit talking about the snooty doctors' wives and all the phony evangelicals. She seemed to forget she was insecure, that she thought she had no career, that raising five kids didn't count. She'd act poised and accomplished, coaching Dreda on interior decorating or making a good béarnaise—things she seemed to have an extraordinary natural talent for. Mercer would talk about his charity work with Doctors Without Borders, and Dad would listen intently. Dreda and Mom would talk about starting a book club.

Ethan tried to steer the conversation back. "Hey, at least your dad and Diane seem rational. They never got snatched up by Jayzus."

"Thank *God*," I said.

Ethan laughed. "Your dad reminds me of Dr. Phil. He's got that same drawl, the pleasant demeanor—well, usually—but always trying to fix people's problems."

"Tell me about it. Always fixing people, always got you on the couch, picking your life apart to see what's wrong with it, so he, the almighty surgeon, can mend it."

"I guess if you spend your entire career playing God, it's kind of hard to shake it."

"Yeah," I said, "but the sad thing is, he has no idea whatsoever how pompous and arrogant he comes across to people."

"Can you say the infamous toilet incident?" Ethan said sarcastically.

"Oh, here we go!" I said, laughing so hard I couldn't keep running. We slowed to a walk. "That goddamned, piece-of-shit, circa-1902 toilet. What a fucking nightmare."

He giggled. "That look on his face when he called you out in the living room, like it was the most grave situation you can imagine."

"Yeah! 'Son, what did you do?' as if I'd fucking killed someone. Gee, Dad, let's see. I ate dinner, processed my food, used the bathroom, and then flushed the toilet, same way I've done a thousand times in a thousand other bathrooms."

Ethan looked at me, wagging his finger. "Ah, but shame on you! You didn't follow his special instructions! 'Cause that toilet is a precision piece of equipment, and you have to have the proper training!"

"Exactly! It's not a goddamned NASA lunar breathing system, Dad. It's a fucking toilet! And hello? It's buh-ROKE-en, old man! Fucking fix it!"

He laughed.

"See, and this is what gets me. He gives everyone this ten-minute fucking disparaging lecture on the toilet procedure, which he knows no one wants to listen to, but see, it's perfect! 'Cause if the toilet breaks, he can point the finger at someone else."

"Why didn't he just say, 'Sorry, guys, the guest toilet is finicky, you kind of have to baby it'?"

"I have no idea, Ethan, other than nothing is ever his fault. It's almost like he deliberately goes out of his way to piss people off. And he always does it the same way: rob them of their dignity and respect . . . oh, and in broad daylight!"

"Yeah, I felt so bad. You looked pretty humiliated in the living room."

"Right, it's like he literally *wants* his kids to hate him. Share anything about your life with him, and he'll find a way to use it against you. 'Son, remember that time after your trip to Europe, when you didn't want to get a job? Tsk, tsk. I guess you can't pull on a weed to make it grow! Har har.'"

"What the fuck?"

"Yeah, he actually said that. First of all, I worked my ass off to save for that trip, and when I came back I had less than three weeks before school started."

Ethan stopped to grab some water from his CamelBak. "That is some seriously twisted logic, dude," he said, passing it to me.

I took a sip but continued my tirade: "'Son, Mike bought a truck with his own money. What do you think about that?' F you, Dad, and your insinuations, 'cause Mike also got an underage girl pregnant and had to pay for her abortion. And he also does cocaine. Oh, but *I'm* the piece of shit? I hardly even drink!"

"Damn, that's what I need right now, a tall cold one . . . cocaine don't sound bad either," he said, but I barely noticed.

"He's such a dick. Goes on like a broken record about 'personal responsibility' . . . like I'm some kind of freeloader."

"Son!" Ethan said in a deep voice. "The world doesn't owe you anything!"

"Ha ha, exactly! Buck up, quit blaming life, quit complaining, and deal with it. Well, gee, Dad, easy for you to say when you are the one who caused my fucked-up life!"

"Okay, man, chill. Sorry I brought it up," Ethan said, looking at me.

I realized I had been pointing my finger aggressively at him. *I hope my face doesn't look like my dad's*, I thought, *all enraged, with those eyes glaring at you like they'll come out of their sockets.*

"No, I'm over it. Just pisses me off that we never got an apology for that shit. Mom never got an apology."

"Oh, right," he said, turning onto the gravel path toward our trailers, "don't hold your breath."

"Well, we had one conversation—one! When I confronted him about it—'Why'd you hit my mom, Dad?'—what's he do? He pulls the 'walk in my shoes' card. Poor me, I had no choice. Tells me one little anecdote about my mom shitfaced one night as they drove home from a party and her hitting him with her shoe. Really, Dad? You couldn't stop the car and walk away? No other options? And what about all the other times? If she was such an alcoholic, divorce her drunk ass!"

A couple of female soldiers passed by us on their way to the chow tent. Ethan fist-bumped one of them, calling out, "Specialist Duerksen!" then pulled out his smokes and lit up.

"And he has the fucking gall to say I have an anger problem, you believe that shit?"

Ethan looked at me as he blew some smoke out. "Uh, you *do* have an anger problem, but Jesus, who wouldn't."

"Whatever," I said.

"So speaking of anger," he said, "you tell your mom about Walker? And what happened?"

"Oh," I said. "No. She doesn't need to know about stuff like that."

"Yeah, true dat. Well, I was thinking . . . you know, maybe Walker is just kind of acting out, reacting to what we deal with."

I glared at him. "Dude, really? Couldn't be he's a complete shitbag or anything."

Ethan cocked his head a little. "I don't know, man. I hate to remind you, but you *did* tell me a story once about when you were growing up. During your parents' divorce. Remember the cat?" He chuckled a little. "The one you tortured the shit out of?"

"Oh, come on! 'Tortured the shit out of'? You make it sound like it was Gitmo."

"Well, it sounded pretty bad, from what I remember."

"It wasn't," I said. But actually it was. A stray cat somehow got into our house, and I chased him all over, trapping him and poking him with a stick. Eventually forced him to jump out of a second-story window. I don't even remember why I did it. I always loved animals.

We arrived back at the trailer and went inside. I turned on the espresso machine as Ethan grabbed his toiletry bag and towel. When he got back from the showers, I finished up my coffee and smoke and got my shower, and Ethan ran to check on mail. Then we headed off to the DFAC for some breakfast.

W e sat at our regular table in the chow tent with Styrofoam plates of sorry-looking ham and eggs and little plastic cups of orange juice.

"If these fuckers are gonna charge eighty-five dollars for what's essentially a fucking Happy Meal . . . ," he said, taking a shaker of lemon pepper seasoning out of his jacket and sprinkling it on top of his eggs.

"Yeah, thanks, FUBAR," I said.

"Fucking crooks." Ethan sounded annoyed. "I could cook better food with a damn spatula stuck up my ass."

I laughed. "So you got your care package from your mom, I see."

"Oh, hells yeah! Lemon pepper, baby wipes, glow sticks, books . . . oh, and a couple cool movies."

Must be nice, I thought. "Excellent. What you got, holmes?"

"*X-Men, Bourne Supremacy* . . ."

"Cool. Let's fire 'em up later on."

We hung out for a little while, talking about stupid shit, refilling our thimbles of orange juice, chatting with fellow soldiers stopping by our table here and there. Right before we were ready to leave, we saw what looked like one of the contractors sitting at a table by himself with a medium-sized cooler next to him. Ethan said he had seen the guy there before, that he always brought a cooler and sat by himself. I didn't really think too much about it; I just jumped at the opportunity to make up a humorous scenario.

"Holy shit, dude, maybe he's from Al's Catering, if you know what I mean."

Ethan laughed politely. "Arr, arr, Al's Qaeda ring. Clever."

"No, I'm serious," I said, acting as ridiculously over-the-top somber as I could. "That guy is working on a top-secret ice cube–based IED."

"You're a funny guy," Ethan said with barely a smile.

I kept going, trying to keep a straight face. "No, listen. This thing blows up and sprays water all over generals and shit, disrupts meetings, ruins toupees—I heard Rumsfeld's deathly afraid of it."

Ethan wasn't very amused. He'd usually play along, but it really had to be fucking hilarious to get him started. "Dude, what does he need a big-ass cooler in the chow tent for?" he said.

I looked over at the guy. He was now bending down to the cooler and putting a few apples and bananas underneath the lid. We watched for a few minutes, trying not to be obvious. He wasn't eating, just looking down at a magazine, never looking up. After a few minutes he took some more fruit and put it under the lid of the cooler.

"Okay, that's it. I'm gonna find out what this fucker is up to," Ethan said, suddenly getting up from the table.

"Ethan," I said, trying to stop him, but he ignored me. I got up from the table and walked over with him. I just had to see the shit go down.

"How you doing? You a contractor?" Ethan asked.

The guy looked up, kind of startled. "Yes."

"I couldn't help but notice you putting food in your cooler," Ethan said, friendly, but with a slightly interrogative tone. I thought he sounded like a traffic cop.

The guy quickly looked back down at his food, then took a drink, apparently to stall for time. "Yeah, just some snacks for later on."

Ethan stood there with his arms folded. "For when you're back at your trailer?"

The guy hesitated. "Yeah."

That was all Ethan needed. He was pissed. "Let me get this straight. You can get all the food you want from the DFAC, controlled strictly by your private contracting company, but you somehow feel a need to hoard away food—meant for soldiers, by the way—which we foot the bill for." Ethan then got bitterly sarcastic. "How much are you making? Just curious."

The guy realized Ethan was not going to let up. He looked around to see if we were drawing any attention in the chow tent. It was apparently too noisy, or no one gave a damn. "Sir . . ." He looked up at Ethan, opening his hand, motioning toward the cooler. "I'm a foreman. I have a crew of Filipinos and Indians, and they're only allowed two meals a day—little bowls of rice and chicken. Same exact thing every single day."

Ethan backed off a bit. He could see the guy was reasonable. I put my hand on his shoulder, hoping he'd just let it go.

"Damn, so you have to bring them extra food? But I thought you guys were making like a hundred bucks an hour."

The guy had now changed his demeanor. Ethan had a way of getting people to open up, even complete strangers, in any type of situation where there was a human interest story. "Yeah, *we* do, but not the Iraqi foreign nationals. It's kind of . . . it's kind of a fucked-up situation." The guy appeared to be holding back a little bit.

"Yeah, I've heard about some things," Ethan said, taking a seat across from the guy.

I kept standing, wondering how long we were going to stay there and discuss shit that for all we knew was completely fabricated.

"One guy was telling me there are Filipino women cleaning toilets in the upper-echelon quarters, and there were cases of sexual assault, mistreatment . . . ," Ethan said.

"Oh, I've actually seen it myself, some of my people."

"Holy shit, are you kidding?" Ethan said, now intrigued.

"You're not from CNN or anything, are you?"

Ethan laughed. "Oh, *hell* no!"

I turned to Ethan. "Dude, there is no way to know if any of this is true."

The guy looked up at me, wide-eyed. He appeared almost offended. "One of my crew came to me one day crying, said her sister had been talked into, maybe forced into, having sex—paid sex—with officers. I know this woman, and she is not the type who'd make shit up."

I had to laugh. "Oh, come on. That is like third-hand." I motioned to Ethan for us to leave.

"No, I wanna hear about this," he said, kind of glaring at me. I just walked back to the table. *Jesus Christ, how the fuck is this helping?* I sat there picking at the last bits of my food. Ethan continued to talk to the fucker. I wanted to just walk out, but I also didn't want to be a baby about it. A few minutes later they were done talking and walked over, exchanging fucking pleasantries.

"Okay, man, nice talking to you. Appreciate you sharing," Ethan said.

"No problem. Good luck to you guys," he said, giving me a smile and extending his hand. I didn't shake it, but Ethan already had his out.

"Thanks, you too, man."

"Stay safe, guys," the guy added.

Ethan and I cleaned the table off and left. To me it seemed like a waste of time even talking to that guy. *We should have reported the fucker for stealing food*, I thought as we walked back to our hooch. Ethan didn't say a word. *I don't know why we didn't. We don't know that dickhead from Adam.*

As we passed by the port-o-johns, I said I had to go. Ethan just started veering off away from them toward the hooches. So I walked alone, wondering what the fuck was up with him. That was how he was. He'd never go off and start screaming at you or anything; he just got quiet, and then you *knew* you'd royally pissed him off.

When I was inside the port-o-john doing my thing, I heard noises and laughter just outside. It sounded like two or three soldiers had come up to take a shit and had started messing around. A few minutes passed, and I heard the door of one of the stalls slam. The laughter turned to what sounded like whispering and suppressed giggling. I shook my head. *These fuck-tards are always up to something.* I looked around for the toilet paper. On the wall somebody had scrawled in black marker:

Today's flavors of bullshit:
A. Bush/Cheney just wanted the oil
B. They just wanted Iraqis to be free
Pick one, bitch

Next thing you know, I heard this huge thump, and the guys outside burst into uncontrollable laughter. I finished up, and when I opened the door I saw three soldiers standing together. One had a small video camera and was pointing it toward a port-o-john lying on its side. I walked over to the ones laughing their asses off. The Asian guy was grabbing the camera away from another guy.

"*Idiota!*" he chastised him. "Zoom in, foo! And . . . heh-woe? Stay in focus."

I looked over at the capsized port-o-john and saw the bare ass of a fourth guy, who was struggling to stand up and pull his pants on.

"Jason, you got two turd hangin' out of your ass," the Asian dude said.

"Fuck all y'alls," he said, fastening his belt buckle.

"We're sorry, man. Was that, like, way over the top?" one guy said, almost unable to talk, he was laughing so hard.

"Hey, check this out," the Asian guy said, motioning to me. I watched as he replayed the video. Two of the soldiers were running as fast as they could before slamming their entire bodies up against the side of the port-o-john. It fell over, the plastic door opened, and the poor guy taking a shit fell right out onto the sand, pants down around his ankles. I tried to laugh along with them, but all I could do was imagine the sludge spilling all over the guy—soaking his hair, getting in his eyes, maybe even into his mouth. It so easily could have gone horribly wrong. I stared at them, wondering how people had the balls to do things like that. But as I walked away I had a sudden pang, like everyone had shit figured out but me. *Those idiots*, I said to myself.

I stopped by the plaza to see if I'd gotten any mail. Just a postcard from Dottie: "Hey, kiddo! Just thinkin bout cha! Miss you terribly. Remember you are not forgotten back home—not all of us are at the mall. Hell, I'm too frail to go shopping!" *No way*, I thought, reading that part. *It's like we're on the same wavelength.* "But the war is on my mind constantly, and as you know I make sure my congressmen know it! Take care, kiddo. Granny Fricket loves ya bunches." I tried not to tear up, but it kind of got to me. When I got back to the hooch I tacked the card over my bed.

That evening, four or five of us crammed folding chairs together and watched *The Bourne Supremacy* on Ethan's tiny laptop screen. I remember thinking how strange it was for a bunch of twenty-year-olds who normally were about as controlled as a litter of stray kittens to sit calmly in their seats, eyes glued to the screen as if they were at an opera. Walker, of all people, was the one who shushed me when I made a remark about one unrealistic scene. *These guys are really taking this seriously*, I thought. *I mean, it's just a dumb movie.* And in the final scene, when Bourne calls the CIA director in her office, obviously after rigging his cell so she can't track his location, he tells her, "Get some rest, Pam. You look tired," and she freaks out and looks out the window. I was thinking, *Oh, brilliant, just tell her you're in the building right across the street!*

When the credits started rolling and that ridiculous music kicked in, Maseth got up and yelled, "Oh, yeah! Jason Bourne, baby, still alive!"

I rolled my eyes, smiling pityingly at him and shaking my head. "Dude, that had like sooo many holes . . ."

The rest of the guys jumped in. "Aw, man, don't be dissin' no Jason Bourne, holmes!" I was clearly outnumbered, and I hesitated to ruin the moment for these fools, but on the other hand, I didn't want Einsteins like Walker getting the impression life was anything like that movie.

"Don't get me wrong, loved the action, but come on, shit like that just does not happen."

Walker started laughing. "Well, no she-ite, motherfucker! Ya think?"

"No, I'm just saying . . . it's like a comic book. I just prefer more edgy, reality-based stuff."

I turned to the others. By the looks on their faces, they were going to let me duke this one out on my own. Walker bent down to get in my face, all smirky. "Oh, reality based? Such as?"

"Like *24*, that's pretty realistic." Before I could finish my sentence, Walker had burst into ridiculous laughter, and a couple of others chuckled. That's how those fuckers were. It didn't matter if they agreed—anything to see a good verbal smackdown between two dudes.

"What? Jack fucking Bauer?" he said. "Oh my Lord Jesus, son!"

I looked over at Ethan, and he had this knowing smile on his face. He was going to hang me out to dry. *Un-fucking-believable.*

"Let me get this straight. Jason Bourne is all fantasy and shit," Walker said, waving his arms in the air sarcastically, "but *24*, with the ticking bombs every damn episode, cartoon good guys and bad guys—*that* shit's real life?" He walked around in a quick circle and faced me, trying to make his point. "Oh snap, you is right, homey! I think I saw something just today in Iraq that was straight out o' Season Four."

"Whatever, man" was all I could say to the dumbass.

I looked over at Ethan again, but he was no help. "I dunno, dude. Despite the excessive juvenile theatrics, Walker has made a surprisingly cogent argument."

Oblivious to the backhanded compliment from Ethan, Walker chimed in with "See, even Co-fag agrees with me."

That should have been the end of it, but for some reason I decided not to drop it. I wasn't even sure why. It just seemed important. Everything seemed important.

"Walker, let me ask you. Do you think, when we're out there on the battlefield, do you think you should have shit like that—ideas that are in that movie—running around in your head?"

"Man, this fucking guy is wack," Walker said, moving toward the door. I guess the conversation was a bit much; two of the guys got up and said something lame about getting some sleep, leaving only me, Maseth, and Ethan.

I ran my fingers through my hair, breathed out heavily as the door closed. Bryan quickly tried to break the tension, clapping his hands, all exaggerated. "Well, *that* went well! Uh, another round, anyone? Coffelt? Beer? Shot of whiskey? Bong hit, perhaps?"

Ethan laughed. "Got any heroin?"

I had to say something. "Look, guys, all I was trying to say is, this war—our mission here—is fucking serious, and every one of us has to have the right head for it. I mean, listen to Walker; he's like a fucking kid! Does he sound to you like he has a handle on what is true and what is bullshit? How's he gonna judge everyday situations on the battlefield?"

Ethan looked at me with raised eyebrows. "This, coming from a guy who wouldn't drink out of a high school water fountain because of a handwritten note . . ."

That took me by surprise. "Ethan, that's totally unrelated. Stay on the subject."

"Oh, no. I think it's related, all right," Ethan said, his eyes widening.

"That was just me being cautious. Anyway . . . ," I said, trying to continue, but Bryan wasn't going to let it go.

He looked at Ethan with a curious smile. "So what happened, now?"

I rolled my eyes and leaned back in my chair. Ethan had center stage, and he was going to tell that stupid story. I looked down at my fingers, picking slowly at a small hangnail on the side of my index finger.

"Okay, so it was our junior year. We were walking down the hall of the Maclellan Building, just got out of chemistry class, and I stop at the water fountain to get a drink. Well, there was a yellow sticky note, and someone had written 'Radioactive, do not drink.'"

"Okay, typical day at high school. Go on," Bryan said, adding his usual sarcasm.

"So Chicken Little over here stops me, exclaims, 'Back off, man! Don't wanna take any chances.' I of course blow it off and go ahead and take a few sips, and he just fucking goes nuts, telling me what a dumbass I am, and I could fucking keel over dead."

As Ethan told the story I tried to smile, to let them know I could take it, but I really saw no humor in it. I mean, taking chances with a life-and-death situation? This wasn't fucking funny to me, 'cause he could have died, when all he had to do was walk two feet down the hall and find another water fountain.

Bryan turned to me, looking uncharacteristically serious. "Dude, can I ask you a question?"

"Yeah."

"Do you think if you know more about what is real here in the Sandbox, that a Johnny Jihad with an IED can't still blow your fucking brains all over the street?"

I looked straight at Bryan. That was an easy answer for me. "It's not about protecting *me*; it's about protecting my fellow soldiers and my country, and I'm willing to die if that's what it takes."

He stared blankly at me for a few seconds, then jumped up and turned slowly to Ethan, doing an impression of Chris Farley's abrasive motivational speaker character, all fat, pulling at his belt to keep his pants from falling down. "Well, hot damn, Co-felt! We got us a regular daggone straight-A student out of boot camp over here!"

Ethan chuckled, adding, "Well, la-dee-freakin-daa!" Then he looked at me. "Sorry, man. That shit was just funny."

"Fuck you guys," I replied, "'cause that's *exactly* what they taught us. Just ask Sergeant Huey. We've got a responsibility here, to watch each other's backs and make sure the missions are a success. How are you gonna do that if you don't understand why we're here, what the overall objectives are? This is important shit, guys."

Ethan raised his eyebrows again and turned his head sideways at me. "Okay, and what if the real reason for being here is not what you believe it to be?"

I could tell he thought he'd got me on that one, like I had no answer. But he didn't realize just how much I had thought this through.

"Then it's my responsibility to find out," I said.

"And you're going to be okay with whatever answer you find," Ethan said, sounding almost condescending.

I wanted to say, *Hey, man, are we forgetting that I talked you into joining? That 9/11 was my calling, not yours? Remember? You were the one who joined because there were no other options, because you'd just been laid off, life in Soddy sucked, your parents had spent the college fund on your six years at McCallie, and the army was your ticket out of there. Ring a bell?* Instead I said, "Of course. If I don't, then I'm not much use to anybody, am I?"

I walked out of the trailer and slammed the door as hard as I could. Something broke off and fell onto the stoop. I headed off toward the south gate, crunching through the gravel. When I got to the dimly lit guard shack, I stopped. It was quiet. For some reason a thought popped into my head that I could go outside the wire, but I didn't. I ended up taking the perimeter road around the FOB, just kept walking and walking.

When I got back I sat in my little spot and smoked until I thought Ethan would be asleep, then peered through the screen door and saw him still reading. Behind him I could see the *Falling Man* poster. *Maybe I should just say fuck it*, I thought, *just relax and be like everyone else. Who cares about higher purpose. Not like I've accomplished shit since I got here. I'm sure Ethan just thinks I still have an anger problem. Fuck that, I've seen anger problems.* I thought of the huge fights my mom and dad used to have. Hysterical screaming and bellowing tones, stomping noises, doors slamming, and finally the sound of something like a body thudding against a wall, followed by wailing and sobbing. My sisters and I would be upstairs, cowering in the bathroom, bawling our eyes out and clinging to each other. The next morning Mom would always fix us one of her elaborate breakfasts, like eggs Sardou or quiche lorraine, and wake us up like it was Christmas morning, talking about the plans for the week with a look of enchantment in her eye. And when we went downstairs, Dad would be gone. A few hours later I might see him walking back inside, and he'd have that look, like he saw through me and I'd better not think the wrong things. But I didn't. There was nothing wrong. We were normal. I'd ask him to play tennis, just the two of us: "I need to work on my serve. Dad, you're such a good teacher! You should've been a coach."

So they both had us. We were like their little liars, the ones who'd play along and smile, define terror as normalcy, anxiety as closeness. I remember a video of Sarah's birthday party. All us kids are at the dining room table, giddy, animated, watching her open her gifts. But several of us have a single hand up at our mouths, picking our lips. Mine used to bleed regularly, I went at it so hard.

It wasn't more than a few days after the conversation with Ethan and Bryan that I got shot. We were rolling in a convoy through the middle of town; I was up top on the .50-cal when some fuckers engaged us from an alleyway next to a mosque. The whole thing lasted no more than twenty seconds—it was *pop! pop!*, little pause, *pop, pop, pop*, one of our guys screaming, "Contact right! Contact right!" and shouting on the platoon radio to the other vehicles, and then the roar of engines as we got the hell out of there. I have no idea where it came from, but in the middle of that split second about a gazillion rounds sprayed up all around me against the side of the Humvee. All I felt was something hit me on the side of the head. Blasted the shit out of my eardrum and knocked my comm wires loose. And next thing I knew, I forgot every fucking thing I had ever known except for the fact that I did *not* want a goddamned bullet or piece of shrapnel to come whizzing into my eyeball and spray my brains all over the inside of my helmet. I scurried down through that turret hole so fucking fast, tumbling into the cab of the truck, and ducked down like mortars were falling from the sky—probably had a look on my face like a monster was coming after me. I wasn't thinking of what I'd said to Bryan before his little Chris Farley routine. It was bizarre; I was actually thinking of the little instruction cards we stuck in our helmets. We had these procedures we were supposed to keep in our helmets at all times, and Ethan and I had been fucking around one night and had taken our cards out and written, "For safety reasons soldiers must at all times keep brain matter off of this instruction card."

When I regained my senses I climbed back up top, trying to ignore the instincts screaming in my head. I had barely heard Sergeant Huey yelling at me to get back on the .50, back on the goddamned .50, but I guess it registered somehow. I manned the gun again and began to fire off rounds into the darkness, not really knowing where to aim, just generally toward the rear. In the madness I thought of that line from the Monty Python movie Ethan and I were always quoting, where the French guy is saying all these mad funny insults: "I fart in your general direction." In this case I was spraying bullets in their general direction. It was complete acoustic bedlam—engines whining as the convoy did ninety through the streets, everyone yelling, small arms fire in the distance, out there in the dark somewhere. I was trying to point away from the shops as we rushed off. There were always little kids running around or men standing in doorways smoking, wearing those goofy white man-dresses. But they took cover as we roared by. Any one of these fuckers could be Mahdi Army, Sunni militants, whatever—any goddamned one of them. But there was no fucking way to know for sure, now, was there? Might as well be back in grammar school trying to figure out which kid would grow up to be Timothy McVeigh. All this rushed through my head. A few seconds later it was over; what more was there to fire at?

We completed our escort at twenty-three thirty. Streets were quiet, nothing going on, such a weird contrast to what we experienced in that short burst. I felt the back of my head. No blood. *Isn't this scenario exactly the same as some forms of torture?* I thought. *Long periods of sensory deprivation interrupted by random spurts of intense fear. It's no fucking wonder so many of us end up with PTSD and shit.* I stayed on my gun and hoped for nothingness. I felt the side of my helmet, dented near the edge with a slight tear now. I played the scene over in my head, grew numb, and stared at buildings passing by like film frames until we arrived back at the FOB.

W elcome back. Have fun?" Ethan asked as I walked into the hooch and dropped my MOLLE pack on the floor. I sat on my cot in full gear, rubbing my eyes and forehead. I bent down and began to untie my boots, pulling uninterestedly on one lace, then stopped and sat up.

"Dude, you okay?" he asked. I heard him stop the video he was playing and walk over to me.

"We took fire, and something clipped my helmet."

"Damn. Really?" He palmed the top of my head and tipped it from side to side, examining my helmet closely. "Yep. There's a big dent in the Kevlar, went through the cloth and . . ." He pulled at the fabric. The shell of the helmet had obviously taken the impact, and whatever it was—AK round or whatever—had been deflected, apparently. I sat there staring at the wall of the trailer.

"Holy shit!" he said, digging his finger underneath the tear in the material.

"What?" I mumbled as I started to unstrap my helmet.

"Check it out, man." Ethan pulled his hand away from my helmet and held it in front of my face. Between his index finger and thumb was a small bullet fragment, all smashed to hell.

"Fuck," I said. I sat there and stared at the thing for a few seconds, took off my helmet, and looked up at him.

He grinned, snatching my Godzilla lighter off the top of my cabinet, and put a cigarette in his mouth. Two little glass eyes lit up with red LEDs as the lighter chirped obnoxiously and a blue flame came out of its mouth.

"Way I see it, this little composite material saved your life today," he said, tapping on the helmet. "When you get back home you should look up the old lady who invented Kevlar and give her a big-ass wet, sloppy French kiss."

I laughed. "I know, right?" I said. "Hey, gimme one of those goddamn things." He handed me a smoke. I sat there taking drags off the cigarette, running my fingers over my scalp, checking.

"So what happened?" he said.

I walked Ethan through the entire experience, second by second, in as much detail as I could remember. Having him there, replaying the experience and laughing a little, really helped. It was like the narration, particularly with the smart-ass commentary, took the danger away, or at least revised it. It somehow split everything into two different palatable stories: one where you play the little mouse running for its life, scared shitless, about to get bitten in half but escaping; the other where you are the badass skateboarder back in high school who just did some ridiculous, idiotic stunt but lived through it, and now you and your buddies are laughing about it.

"Well, at any rate," Ethan said, "best you should know, the Kevlar lady is about a day and a half older than Methuselah."

"That's fine," I said, giggling. "She can have my awesome body for one night; we'll call it even."

After we got done joking around, I did my usual routine: stripped down to my boxers and splashed water on my chest to keep myself cool for the night. Ethan opened the package of glow sticks and hung one over the window, then sat on his bed reading his Stephen Hawking book. I looked in the mirror, turned my head to the side, and rubbed my temple. *Damn, I'm alive.* For a brief moment I had a feeling of giddiness—a huge rush, like I'd just taken a hit of something. I decided to throw on some shorts and grab another smoke before I turned in.

I leaned against the side of the hooch, looking out at the night sky. I thought about the first time I felt like I'd cheated death, back when I was eleven. I was riding my purple BMX bike and got hit by a car in front of our house. We lived on a winding road on Lookout called West Brow, right along the edge of a cliff. I came pedaling like crazy out of the driveway and straight into the road, just as a big Land Rover rounded the corner. I smacked into the right front bumper, which instantly popped my front tire, dragging my bike down the road in a crumpled mess. Meanwhile, I went cartwheeling across the front windshield and landed on the other side of the street. I was almost completely unharmed, except the front wheel of the SUV had pinched the toe of my tennis shoe and managed to rip my toenail clean off. And there I was, standing on my good leg a mere two feet from a spiked wrought-iron fence, peering over in amazement at the sheer drop-off on the other side. *Wow,* I'd thought. *God saved me. He must need me to stay alive.*

I put out my cigarette and headed inside. It was a weird feeling; stupid, really. What had happened to me was nothing. Shit way more serious happened dozens of times every day in the Sandbox, and no one else had really even noticed my deal. But I couldn't help myself. I felt so . . . invincible.

When I lay down on my cot, I looked up and saw the poster, and suddenly everything I'd been thinking blew up in my face. *I am such an asshole. How disrespectful, thinking that shit. Who was there to keep Mercer alive, huh? You self-righteous, self-important prick.* I kept staring at the poster. *He was actually doing something useful. What have you done? Fucking nothing. Maybe you should have died, you useless piece of shit.*

I closed my eyes and breathed in deeply. *Get a grip, man. Goddamn. You haven't been here long enough to get messed up in the head.*

That night I had a dream about the time Dad kicked through the bathroom door. It started out exactly as I remembered it, from when I was ten. Mom had locked herself in the bathroom after one of their fights. She was screaming that she was going to take pills and kill herself. My sisters were all in my parents' bedroom, bawling, scared, confused. Karen was huddled in the corner next to the door, her knees pulled up underneath her nightgown. She was screeching as pieces of the wooden door broke off and fell next to her. In the dream, I was watching, trying to figure out what to do. All of a sudden my friend Andy stepped inside the doorway of the bedroom, totally out of context, like he was walking onto a movie set unannounced. Everyone stopped what they were doing and turned toward him. He motioned to my sisters and said, "Come, come! That door is just Kevlar." My sisters got up off the floor and went running to him. Andy gathered them together right outside the bedroom and gave them beer. They all started drinking bottle after bottle and got drunk. I didn't run like them but just stood there frozen while Dad got back to kicking the door in. Then he turned to me and said, "Just standing there, I see" in a disparaging way, as if I should follow Andy because at least he was taking action.

I woke up abruptly, thinking I needed to come up with a quick excuse, some kind of justification, a defense, and then I realized where I was. I lay there in the dark, agitated, trying to figure out why I'd had such a vivid, symbolic dream. The door thing was something I'd almost forgotten about. My mom had told me a long time ago I would suppress some memories, that it was natural, for survival. *The door. It was Kevlar . . . oh, right, like my helmet, but because . . . 'cause it represents protection, I guess? Okay, what about Andy?* I hadn't thought of him in months, and he had pretty much fallen off the radar years ago. He was kind of shitty about keeping in touch after we graduated. Went off to some no-name college in middle Tennessee. Biblical studies, apparently. Found a new, non-secular set of friends, I guess. Never gave me his email address. I'd even called his dad, Reverend Stoops, two months before I left for Iraq, asking him to tell Andy about my deployment. He had just let out a chuckle and said that Andy hadn't been home recently and that he didn't know his cell or contact info. What? I remember I paused for a moment, picturing Reverend Stoops on the phone in his church office—the red beard, smoking his pipe with that permanent jovial grin on his face. His chortles always translated to something; in this case it was "That Andrew, what a character!" I tried not to take it personally, not to read too much into it. But sure enough, Andy never called or even emailed, and I never knew why. Maybe his dad hung up the phone with me and just got back to working on his sermon; maybe Andy did get the message but scrawled down my number and couldn't read his own handwriting; or maybe the napkin fell on the floorboard of Andy's Triumph Spitfire and got buried underneath his Camus books and beer bottles. I'd never know.

The beer. What the hell was that about? I thought, stepping outside to grab a smoke. I was careful to ease the door shut so I wouldn't wake Ethan. I lit up a cigarette and stood outside. The dim light of the glow stick shone through the window.

I thought about the break-in incident. Dad, Diane, and I were on vacation in Europe. Andy and his foreign exchange friend, Heiner, got drunk off their asses as usual and got into Dad's house through an old painted-over window that wouldn't lock. My stepmother had arranged for her parents, who lived five minutes away, to keep an eye on the house, and they had apparently interpreted this as "patrol the house every two minutes." So of course Andy and Heiner were busted. The way Andy described it to me, the two of them were passed out all over the living room floor, heard a vehicle, and jumped up in a panic right in front of the windows just as the gramps pulled up in the driveway going three miles an hour in their monster Cadillac.

Diane's parents decided to keep it to themselves until we came back from Europe, which was pretty generous of them, I thought. But when we returned I got a nice, long sit-down talk with Dad and Diane at the Victorian dining room table, including an academic discussion of the dynamics of property ownership and respecting other people. My dad saw this as an opportunity to present another object lesson and remained calm. I sat there and listened intently. I felt bad about what they had to deal with—their first year in that big dream house, worrying about us punk-ass kids spilling shit by accident or knocking over antiques. I felt guilty even living there. I felt responsible for Andy breaking and entering—even though I kind of knew I had not done anything—and I thought the least I could do to make it up to Dad and Diane was to be accountable for what my friend had done. But my stepmother had a look on her face I would never forget. It was a mixture of rage and resentment, as if I was a pain in the ass she had not signed up for, and neither me nor anyone I was associated with would be tolerated. My dad and his wife were captains of the royal fleet of parenting. They were both MDs, and they were used to more than just respect. More like reverence.

The alarm went off on my Nokia. Zero six hundred. Ethan was already up, watching Bill Maher episodes his mom had burned on DVD. I dragged myself out of bed and got my gear together. We went out on another checkpoint, stationed near a highway exit, stopping the cars that came by every so often. Mostly we just stood around in the sun sweating, smoking cigarettes. Ethan did his parkour thing, vaulting over jersey barriers and doing flips off the roof of the guard station. A minor dust storm came in but cleared up pretty quickly. At noon he and I grabbed a couple of MREs and sat against the sandbags and ate chow, and I told him about the dream, trying to prompt him for a psychoanalysis.

"Hmm, that is interesting. The Kevlar door, Andy with the beer—how fitting—your sisters . . ."

"Yeah, definitely means something," I said.

"Don't know, dude. I think Carl Jung might have to rework his entire theory over that one," he said, biting into his burrito.

"Can you believe Andy wanted to be a preacher?"

Ethan shook his head, laughing. "Pfft, for God's sake, just don't put him in charge of providing the wine for Communion!"

I laughed. "Hey, do you remember the time he and Heiner got busted breaking into Dad's house?"

"God, dude, how could I forget? You got the big guilt trip, and you weren't even there, right?"

"We were in Europe."

"Oh yeah! Your folks met you over there. I remember. You worked your ass off all year saving up for the trip, but Andy fucked up and blew all his money, so he couldn't go."

"Yep."

Ethan looked amused. "Man, I remember how fucking pissed you were when Andy bought a rose for Diane and made you look like a dick."

A couple of days after Dad and Diane found out about the break-in, Andy showed up at my dad's house with a yellow rose for my step-mother and rattled off a bullshit apology, and he was instantly cleared of all charges and forgiven, no questions asked.

"That fucker set me up," I said half seriously.

"Uh, son, we'd like you to look at what Andrew did, because that is the shining example of what a son *should* act like," Ethan said, imitating my dad's voice.

My dad loves to tell the story, beaming with excitement when he gets to the part about the rose. He'll form his hand into the okay sign, looking you straight in the eye as if delivering the most profound words ever spoken on earth, and say, "Now *that's* atonement."

"Oh, never mind that I didn't have a drinking problem, didn't do drugs, barely had even smoked pot, didn't have sex, never got arrested and thrown in jail . . . Jesus!" I said.

"Right, you were like the ideal son. Andy commits an infraction far worse than you would ever even *think* of doing, and with one brown-nose gesture he's not just cleared of all charges, but he sets a standard for *you* to follow! Yeah, that was pretty fucked up."

I impulsively threw in a jab at Ethan. "Yeah, it's not like I broke into the nuclear plant guard shack and placed a long-distance call to Russia or anything."

Ethan laughed. "Senator, I do not recall the incident to which you are referring."

"Rrrright. 'Uh, ma'am, this is AT&T, looks like the call your son placed was from Friday at midnight to about, uh . . . oh, here it is, *Monday fucking morning,* when the plant opened back up! Now, will this be cash or check?'"

"Don't remind me," he said defensively. "I think I still have scars on my ass."

"Well, I still don't see what that fucking dream meant. Dude, my dreams never make sense like that."

Ethan gave me a sheepish look. "Uh, I think it means your head ain't where it should be, soldier."

"No, seriously, Ethan. It made sense, it was like real life, not just random nonsense images. And it meant something, I just have no idea what."

"Well, uh . . . Kevlar, that is what saved your ass. Andy said the door's Kevlar."

"He said, 'It's just Kevlar,' and then he tells my sisters to come with him."

"And they go get wasted. Typical Andy way of handling his problems, maybe?"

"He's gotta represent the church . . . religion. Ah, so my sisters go running to religion, okay."

Ethan laughed. "There ya go. They's drunk on Jesus!"

"And I don't go with them, I don't follow Andy," I said.

"Hey, if it'd been my ass, I'd be like, 'See ya!' Zing! Out the window!"

"Ha ha, I know, right? For some reason I stayed, and Dad ridiculed me for it."

"Dun, dun, duuun! Now we're talkin' *Mama Day* level of symbolism. You stayed. What's that represent? Sorve diss ploblem, grasshoppah, you will know thyself!"

The next week we started doing night convoy escorts, rolling out late in the evening, the sky dimly lit by flares from helicopters in the distance. It was nice not to have to deal with the debilitating heat or drink bottled water like we did during daytime missions. The smells were worse, though. Piles of burning trash, open sewage, bodies floating in canals, and God knows what else caused a nasty, nauseatingly sweet rotten-egg stench to fill the air.

With the evening schedule I was able to stop by the internet hut every day to check email, but I wasn't getting much. I'd given my family the email address I'd set up just for Iraq, but they were either not into computers or afraid of the technology. One of my sisters even summarily stated she preferred not to have an email account. I did get an email from my uncle. He wrote to tell me they'd had to take Dottie to the hospital, but Glenn hadn't called him back, so he didn't know more. No one else emailed me, so I wasn't worried. I figured surely they'd email me about that.

One evening we were on a stretch of road just outside town. We were in the lead vehicle. Bryan was at the wheel, I was riding shotgun, and Huey and Walker were in the back. Ethan was with the platoon commander in the rear Humvee, behind two KBR tractor-trailers. Everything had been quiet; all our stops had been routine, with no incidents whatsoever. We just rode along, trying to stay alert, listening to the radio crackle calling out checkpoints. I remember feeling I should be glad that it was boring.

As we approached a small group of houses, a couple of little girls walked up to the road from between some bushes next to what looked like a path that led into the hills. At first I saw them in the distance, with three goats following behind them, tethered by ropes tied to the girls' waists. It occurred to me how odd it was, and just before we began to pass them it looked as if they were going to walk along the road in the same direction as us. But the one taller girl was yanking the other one's arm, trying to direct her. She must have been so focused on controlling her sister that she didn't think about how wide the trucks were. In a split second they stopped and began turning around in the small space between the bushes and the road.

"Shit!" Maseth yelled as we roared past, the side mirror barely missing one of the goats. I shot my head out of the window and looked back as one of the goats was struck by the front of the tractor-trailer. The little girl was yanked up by the rope and slammed against the side of the truck. I heard two horrible thudding sounds and the skidding of tires, then saw what looked like the older girl hurtle herself over the bushes and into the dark.

I turned back around and looked at Maseth.

"What the fuck was that?" Walker yelled from the back.

"Stop the vehicle," I said.

Maseth was trying to look over at me while still watching the road, but he wasn't slowing down. "We can't do that, man."

I lost it. "Bryan, pull this vehicle the fuck over!"

Sergeant Huey leaned into the front seat. "If we slow down, they fucking RPG our asses, you guys know that."

"Fuck this goddamn . . . oh my fucking . . ." I shouted, trying to form a sentence. My lips quivered, and tears ran down my face and over my chinstrap. The convoy kept going, even slightly faster than before.

A voice came on the radio. "What the fuck? Victor One, were those little kids?"

"Affirmative, plus some sheep or goats or something."

"Do *not* halt convoy. They're fucking dead," the convoy commander said.

A bit of vomit came up into my mouth and spilled onto my chin. I wiped it off with my sleeve and coughed, then cleared my eyes with my fingers and looked out the window behind us again. I turned back around and stared at the road. My mind was a blur; it felt like I had been drugged, like I was lost in a nightmare.

Sergeant Huey leaned forward again and looked at me. "Look, man, there's nothing we could do. And it was their fault, not ours. They should have—"

"Oh, thanks, Sergeant, I feel great now," I said in a low voice, pausing for a second. Huey sat back down.

"He's right, man, ain't nuttin' we coulda done," Walker said.

I sat for a few seconds, staring forward, then punched the windshield so hard I split the seam of my glove. "Oh, well, fantastic, guys! Let's go get a FUCKING ICE CREAM!"

We drove for another forty-five minutes, stopping by checkpoints and moving on. I focused on staying alert, trying to forget what happened like everyone else had seemed to. I saw a dog run into the street and then scurry away as we approached. A small figure sat on the curb under a palm tree. When the lights of the truck shone there, I could see it was another little girl; it looked like she was five or so. It almost made me explode to see her. I couldn't take it. *Those innocent little girls, poor, innocent, cute-as-a-fucking-button little girls, smashed by a truck hauling stuff to wipe our asses with. Toilet paper, or paper plates, cups, boxes—things we could easily buy from the locals for two goddamn cents apiece to help them out, give them money to feed their goats . . .* The tears started coming, and I just lost it, and I didn't give a fuck what these assholes thought of me. *Cute little innocent girls walking their goats. This fucking sucks. This fucking sucks.*

Bryan kept driving and left me alone for a while, then asked if I was okay. I tried to get back on track and keep him from being affected by what had happened.

"Yeah, I'm good," I said, pretty sure he wouldn't believe me. He didn't respond, just kept driving. A few minutes before we arrived back at the FOB, he spoke up again. "Listen, man, we're gonna see some fucked-up shit here."

"I know," I said. "I heard stories about convoys before I left, most of it probably bullshit, exaggerated or whatever."

"I don't know," he said doubtfully. "My buddy in Echo has done all sorts of escorts. He says they run vehicles off the road all the time, fire at 'em, mad crazy shit like that."

I took a quick look in the backseat. Sergeant Huey was staring out the window, smoking. Walker looked up at me. He didn't have the same gangsta expression. "You a'ight, man?" he asked.

"Yeah," I said, turning back around. "Bryan, you seem okay. How much have *you* personally seen?"

He pulled a cigarette out. "I've only seen one thing, really," he said, pausing. "Okay, let me put it this way: if I make it out of this motherfucker alive, and I get back home, and a few years later I'm cuckoo for Cocoa Puffs, in a straitjacket and a padded cell, it is because of one specific thing I saw."

He paused, taking a deep breath—seemed to be thinking of how to say it. "So this one time, this old Iraqi woman approached our vehicle, looked like she had something in her hand. We told her to stop. I kept telling her to stop. Bitch wouldn't stop, kept coming at us."

"You all had to take her out, I assume."

"Well . . ." Then Bryan stopped talking. I looked over at him. He checked the rearview mirror, sniffing as if to shrug off the thought. I started to interrupt, change the subject, but he blurted out the rest of it.

"It wasn't 'we,' okay? It was me. I took her out. I took the first shot . . . and then, then everyone just fucking unloaded on her, tore her to shreds."

"Damn, dude."

"Yeah, so I lied, it wasn't what I saw, it's what I did. I killed that hajji woman, and come to find out, the bitch wasn't even . . . it was a goddamned blanket she had in her hand."

"Fuck, man, that is messed up."

"Yeah. What are ya gonna do? She's dead. I'm alive. I got her blanket."

"What? You kept her blanket?"

"Yeah, I held on to it, tried to find out who she was so I could maybe give it back to her family."

"That's pretty cool of you, man," I said.

"'Pretty cool,'" he said absentmindedly, then added tersely, "Nothing about that day was pretty cool. But what really fucks with my head is, what if the shit happens again? It happens again just like before, but this time I hesitate, and it turns out it *is* an insurgent, and one of us gets taken out 'cause I fuckin' froze up."

"Yeah," I said, trying to sound like I understood, "but I'm sure you—"

"How the fuck do I live with that, huh? Or what if I'm so worried about freezing up, I jump the gun again and shoot a fucking kid or something? Oh, that would be just peachy to live with."

He sniffed loudly and looked out the window. I started to say something, but he turned to me. "You know what? Most of the time I feel like I'm on a fucking tightrope. You either fall this way or you fall that way, but your ass is gonna fall—unless you got some kind of perfect Zenlike concentration. So every day I tell myself, Man up, pussy. Keep your head together and don't look down. Keep walking, 'cause every step I don't fall I'm closer to rotating back stateside. Once that happens I can cry like a little bitch to a VA shrink all day if I want to, but while I'm here in the suck? Just try to stuff it away, put it in a box, and I can open it later, maybe at a time when one little mistake won't mean somebody gets killed."

It was then I saw a side of Bryan that surprised me. Besides being a pretty damn good soldier and goddamned hilarious, he was apparently a decent human being. *Why would he want to hang out with Walker?* I wondered. Maybe he needed the contrast to feel better about himself. Maybe Walker helped him suppress shit, helped him put it in a box, as he put it.

Even though I knew intellectually that what Bryan was saying made sense, emotionally I was still unable to get the image of those girls out of my head. When we finally finished the run and got back to base, I got out of the truck like a zombie and headed for the showers. As I passed the rear wheels I noticed their size, the huge treads, the solid metal fender. I looked away as horrible details popped into my head. Dazed and gut-sick all over again, I muttered to myself, "Put it in a box . . . yeah, right."

The next day we were put back on checkpoint duty again. I assumed it was because of what had happened during the escort, but Huey didn't mention it in the briefing. He just gave Ethan the coordinates to another highway exit, and we spent the day stopping cars every half hour or so. The temperature was well over a hundred. Mirages hovered above the surface of the pavement, shimmering with invisible flames, and sparrows chirped in the sparse trees nearby. Bryan, Ethan, and I tried to stay in the small cement structure behind the barriers, where at least we had shade, but we got bored, so we kept stepping out onto the patio. That was nothing but a small slab of concrete surrounded by a four-foot-high wall buttressed with sandbags, but it was all we had. Walker stayed outside on the off-ramp, fifteen meters away from us, walking from side to side on the pavement and waiting for vehicles to come.

"Gimme one of those Poland Springs," Bryan said to me, putting his helmet down on top of the wall and wiping the skin on his head with his hand. "Coffelt, did you see what happened to those little girls?" he asked. He squeezed some water out of the bottle onto his hand and doused his face.

Ethan walked outside the enclosure, adjusting his M4 sling over his shoulder. "Dude, I'm rapidly accumulating a fuck-long list of experiences I want desperately to forget here in this godforsaken hellhole, and that shit yesterday is right at the top of the list, ya feel me?"

"That was some fucked-up shit," Bryan said, turning to look at me before he put his shades back on. "I wish we could have stopped, helped 'em out." He sounded so aloof, so unaffected, like he was trying to feel something, say the right words, but there was nothing behind them.

I looked down at my hands, checking out my fingernails, then bit at the side of my thumb, where the edge of the nail was uneven. Bryan slapped my shoulder. "But Mister Sensitive over here sure was pretty messed up over it," he said, giving me a sympathetic smile. "Naw, it's cool, man," he said. "It kind of got to me too. I mean, those little girls went flying. God, who *knows* where they ended up . . . wonder if somebody—"

"Ended up?" I blurted out. "They *ended up* dead, dude. Thrown a hundred feet, smashed to shit, okay?"

I turned around and went back into the shelter. Bryan paused for a second, then said something to Ethan. A few seconds later I heard suppressed laughter, just a little. I knew it wasn't that big of a deal, just their way of handling it. But I still went to the window and leaned on the sandbags, near enough so they knew I could hear them.

Bryan glanced over at me and then asked Ethan something, and Ethan motioned toward me. Bryan looked at me again. "Dude," he shouted, "did you really see everything—I mean, that much detail?"

I looked away from him, across the wall toward Walker, focusing on his pacing back and forth and swatting bugs away from his face. In no way did I want to replay those goddamned images in my head. I turned back to Bryan but kept my eyes straight ahead.

"Yes, I did," I said. And that was that. I guess no one felt like saying anything else about it. Ethan reached into his knee pouch and started packing down his cigarettes on the top of the wall. Bryan swatted at his temple, swearing about "fucking gnats." I remember thinking this was such a typical male gesture; when a buddy is upset, act pissed off too, to show your alliance. I saw through it, but still, I appreciated him doing that.

Later, when we broke for chow, the three of us stood leaning against the wall, opening up MREs. Bryan called over to Walker, asking if he was hungry, but the psycho said he'd already had baby lamb and kept pacing back and forth. We'd been with him. We knew he hadn't eaten yet.

Bryan just shook his head. "That boy's worse off than you, that's for damn sure," he said, scooping up some beef ravioli. "He's seen shit like you don't even wanna know."

He was right. I didn't.

In the first week of August, I got a small package from my sister Kelly. I pulled the tear strip, and inside was an envelope and a small box gift wrapped in Winnie the Pooh paper. On the envelope were the words "Pathetically belated and not even store-bought Birthday Card. Sorry!" next to a smiley face. I opened the card first: "Hey Bro, Happy Birfday!!!" The B was written in huge bold print with a red crayon.

> I am sooooo sorry I am mailing this card late. You know how it is, takin' care of a young'un! He's quite the handful these days. Ooo but he's so cute! Sorry I don't have photos. We've been very dissatisfied with daycare in the area and have been frantically looking for a new one—and guess what? We found one!! Word of Life Christian. Phew! What a relief. Oops, sorry, looks like I am almost out of room. Happy birthday, bro, we miss you and stay safe. Love, Kel.

In the margin she wrote, "Again, so sorry this card is late, I feel reeeee (e times 1000)-ly bad."

Inside the gift wrap was a colorful box with a cellophane window and a picture of a bear dressed in fatigues. The bear was saluting in front of a cake with all his friends, about to blow out candles. The chocolate inside had melted during shipping and pooled at the bottom of the box, filling it halfway up the cellophane window. I guessed it used to be in the shape of a beehive or something.

I put the card next to my boots and swept off the bed with my hand. I lay down and thought about what she had written. It seemed a little off somehow. How many times had she written "sorry"? Did she really think, being in Iraq, I would care if I got a birthday card late? I remembered how growing up we were so close, how we'd spend all day thinking of some daredevil stunt—walking on the roof of the house, learning to ride a unicycle, or trying to go the entire weekend climbing around the house without touching the floor. The summer when I was about eight years old, we spent a week at our grandparents' in Nashville, sneaking around and holding secret meetings we called "children's conferences" to talk about my paranoid grandmother accusing us of stupid things like laughing at how she chewed her biscuits or "getting any ideas" about her stamp money—a baggie with exactly thirteen pennies in it. A few years later we would hide outside Mom and Dad's room for hours listening to their horrible fighting, and I would convince my sister we should sneak my dad's handgun for our protection.

Now it was so different. She *sounded* the same—I could hear the same voice that had always connected us—but the words were off, as if she didn't know I was in Iraq, like there was nothing at all to be serious about. Where was the sister who'd been the closest to me during all that trauma? Gone. Fucking gone.

Maseth walked in the door and saw I had opened a package from home. "Hope those aren't druuugs, mmmkay?" he said, imitating Mr. Mackey from *South Park*, "cuz drugs are bayud, mmmkay?"

"It's chocolate," I mumbled, trying not to start a conversation.

He laughed sarcastically. "Chocolate? Uh, don't they know it's like two hundred degrees here in the shade, over dry ice with a fan blowing?"

"Fuck if I know." I tossed the card aside, wadded up the wrapping paper, and grabbed the boxes and everything else, then walked out of the trailer to go get a shower. On the way out I opened the trash bin and threw it all in, letting the lid slam behind me. My sister would have cried her eyes out if she'd known I'd done that, but Jesus, what was I supposed to do, unfold the box and lick the chocolate off the cardboard?

W e had been on a daytime schedule ever since the accident with the goat girls. Mostly checkpoints, with a few cordons here and there. Our situation seemed stable. I tried not to overthink it, 'cause shit could go down anytime. But for now things were routine and uneventful. We could afford to relax a little.

One afternoon we were at a highway exit, leaning against some jersey barriers, eating chow.

Ethan leaned over with a smirk, peeking inside my MRE. "Mmm, is that tagliatelle or orecchiette? I can't quite place it."

"Well, let's see," I said, turning up the bag. "Spaghetti with meat and sauce."

The guys laughed. "Excellent choice," Ethan said dryly. "Me, I prefer my exquisite quote-finger pasta with cheese-flavored goo."

We sat for a few minutes, chewing, swatting insects away from our faces.

"Hey," Bryan said, "you guys know that guy Stuart they call Big Country?"

"Big Country?" Ethan asked.

"He's in Gafni's platoon, looks like a linebacker, got a thick southern drawl . . ."

"Never met him," I said, tearing open a Gatorade packet.

"Well, I heard he got the call from his fiancée yesterday, said she's bangin' Jody now. He's pretty messed up about it."

"Daaamn!" Ethan exclaimed. "No Dear John letter, she actually *called* his ass?"

"Yeah, long distance from Nashville. Dropped the Jody bomb on his ass. Boom, baby!"

"Goddamn," I said. "Model military spouse there."

"So a few of us were going to get together, try to throw him a little fuck da bitch party. You guys are welcome to come."

Ethan broke into sarcastic laughter. "Gee, I'll have to check my Day-Timer." He mimed opening up his organizer and pointing to a calendar, then curled his lip and shook his head, mocking disappointment. "Yeah, looks like I have a war going on that day."

"No, Co-tard, we're just going to pick a slow night, make sure there are no briefings, and hang out for an hour or so. My Asian Mafia connection's gonna try to snap some Iraqi hooch."

"Wow," I said. "Are you serious?"

"Yeah, they already got the okay from the commanders and shit; they know what the situation is. They're going to look the other way, might even stop by to make sure nobody gets too wasted."

Ethan's eyes widened. "Uh, hello? General Order Numero Uno? No alcohol in Muslim countries? And who the hell they gonna get it from? I thought it was outlawed by the Mahdi Army."

"Hail, I don't know, Co-fag!" Bryan said sardonically. "But they can. Said it comes from Diyala Province."

Ethan chuckled. "Hmm, I don't know about that."

I looked at Bryan and kept chewing. *He cracks me up*, I thought, *but Jody fucking your girl while you're here in Iraq? That just isn't funny.*

"Don't worry, boys. You ain't gonna get no Article 15 for drinkin' just this once."

"No, it's not that," Ethan said. "If I were this guy—my woman cheated on me—I would *not* want dudes throwing me a damn party. Just leave me the fuck alone in my misery. You sure he'll be okay with this?"

Bryan tore an MRE pouch open and emptied a few crackers into his hand. "Yeah, I thought the same thing, but apparently he doesn't care. He's already told his whole squad about her cheatin'. He really just wants to drown his sorrows."

"And how exactly will this help our mission in Iraq?" I asked.

Bryan sprayed a few cracker crumbs out of his mouth, all goofy and exaggerated. "Jesus, man, the dude just lost his fiancée. Give him a ten-minute break from the fucking mission in Iraq, for God's sake."

I didn't know what to say to that. *Bryan has a point,* I remember thinking. *He's a pretty cool guy. But how naïve can you get? Chances are the guy is making the shit up, too scared to fight, wants a discharge or something. A Jody call? Come on. We all sang those stupid cadences during basic: "Ain't no use in callin' home, Jody's got your girl and gone." Bullshit like that. They're just cadences. Jokes, essentially. Because shit like that just doesn't happen that often in war. Most loved ones at home wouldn't just turn on a soldier who's serving his country.*

The day they decided to get Stuart wasted, the squad leaders coordinated to make sure everyone was a go for that night. We were told to meet behind the port-o-johns next to the supply building, where no one was likely to walk by or hear anything. While Maseth was off helping to get Big Country to the party, Ethan and I secured a few folding camp chairs, a small plastic table, and a portable lamp. We went and set up the stuff, then smoked cigarettes and chatted about some brilliant astrophysicist Ethan saw on Bill Maher.

About fifteen minutes later we saw lights near the corner of the building. We looked over as Bryan and an Asian guy came shuffling around the corner, holding two ends of some big-ass crate or something. One of them dropped his end, and the sound of clinking bottles echoed off the building. "You thuuupid muthah . . . ," the guy quipped at Bryan. They resumed inching toward us, bent over and straining.

Ethan was in a good mood. He let out a puff of smoke and stood there staring as they got closer. "What is this, bring your own fully loaded treasure chest?"

Bryan let out a short burst of laughter and started losing his grip. "Oh, *that* helps," he said as they took quick baby steps and plopped the thing down next to the table. "Thanks, Tuy."

I recognized the Asian guy. "Hey, I remember you. Port-o-johns prank, right?"

"Which one?" He smirked at me with one raised eyebrow and made a self-satisfied giggling sound like SpongeBob.

"Where's the guest of honor?" I asked.

"Dewango and him are on their way . . . oh, here they come," Bryan said, looking past me toward the building.

"So there's six of us total?"

"Plus Mr. 'Fucking Arab.'"

"Oh God, no. Butterbar Gafni?" Ethan said, turning to me. In the dim light I could see a look that said "what the fuck?"

"I know, right?" I held my hands up as if in warning. "Whatever you do, men, do not spill any coffee on yourselves tonight." Bryan wasn't paying attention. He was bent over, taking bottles, Styrofoam cups, and ice out of what I could see now was a wooden ammo crate they were using as a cooler.

"Oh, hey, guys, listen up," Bryan whispered, motioning everyone to huddle up. "Before they get over here, be aware Big Country is a fucking mess, okay? So be cool. Don't be dicks, okay?" Then he added, "Well, you can be dicks as usual, just not to him."

"Of course. No problem," I answered. I was glad he'd said that. To me it went without saying—it wasn't the time to act like locker-room assholes—but it said a lot about Bryan, that it was important to him to take care of a fellow soldier. And it made sense too, to make sure all of us maintained the best possible mental condition for the battlefield. I was impressed.

Ethan and I noticed a square bottle with a yellow label written in Arabic, and I got started pouring it into the Styrofoam cups. Bryan picked up a couple and handed them to Thiessen and Gafni as they walked up to the table. Stuart followed behind them. Slightly heavyset, shaved head, he managed a half smile as he grabbed his drink.

"Gentlemen," Bryan announced, exaggerating his drawl, "this right here is some gen-u-wine I-racki hooch—aka two-hundred-proof camel piss! Enjoy."

Everyone grabbed a chair except Tuy, who set up some music on a laptop, then stood by the table examining one of the bottles. Bryan started telling us how Tuy had gotten the stuff smuggled in through his Iraqi connection. It was actually pretty interesting how it worked. Nothing sophisticated. Just some old guy who drove the produce truck to the DFAC. KBR contractor, cheap labor. He spoke just enough English, was well known at the FOB, and happened to have a nephew from Diyala. It didn't sound like he dealt in anything super-illegal, just some porno mags from kids on the streets of Baghdad, whiskey, and maybe a little hashish. The whole time Tuy seemed totally uninterested, except when Bryan referred to him as an ex–5T gang member. "Jumudda!" Tuy muttered.

"I heard the guards at the main gate are doing the same type of shit," Delaney said. "They take morphine, Percocet, amphetamines from the med units and sell them."

Bryan laughed. "Well, shit, son. Git us some contacts. We're talkin' cha-ching!"

"Right, and get my ass thrown out, dishonorable. I don't think so, Cookie Dick."

The conversation continued like that for a while, getting stupider as the alcohol began to take effect. Then Gafni spoke up. "Okay, so you fuckin' Joes convinced me to look the other way so you could get one of my men shitfaced," he said, getting up and walking slowly to the table, "but let's just get a few things straight: (a) tonight didn't happen, (b) I was not aware of any party with alcohol, and (c) I sure as hell didn't drink any of it." Then he turned around dramatically and looked at Stuart, who was holding a plastic bottle marked "Listerine." "All I saw was Big Country chugging a whole motherfucking bottle of mouthwash!"

Suddenly the noise was uncontrollable. We were all way more drunk than we'd expected to be at that point, and the idea of Stuart chugging sent us over the top.

"Chug! Chug! Chug!" we chanted.

Stuart took the bottle and twisted off the cap. "If this shit ain't got alcohol, I'm gonna kick y'all's ass into next week." He tipped it up and drank for a few seconds, then passed it around. I was glad he didn't keep going. I finished what was in my Styrofoam cup, looking around the perimeter to make sure their yelling hadn't alerted anyone. The hooch was nasty—tasted like soap-infused nail polish remover. I stood up, bracing myself on Ethan's shoulder, and walked over to the table. Tuy was holding an upside-down glass, apparently full of some kind of alcohol, against the surface of the table.

What is this fucker up to? I thought, looking at the glass sitting near the edge. He struck me as one of those weirdos at a party who doesn't want to be in the midst of people but just can't help trying to draw attention to himself.

"Do you know how you can turn the glass right side up without spilling the liquid?" he asked.

I reached down to the crate to fill my cup. "No idea, dude." I rustled through various bottles, looking for something a little more palatable. "Anything in here that doesn't taste like ass?"

The guy ignored me and continued to try to get my attention. "No, seriously, most people don't know how to do it, and it's so simple."

I found another Listerine bottle. *Straight vodka might taste like jet fuel, but that'd probably be an improvement.* I poured a little in the cup, swirled it around, and emptied it on the ground, looking sideways at Tuy. "Real tough," I said. "You lift the glass and the table together and turn them upside down."

He was messing around with the portable lamp now and replied bluntly—matter of fact, yet almost indifferent about it—"No, that's against the rule. You can't move the table."

'Against the rule'? I thought. *Nice plural.* I glanced over at the group to see if they were talking about anything interesting, then turned back, folding my arms. "So what's the answer, Confucius?" I said.

He seemed to know exactly what I was thinking. "Dude, it's not a trick question," he said, as if warning me not to make an idiot out of myself.

"Whatever," I said, wondering what his comeback would be. But instead he was reaching his hand in his pocket to answer his cell phone. He flipped it open. "What up, fool?" He began walking toward the building, talking smack with whoever was on the other end. Sounded like a friend from back home. *How's he calling stateside?* I thought.

I leaned against the table and sipped the vodka, watching the guys bullshit each other and fall over in their chairs. They began telling quick anecdotes about times they got dumped or cheated on. Delaney and a couple of others joined in and tried to tell the most god-awful, lewd cheating stories they could. Tuy came back to the table, snapping his cell shut and slipping it into his pocket.

"Well, did you figure it out?"

I hadn't really thought much about it, and no obvious answer came to mind. *But what the hell*, I thought, *I'll play his game.* "Okay, how about you flip the glass over super fucking fast?"

He gave me a humorous look of exaggerated disdain. "*Idiota.* You'd still lose at least *some* liquid that way."

"But you'd get most of it."

"Right, but how can you get all of it?"

I stared at the glass for a few seconds; he had convinced me this wouldn't end up being some stupid, hokey trick question. "Hmm, can't move the table?"

"No. Look, think of the liquid. Think of what the liquid wants to do."

I processed what he said. "'What the liquid wants to do' . . ."

"Yeah. Allow the liquid to do what it wants to do."

"What?" I totally didn't understand. "Fall to the ground?"

He put his hand around the glass near the rim and carefully slid the glass toward the middle of the table, leaning over and positioning himself as if setting up for a pool shot. "Okay." He chuckled at himself. "Now, uh, I've never actually"—cough, cough—"done this or anything!"

I rolled my eyes. "Nor has anyone else, probably."

"Hang on, hang on," he said, looking back and forth along the tabletop. He moved the lamp near the edge so he could see both the surface and the ground.

"You dern crazy Chinaman!" Maseth yelled, looking over from his chair and standing up to come over. "That better not be vodka, holmes."

"Uh, oops. Sorry, bossth," Tuy said, staring into the glass, motionless. Then all of a sudden he slid the glass across and off the table in one smooth motion, letting go as it reached the edge, except to tip it into a rotation. The glass and vodka fell in a parabolic arc, at which point he gripped the glass tightly and let his hand and the bottom of the glass land safely on the sand.

"Oh my fucking God, dude," I exclaimed. "How'd you do that?"

"And what was the point of all this?" Bryan asked. Tuy started looking for something around the crate.

"Turn the glass over without spilling," I answered.

"Hey, where's that laminated instruction sheet or whatever?" Tuy asked.

I looked over and saw something leaning against the crate. "This?"

"Yeah," he said, taking it from my hand and covering the glass with it. He then flipped the glass and the laminated sheet facedown onto the table, pulled the sheet out, and dropped it in the sand. "Who's next?"

I turned to Bryan. "What the fuck, I'll give it a whirl." If this guy had done it in one try, I didn't see how it couldn't work, yet something told me it wasn't going to be good. I just had a bad feeling about it. Sure enough, I positioned myself, concentrated, and thought about the physics and everything, but at the part where you loosen your grip and let the glass rotate, the damned thing slipped out of my hand and tumbled onto the ground, vodka spilling everywhere.

Bryan started laughing but also wasn't too pleased. "Fucking brilliant! Only alcohol in the entire FOB. Go ahead and just dump the shit on the ground. It's all good."

Tuy showed only slight amusement, grabbing the laminated sheet off the ground. "Okay, maybe we should use water for you—ahem—noobs."

"Okay, Maseth, *you* go this time," I said, then looked over at Ethan. "Hey, dude, come see this shit."

Bryan grabbed the glass and slid it off the table, rotating it okay, but it hit the ground hard and most of the water spilled out of the glass.

"Way to waste precious water, duuude," I said with a surfer accent, laughing my ass off.

"Okay, wait. I gotta try that again," Bryan said. Tuy poured some more water and set the glass up again. This time the glass slipped out of Bryan's hand and tumbled across the ground. Maseth tried a couple more times with no success, and then I went again. The others came over and made attempts. We kept at it for half an hour while Tuy stood patiently by, coaching us on our technique and the physics involved. Ethan watched us, sipping his hooch, and seemed amused by all of it.

"This shit is impossible," Bryan said. "Hey, Coffelt, why don't *you* try it?"

"Uh, I am, like, reeeal drunk, okay? So promise not to laugh," Ethan said, setting his drink down and walking to the table. He grabbed the glass and paused for a few seconds, looking back and forth, planning out the trajectory. In one swift motion he slid the glass, turned it over to catch the water, and smoothly brought it to a stop before it hit the sand.

"Damn! And Coffelt comes out of nowhere, takes the gold!" Bryan exclaimed. Ethan walked back over to me and picked up his drink. I turned to him.

"Dude, how the fuck?" I said, frowning.

"Wasn't that big a deal, man," he said casually.

I shook my head. *This is bullshit. Everybody attempts the thing a hundred times, and these two fuckers waltz in and do it on the first try.*

The guys walked back and sat down. Some of them began opening up, telling more cheating stories. The banter continued as Ethan and I hung out at the table watching Tuy cut through something with a Swiss Army knife. Then Gafni stood up and waved his hands melodramatically, raising his voice over everyone else's.

"All right, all you guys just shut up and listen," he said. It wasn't aggressive or full of rage, like we had seen at the cordon and search. This time his voice sounded nervous, insecure. He seemed to be trying real hard to be the cool guy in the group. "A few years ago I met this one girl at the gym—hot as hell, super-toned, so I asked her out for a drink, took her to a bar I know."

As he began to speak I noticed his body language: hands moving furiously yet awkwardly, eyes darting from one person to the next. It was as if he were a habitual lousy joke teller who had more enthusiasm than Chris Rock.

"At one point I got up to use the bathroom. Now, here I am at this bar, showing this chick a nice time. Expensive drinks, hors d'oeuvres—I'm doing it up right. Okay? So I get up, go to the bathroom. I guess I was in there a few minutes. Anyway, I come out of the bathroom, walk back to the bar, and she is"—at this point Gafni got all animated, enjoying his own story—"and what's she doing? She is talking to some dude!" He let out a huge guffaw. It seemed he expected everyone to react on cue and all shout, "Whoa! Say it ain't so!" Instead, everyone just sat there, but Gafni continued, repeating himself for emphasis, mouthing each word slowly: "What is she doing? She is talking to some swinging dick!"

Again, no one really reacted too much.

"So as I walk up to her, I'm wondering, what the fuck? And guess what, she's handing him a napkin with her goddamned phone number written on it!"

"Oh, dude, that sucks," someone finally said.

"Sucked? It was a fucking nightmare, man," Gafni replied, almost protesting the guy's subdued reaction. Gafni sat down formally, looking like a contestant on *American Idol* trying to appear confident to prevent himself from being eliminated in the next round.

A couple of guys got up to get more drinks, and when they came back, Thiessen asked who else had a story. I looked over at Stuart, wondering what was going on with him. He seemed so quiet. A few times he seemed to be staring off, smiling reflexively when people laughed, but you could tell he wasn't listening.

Bryan spoke up and told us about dating a girl who bragged to him that two weeks before she met him, she had gone to a bar, hooked up with a strange guy, gone to his place and had sex, then had driven back to the same bar and gone home with a second guy, all in the same night. After several "holy shits" from everybody, people doing fist bumps with Bryan and clinking glasses, I looked over at Stuart and saw he had tuned in just a little bit, was smiling, sort of. But when he turned the Listerine bottle up, I saw in the light where a tear had run down the side of his cheek. Everyone was laughing, and Bryan was getting a kick out of putting his ex-bitch in her place. I felt like I was the only one who really understood how serious this shit was for Stuart. He was sitting there acting polite about our little emotional rescue operation, being a good sport and everything, but I kept my eye on him, wondering if he was just playing a part for us.

No one asked Stuart directly about what had happened. It seemed understood that we were just there to share the nastiest, ugliest personal experiences we possibly could—nothing more—so Stuart wouldn't feel like *his* experience was such a fiery auto wreck. Finally he did open up to us, though, talking about first meeting his fiancée and how cool and interesting she was: an artist who listened to the Pixies and Édith Piaf and painted poems on the walls of her apartment. He said he loved how she was such a free spirit, that he wasn't bothered by the fact that she'd slept with a bunch of people before him—one-night stands, married men, even a girlfriend once. Apparently she'd told Stuart all about her sexual past—casually, enthusiastically, as if she were talking about someone else's life, someone enigmatic like Frida Kahlo.

Stuart seemed to be the least devastated when he told these stories, as if he were being brought back to life by their retelling. There was excitement, nostalgia in his eyes, like he was falling in love or something. It was almost as if he had no recollection of her heartbreaking betrayal just a few short days before. I thought it was pathetic. Not that I had never had that shit happen to me; it just looked so sad to see him paint the picture, like all of a sudden, out of the blue, this sweet, innocent girl had woken up one day possessed, and cheated on him. Five minutes before, he had described this girl's sordid past—which sounded pretty damned lewd, in my opinion—so to me he was actually shooting his own argument down. *Jesus*, I thought, looking at his face. *What was this poor, sweet, innocent teddy bear doing dating some chick who was obviously a serial freaking slutbag?*

"You know what your problem is, dude?" Bryan interrupted him, a big grin on his face. Stuart looked up at him. "This sounds like the same situation I was in one time. I told this one girl—right before I kicked that, uh, *bitch* to the curb—I said, 'Honey, it's all good. The way I see it, all we got is some minor religious differences. See, I myself, I was brought up Christian.'" He paused for a second. "'And you are the *fucking devil!*'"

Laughter erupted again. "Yeeeah, suck on dat, bitch!" someone said. We were all rolling. Even Stuart finally laughed out loud. He stood up, waving his bottle, almost toppled over, and tried to chime in, slurring, "Hail yeah, git the fuck out, you fuckin'... ardist."

That night I lay down and felt the bed spinning horribly, passed out, and then had the most bizarre and vivid dream. I was back home having a conversation with Reverend Stoops, Andy's father. I had flown all the way from Iraq to meet him for lunch at the mall in Chattanooga. We sat in the food court, which was crowded with super-skinny teenagers. They were all walking past us, holding several shopping bags on each arm, in a big hurry but with no clue where they were going. I was dressed in full combat gear, barely able to fit in the tiny plastic chair, and they kept brushing up against me, hitting me with their bags. At first I was just surprised, but after a while I started mentioning how inconsiderate it seemed. The reverend was sitting comfortably, all gleeful as usual, giving that boisterous laugh after each little thing I said. I watched as one girl rushed by us and turned left at the corner, walking past the mall directory. A few seconds later she doubled back, obviously having gone the wrong direction. She went right by the directory again and walked briskly down the other hall. I was puzzled and asked if the reverend was going to help the kids, and he just laughed merrily, not a bit curious about any of it.

The strangest thing was that the character in my dream was not entirely Andy's dad. He was also that evangelical Christian guy who wrote all those books on marriage being sacred and focusing on the family. Right after my parents got divorced, my dad obsessed over the guy's radio program and talked about his theories constantly to me and my sisters. His marriage had shattered into a million pieces, and Dad, to his credit, at least saw we were bleeding to death. But as usual, his instinct was to fix us. Never mind what was causing the injury; he was a doctor, so let's operate. All he needed was a tourniquet, and that Christian guy seemed to be selling one.

But in the dream I knew the purpose of meeting at the food court: for Reverend Stoops to fill me in on what was going on back home. He told me about the youth groups at church, how kids were getting into texting and iPods, and who would win *American Idol* this year. He gave his same flippant laugh as he said these things, and as he went on I became concerned he was leaving something out. I kept adjusting my uniform, expecting him to get the hint, but he just smiled from ear to ear, making blithe comments about how his congregation didn't watch the news, they got together to discuss homeschooling and prayer groups. It got worse and worse until finally he revealed his own twisted world view, saying he'd been a preacher for many, many years, and this was the nature of things: "Folks have a baby, I do a baptism. If a baby dies? Well, ha! I guess I do a funeral . . . Couples get married, they divorce; little girls get their awards in Bible class, then they get pregnant . . . It's all part of the Lord's plan, right?"

I sat there in shock, horrified by what he was saying.

"So folks need something to soothe them, to get them through it all. Kind of like booze! Ha! Well, so, if you think about it, that's what Communion is, right? The priest doles out the wine? 'This is my blood . . .'" I was shaking my head for him to stop, but he kept going. "Boys fall in love, their girlfriends cheat on them . . . Mothers have sons, those sons go off to war and—"

Suddenly he stopped, and his demeanor changed completely. He leaned over the table and looked me in the eye, whispering in a chilling tone, "Psst. I am the devil."

As if to demonstrate it to me, he got up from his chair and stood next to the table, holding his arms straight out. Then he began to levitate slowly, all the time staring at me with eyes that had turned black. This had a devastating effect on me. I was so upset I began to vomit, which woke me up coughing, and I completely panicked. I sat up in the bed, looking around the dark of the trailer, and saw the dim green lights on Ethan's watch. It took a few seconds to realize where I was and that the alcohol hadn't worn off yet. I wondered why I was starting to have so many weird dreams. *I've never dreamed this much in my whole life.*

The next morning I was up before anyone else. I stepped out of the trailer in my boxers and lit up a cigarette. A blanket of gray hung low in the sky, which probably meant rain was coming, but it looked pretty cool anyway. I felt surprisingly good. No headache or anything. I enjoyed the quiet and watched the rays of sun coming up slowly over the mountains, illuminating the clouds. I tiptoed back inside, careful not to wake Ethan, and threw on some shorts and a T-shirt. Then I stepped outside again and headed toward the port-o-johns.

I could feel the cool sand through my flip-flops as I made my way around the chow tent. No one seemed to be up yet, and the only sounds came from a few birds chirping in the brush behind the supply building. But as I rounded the corner I heard music coming from our party spot. At first it looked like we had cleaned up everything except one folding camp chair in the middle of the clearing. But I quickly realized there was somebody slouched in it, facing away from me. I stopped for a minute to see if he would move, then figured he must be sleeping. I was sure it was one of the guys from the night before, so I turned to walk over there. His phone was sticking out of the sand at his feet. I recognized the song: "Maps" by the Yeah Yeah Yeahs. As I got up close I could see by the big bald head and the few rolls of fat on the back of his neck that it was Stuart. *He must have passed out last night and no one could lift his big ass,* I thought.

"Wait," the girl's voice in the song crooned in desperation, "they don't love you like I love you . . . wait!"

"You awake, Big Country?" I said, coming up behind him.

"Mornin'," he said, being friendly to whoever I was. He leaned down and paused the music, then turned his head to the side.

"Damn, dude, did you sleep out here the entire—" I began to ask.

"Holy shit!" Stuart yelled, seeing my face. He jumped up from the chair and stood back like I was holding a knife.

"Jesus, man, relax!" I said, smiling. "It's just me." It was kind of funny seeing the big guy get the shit scared out of him.

He frowned at me, still holding his distance. "Why'd you come over here?" he said with his twang.

"Uh, needed to take a shit?"

"Naw," he said, shaking his head and pointing emphatically, "the crappers is over *there*."

"Chill, man, I saw somebody sitting here and walked over to see who it was, that's all."

"Well, I'm totally fuckin' freaked out right now," he said, gesturing with his palms toward me. "I had a vision last night, and you was in it, plain as day."

I laughed. "Hey, I had a vision too, dude; it's called getting goddamn stupid on Iraqi hooch."

"Naw, this wasn't cuz o' drinkin'. This wasn't no dream," he said. He looked upset, very serious and concerned.

"Okay, so you had a vision and I was in it. So what? Didn't we talk a little last night? Makes perfect sense to me."

Stuart sat back down in the chair, holding his temples. "Look, you just don't understand. This ain't happened in a long time. I thought it went away."

"Went away? *What* went away?"

"The visions," he said, hesitating. "I used to have 'em a long time ago. I saw things. People said I was crazy."

"Oh," I said, "so you saw, like . . ."

"Sometimes it was good things, most times horrible things. Some folks said I was touched by God; some said it was the work of the devil." A weird little smile had worked its way onto his face.

I briefly remembered my dream, with Andy's dad turning into the devil. I stood there staring down at Stuart, not knowing what to tell him. I knew he was messed up over getting dumped, but I couldn't see that causing him to have visions about some guy. *Maybe he's secretly gay*, I thought.

Stuart's smile evaporated as he continued. "But I was never wrong.

Every time I saw anything"—he breathed in sharply through his nose, his eyes focusing in like lasers at me—"it came true." The way he said it just creeped me the fuck out, especially after the dream I'd had.

"So what the fuck did you see?" I asked, no longer sure if I really wanted to know.

"No. It was . . . this little girl. A little girl dressed up like a flower . . ." He stared down into the sand, shielding his face. "And you and her was way, way up in the air, fallin'. Like forever. Tumbling over and over." He shook his head again. "Over and over."

I looked at Stuart, feeling sorry for him again. It was obvious he'd seen some bad shit, and his fiancée cheating on him must have just pushed him over the edge. The image of the goat girls flashed in my mind, but I shrugged it off.

"So," I said, "what's so bad about that?"

"It . . . ," he said, glancing up at me finally. "The force, it was so powerful. Like a big magnetic field or something. I could just feel it. I ain't *never* had a vision where I could feel stuff." He thought for a moment. "It's one of the weirdest things I ever seen in my life. Made me sick. Couldn't get to sleep."

"Damn, dude. Sounds like *Sixth Sense* kind of shit," I said.

He slapped his hands down on the armrests. "Goddamn it! This ain't a fuckin' movie!"

I felt like laughing, he sounded so ridiculous, but I didn't want to be a dick. "Calm down, I'm not saying you're . . . ," I said, trying to think of something. But I wasn't able to hide a slight smile, and that just aggravated him more.

"Yeah, you *are* saying. You think this is the first time I seen what people do when I tell 'em I had a vision? I know what you're thinking. You think I'm full of shit."

A few moments passed. I figured I could be real with him, and maybe that would help. "Okay, you're right. This supernatural stuff, I just don't believe in shit like that. Sorry."

He looked at me with disdain, shaking his head. I was surprised that he could act condescending. "Yeah, it's like clockwork. They all say the same fuckin' thing. Every time."

"Exactly, 'cause it makes no sense. It's called zero scientific evidence." He chuckled, turning in his seat toward me. "No. You know what makes no sense? Is there evidence that it is *not* true?" he said, cleaning up his accent.

"No, but I didn't say it was proven to be *not* true, I just said it—"

"Right, but you already chose one of 'em to believe. See, either one *could* be true, which you admit, but you already went and believed one of 'em *was* true."

I stopped for a second, thinking, *Yeah, exactly, you big dummy. I don't just jump to conclusions.*

He stood up and pointed to our party spot, where the table had been. "Look, I was talkin' to Tuy last night, after y'all left. Told him about me and my fiancée. You know what he said? Said I chose the wrong lie. I was like, what? He said the first assertion is that she might be screwin' around on me, and that's a lie cuz it would be so devastating, it couldn't possibly be true. Second lie is the one I told myself: that she was absolutely not cheatin' because she wasn't that kind of girl. There ya have it. Two different things I *could've* believed, and I chose the wrong one. On purpose."

"Gee, maybe to give her the benefit of the doubt?" I said.

Stuart laughed mockingly. "Doubt? Bullshit. More like flat-out lies. She was telling me lies. 'You're the best-lookin' guy I've ever seen'—lie. 'I'd never cheat on you, baby, never, ever'—lie. Meanwhile, even her own girlfriend was telling me she was rollin' in the hay with every artist in Nashville. Another lie? So what I'm talking about is which lie I chose to believe." Stuart looked at me, raising his eyebrows.

I guess that kind of makes sense, I thought.

"Ain't nobody gonna FedEx the evidence to your doorstep. You gotta go and get it yourself. Meanwhile, make for damn sure you call the right lie the truth," he said, staring through me, motionless.

Wow. That is fucking deep, I thought. *Call the right lie the truth? This dude is seriously into some Zen shit.*

"Okay, so your vision could be true, all right?"

He seemed somewhat placated. "It's come true all the other times."

"Yeah. Well, I really need to go now, before I crap my pants."

Stuart smiled. "All right, man," he said, slapping my shoulder endearingly. "You did totally freak me out, though."

"I know, right?"

"Wish I had more details," he said.

"No, it's okay. I'll let ya know if . . . uh, you know . . . *when* something happens." I didn't believe it; I just said it for his benefit. He smiled, and I turned around and walked toward the port-o-johns.

D uring the entire time I was in Iraq, only a few times did I get to see anything from the air. A week after our party we were called in to assist the transition team that patrolled the Iraqi-Syrian border. There had just been an incident between US forces and Syria, and they wanted to step up security and crack down on smugglers and insurgents walking across the open desert. We loaded up in a UH-60 Black Hawk helicopter and flew west one chilly morning just as the sun began to come over the horizon. Strapped securely in our metal seats—two rows of four, facing each other—we stuck our necks out, trying to look out of the open doors. We flew low, first over buildings and city streets, then over farmland toward the Euphrates. All the guys were smiling and making hand gestures to each other, obviously getting a big thrill as we banked and turned. Ethan sat on the end, across from me, with one boot on the edge of the door frame, and waved to people as they looked up at us. Kids on bicycles, old men walking down dirt roads, fishermen—the scene changed dramatically from one minute to the next, until suddenly we crossed the river and there was a vast open desert. The brownish-yellow sand stretched endlessly, completely flat except for subtle ridges or dried-up streambeds here and there. We flew straight on for a while, then flew over the tip of Habbaniyah Lake. At one point the crew chief turned around and handed her map to us, signaling us to pass it around and show everyone where we were going.

Before we took off, one of the pilots had given us an informal briefing. The border extended over six hundred kilometers, most of which was marked by nothing more than a sandy berm. Insurgents were coming in from Syria on what our guys called "rat lines," routes that ran all the way to Baghdad. The Iraqi border police had stations every so often, either small brick buildings or, in many cases, small tents. Usually these guys were equipped with only a handheld radio, a rifle, and a flashlight. As I stared out across the desert I thought about the mission, how incredibly important it sounded, keeping foreign fighters out of Iraq. This was the type of thing we came here for, to do something that really meant something, made a difference for these people.

As we got closer to our insertion point, I looked down and could barely see the contour of the border snaking across the desert randomly, separating a patchwork of areas that looked nearly identical except for slight variations in tone. We dipped into Syria, banking sharply to the right to follow the border northeast. It seemed like we were tilted completely sideways, and I could see straight down to the sand streaking by just below us. This might have been routine for the flight crew, but for us it was a thrill ride. Although no one could hear over the high-pitched whine of the rotors, we were all yelling with excitement as we held on. I glanced over at Bryan, who was making devil horns and shouting what looked like "Fucking awesome!" Walker was next to him with his video camera, panning around to get everyone's reactions. I remember thinking we had been suddenly transformed into eight-year-old boys, excused from the war for a moment, allowed to just enjoy an experience few would ever have in their lifetimes.

The next moment I saw a group of white-and-gray forms ahead of us, lining a dirt road that crossed the border. As we flew closer we slowed down, and I got a better view: more than a hundred small tents huddled together in the middle of the desert. Along the edge it looked like a city dump, with white trash bags and plastic bottles all over. As we passed overhead, a bunch of kids poured out of tents and came running, shouting up at us. One of the smaller ones tripped on a plastic container and did a face-plant in the dirt. I noticed cardboard boxes scattered everywhere, and clotheslines draped between each of the tents. It was obvious people were living there, but for no reason I could think of. The camp was in the middle of a huge expanse of absolutely nothing. Only a narrow makeshift road led into it, like a faint brushstroke a sandstorm could easily blend into the desert.

I gave Ethan a confused look. At first he shrugged his shoulders, but then he motioned to me and leaned forward and shouted, "Refugee camp."

I rolled my eyes at him. *No shit. But why here?* I planned to ask someone as soon as we landed.

A half hour later we arrived at our insertion point. I looked around as we descended, expecting the helicopter to turn and an outpost or building or something to come into view. Instead there was nothing but another dirt road leading across the sand berm. There was no village, no Iraqi border patrol, no vehicles, nothing. The helicopter touched down for only a few minutes, just enough time to drop four of us off—me, Walker, Bryan, and Ethan—before taking the rest of the squad to the other location. The plan was for us to check cars coming across the border and make sure no one tried to cross by going around us. It sounded like a good plan, and I was looking forward to assisting the transition team.

The entire morning, we paced back and forth in the blistering heat, guzzling bottles of Poland Spring water, watching for activity in the empty desert. By noon we were completely bored and figured we wouldn't be seeing any vehicles. But soon after, a small Toyota truck appeared, driving slowly in from the Syrian side. Ethan walked up and signaled for the driver to stop a safe distance from us, and two men and a small boy got out and walked toward us. They appeared to know the procedure: hand us their IDs, let us inspect their vehicle while they stood there. The men wore black gowns and red-and-white-checkered headdresses, and the boy was dressed in a white gown.

Bryan decided to be our impromptu border patrol officer and extended his hand to the older man and smiled. He used very basic English with them, but their only responses were smiles and phrases like "thank you," which were horribly mispronounced. As Walker and I stood back a few feet, Bryan continued to ask simple questions about where they were going, if they were visiting friends, if the kid was their son, but they understood none of it, just kept smiling and making agreeable or submissive expressions. Ethan finished checking the vehicle and gave me the thumbs-up, so I put a hand on Bryan's shoulder.

"Vehicle's good."

"Cool," he said, handing their IDs back to the older man.

Walker immediately stepped forward, grinning at Bryan. "Hey, man, check this shit out."

He began overacting, pointing to one of the men like he was having a hard time remembering something. "Now, uh, which one of y'all was the po' fool with the two-inch schlong?"

"Walker, come on," I said, trying not to have a disturbed expression on my face.

Walker kept smiling and focused on one of them. "Oh, it was you, homey? Now, you mind if I go ahead and git freaky wit yo' bitch?" He chuckled. "'Cause you know she prob'ly need it, right?"

The men laughed along, obviously clueless. Walker couldn't just stop there, though. He had to keep entertaining himself. "Now, lemme ax you, does she get all freaky and shit? Is she like a wildcat? You know, head, up the booty, threesomes and shit?"

"Yes, yes, thank you, Amreekee," one of the men said.

Walker busted out laughing, looking at Bryan. "Well, damn, son! You folks is all right," he said, shaking their hands good-bye. Bryan told them good luck and waved as they walked back to their truck. Walker was still in stitches, trying to get Bryan to laugh with him. I went over to the other side of the road and sat down next to Ethan.

"Walker, our resident shitbag."

Ethan chuckled. "You gotta admit that was pretty funny."

"Yeah. Mocking the locals. Real funny."

Bryan and Walker walked over to us, in hysterics. "Yes, yes, Amreekee!"

Bryan giggled. "Dude, you should have YouTubed that shit."

I looked up at both of them. "Yeah, fucking brilliant. Let's tell the whole world US soldiers make fun of Iraqis."

Suddenly Walker exploded. "Goddamn, son! Again? You *always* frontin'?"

I glared at him. "Let's see. Muslims are deeply offended by, hmm . . . oh, that's right, *any* sexual reference whatsoever, no matter how harmless. So fuck, I got an idea: how about we talk about their wives whoring around and doing it up the ass, and hey, let's blast it all over the fucking world!"

Walker moved aggressively toward me and stood right in front of my boots. I continued staring him in the face. He looked like an animal. His eyes were wide, and his lips were formed into a ridiculous little snarl. Bryan stepped in, waving his hands and doing his fake drawl. "Now, you two Duke boys, don't be getting into no tussles."

"We're not going to fight," I said.

Walker turned to look at Bryan, then quickly back at me. "Aw, damn, dog, we ain't?" he said with a sneer.

"Jesus, what is this," Ethan said, "an outtake from *Fast and Furious*?"

Bryan started laughing and opened the cooler, grabbing a water bottle. "What is it with you, man?" he asked me, twisting off the cap and taking a sip.

Walker turned to walk away from us. He slid his boot to the side just enough to bump up against mine, but I ignored it.

"With me?" I said, waiting for Walker to get out of earshot. "It's you guys who don't think this shit is serious." I was expecting Bryan to get offended and pissed off at what I said, but instead he said something far worse.

"Serious?" he said, pausing for a second. "You know what? Bingo, motherfucker!"

"What do you mean?"

"We *don't* think this shit is serious. And you know why? 'Cause this war is a big fucking joke, that's why. It's like a goddamned skit on *The Daily Show*."

I shook my head. "Come on."

"Oh, really?" Bryan mocked me. "So tell me, just how many foreign fighters have we caught coming across that border?" He pointed out toward the sand berm.

"Who knows, man. I'm guessing . . . a few hundred?"

"How about zero. Zip. Nada," he said.

"How is that?" Ethan asked Bryan, sounding neutral.

Bryan looked at him confidently. "We don't catch shit, just small-time smugglers. Old, poor guy on a donkey trying to feed his family. To this day we've never caught a single foreign fighter actually crossing the border."

This sounded like bullshit to me, except Bryan seemed like he knew something about the subject. "How the fuck would you know that?" I said.

"Gee, only the lieutenant colonel, head of the entire transition team. I saw him giving an interview about it."

I didn't have an answer. I looked up at Ethan, expecting him to at least challenge Bryan a little. But he was dousing his face with water and didn't look like he was that engaged in the conversation.

Bryan continued, "Oh, and how'd you like al-Tanf, that Palestinian refugee camp?"

"I thought they were Iraqis," I said.

"No, dude." He laughed. "See, Iraqis can actually *leave* Iraq. Those were Palestinians who used to live in big cities like Baghdad."

"Oh, illegal immigrants?"

"Uh, no. Refugees. Hello?"

I gestured to him with open hands. "I don't get it."

"Kicked out of Israel in 1948, fled to Iraq. Now they have to leave again because they're not Iraqi. Shia militia came in, said, 'Iraq is for Iraqis, now get the fuck out.'"

"Don't forget the 1967 war," Ethan added. "Plus, during the Gulf War, kicked out of Kuwait 'cause people were pissed off at Arafat."

"Right, Co-felt, so they're triple or quadruple refugees."

"So what's your point? That's not *our* fault."

Bryan shook his head humorously to act condescending and put his hand on my shoulder. "Good God, son. What *did* they do to you?"

I pulled away from his hand and looked up at him. "No, Bryan, seriously."

Bryan laughed. "Okay, so why don't you take a guess who made sure the poor Palestinian bastards had a place to live, before we came along?"

I paused, then looked up at Bryan, squinting from the sun. "I give up. Who?"

"Good ole Sadd-um," Ethan said, doing an imitation of George Bush Senior.

Fuck, I thought, *how do they know all this shit?* I brought my hand up to examine my nails, sitting there listening as Ethan and Bryan exchanged a few political quips about the Gulf War and then started doing Bush impressions. I tried to sort out the information and say something back to Bryan. But what could I do? It was two against one, and I didn't have the debate skills to dress them down. *Fucking politics.* I just sat there as they joked around. Sat there and picked at my fingers.

Later that evening we were hanging out at the trailer, me inside cleaning my weapons and straightening up my area, the three of them playing cards and fucking around outside. At some point I stepped outside for a smoke and saw them laughing their asses off, acting out a skit.

"So I'll play the IO," Maseth said, "yelling at the top of his fuckin' lungs like the sergeant tearing Gomer Pyle a new one." He giggled, looking at Ethan. "Now, Coffelt, you be the Gomer Pyle character. Let's call him . . . Peabody."

Ethan nodded.

"Okay, now, here's the scene." Maseth paused to think it through. "Okay, the officers' tent is packed with four-star generals. Rumsfeld's pissed, wanting answers, and right goddamn now!" He tipped his water bottle up.

Ethan added, "Where's my quagmire?"

Maseth cracked up, almost choking. "Exactly. And Peabody royally fucked up, 'cause he decided to call for only five units to cover the entire six hundred kilometers of goddamned border."

Maseth goose-stepped in front of Ethan, then stopped and shoved his nose in Ethan's face. "Peabody! What the flying-ass fuck were you thinking? Don't you know these hajjis have contacts who tell them the precise locations of your men, and they know the terrain and just detour around you?"

Ethan snapped to attention. "Five units were all I was allowed by the command, sir," he said, all over-the-top scared shitless.

Maseth cut him off. "Bullshit, Peabody! You go to war with the army you have."

Ethan ad-libbed quickly. "All due respect, the army you have sucks, sir!"

Maseth laughed. "That's a good one, Coffelt." He paused again. "Okay, no, no, here we go; the sergeant is one of those bizarre born-again military types. Tough as nails, all World War II and shit, but has his Bible study every single day, and he never drinks or swears." Then he continued his barrage. "Peabody, I don't give a freakin' goll-dern *what* the command allowed! Your task was to guard that entire border!"

"Yes, *sir!*" Ethan answered with a smile on his face.

"Are you good at fourth-grade civil engineering, Peabrainy?" Maseth barked out.

Ethan thought up a quick line: "Graduated honors—first in my class, sir!"

"Well, good!" Bryan said with a sarcastic grin. "Here's a math problem for ya. There's a creek behind your grammar school, ten feet wide. You and your little gay playmates decide to build a dam. You go to yer daddy's workshop to get a piece of plywood to stick in the mud, block the water." Bryan paused to suppress his laughter and think of more dialogue.

"Final exam question, Peabrainy! Does that piece of plywood need to be (a) eight feet long, (b) ten feet long, or (c) a flimsy, rotted-out piece of crap with more holes in it than Swiss cheese in a skeet shoot?"

Ethan was drinking from a water bottle and spit a big mouthful out on the gravel, laughing so hard he started to choke. Bryan was on a roll.

The whole time I just stood off to the side in my little smoking area, leaning against the corner of the hooch. I looked at each of them, trying to smile like it didn't bother me. But I felt like I was going to lose it, go completely postal. I even pictured smashing their faces in but caught myself. I just grabbed smoke after smoke until they finished, then stayed out there until Ethan had gone to sleep.

L ate Wednesday afternoon, the third straight day of keeping to myself, I got an email from my uncle in Atlanta. It was terse and unemotional, even for him: "Dot was admitted to hospice, it appears to be serious and I thought you should know now since you're not as reachable and there's no way to be sure if/when something will happen."

I sent him a quick thanks, logged off as fast as I could, and began asking around for who I should see to request emergency leave. Luckily a guy near the plaza seemed to know his shit, telling me I needed to go see SFC Bartlett at the PAC office, whatever that was. Bartlett was in charge of vetting leave forms and submitting them to the battalion commander for approval. I rushed over to the PAC office, which was housed in a trailer on the other side of the FOB, but it had closed at seventeen hundred.

The next morning I went back over there and sat on the concrete slab in front, smoking cigarettes one after another, hoping maybe just this once they would open the office early. Instead the guy ambled in at almost ten o'clock, fumbling with his keys, beef jerky dangling from his mouth under a ridiculous Charlie Chaplin mustache. First thing he said was "Smoking is prohibited within fifty feet of the trailer, Specialist."

I apologized, ditching my butt, and gave him the quick synopsis: my grandmother is in hospice in Georgia, I'm interested in filing a leave request, I've already run it by my sergeant, I'd like to see her before she dies. Only I didn't get to the words "before she dies." As he booted up his laptop and threw an old cup of coffee in the trash, he rattled off what seemed to be a rote response—"If it's got a 'grand' or ends in 'friend' . . ."—and shook his head.

Oh God, please. Not one of these insensitive bastards, I thought. His little quip sounded like some stupid cliché. *What the fuck does "gotta grand" mean?* The guy's body language was so obvious: no eye contact, busy untangling his little ear buds, not a care in the world. I wanted to grab the guy by the collar. *Hey, tool, nix the fucking cheeky catchphrases. We're talking about my grandmother here.* But I tried to stay calm. I had to try to win this guy over somehow.

"Austin Powers. Hilarious movie," I said, chuckling and motioning to the poster behind his desk. Mike Myers was in that crazy bright-blue suit, white sash around his neck, smiling at us, all cheesy, showing off his bad British teeth.

"Not my poster," he said, looking at the screen as he logged in for the day.

Jesus, how bad can this possibly be? I thought. "Sergeant, would it be possible to get a copy of the form? I'd really like to see my grandmother before—"

"Sorry for your loss, but if it's got a 'grand,' it's not getting by Holshek's office."

I immediately felt a shock. *My "loss"? She's not dead, you little prick.* But I couldn't get pissed, and I sure as hell couldn't cry in front of him, so my face started burning. I breathed in quickly through my nose and managed to continue, almost whispering. "'Got a grand'? Sergeant, what does that mean?"

He seemed annoyed at the question. "Grandmother, grandfather, grandson, grand-niece of gay Aunt Denise's second wife twice removed . . . the battalion commander don't give a damn. He's not very liberal about these things," he said in full voice.

"Sergeant, I understand they can't allow leave for just any circumstance, but aren't requests approved on a case-by-case basis? Can't I apply anyway, and depending on my squad assignments . . ."

He took a very long, deep breath, moved forward in his chair, and looked at me as if I were a shitbag trying to weasel my way out of my duties. He even put his elbows on the table and clasped his hands. *This is un-fucking-believable.*

"Specialist, does the word *grandmother* got a 'grand' in it?" he said under that stupid mustache.

I paused for about five seconds, wanting so much to say something, when of course I was supposed to sit there and *not* answer, because it was a non-question. And all of a sudden he did one of the most ridiculous things I have ever seen in my life. He winked at me. The fucker looked me straight in the eye, flashed the stupidest smart-ass "I'm a complete assbag" grin ever, and actually fucking winked at me.

With that, I immediately raised my M4 and blew his fucking brains all over the goddamned file cabinet, grabbed an application, and walked out.

Except I couldn't do that. I was powerless—there was nothing I could do—and I was forced to watch him enjoy seeing me be powerless. And I was not allowed even the common decency of knowing why on God's green earth someone would actually enjoy putting another human being through that.

At that point it was over. All I could do was make it obvious that I hated his goddamned guts. I jumped up from the chair and was planning on literally running out the door. But as I got up, the chair fell over, and I made the mistake of stopping.

Bartlett reacted within nanoseconds. "Specialist, you are to return that chair to its exact original position."

I stood in the doorway; here was the chance to say, "Fuck you." A few seconds went by as I tried to assess what could happen to me. This time he yelled out at the top of his lungs, "Specialist, you are to return that goddamned plastic chair to its original goddamned position!"

I leaned over and turned the chair upright, looking at him with a plan to smile and wink. But he had turned sideways to face a file cabinet, perfectly able to move on to his next task. I hadn't been in that trailer five minutes, and every hope I'd had of seeing Granny Fricket was gone. I was fucking furious, and some complete asshole had just had the most joyful day of his life.

I double-timed it back to the hooch, hoping I wouldn't run into anyone. The tears were hard to stop—the frustration and anger, the thought of not being able to see Dottie one last time. I came up on a guy from my company walking toward me in the bright sun. I looked down at the gravel kicking up at my feet as I passed him. Maybe he saw my face; I didn't care. I just couldn't stop. I felt the guilt already. *How many times did I miss an opportunity to talk to my grandmother when I was younger?* She and Paw-Paw would drive all the way from Dallas, come in for Christmas. They'd call and say they'd try to arrive in Chattanooga by Sunday, then would surprise us and show up Friday evening. My mom would burst into tears and yell, "They're here!" sending my sisters running, squealing in excitement. *Did I spend enough time with them?* They were such generous grandparents, always showering us with gifts, way more than they could afford. "At what price, happiness?" Paw-Paw would always say.

Think, what did I do, just tear through the wrapping paper, grab my PlayStation games, and run off? No. I probably made a ridiculous deal of it, hugging them, getting all cornball and saying, "I love it sooo much," like they had just donated a kidney for me. That's what we did in our family—act effusive, drown each other in saccharine. *So did Dottie feel like she even knew me? Why can't I remember going for a walk with her, just the two of us? None of this would matter if I could only see her one more time. Just one more time, please.* I stopped for a moment to catch my breath, then ran again. Tuy and a couple of guys came out of the DFAC as I went by. Tuy yelled, "Run, Forrest, run!" I just kept looking down, watching my boots stroke through the sand, contemplating not seeing my grandmother ever again.

I swung by the internet trailer just in case. I knew they were closed Thursdays but thought maybe they'd be open this time. Nope. Not a chance. *Of course not*, I thought.

Ethan was propped up in his bed reading when I came into the hooch. I walked over to my area and started straightening things, even though I knew everything was already set. I moved a box of baby wipes to the top shelf, refolded a shirt, and wiped off the mirror, then stopped. I could feel Ethan staring at me. I put my hands against the metal cabinet and dropped my head. "I'm such a fucking OCD loser,"

I said, my voice cracking. I wiped my eyes on my sleeve. "All I ever do is clean and straighten up . . . clean the fucking sand in here, which we'll just track in again, clean my fucking piece-of-shit M4, fold all this . . . quote-unquote clean laundry—thanks, FUBAR, you fucking . . ." I took a stack of T-shirts and threw them across the room.

"Dude, you all right?" he asked.

So of course I spilled my guts. Told him the whole thing. Never mind he had let me look like an asshole the other day. Never mind I had opened up to everyone the night we watched *Bourne* and let those guys see how personal this war was to me, and my own best friend didn't back me up. No. As usual, I would suffer silently, hold it inside for a short time. But just say boo to me and I'd let it all come pouring out. *What a pussy*, I thought.

"Sucks they won't grant you leave, man. But she's what, ninety-something? She's lived a good, long life," Ethan told me, lying there looking all content and peering over the book his mom had mailed him.

Oh, is that it? I wanted to say. *I guess it doesn't matter when people die. It's no big deal I can't tell my grandmother good-bye. No big deal, we're not doing shit right now in Iraq, and there is no reason whatsoever I cannot take a quick flight stateside, be back next week probably. No, no, everybody dies, that should be a comfort.*

"Phew, what a relief!" I said, glaring at him. I looked at the 9/11 poster. *My entire life is a waste. I have done absolutely nothing since I have been here. Nothing. And now I fucked up and won't even be there for my grandmother when she dies. I am fucking useless.*

"Huh?" He looked confused. I didn't bother. Why waste my breath if no one could change anything, and all I'd get were doses of reality that never cured anybody of anything. I grabbed my smokes and sunglasses and walked out. "I've gotta find someone with a video camera," I said, stepping out the door, "so my grandmother can at least see my face before she fucking dies."

"Maseth's got a Sony Flip," he shouted as the door slammed. I put on my shades and treaded through the gravel toward the chow tent.

found a nice backdrop for my video in front of the KBR office. There was a simple arrangement of yellow and purple flowers and a makeshift wooden gazebo, plus a white rosebush growing up a trellis behind the bench inside. My grandfather had loved roses. I remember a backyard full of them at their house in Dallas, and even after Paw-Paw died my grandmother kept up the tradition when she moved to her condo near my mom's house. I also managed to find a semi-antique chair. It wasn't Victorian like Dottie's collection, but it was better than nothing. Bryan not only let me borrow the Flip plus a camera stand, he also helped me set it up and then stayed for a few minutes to make sure I knew how to record myself. I gathered my thoughts, then hit record and sat back in my chair.

"Hi, Granny Fricket," I began, trying to imagine her there as I stared into the tiny lens surrounded by its glossy white plastic case. *Shit, the sunglasses.* "Oh, this damn glare," I said, finding myself saying it exactly the way my grandparents would have. They absolutely never swore, not because they tried to be prim and proper, or for dumb religious reasons, but simply because they were considerate of others. Dot and Paw-Paw were just inoffensive people, period. Nevertheless, they would blend "hell" or "damn" into almost every conversation, and somehow it always sounded endearing and humorous.

"Sorry, the sun is so bright, I'm going to have to leave my sunglasses on. Anyway, I hope this video gets to the States soon. I'm sure you've heard by now they wouldn't let me go on leave. Not sure why the hell not. We're not doing a damn thing here at the moment. But I just wanted to tell you in person, kind of, how special you are to me and how much you mean to me. I remember you and Paw-Paw Frank driving in from Midland or Dallas those many times—driving all the way to Tennessee—and surprising us by showing up a day or two early. And you'd fill the back of the car with five or six big cardboard shipping boxes, each packed neatly with Christmas gifts with the bows taken off so you could squeeze more in there. I remember you guys hanging out in the living room, drinking gin and tonics, telling stories with Mom and Dad, laughing. Paw-Paw doing one of his comedy routines for you guys, with his Cajun accent. I could always hear the laughter all the way upstairs."

I paused for a moment, having a hard time swallowing. It was always a bad idea to say things this way, starting off all nostalgic and rattling off the most touching memories. It was the quickest way to get choked up—another stupid habit I'd picked up from my mom.

I cleared my throat and continued. "But mainly I wanted to tell you I . . . have been having a hard time here in Iraq. I came here expecting certain things, wanting to make a difference, and things haven't been . . . things have been very messed up here so far. I want you to know how much your letters have helped me. I have needed someone to understand what it is like here and what I am going through, and you have kept informed and involved, and you have been with me." I started to choke up. "The *only* one with me."

I paused again, wanting to make sure I didn't forget anything. I tried not to think about her being gone or these being our final words. "God, I wish I could call you. Uncle Frank said you weren't able to talk on the phone right now . . . Dottie . . . you used to say ten years ago and even fifteen years ago that you were not sure why God had kept you on this earth for so long." The tears finally started streaming down my face as I tried to stay still. "I look forward to you saying that again when I get back home, and in another five years, and in another fifteen. I love you very much. Get well soon. Bye. See you soon."

Sometime after Dottie died, I started getting into meds. I'm not sure exactly when it got out of hand, because everything began to run together. Days on patrol, days off. Outside the wire, inside the wire. Screaming down city streets, waiting to get shot at; lying on the cot, staring at the glow stick. It all just blended together. But I know how it started. Ethan was bedridden one day with some nasty bacterial infection and sent me over to Walker's hooch to pick up something that, as Ethan put it, the geniuses at FUBAR didn't feel the need to keep in stock. I remember walking in and seeing Walker standing in front of an easel, shirtless, tats all over his arms and back.

He was oil painting, of all things, and some rap metal song I'd never heard was blaring. He was being cool with me, so I chatted with him while he cleaned up, and I asked what band it was.

He stopped and looked at me like I'd just said the magic words. "Shit, son! You ain't ne'er heard Rage Against the Machine?" He thumbed through some beat-up spiral notebooks on his shelf, found an old CD, and handed it to me. "Every song on there . . . off da hook, son!" The cover pictured a clean-cut Americana white kid in a superhero costume. He had a cape and the letter *e* on the front of his shirt, with a banner underneath that read "Evil Empire." Walker broke down the meanings of some songs on the album: right-wing radio, propaganda, Ollie North and Iran-Contra, references to *1984*. Said some shit about how "we all gots to wake the fuck up" and said he used to be like everybody else, but once he allowed his eyes to open just a sliver, what he saw opened them up the rest of the way. I wasn't really into what he was saying. I was just there to pick up Ethan's medicine. When Walker went to get it, he showed me a big blue tackle box full of pills—tons of all different kinds of painkillers, antidepressants, sleep aids. I didn't jump up and down saying, "I want me some of those," so he shut the box and opened his locker to hand me Ethan's antibiotics.

"Tell Coffelt I got the other type too, if he need it," Walker said as I started toward the door.

"Okay," I said.

"Hold up," he said, reaching back into the blue box. "This is fuh you, son." He handed me a bottle. "Might can help you . . . cope." Then he held out his hand and gave me the "we cool" look. I slapped him five and started to walk out.

"Hey, you ain't gonna take this?" he said, holding up the CD.

"Oh yeah," I said, and he tossed it to me.

I didn't have to ask Walker what meds he'd given me. I'd heard a hundred times about soldiers and what kind of shit people were on: Seroquel, Oxy, Vike, Xanax. I don't think I even hesitated to take whatever the hell it was. The squad had another patrol planned that night, and as soon as I got geared up I walked to the cabinet and popped a pill in my mouth, tipping up my water bottle. Ethan was right there. He didn't have a clue. Less than an hour later I was riding shotgun with Maseth, mellow as fuck, smoking a lot more cigarettes than usual but otherwise pretty much normal, I thought. Just not so much in my own head.

A few days later I tried another one.

One night I sat in bed, staring at the glow stick, and started thinking about Dottie and how I'd missed out on her last moments on earth, and I just needed something. I accidentally tipped the pill bottle over, and Ethan looked up from reading, asking if I was sick. "Just a headache," I said. I wrapped the bottle up in Kleenex and put it back in the box on top of the Rage CD.

It went on like that for a few months. I'd hit up Walker, he'd sell me a bottle, and I'd say it was probably the last one I'd need, or I'd say the drug was actually pretty mild, or I'd talk about how it could probably help soldiers focus on the missions by relieving combat anxiety. I felt totally normal, like I could function and everything; I just took one every so often to switch to a different mode, kind of like autopilot, so I could go somewhere else for a little while. Away from memories that kept popping into my head—summer vacations, Dot in her big sixties sunglasses, clipping Paw-Paw's rosebushes along the tall wooden fence around their backyard in Dallas. New Orleans. Dad knocking over a plate of beignets—fancy French doughnuts—at Café Du Monde and Mom laughing hysterically as powdered sugar sprayed all over her red pants. Pensacola with the Geislers. All seven of us kids crammed in sleeping bags on the floor of the beach house. The sounds of the waves on the beach, the subdued voices of the adults, the clinking of martini glasses. These memories were there to threaten me, remind me of what was just around the corner, what always came after such happiness. Sometimes I'd take a pill and be fine, only to sleep for an hour and then wake up, staring at the glow stick, scenes flashing. Then it would stop, and I'd be okay. I wouldn't need anything.

Pretty soon it was Christmas. They had some kind of service at the chapel. None of us went. Right before noon Sergeant Huey walked around the hooches handing out mail to people, which I guess was how they tried to make it special for us. Ethan and I were about to go get into the chow line, when we heard him bang on our screen door. I was still near the back of the trailer putting on my boots, but I looked up and saw Huey hand Ethan a few colored envelopes. I was already on my second Oxy for the day.

"Looks like you got a few holiday cards," Ethan said, flinging them randomly in my general direction.

"Damn. Perfect timing. Christmas cards arriving on Christmas," I said.

Ethan chuckled. "No, smart-ass, they probably held on to them. Fuckers like you have no self-control, would've just torn into them right away."

I laughed. "Oh, right, that's me, no self-control," I said, picking the cards up off the floor and bed. "I better leave 'em here so I'm not tempted during lunch." And I plopped the cards on the table as we walked out.

After chow I sat on my cot and opened the cards from my family. I didn't want to. I knew it might mess with my head. But I couldn't stop myself; there was some kind of desperate need, like I was afraid if I didn't, I might not see their fairy-tale world again. So I did, and it hit me worse than I'd expected.

In the first card my sister Madeline had drawn a picture of our backyard at the Lookout Mountain house—what my mom used to call the secret garden—complete with the ivy trellis and the grass and the stone walkway. Pretty detailed. A big Christmas tree was in the middle, with Easter eggs all around the base, colored in with crayons. It was so creative. Below her drawing she wrote, "Remember? You made that my best Easter ever." I sat there staring at the card, smiling. I *did* remember. Maddie had been probably six or seven, and I had come up with an elaborate "resurrection scavenger hunt"; I had dyed a bunch of eggs and written words on them, and I'd made maps for Maddie and Sarah, with hints and puzzles. My mom was incredibly impressed and was overjoyed I had done something so special for my sisters. We watched them walk around in their white lace dresses, bending down in the grass, holding their little papers, running back to me to ask, "What does *Magdalene* mean?" When I glanced over at my mom, she'd given me that smile—warm, endearing, yet so deeply moved she looked like she could break down sobbing.

And that was what I started to do. I pressed my hand up against my mouth so Ethan could not hear anything, and tears poured uncontrollably. The other cards were just as bad. My older sister, Karen, had sent pictures of me and her at the airport the day I shipped out. I was holding the little pewter coffee scoop she'd bought me. My dad had sent me a copy of the photograph he had given me for high school graduation—I was standing in a pile of snow in front of our house in Boston, must have been no more than three years old, wearing one of those oversized down coats. I had my arms outstretched and my face all scrunched up, and I was crying miserably. I did *not* look happy. For my McCallie graduation card my dad had glued the photo on the inside and written, "The road ahead may be long and cold . . ." I remembered being overwhelmed by that card, so impressed my dad had put something together so artistic and sentimental. I'd cried then, and I cried again seeing that picture in Iraq. His note read "I forgot to mention some roads might be hot as all HELL! haha. Merry Christmas, son. We love you."

Ethan got up and said something about hitting the bathroom, and I went to the cabinet and took another. I pulled the blankets over me and turned toward the wall, and when he came back and asked why I was in bed, I acted like I was asleep. Finally the meds kicked in, and I did actually sleep.

Y ou listen to them tunes yet?" Walker asked me as soon as I walked in the door of his hooch. "Oh. Uh, no. Not yet," I said. He bent down to grab the blue tackle box. "Come on, now! Rage got some shit to tell you, son!" I handed him a wad of cash, and he set a bottle on the desk in front of me. I noticed one of his T-shirts draped over the chair. The artwork was a spray-painted outline of a thug in an oversized coat, holding his fist up in solidarity. I read off the title: "Battle of Los Angeles."

"Oh, hey, check this out, son." He twisted around in his seat to grab his phone. "LA concert. Backstage. Yours truly got to meet err one o' them cats." He pulled up a pic of him next to a guy with full dreadlocks, his arm around Walker, smiling for the camera. "That's Zack. Lead singer. One cool muhfucker."

"Looks kinda like Marley," I said.

"Listen up. So I told Zack I was goin' to Iraq, right? Asked him for an autograph. You know what he did?" Walker pulled up his camo tee and pointed to his chest. It looked like someone had written in cursive marker, but it was actually a tattoo:

Yeah, they rally round tha family . . . wit a pocket full o shells

Walker looked at me with his Ving Rhames eyes. "He wrote them lyrics himself . . . with a black marker. I made it into a tat. Muhfuck-ahs didn't see this shit 'til after basic, almost kicked my ass out."

"Oh, really?" I had no idea what was so bad about the quote. Then again, I wasn't sure what the hell it meant. But we kept talking. He showed me his bookshelf: *Confessions of an Economic Hitman*, *The Nation* magazines, and *Boomerang*, a book about covert wars and terrorism. He opened up a little about why he'd gotten into pharming. He said he'd always stayed away from drugs, even back in the hood, but it had started on his first tour in Iraq, before joining up with our squad.

"I already seen niggas dying an' shit. That was no big deal. It was that goddamn airport road with all them IEDs blowing up errbody. *That's* what fucked me up."

"Oh, you were doin' escorts? How often?"

"Huh." He sniffed sarcastically. "Nigga, we did escorts maybe three, fo' times a damn day. Did that bullshit ten whole weeks."

"Damn," I said.

He chuckled. "Hey. *You* try playin' Russian roulette that long wid-out takin' drugs!"

It struck me that he'd actually thought about the reasons. He also mentioned throwing the flash bang at the sheep. He said that right after that incident he took enough pills to kill most people, but Maseth ran him to the clinic to get his stomach pumped. "It's like vines," he said, motioning toward the outside. "You know . . . growin' around your house? Sometimes they just ain't no way to kill 'em. You just gotta keep 'em from gettin' inside. Makin' a man go crazy."

He shook his head and stood up, handing me the bottle. "That's what these are for. Help with the vines."

"Yeah," I said, and left.

W hat Walker had said began to mess with me. The vines. The notion that there could be something right outside my door, ready to come in, that would never go away and I could never get rid of. PTSD. That is what he was really talking about. *That's fucking scary*, I thought. *PTSD is already inside my head? Jesus, I've got enough inside there already.* I imagined the vines slithering in through the windows, filling the room, twisting and crawling ever so slowly at my feet. Creeping up my pant leg, wrapping around my head, trying to take over. *Goddamn it, stop*, I said to myself as I stared at the ceiling. *Quit thinking so much.* I was desperate to take one that night, but I didn't. I wanted to prove to myself I could do it by myself—fight the vines.

T he morning of the day they got inside, we gathered at the motor pool, smoking cigarettes and checking our gear. There wasn't much talking, just the zipping sounds of Velcro as we adjusted our body armor. Except Bryan, who mumbled, "I can hear Higher now: 'Okay, so wait 'til they think they know their orders, then hit 'em with another FRAGO,'" eliciting laughter from the group. I was feeling pumped. An entire week without taking anything. I even wondered for a second if I was done with the meds for good. I shivered as I took a sip of coffee from my Styrofoam cup, looking out across the palm trees toward the city. The light of the sunrise illuminated some of the minarets downtown, where they stood like silent giants in the morning chill.

"Move out," the CO yelled, and within minutes we were rolling down the main drag away from the FOB. The radio crackled with voices. Our job was to provide support for a marine unit securing an AO inside the city. We were second in line, followed by the rest of the convoy. Ethan, Bryan, Walker, and I sat facing each other in the back, getting jerked back and forth as the Humvee crunched over debris and potholes in the road. During the half-hour ride into town I looked over at Maseth and Walker. They were sitting in wait mode, staring forward. Too much noise to talk. Maseth gave me this sarcastic "gee, ain't this just loads of fun" look. I smiled and glanced at Ethan. He was trying to get some Zs but kept lurching over and hitting my shoulder.

After slowing down for a few turns, speeding up again, engines revving, and then slowing down for a final turn, we came to a sudden stop. "Dismount left!" Sergeant Huey yelled over the net. The tailgate dropped down and we piled out, taking up position alongside the vehicles. The marines ahead of us had been clearing buildings for a few hours, but there were still insurgents scattered around. We could hear random AKs from the rooftops, followed by the sound of our guys. Our fire team leader came around back to us and knelt down. "Okay, restraint, guys. There's a mosque at the end of the street. We are not to engage unless fired upon." He ordered us to take up positions on the roof of the building in front of our Humvee. We moved quickly and made our way up the four flights of stairs to the rooftop.

Once we were on the roof, we saw we had an excellent vantage point; no one would see us up there, much less be able to target us easily. First thing we did was set up security at each wall and see what was around us. Our building was connected to a shorter, white apartment complex to the north, where we could see what seemed like one hundred satellite dishes placed randomly all over the roof. Maseth and Walker set up along the easterly wall, which overlooked the small fields that lined the river. On the opposite side, on the west side of the street, there was a row of slightly shorter buildings facing us. A tangled god-awful mess of wires draped between our building and theirs.

Ethan and I quickly scoped out the windows of the apartments, peering over the three-foot wall along the perimeter of the roof. There was almost no sound for the first few minutes as our guys whispered together, crawling against the wall, carefully readying their weapons. Ethan had the binoculars and was methodically scanning each window. A few minutes passed, and he whispered, "Hey." I must have hesitated, because he quickly snapped at me, "Quit jerkin' it and get over here. I got something." I scooted over to him and grabbed the binos. "Puke-yellow building. Top floor. Third window from right."

I quipped back with a British accent, "Could you be a bit more specific? The whole bleedin' country's puke yellow."

"Okay, butt munch, the *pukier* yellow building."

"I see him. Guy in black?"

"Yeah."

"Something's in his hand?"

"Grenade," Ethan said. "Fuck, and he's watching our guys."

I called out to our team leader, who was near the middle of the roof, "Sergeant, we've got a hajji two buildings down, west side of the street. Request permission to engage."

"That is a negative. Stick to your ROE and keep an eye on him."

"Sir, he has a grenade, and he's—"

"Shit. Marines are Oscar Mike," Ethan said, "about to be underneath him soon."

"Sergeant, Marine squad moving directly toward the guy," I yelled.

There was a long pause as we watched our guys approach under the building.

"Take him out."

I scooted back to Ethan, who was holding his rifle motionless. I peered over the wall. He pulled the trigger, peppering the window frame and the flimsy curtain. We heard a noise that sounded vaguely like screaming, but it took a few seconds for the dust to clear away from the window frame. Ethan had blown the shit out of the window and curtains, and all I could make out inside was the edge of a table. No movement. A few seconds later a corner of what remained of the curtain blew outside the window and folded against the frame. We could see blood splatter clearly on the material. Ethan turned around and sat down against the wall.

"Okay, I think I got him," he said matter-of-factly.

We looked around to assess the situation, scanning the buildings and street below. All of a sudden an RPG blasted out from the top of a tree to the north, halfway down to the mosque, in a small park between the buildings. The RPG careened off way above us, but it started a flurry of activity on our roof. An M240 gunner and several other soldiers with M4s took positions next to Ethan and me. "Holy fucking—" I heard someone yell out. "Ortiz, light that shit up!" I turned to my right to the guy who must have been Ortiz; he had the M240.

"Oh, you firing from the trees now? Is that it?" he yelled, and just fucking unloaded on that tree and everything around it. Several others joined in. What seemed like thirty seconds later, the rounds quieted as everyone stopped to reload and assess the damage. Through the binos I could see the tree had been completely effed up—branches lopped off, hanging free, shit on the ground, leaves fluttering everywhere.

Ethan was giggling. "Dude, that RPG looked like our launch of Vostok II," he said, a reference to our epically failed launch of the model rocket we made one time, using a cardboard paper towel tube, an Estes engine, and Elmer's glue. Fucker shot up, cartwheeled madly out of control, and ended up across I-24, snagged on top of a big-ass pine tree like nine hundred feet up.

"Ha ha, I know, right?" I looked through the binoculars again to confirm the kill. I scanned the base of the tree to see if the shooter had fallen, but there was just debris. I kept looking around, up in the tree branches, near the edge of the building to the left. Nothing. "Where is the shooter?" I asked, continuing to scan. Everything was clear and discernable; just nothing looked like a body. "Weird," I said, about to hand the binos to Ethan. "Wait, there's some kind of board just behind the big branch at the base." I let Ethan take a look. "See it?" I said. "There's a few nails sticking out."

"Yeah," Ethan said, concentrating for a few seconds. "There is a piece of bark stuck on one of the nails . . . hold on . . . okay, these dorks must've stuck a two-by-eight out of a window of that building and secured it to the tree."

I burst into laughter. I knew the guy had probably run down the plank into the window after firing the RPG and could be aiming at us at that very moment, but it was just so utterly stupid.

"*Marhaba*," I yelled out, "*shoof huna, ethwel!*" I turned to Ethan. "Yoohoo, over here, idiot."

Ethan shook his head. "Damn, dude. You sound like a frickin' native speaker." I smiled.

We scanned the building, the area behind the tree, and the park, but there were no obvious places for the shooter to fire from. Suddenly a guy came walking out of the building directly across from Thiessen's team. He was holding his AK like Rambo and had this ridiculous scrunched-up face—half snarl, half crazed maniac. It took about two seconds for Thiessen's guys to mow him down. Our guys just peered over the wall of the building, didn't even need to assist, it was such a joke. I watched through the binoculars. First his legs were shot up—well, basically off—and he fell to the ground. Must have been on drugs, though, because he still seemed to be lunging forward, firing away. That is, until the spray of bullets hit his upper body. I felt a huge rush of giddiness. A couple of guys next to me reacted with what sounded like shocked laughter, like they felt bad but couldn't help but get tickled, it was so over-the-top gruesome.

"Oooh!" I said, making a comical wincing expression. I turned and sat down against the wall, handing the binoculars to Ethan. In my periphery I could tell he was looking at me, trying to read my reaction to what I'd seen. I burst out laughing. "It's only a flesh wound!"

He responded, sounding guilty, "That's sick. What the fuck was he trying to do, anyway?"

I didn't answer for a few seconds, marveling at the sea of brass casings spilled all over the roof and the fog of gunpowder drifting across it. I turned back around to peer over the wall. "Doesn't matter now, does it?"

A group of insurgents had made their way to the top of the yellow building and began firing down at the apartment roof next door. We could see the ends of their AKs sticking out, angled down and to the right of us. My first thought was that we had no men on top of that roof with the satellite dishes. What dumbasses, firing at the wrong roof.

Ethan tapped my shoulder. "Hey, where the hell are Maseth and Walker?"

I turned to look at the east wall, where they were supposed to be. Some soldier I didn't know was over there scanning the field behind the building, using his riflescope. I yelled out, "Hey, where are the two guys who were on that wall?" The guy motioned toward the rooftop with the satellite dishes.

"Holy shit. Ethan! Cookie Crisp is on the fucking roof next door."

The insurgents across the street had a clear shot of the roof, and I could hear pinging sounds as the bullets struck the dishes. We relayed this to the team leader, who was over with Sergeant Huey, and they told us to go check it out. Ethan and I crouched and made our way to the back edge of the roof. I peered over and looked down at the roof of the other building. Nothing. The dishes, a few antennas, a small metal-framed bed, a water cooler against the edge, next to the door. A steady stream of water flowed out from underneath. No Bryan. A few more rounds fired off, striking the far wall and the tank, bouncing off the gravel.

"Fuck. What are they shooting at?" I said, turning to Ethan.

He pointed. "Hey, look, Maseth's PowerAde bottle."

"Okay, they must have gotten pinned down at the front wall, then somehow got to that door." I looked down along the wall. No ladder to climb down; we'd have to hold on to the edge and drop down.

"Yeah, ain't no climbing back up this bitch." I paused for a second. "Fucking goddamned Maseth," I said as Ethan swung his leg over the edge. I yelled into my headset, "Sergeant, Maseth and Walker went north one building, don't know where they are. We're going after 'em."

I swung over the wall and dropped down next to Ethan. Then we crouched and ran up to the front wall. For a brief second I could see the roof of the building and guys with black headscarves. They missed seeing us, luckily. We stopped at the front wall, ducked down, and checked out the route to the door. We'd definitely be visible to the insurgents for a few seconds—that entire north wall was completely exposed. In fact, it had bullet holes all over. I could see chips of blue paint scattered on the gravel. No blood, at least.

I remembered an off-duty game of paintball I was in one time. It was capture the flag, two teams of six, each with its own little fort separated by an open area. Everything moved so slowly. People were crouched down, peering out from behind wooden barriers, log piles, and such. It seemed so predictable; the tactics and positions were so obvious. So I decided I'd just do something crazy abnormal: I jumped up and sprinted down the middle of the open area, passing each barrier and shooting whoever happened to be crouched behind it. I took out the guard with an easy shot, ran straight into their fort, and saw two guys sitting on the floor pointing at a map. *Bam, bam.* Just like that.

I looked at Ethan now. "Run straight across?"

He was thinking the same thing. "Yeah, fuck trying to sneak over there, just minimize the distance and run like a motherfucker!"

I smiled. *Now I feel alive*, I thought. "Ready?"

"Yeah."

We took off. I heard some yelling in Arabic behind us as we skipped through the satellite dishes, trying not to slip on the gravel. Ethan reached the doorway just as I heard the first shots ring out, and I felt something hit the back of my leg. I kept running as chips flew off the blue wall. It wasn't exactly an army move, but I stuck my legs out and slid through the doorway like it was first base. As I got to my feet, Ethan was laughing his ass off. "And A-Rod is . . . *safe!*" he yelled, motioning with his arms. I checked my leg and found it was just some gravel that had ricocheted against my skin. No big deal.

The power had been knocked out in the building. I pulled a Maglite out, and we looked down the stairwell. Nothing to see but concrete and dirt. We carefully made our way down to the top-floor hallway, which looked clear but dark. There looked to be four apartments on each side, all empty, of course, unless insurgents were hiding inside, ready to mow us down with AKs. We crept down the hallway, listening intently for any sounds coming from the apartments.

"Cookie Crisp!" Ethan called out in a half whisper.

"Oh, like using nicknames will make it harder to hear us," I whispered.

He gave me a look of acknowledgment, stepping forward cautiously. A dim light shone through the window at the end of the hall. It was eerily quiet. The only sound was the muffled popping of small arms fire outside. I whispered to Ethan, "Check each apartment?"

"Fuuuck no," he said. "Take too long."

We walked back toward the other side, passing by the stairwell. Ethan pointed to the apartment at the end. The door was wide open. He put his finger to his mouth to give the "quiet" signal, trying to be stupid, so I smiled. We crept along, hugging the left wall. I remember looking down at the hideous Berber carpet and being so glad we had a quiet surface to walk on. We got past the third door and peered into the apartment. There was a small entrance area with a thick brown curtain blocking our view into the main room. I immediately felt this weird sensation come over me. My face shook—like all the muscles that control tiny movements tensed up all at once. There could have easily been a guy sitting on a couch behind that curtain, pointing a goddamned AK-47 right at us. *Fuck it*, I thought, and just yanked the curtain open. There it was, the couch I expected to see. It was turned a different way, though, facing away from us, toward a small table and TV that were pushed up against the window. Pretty small apartment, not even a bathroom. The kitchen was nothing more than a nook in the corner. On the right there was a shallow step-out balcony with its glass door left open. I walked over to look out, see if anyone had gotten out this way, maybe jumped over to the outside wall. I noted the narrow decorative ledge. We were three floors up, but it would not be impossible to leap over there, sidestep over to the drainage pipe, and climb up to the roof with the satellites. I paused for a second, then leaned over the balcony to look down.

"Holy shit, I think it's them!" I heard Ethan yell out. He had opened the other window and was standing on the table, leaning over.

I looked down and could see one of our guys below, lying on his back on a concrete slab at the base of the building. Another one of our men was leaning over him, propping the guy's neck up. "Walker!" Ethan shouted.

The guy looked up. "Need some fucking help here!"

I shouted back, "Is this building clear?"

Walker yelled, "Yeah, just get the fuck down here!"

He sounded upset, even panicked. Ethan and I ran down the hall and to the stairwell, and within a minute we were outside. I wasn't sure what we'd see when we got down there. Not that there was much time to think. It was all autopilot, nothing but motor skills—one boot in front of the other, fast as shit, make sure no insurgents had flanked us, go check on the fallen soldier. Battle drill. Buddy care.

As we ran up to them, we saw Bryan. He was lying down, eyes closed, sunglasses hanging down over his mouth. "What the fuck happened?" I asked Walker, kneeling down on the concrete next to Bryan's shoulder. Walker turned to us. His expression was totally out of character. Disoriented, in shock, completely rattled. He pointed to the ledge I had been looking at.

"He fell . . . I think he . . . concussion maybe, I don't know."

Ethan was smacking Bryan's face. Bryan looked lifeless. His forehead was all scraped up, red specks of blood mixed with dirt and sand.

"Bryan! Can you hear me? Wake up, bro!" Ethan yelled, opening each eyelid with his gloved fingers. Walker felt for a pulse. I stood up and began scanning the back of the building for insurgents. "I woulda radioed," Walker said. "Fuckin' headset was broke."

I took a few steps away from them to look south, see if we had a clear path to our vehicles, which I figured should be just around the corner. "Where the fuck's the medic?" I called out on my radio. No answer.

"Let's get him up," Ethan said. The three of us lifted, grabbing under each arm and under his legs. "Watch the neck . . . Walker, make sure his head is straight."

We double-timed it behind the building, down concrete steps, and across patios. When we rounded the corner of the building, we could see the Humvees parked exactly where we'd left them. "Oh, thank fucking Christ!" Ethan muttered, out of breath. The medic met up with us, and we loaded Bryan into the Humvee ambulance, laying him down on one of the litters in the back. We radioed Sergeant Huey and gave him a quick SITREP, and he arranged for Bryan to be taken to the battalion aid station.

The three of us stood there and watched as the vehicle drove off. Stupid as this sounds, I wondered why they couldn't arrange to radio us and give us an update on Bryan's condition. Instead, we were ordered to rejoin the squad up on the roof, and we spent the rest of the day in the same spot where we'd been before. I felt this strange sense of monotony—unfeeling, robotic. I didn't really care who I was shooting at, didn't care about killing some guy with an RPG sneaking behind a jingle truck. And I didn't really care if they shot at me. I tried to snap out of it, but the numbness crept in. All I could do was crouch behind that same wall, fire when the others fired, stop shooting when I heard "Cease fire." *Why didn't I take something today?* I thought.

That night Ethan and I hiked over to the clinic to see Bryan. We'd heard they'd gotten him to wake up, and he was in stable enough condition that they'd transferred him from the aid station. I just knew he'd be okay. I took a Xannie, of course. Ethan had said something about Bryan that showed how worried he was. He sounded depressed, resigned almost, like Maseth could definitely die. Scared shitless to find out. This put me in rescue mode. I laughed cheerfully, trying to be convincing. "Dude, he fell—what?—twenty feet? People don't die from that." But neither of us knew much, really. We hadn't had a chance to talk to Walker. Ethan didn't say anything, just kept trudging across the gravel toward the clinic. It seemed to take forever, and my legs were aching like shit.

When we got to the room, Walker was talking to Bryan, who was sitting in the bed in a neck brace, an IV sticking out of his arm. We were immediately relieved and launched into a tirade of laughter, shouting out, "High five!" like Bryan always did in his Borat accent. Bryan managed a smile.

"So what the hell happened, holmes?" Ethan asked, plopping

down in one of the chairs. Bryan sat still and just moved his eyes toward whoever was speaking, maintaining a slight smile.

"I fucked up, is what," he said with his southern lilt.

Walker tried to help out. "Asshole climbs out the window onto the ledge, tries to climb up to the top to shoot at those muhfuckahs."

"What?" I said in disbelief. I turned to Bryan.

Bryan answered slowly, "Yeah, I was trying to get behind the water tank. Woulda had an excellent shot at them, too."

"Slipped?"

"Yeah, fell right on one of my ass cheeks." Bryan gave his devilish grin as best he could. I could see it in his eyes. "Now my dumps come out half moon–shaped."

I shook my head, turning to the other guys. "The guy breaks his fuckin' neck, and he's still writing comedy routines . . . Dude, the neck! How'd you break the neck?"

Bryan continued, "So I hit my ass on the ledge, and it flips me completely over, three hundred and sixty degrees, and I land on the top of my head. Heard this big snap!"

"A hundred and eighty degrees," Ethan said.

"Whatever, Co-fag. So I flipped over twice, fucker!"

Everybody laughed. I could see Bryan's cheek muscles strain a bit as he smiled under the bandage. *Jesus. The guy almost dies, and look at him, doesn't miss a damn beat*, I thought.

"Hey, so what did they say, what kind of damage was there?" I said, pointing to the back of my neck.

"Said I was a lucky sumbitch, that's what," Bryan said, half laughing some more. "Said if I'd broken it slightly higher, it woulda fucked up my breathing."

"Phrenic nerve," Ethan added.

"Yeah, exactly, Coffelt. That's what they said, phrenic nerve."

"Goddamn, son! Stopped you breathing?" Walker said, shuddering at the thought.

It seemed like we all had a brief moment of total seriousness, thinking about how Bryan had just cheated death. Then some soldiers and COs rapped on the door, so we said our good-byes. I stayed a few minutes to track down the doc and ask a few questions. Dad being a general surgeon, I guess I needed to know just a little more, feel like I had done absolutely everything I could. The doctor told me Bryan was very stable, little to no chance of lapsing into a coma or anything crazy. She was very helpful, almost shocking how she addressed every one of my questions, explaining everything. I knew he'd be okay after that. I got back to the hooch, then snuck back out to grab a little refill from Walker. But I didn't take any.

I dreamed about it that first night—Bryan in a neck brace, lying in bed with vines sticking out of his head, fanning out in all directions and wrapped around all of us: me, Ethan, Walker, Thiessen. But it wasn't exactly Bryan's body. He looked just like my mom that time she went to the hospital. It was after Mom and Dad had a huge fight and we all woke up and stood crying in the hallway. Mommy slipped on the stairs, they tried to tell us. And in the dream all of us standing around Bryan were supposed to be my sisters gathering around my mom in bed, when she had that drooping smile that scared me, because they had her on morphine. Weird. I told Ethan about it over chow the next morning, but he shrugged it off, sounding annoyed. He told me stress was normal; I just needed some self-restraint. When I asked what he meant exactly, he said I wasn't the same lately. "Probably 'cause of that shit. You need to ease up," he said.

I hesitated for a second, not sure he knew. "Ethan, the place is getting to all of us. Most people are probably doing it."

He looked at me with his patented glare. "Uh, no. I think it's just you."

With that I tipped my milk up and gulped the last of it, tossed the empty carton on the tray, and stood up. I wasn't sure why, but that just completely pissed me off.

"Gee, I just can't imagine why anyone would need to!" I said. I scooped some stuff up off the tray and threw it in the air, making an explosion sound. "Fucking IEDs, mortar rounds, little goat girls getting run over, fellow soldiers almost dying . . . not getting to see your own fucking grandmother before she dies!" I yelled the last part, and a few people looked up from their breakfast. *Nosy pricks. So a guy raises his voice a little, big fucking deal.* Ethan didn't say anything, just kept staring at me.

"Fuck it, I'm done," I said, and I walked out. I went over to Walker's hooch and hung out. Told him I was not there to get any meds. "Dass cool," he said. One of his buds stopped by, and the three of us played some music, thumbed through mags, shot the shit. It was cool until Walker's dumbass friend opened his big mouth.

"War of aggression," he said, tapping the article he was reading. "Hail yeah."

"What, Iraq?" Walker said.

"Hail yeah, muhfucker. Dass all this is. Feel me?"

Walker let out a chuckle. "Nigga, don't be frontin'. You in it too."

"Oh, I know!" he said. "We the worse ones. We da assholes who got pimped."

Walker shook his head. "No, we nuttin' but fuckin' punks. You a thug, I'm a thug . . ." He waved his hand at both of us. "Might as well be in the hood. You. Him. Me. We all just low-life niggas, goin' around waving guns, scarin' people, scarin' poor women. Ain't accomplishin' shit."

"Uh-huh," his friend said, laughing. "We ain't savin' nobody! Nigga, we pissin' the whole world off, is what!" Walker laughed with him.

That was it for me. "Are you guys fucking high?" I said, standing up to walk to the door.

Walker thought that was so hilarious. "Fo' real? This is *you* askin'?"

"I'm out," I said, opening the door.

"Hey, man," Walker said, "we just playin'. But I'ma be straight wit chu," he said, nodding at me. He looked pretty sincere. "Maybe if you open your eyes to what we sayin', you won't need all them Oxys and shit."

I walked out.

E verybody was happy about Bryan. The company commander made an announcement at our next briefing, and people were cheering and yelling "Cookie Crisp!" and clapping. It was pretty emotional. There seemed to be an understanding of who Bryan was. Hell, the guy knew people every goddamn where: army, MPs, contractors, women, men, everybody. I realized how much he kind of held our squad together, and now he was flying back stateside. It sucked for us, really. I was glad he could leave the sand pit, but I wished more that he could stay around.

For the next two weeks, until they could arrange for a flight to Ramstein, Bryan would stay at the clinic. They could watch over him there, make sure he didn't have blood clots or whatever, and a new wing had just been built that had a shower facility that he could get in and out of easily.

Bryan started doing a bunch of crazy YouTube videos. They were funny as hell, became kind of a cult classic overnight around the FOB. He'd interview soldiers, usually rookies, asking them obscene questions like "How often do you jerk it?" Totally straight-faced, he'd continue, "Okay, now, Private, do the spank fests usually occur at night in the privacy of your jerk shack, or do you prefer the urine-stained, feces-encrusted port-o-shitter?" The soldier would start snickering and try to hold it together enough to answer. Bryan would just go over the top, insisting it was a very serious matter, and please just answer candidly because we're trying to show folks at home what life's like here in the suck, and people like your mom need to know these things. Of course the soldiers couldn't act, so they just burst into hysterics, but that was fine with Bryan. It seemed like that was what he wanted them to do anyway, like he couldn't care less about making entertainment. He just wanted to mess with his poor interviewee. Word spread quickly, and within a day or two people were ripping DVDs of Bryan's skits and watching them at night huddled around a laptop.

It was on one of the nights we had watched one, in fact, when we got the news about Bryan. I remember there was a checkpoint that day, because it was at the same highway location we were sent right after the goat girls, where Bryan and Ethan and I stood outside on the patio while Walker paced back and forth. I had finally fallen asleep after lying in bed for a couple of hours after Ethan had put his book away and turned off the light. He and I hadn't talked much in a few days. It must have been three or four in the morning. Someone started banging frantically on the door. Ethan jumped up and ran over to open it. I heard Sergeant Huey outside, talking in a strange tone of voice. It wasn't loud or commanding like I had expected, because I was thinking there must have been a mortar attack, or we were getting called up on a night mission.

I heard Ethan say, "What the fuck?" in a solemn tone, and I slipped a pair of shorts on and walked over to the door. From the dim light of the outdoor bulb, I could just see enough of Huey's face to tell something was wrong. In that split second I ran through a few possibilities: an IED attack had killed one of our men, someone was killed out on patrol, someone from the battalion went missing, things like that. But if he didn't need us to ready up, why wake us in the middle of the night, why Ethan and me? Something inside me knew the answer.

"What's going on?" I asked. Huey paused for a second. I'd never seen him like that, with that expression. He looked like he was unprepared for a speech, and talking to us scared him to death.

"There was an accident. Bryan . . . was in an accident. They found him in the shower."

Huey's stupid look didn't seem to match his words, and it annoyed the fuck out of me. "So? What, did he slip out of his little cushioned shower seat? Get soap in his eyes? What?"

"Uh, electrocuted. He got some kind of electrical shock in the shower. They don't know how, exactly."

Huey stood at the bottom of the steps, looking up at me like some assbag, trying to be all noble and respectful.

"He okay? Where is he?" Ethan asked, lighting up a cigarette. I could smell the phosphorus of the match, but it didn't really register.

"He's still at the clinic. They wouldn't say. I did run into a med—"

"Is. He. Okay!" I blasted out, thinking, *This fucker ought to know there's only one thing we care about hearing right now. Cut the bullshit.*

"I said, 'They wouldn't say'!" Huey snapped, raising his voice over mine.

"So you don't know," I said.

"No, *Specialist*. But it's pretty serious."

Ethan lifted his hand in front of me, trying to get me to back off. "Dude . . ."

"Thank you . . . sir," I said. "So, bottom line: no one knows." I turned and yanked open the screen door to walk back inside.

I heard Ethan continue the conversation, asking about possibly going to visit Bryan. I thought they might think I was an asshole for not asking that. *But what the fuck does it matter, anyway? God let my friend get electrocuted; what the fuck difference will it make if I go stand next to his hospital bed and stare at tubes and a beeping machine?*

The answer is, it ended up not making a fuck-all bit of difference. Ethan stood outside for a few more minutes, then came in and saw me at the cabinet. He let out a loud breath, and then I heard a jingle as he started to put on some pants. "So," he said cautiously, "you wanna head over to the CSH? I'm going." I didn't respond, just shut the cabinet and threw on some clothes. Ethan waited for me, and we headed toward the gravel path to the clinic.

I remember the time when I was twelve, walking down West Brow Road, at the same spot where I'd been hit by a car while I was riding my bike. I was crying about my friend Timmy, whose mom was dying of breast cancer. My dad had operated on her, so I kept hearing about things getting worse and worse. I just walked aimlessly down the street by myself, praying to God: *Please let her live, please do something, intervene, please take care of her.* But something told me it didn't make any difference. There were far more powerful forces acting, and nothing—no painful tears, no prayers or being a good little Christian boy or even loving my friend like he was my own brother—none of those things would change the answer one bit. Somehow I knew this, even at twelve. And there I was again, walking into the clinic, about to be handed another verdict.

When Ethan and I got inside, they sat us in a tiny waiting room with a ridiculously large HDTV playing Fox News. We'd told them Ethan and I were really close friends of Bryan, so they were all nice to us. Of course, they had to be, since they probably knew already. They just had to do their sympathy bullshit, and, oh, could we wait just a few more minutes, and someone would be right out to talk to us about Bryan. Five minutes later, sure enough, they sent out a fucking chaplain. Some fat, prissy motherfucker with sympathetic eyes. They might as well have lit up a neon sign above the doors where they'd taken Bryan with the word *DIED* in big, bright, buzzing, blinking red.

"Oh, fucking *hell* no," I blurted out to the guy as he clasped his hands and locked his eyes on Ethan and me. "We want to talk to the doctor," I said. "Send Bryan's doctor out here." I was not about to even stand up.

The fucker's voice was so calm and soothing. "No problem, but I'd like to just sit with you guys for a few minutes, okay?" As he said this he squatted right in front of us to be on our level.

"Fuck this," I said, jumping up and turning toward the exit.

Whatever they had to tell me through a goddamned man of God, I had no use for. If Bryan was dead, I wasn't going to get the news delivered to me like I was a fucking punk. I just walked out. At some point I remember thinking Ethan would probably follow, but I kept walking regardless. The FOB seemed sterile and soulless, nothing but the sound of my boots trudging through the gravel. I walked inside the hooch in the dark, opened the cabinet, took two, maybe three of whatever was in the bottle, felt around for the bed, and lay down. I took a fresh pack of cigarettes out of my shoulder pocket and lit the first one up, then just stared at the ceiling with my gear on. It seemed like a couple of hours later when the screen door creaked open and Ethan walked inside. I didn't say anything, just kept still and waited for the pills to do something, which they never did.

I didn't attend the service they held for Bryan. I wasn't sure why. I knew I should have. But somehow, in my mind, doing that would have been to give in, to sign off on the reality, when I knew very well it was complete bullshit. To have to stand there solemnly at attention, the same way everyone had the countless times that shit had happened. What a cliché. Like some stupid play with known characters and known lines, and no one's allowed to improvise or do anything different. *Fuck that. I didn't come six thousand miles all the way over here to accept shit for how it is. I came here to change things.*

For a few days I even had this strange notion that it wasn't a done deal yet, that Bryan could still be brought back. It was like there wasn't much time left, but if I acted quickly and played things just right, we could find him alive. Maybe there had been a mix-up at the clinic; they got his name wrong or something.

All the normal details of those next few days were lost on me. I don't remember much, just cleaning my rifle and sleeping. And of course the meds. Lots of meds. In my mind I had to take them just in case my notion was wrong. I did this deliberately, consciously. I even talked myself through it logically in the port-o-john: *Fact: there could have been a mix-up. I am not making this up; I am simply choosing to believe there was a mix-up. Just because I am back to taking pills doesn't mean I don't believe he is alive.*

"I'm just covering all my bases, that's all. Just in case," I said aloud.

Thump! Thump! The plastic door rattled loudly as someone pounded on it in rapid succession. "Who the fuck you talking to?" some guy said. I heard mischievous giggles fade as he took off running, followed by laughter from a couple of other guys.

Because of the meds, I was also back to smoking all the time. I would wake up, take a blue, drink espresso all day, smoke two packs, then pop a Vike or a Perk or something. Because of the caffeine, I either couldn't get to sleep or would wake up ten times during the night, and it seemed like every time I woke I'd be thinking of the beach and have a migraine and be burning up. I'd lie there in my boxers, sweating, remembering Dr. Geisler and the phone call, and get that same instantaneous fever. I don't even think the temperature was that bad in Iraq, it was something weird with my body. I had no idea what was going on, but it was like that every night, and it freaked me out. Memories were popping into my head again, over and over, like ADD. Low frequencies of voices through the walls. Shouting, escalating in pitch. Mom storming out of her bedroom with blood-shot eyes, sneering, "Since when did *you* ever satisfy a woman?" at my dad, me standing there shaking uncontrollably, trying to ask what was wrong. Her snapping at me viciously, the smell of alcohol, her nightgown opening slightly, carelessly. Me seeing too much.

And then there was the neck brace. It kept flashing into my mind—Bryan sitting there in bed, awkwardly upright, with that foam thing crammed under his chin and wrapped all the way around. I tried not to visualize it, but it wouldn't stop. One night I was staring at a hand towel hanging on the door, just staring at it like a zombie. In the dim light it looked just like the neck brace. Suddenly—and I was totally awake during all this—I started hearing this whooshing sound, like slow helicopter blades, coming at me from the side. It was the neck brace, unfolded, flying like a boomerang toward the side of my face, the whooshing sound getting louder. I couldn't see it; it was invisible, 'cause it was nothing but a concept, really, but I knew exactly where it was, and just as it was about to hit my head, I was compelled to turn my face to the side. And then it would go in a straight line, way off in the distance, loop back, and come at me again, and I'd have to turn to the other side. It went on like that for a while. I thought I was going insane. I finally jumped up and went to my locker and turned the Maglite on, then opened a water bottle and splashed it into my eyes, rubbing the shit out of them.

"You all right, man?" Ethan called out. He was sitting at his computer.

A few seconds went by; I glanced at my watch and realized it was only midnight. I leaned in close to the mirror. My eyes had little red splotches. "Yeah," I said, clicking the flashlight off, "I'm good." I flopped back down on my bunk, and for a few minutes I was okay, but then it started again. Like frames of a movie reel: Bryan sitting there with the goddamned neck brace, which felt so familiar. *Did I dream about this recently or something?* I'd seen it before, somewhere. *Maybe it was Brazil, must have been Brazil,* I thought. *What the fuck was it, and why would I be going mental like this?* It scared the hell out of me. I wanted to tell Ethan about it, but I felt myself breaking down, and I didn't want to affect him. He might have been in worse shape than me, for all I knew. I couldn't risk burdening him with my problems.

Plus, I'd been such a dick I couldn't ask him for anything. He was right; I just needed to get a grip. I had to try to fight off the vines.

I don't know how many days this psychotic shit went on. By day I would go on patrol, a couple pills in me. I'd be leaning against a wall watching for vehicles, and I'd hear someone call on the radio. I would instantly play this scenario in my head where I was hearing them shout, "We found Maseth!" And when it wasn't that, I'd morph the scenario into making sense, thinking that realistically they wouldn't place a radio call just to let my dumb ass know about Bryan; they'd wait 'til I got back to the FOB to tell me. Later I'd hear the radio crackle again, and I'd do the same thing, kind of forgetting about earlier. At night I'd sit in bed with another pounding headache, staring at the poster.

I t eventually went away. I have no idea how long it took; somewhere along the way I lost all concept of time. There were some days I did things I barely remember. In fact, I know I blanked a lot of things completely out. Entire conversations, entire missions, entire days. Ethan said he woke up one night to me yelling at the top of my lungs. He said I was holding my neck like I was choking. The next day he told me about it, and I was clueless. I went on a five-hour cordon mission and forgot it happened. I did checkpoints and forgot. Ethan said he was so fucking close to talking to someone about me, but then one day he saw some signs like I might be getting better.

He told me later he had gone to Walker, first to ask him nicely to stop selling me so many meds, fully prepared, as he put it, to go Jackie Chan on his fucking ass if needed. But Walker told him I wasn't buying that much anymore. I had been going over there a lot, but mostly just hanging out with Walker and asking him about politics and the war, listening to music, and even doing some poetry. Ethan said he hadn't been sure he believed that, but Walker had given him a poem I wrote. Ethan said he could tell it was mine, and it was some pretty trippy shit.

But apparently I had gotten so low on cash I'd hit up Ethan, and he had given me an unequivocal "Fuck no," he would absolutely not sponsor his best friend killing himself. Meanwhile, we had three or four weeks with no patrols or escorts, which must have given me enough of a break from combat that I didn't need so many pills.

I n the weeks that followed, once I woke up, everything seemed like it was different, like it had changed colors or something. The other guys may not have seen it—in fact, I'm sure they didn't—but I did. More like felt it. It was like a low, vibrating tone, a hum, must have been in the background before, barely audible, and someone had been tweaking the knob a teeny, tiny bit once each day. I'd been so messed up I hadn't noticed, but now it was obvious. I could sense it. The guys in our squad were not who they'd been before.

We'd do the same things we'd always done—smoke and talk as we waited at the motor pool, eat MREs at a checkpoint, play cards outside the hooch, whatever—but I watched as the guys joked around. I saw their faces and could hear it in their voices. It might be the same sarcastic expression as before, but there'd be a hint of something, or an outburst of laughter, like the frequencies were just a tad off. It reminded me of Paw-Paw's funeral, how odd it seemed to me that people would not sit solemnly and quietly. I noticed several people smile, not the sympathetic funeral smile everyone makes, but an almost joyful smile. Not that I thought it was inappropriate, just out of context. Even Mom and Dottie. On the way to the grave site they were smiling, acting playful, even yukking it up; I couldn't believe it. I'd been asked to help by driving Dot's car for her: "Careful, son, she's precious cargo," Mom said, directing me cheerfully. And I was glad to do it. It made me feel trusted, them allowing me to drive when I only had my learner's. My cousins jumped in, then Mom decided to ride too, obviously to be there for my grandmother. So the whole way Mom tried to play the strong one for everyone's sake, which for the Marwood side of the family meant making jokes about everything. "Damn you, Paw-Paw!" she said, looking up at the thunderclouds. "Well, I guess he's still got his sense of humor!" she chuckled, turning around to each of us. Of course, the standard Marwood thing was to respond in kind, ante up, be a team player. You had to take the joke and run with it or at least laugh hysterically, showing your solidarity. But I just couldn't chime in; I wasn't feeling it. I appreciated what Mom was doing, trying to keep Dottie's spirits up, keep everyone's up, to maintain that "celebratory spirit," as Paw-Paw used to call it, but it still seemed bizarre to me to be laughing at a time like that. Still, before I knew it, Dottie joined in as we sat idle in traffic; I had just begun to worry we'd be late for the service. "This better to hell be open bar!" she said dryly—another Marwood standard. I jerked my head around toward my grandmother, who kept her straight face for added effect. Mom burst into hysterics and touched my shoulder. I managed a smile, but God, it was weird.

That is how the guys seemed to me. No somber moods, no dark clouds hanging over everyone's heads, no soldiers sitting off by themselves, staring bleakly into the distance. Sergeant Huey pulled his pranks just like before; Ethan made his tongue-in-cheek derisive remarks whenever the new guy pulled a rookie move; Walker continued fucking around with the Iraqis. *The vines*, I thought, *they're different from what I've been imagining.* It wasn't like you looked in the mirror one day and said, "Hey, what's this ivy growing up my neck? Maybe I'm getting PTSD!" It's more like some alien virus from space— stays dormant for months and months, and you think you're fine, and everyone thinks you're fine, but in reality you've gone all *Body Snatchers*, and one day after the war is over you wake up next to your sleeping wife and kids, walk into the garage like a zombie, and hang yourself with a garden hose.

A few weeks passed, and it began to get hot again. I remember thinking I was back to normal, for the most part, although I was left with a sense of unease—a threatening feeling—that I had almost lost it, may have come close to going batshit crazy. No one else seemed to need painkillers or have flashbacks or hallucinations or whatever. *Maybe that's good, though*, I thought. *Hopefully it will never totally get to them. Let me be the one to take the psychological trauma. I gotta stay strong, be an example.*

As a kind of apology to Ethan for acting like a dick to him and keeping to myself for so long, I started talking about high school and all the crazy stuff we used to do back then. We'd be doing some detail work like hauling shit barrels to the burn pit, and I'd say, "Fuck diss shit!"—a reference to one time when Ethan and I were hanging out in the back at Dad's place and heard the garbage truck pull up in front of the house. We could hear the clanging of metal cans and the hydraulic brakes and everything. The next thing you know, we heard one of the dudes yell it out: "Fuck diss shit!" We just busted out laughing, only imagining what must have happened. He must have lifted up a trash can and some kind of nasty syrupy, stinky goo dripped out and got on his crotch or something. So from then on every time a teacher or boss gave us something to do, we'd rattle off that quote. One time Ethan even dissected the etymology of the phrase, just to crack me up: "It's actually a form of sophisticated shorthand: 'My, but this task is tedious! Might I suggest we discontinue?'"

Ethan seemed a little distant at first, but I understood. I imagined it was disturbing having to watch as his best friend slowly went psycho. I may have felt sure I was over it, but for him it was probably different. He would have to be cautious, guarded. No worries, I was getting my shit together.

I sat in the passenger seat with the window up, sipping coffee with gloves on, staring out at the morning. The streets were mostly empty, just men in white dishdashas opening up their storefronts, a few leaning against taxis, smoking and waiting.

"Wonder what those fuckers think of us," Ethan said, leaning over the console to look out my window. "I'd love to stop and ask each and every one, 'Hey, do *all* y'all hate us, or just some of you? What are we up against here?'" I didn't say anything, just noted his curiosity. I turned back to look again, and Ethan continued, "Like that old dude with the beard and sunken eyes. See him?"

"Yeah," I said, watching the guy turn his head slowly as we rolled past.

"Fucker looks like a damn caricature of an Arab! Well, okay"—he chuckled— "that is just my own bias or Western perspective, but still! The guy just stares at us, and you can't even tell if that's a glare or not. Not a single facial muscle contraction. Jesus, dude, let's see a risorius muscle twitch or something. Come on!"

"You hungry?" I said, motioning to the stash of snacks.

"Sure, I'll take one of those fruit and nut bars."

Ethan fumbled awkwardly with the wrapper with his gloves.

"Shall I have that peeled for you, my liege?" I asked, quoting a *Three Stooges* episode he knew.

"Nah, I'm good," he said, tearing off one side with his teeth.

"Man, I'd kill to be stateside watching *The Stooges* right now." I looked over to Ethan to get his reaction.

"Yeah," he said absently, checking the side mirror to make a turn.

I went back to staring outside, picturing us sitting in Dad's porch room in those wicker chairs, eating Arby's beef and cheddars, slurping down cans of Coke and watching an entire DVD of *Stooges*. I remembered how Dad would drive up in his Mercedes, just coming home from work while we fuckups had been out of school for hours. We'd see him pull around back and park in his "Doctors Only" spot, and then he'd walk in, looking all austere with the stethoscope around his neck, and say, "Gentlemen!" as if we were hardly that mature by any stretch, but he was feeling magnanimous. But there was one afternoon I'll never forget. He walked in the porch room and suddenly got all excited when he saw *The Stooges*, plopping down and telling us how he used to watch those vaudeville acts when *he* was an "adolescent." He was trying to connect with us, playing the hip dad, the cool, relaxed, nonauthoritarian dad, able to appreciate three complete morons making a total mockery of responsibility and seriousness. It was awesome seeing him that way, even if it was a little forced.

I wondered if Ethan had noticed the same thing about my dad back then. As we passed through a shadow of a building, I saw his reflection briefly in the window, and he just looked somber. Then I remembered Bryan and felt horrible. *Jesus*, I thought, *he's probably thinking about Bryan, and here I am quoting the fucking* Three Stooges? *What a dick I am.* We passed another group of men standing facing the road. I pictured myself jumping out and drop-kicking one of them to the ground. "Wipe that fucking glare off your face, motherfucker!" I said aloud, as if they could hear me. "We're here to free your asses; least you can do is smile at us." I was hoping Ethan would say something, but he didn't, just kept driving.

We got back to the base, and I decided to try to talk to Mom. I didn't have the money for it, but I didn't care. A new guy in our platoon overheard me telling Delaney how crazy expensive it was calling stateside and asked if I'd talked to Chino Loco yet. He seemed almost amused and condescending when I asked who that was.

"Dude! Chino Loco? Crazy Vietnamese guy? You never met him? I thought *everybody* knew Tuy."

I looked at Delaney.

"Asian guy from Stuart's party," he said. "Looks kinda like Bruce Lee?"

"Oh, him," I said. "What's the deal, does he have a calling card?"

"He's a tech wiz," the new guy said. "Go talk to him, he'll hook you up."

I found Tuy outside his hooch with a bunch of rookies. You could always spot new guys 'cause they looked like nervous rabbits, constantly peering around to see if a predator was sneaking up on them. It took about a month for new guys to relax, even inside the wire.

These guys were all gathered around a plastic card table, with Tuy in a chair holding a whole deck of cards fanned out in his hands. It seemed kind of bizarre—Tuy the center of attention, noobs looking on, totally enthralled like he was David Blaine or some shit. I folded my arms and waited for the little show to wrap up, which it did quickly when Tuy pulled out a card and the dumb shits all yelled out, "Ho!" and started laughing their asses off. One guy even doubled over choking, getting Red Bull down his windpipe. It looked like what Bryan used to always do. When the guy stopped overacting and stood back up, I glared at him and walked over to the palm tree. I lit up a cigarette and stood waiting for their bullshit to finish. Tuy had this subdued look of self-satisfaction on his face, like he was only mildly amused that he looked infinitely more intelligent than these recruits. They were all slapping bills down on the table in front of him.

"No, Santos, only fifteen for you," Tuy said, grabbing a five and handing it back to one of the guys. The guy took the money, looking like he was struggling to do the math, but then quickly played it off like he got it. Tuy immediately jumped to the next thing.

"Hey!" he called out, waving a twenty at two guys walking away from the table. He turned to Santos. "What is that crippled guy's name? Hey, gimp!"

One of the two guys turned around as Santos answered, "That's Forrester."

Tuy paused for a second. "Hey, Forrest Gimp. Take this."

The guy walked slowly to the table. Looked like he had a slight sprain in his ankle. "What for?"

Tuy smiled condescendingly. "Consider this your boot camp. But it'll be double or nothing next time, fool."

The guy smiled and took the money but didn't appear entirely pleased at being shown up. *Damn*, I thought, *why do they treat this guy like some kind of Mafia boss?*

Santos stayed to ask Tuy a couple more questions about the bet, and Tuy gave him a quick remedial lesson. Santos didn't seem to fully understand, just sat there in amazement. "It's all just math, dude," Tuy said, squaring up the cards and slipping them back in their case. Santos stood up, shaking his head.

"You'll get it," Tuy said.

"Coolio. Thanks, Tuy. So, poker next week?"

"Yeah, or somethin'. Call and remind me."

Tuy looked over at me as Santos left. "You waiting for me?"

"Yeah, I heard you can hook me up. I want to call home."

Tuy wasted no time starting in with his shtick. "Somebody need to call their mommy?"

"Yeah, whatever, can you just hook me up, man?"

Tuy gave me a quick smile that seemed condescending but friendly. "No, it's cool, it's cool. Important to call the moms."

It was annoying to have this smart-ass read my mind right off the bat. Of course, it was more like a lucky guess. Who else do soldiers usually call?

"The best I can do is Skype. I got a SAT phone too, but Jason or somebody has it."

Gee, way to be responsible, I thought.

We walked over to the internet hut and he set me up with Skype, which allowed me to call home for free.

"You're good now," he said. "Sound only. Video's too slow. Remember, Alt+F4 to close the shit quickly. Do *not* get caught. They'll block VoIP for everybody."

I asked if he wanted some money, and he seemed totally uninterested. It was like all he wanted was to help people out. *Probably likes making himself look important*, I thought. *Whatever.* I was just glad to be able to call Mom and save some money. But for a moment I wished I could be like that, totally oblivious and immune to the nightmare that was going on in Iraq.

"Thanks, man." I put on the headset and typed in the number on the keyboard. As it rang I anticipated how she'd sound this time, if I'd feel free to tell her what was going on with me. So much had changed. Maybe I'd just spill everything. And she'd listen; she'd be okay hearing what I'd been through. She'd reassure me I'd be fine now.

Finally someone picked up. It was Glenn. His voice was cheerful and pleasant.

"Hey, G, it's me."

"Oh," he said, sounding caught off guard. "Hold on, let me get your mother." His tone was now distant. *Oh God.* I'd seen this before. This was what he did when Mom was pissed off at someone. Didn't matter why, or even if Glenn knew dick about the situation; he had no opinion of his own. Just a mirror of hers.

A couple minutes later Mom got on the line. "Well, it's nice to finally know you're alive," she said, all sarcastic and bitter.

I can't believe this shit. "What?"

"We haven't heard from you, son. We've been worried sick."

"Uh, hey, Mom, news flash: I'm in a war, okay? I emailed you."

I paused, trying to control my voice. I looked around the hut; thankfully there were no other soldiers, just the check-in guy way in the front. He was facing the other direction, watching a small flat-screen hanging from the plywood ceiling.

I'm not letting this shit go. "Did you email me back? No. Did I get any letters? Care packages?"

She played the defensive "poor me" card. "Well, gee, I am so sorry, son. I guess we're from the wrong generation. Not computer experts like you all."

"Oh God, Mom. I showed you guys how to do email . . . twice! Remember the sticky notes? Step one: push the power button. Step two: open the browser. It's like four goddamned steps!"

"Don't be disrespectful," she said.

Pfft, what's there to respect, I thought. Then of course I felt guilty. "Look, Mom, I'm sorry if I haven't called. It's just been really difficult for me. Dottie . . . she was such a great . . ."

"I know, you all were really close, considering," she said, sounding detached. "You didn't know the Dottie I knew—the *mother* I knew."

I rolled my eyes. "What's that supposed to mean?"

She paused and let out a deep breath. "Son, your grandmother was in many ways a very cold person, and a very disloyal person. She defended your father during the divorce—did you know that?—rather than her own daughter."

Jesus Christ. Dottie just died. Talk about disrespectful.

"Mom, all she ever said was Dad had to deal with your drinking."

She immediately launched into her typical hysterics. "Oh, so the divorce is my fault because I drank?"

"Not what I said."

"Well, what *did* you say, son? Whose fault was it?" She paused for me to respond. But I was done. *Just wait it out, let her finish her fucking seizure.*

"Well? You're going to have to decide what you believe, son. Either poop or get off the pot, decide whose side you are on. Maybe that's why you've been so—"

"Not yours, that's for sure."

"Oh, well, bravo!" she sneered. "You finally admitted what I always knew."

I put my fingers against my temples and pressed down, stretching the skin. The frustration was unbearable. "Oh, and before you fucking say it, I'm not on Dad's side either."

She laughed sarcastically. "Well, gosh, what other side is there? After all these years you can't—after seeing for yourself what kind of person your father is, and you're still . . ."

"Bryan's fucking dead!" I started to yell, except I stopped myself. All that came out was "Bryan's." I couldn't say it. There was a long pause as I felt myself sliding back down again. *Bryan's dead, Dottie's dead, the little girls are dead, the Pakistani guy's dead. Fuck it. Don't think. Put it in a box. Don't let the vines get in. Don't tell Mom anything, or she will have one of her nervous breakdowns. Lie. Lie. Lie.*

I would never get what I needed from her anyway. I sat there leaning over the keyboard with my hands on my forehead, feeling tears course down the side of my nose and drop onto the letter *g*.

"What?" she asked somewhere in between.

"Doesn't matter," I managed to say.

"Are you okay? Who is Bryan? Did something happen to him?"

"I'm fine," I said finally. But I hoped she knew I wasn't, as if I still believed mothers could always sense these things. Of course she couldn't, and all the times I thought she could were nothing but a fantasy built on childish impressions. I imagined how she would feel, hearing about Bryan, how she would worry herself sick and be even more of a basket case. *Jesus, what did I expect? Like I could call her up and blurt it all out like when I was twelve? "Mommy, Timmy's mom died. Boohoo! Make it all go away."* I sat there with my head in my hands, staring at the watery keys. Seemed like three or four minutes. Mom had changed the subject, begun talking about her church group praying for the troops' safety. I wasn't really listening; I was only in tune with her inflections and how normal, unaffected she sounded. All I could do was keep saying, "Okay . . . sounds good," and act like I wasn't crying.

The attendant's ring tone started blaring that stupid "boot in your ass" song, and it echoed off the plywood walls. I looked up and saw him snatch the cell off the counter. "Bromley!" Then the door to the internet hut swung open and two guys rushed in, waving their M4s at him.

"You gay-tards!" he shouted.

The guys snickered, lowering their weapons. "Bromley, you'd be sooo dead by now."

"Pfft, yeah, right. Whatevs."

One of the guys looked toward the back and saw me there as they continued messing around.

"Are those your friends, son?" Mom asked.

"No, Mom, I'm in the internet hut."

"Internet hut?"

"Yeah, the public call center. People are coming in. I gotta go."

"Okay, love you, son."

"You too. Bye."

S o did you get *any* sleep last night?" Ethan asked, spooning up his scrambled eggs from the Styrofoam compartment.

"Not really. Why, did I keep you up?"

"You were shifting, jerking your body around, making these agitated snorting noises."

"Sorry, man."

"It was like you were mocking someone, jeering. You kept saying, 'Cover me. It's only your fucking job.' You sounded pissed off."

I took a sip of my espresso. "Yeah, I remember. I didn't have enough blanket. Mom kept pulling it off me."

"Your mom, huh? How oedipal," Ethan said, raising his eyebrows.

"No. Not like that. She wasn't *in* my bed, she just kept taking the blanket. She needed it. That's all I remember."

"Hmm, that is interesting."

I looked around at the other tables—soldiers finishing their coffee, getting up to carry their trays to the back. "Look, as you know, I have been having a lot of dreams lately. They are really freaking me out. Extremely fucked up and disturbing, but somehow related. There's some kind of significance."

"What, like *Vanilla Sky* kind of shit?"

"Yeah, exactly. Like, awhile back I had one. I was back in Brazil, at the Teen Missions camp. Bryan's neck brace was this *thing* that was after me, hovering around me, terrorizing me."

"Wow, really? His neck brace?" Ethan paused to take a bite. "Seems odd. Obviously it's about Bryan, but it wasn't the neck brace that was . . . evil."

"No, that's just it. It wasn't about Bryan. It felt like it was more about Brazil."

Ethan raised his eyebrows again. "Dunno, man. Sounds drug induced to me."

"No. It's not just 'cause of that. I can tell. It means something. I just can't figure out what. I mean, what would Brazil have to do with it?"

"Well, I remember two things you told me about Brazil. One, you went there with what's his name—Joshy—to save the poor heathens; and two, you were in Brazil when you found out your parents were breaking up. You came home to a fuckin' war zone."

I ran my hand over my head. "Yeah, but the neck brace. It fits in somehow. What the fuck, dude?"

"Man, you just need to quit obsessing over the past. I'm not a gestalt psychologist, but that would be my advice. Man, you think way too much sometimes."

This was vintage Ethan. Don't spend a second of your life worrying about shit, no matter how horrific or tragic it may threaten to become. Don't worry about it, because it is bigger than you. It's all in God's hands . . . *Footnote: there is no god.*

"Oh, great, so just stop thinking. Well, holy shit, you did it! The case cracker!" I said, throwing my hands up sarcastically.

Ethan looked annoyed. "No, that is not what I said. Point is, you are overanalyzing, driving yourself batshit, driving *me* batshit." He wadded up his napkin and tossed it on the tray, leaning back in his seat. "You're obsessing, dude. Taking shit too seriously."

"Well, shit. We're in a war. I'd say that's pretty serious. Bryan, the goat girls. Refugee camps . . . Who else is gonna step up and figure this shit out?" I waved my arm toward the trailers. "Those fuckers in denial? Huey, with the practical jokes?"

Ethan smiled but immediately suppressed it, as if he thought that was ridiculous. "No, it's okay to do what you can," he said, "but for God's sakes, man, stop trying to fix the whole fucking world."

"Oookay. Here we go," I said, feeling the blood rush to my face. "Jesus, man, what is wrong with trying to change the world?"

Ethan now looked uncomfortable. "Hey, it's okay, dude. Don't start throwing shit again. If you want to be Gandhi, I'm not gonna hold you back."

I sat up in bed, turning to point my flashlight toward the clock. Three in the morning. Ethan was snoring a little. I shined it over at him real quick. He looked content. *He's so lucky.* I clicked the light off and sat staring into the darkness, the sound of the generator next door my only company. I wondered why people had no control over nightmares if it was their own thoughts. Then I thought about Ethan saying I was obsessing. *I can't even control my thoughts when I'm awake. Maybe we are all just automatons, just inputs and rote responses. Knee-jerk reactions; nothing we do is voluntary.* I worried I'd have another nightmare that night. I stared at the glow stick. It looked like it was getting dimmer.

I don't remember if I even fell asleep that night.

The next morning we were called to a briefing that seemed to have the whole company present. We'd been to several of these. Captain Garza would walk in casually, taking time to shake hands, greet us, thank us for doing a kick-ass job, stuff like that. But this time we heard the doors in the back slap open, the room was called to attention, and Lieutenant McLoughlin, the assistant S2, stormed in, his boots clomp, clomp, clomping down the aisle. When he got to the front he grabbed a marker and printed bold black letters in the center of the whiteboard: "CONCERNED LOCAL CITIZENS = ____?"

"The CLC," he said, enunciating each letter with a slight accent. Sounded cool to me; New England, I was guessing.

"Anyone here know what that means? Who are they, exactly?"

A guy spoke up in the back. "Iraqi citizens working with coalition forces to maintain security."

McLoughlin looked down and paced a few steps back and forth. I leaned over at Ethan and whispered, "This guy is good."

Ethan shot me a quick, confused look. "And you know this . . . how?"

"Well," McLoughlin said, going back to the whiteboard, "I see *someone's* been getting his news from *The View.*" The soldiers laughed. He erased the blank line and the question mark and replaced them with the words "BAD GUYS + $," then turned around to face the crowd.

"That simple, folks. Bad guys plus American dollars. We are basically paying off these tribal sheikhs so they'll stop aiding insurgents and come help us and the Iraqi security forces, which right now ain't too secure and ain't too forceful."

He paused again, pacing. "It is very important for you to understand this. These folks—this Sunni Awakening, as it's called—are nothing more than insurgents, guys who were shooting at us only weeks ago. The minute we began this initiative, started waving around American dollars, oh, suddenly every jagoff within a hundred miles claims he's got tribal connections, wants money to build a school, sewer system, etc."

He went on like this for thirty minutes, telling the long, complex history of sheikhs, tribal leaders going way back in history. Sunnis, Shiites, Abu Risha, Muqtada al-Sadr, and all sorts of names I'd never heard. Everybody seemed to be paying close attention, like there'd be a test later. One girl was even taking notes. At one point someone in the front raised his hand and murmured something.

"Good question," the lieutenant reassured him. "The question was 'How do we know which ones are the bad guys?'"

Another collective chuckle came from the crowd. Without warning I felt my body move, almost of its own free will, until I stood up halfway with my hand raised. Lieutenant McLoughlin took notice and pointed toward me.

"There *are* no good guys or bad guys," I said, suddenly aware of the sea of faces now zeroed in on me. But I knew this was the one chance I had, and these guys probably could use some common sense. Still, I felt my face flush.

"It's . . . not that simplistic," I said, trying to project my voice, which I sensed was quivering. "Not like in World War II, where we had a clear battlefront. Here we have to have a different approach. Destroy the enemy, make him your friend."

I thought maybe the last part sounded funny, so I quickly added, "That kind of thing."

But soon I wished I hadn't been so near to the front, because I was paying close attention to McLoughlin's face to judge his reaction, and it wasn't at all what I had expected. Soldiers picked up on it, too. In the back they started making giggling noises and deliberately coughing. All at once I felt both way smarter than everyone and like a complete fucking dumbass.

"Or," McLoughlin said, "you could take a seat and let me finish, or would you like to continue your lecture?"

"Yes, sir."

I sat down, feeling Ethan's stare, knowing he must have had a completely dumbfounded look on his face. He whispered something to me, but my mind was a blur. I couldn't hear the lieutenant anymore. All I could do was stare at the guy sitting in front of me—stare at the back of his head—feeling my body tremble from my heartbeat. *What's your fucking problem?* I wanted to say. *I was supporting your point, asshole. Thanks for making me look like a complete douchebag.*

Then it was over. The briefing ended. Everyone stood up and began shuffling out of the room. Ethan was behind me. He slapped me on the shoulder. "Good job, man. I think we're on the LT's Christmas list for sure now."

I had a quick comeback, but the words started coming out wrong, so I turned back around and kept walking. I heard the guy next to Ethan say, "All righty then!" in that sarcastic Jim Carrey voice, like I was a big fucking joke. *Just like at McCallie,* I thought. *Try to be cool, make a connection with one of the teachers, do the fist bump thing, and—slam!—you get shot down right in front of your friends. Punishment through humiliation.*

When we got outside I intended to walk back to the hooch by myself, but Sergeant Huey called out to me. I turned around. He did not look happy.

"That shit you pulled in there? When Captain Garza hears about it and comes and tears me a new asshole, I'm going to go so goddamned medieval on your ass, you'll *wish* you'd shut the fuck up in that briefing. You got that, Specialist?"

"Yes, Sergeant."

He turned around and called the others over for a quick squad meeting. Talked about a mission the next day, pulling the same security escort the lieutenant had mentioned. I realized I had missed that part of the briefing and was going to have to ask Ethan to fill me in, even though I'd sat right next to him at the meeting. *Fucking great. Even more humiliation.* I just stood there, barely in the circle, and tried to listen closely this time. I didn't want to think about having to ask Ethan what the hell critical info I'd missed in that goddamned briefing. *No fucking way am I gonna ask him right now. I'll wait. Maybe I'll overhear someone talking about it and won't have to. Fuck it, who knows if we even need the info.*

In the split second Huey broke the huddle meeting, I had turned around and was walking back to the hooch. When I got there I started straightening up my area, touching up my M4, making sure it was clean. But not five minutes later, Ethan came walking in, bringing Tuy with him. I looked over and gave Ethan a halfhearted "Whassup," then got back to wiping down the barrel. They started talking about Ethan's laptop and some issue he was having. Tuy said something smart-ass about Windows being a fucked-up operating system. "But fucked up is where I do my best work," he said, making a weird little self-satisfied laugh that sounded like a deranged motorboat.

Ethan laughed and walked over to my bed, where I was sitting against the wall. "Dude, you okay?"

"Sure, whatever."

Ethan paused for a second. "Hey, so you got dressed down a little, no biggie." His eyebrows were raised just slightly. I could tell he was trying not to act like he was patronizing me.

"Fucker totally sold me out," I said. "There I was, supporting everything he was saying, and he fucking makes me look like an asshat in front of everybody."

Ethan kind of smiled, trying to hide it. "Dude, 'asshat'? It wasn't *that* bad."

"Yeah, right. I heard the snickering. I was a fucking joke."

Ethan frowned and shook his head. "I didn't hear—"

"Bull-fucking-shit, Ethan!" I sat up straight and looked over at Tuy. "Dude, you were at the briefing. After I stood up and made my comments, were they or were they not all laughing?"

Tuy was staring at the screen. "Yeah. Fuckers were pretty rude. I told 'em keep it down while people like me trying to sleep."

Ethan let out a short laugh. "Dude, you were actually sleeping?"

"Trying," Tuy said.

I looked at Tuy's deadpan face, with his eyes half closed, staring at the screen. *Is he fucking with us? Trying to act cool? Just spouting off random bullshit?* He was impossible to read, but somehow I got the sense he was not a poseur. He didn't even seem capable of trying to impress anybody. The guy simply didn't give a fuck.

"Mmkay," I said sarcastically. "Model soldier there."

Tuy let out another ridiculous giggle. "Yeah, dass right, beeyatch, they call me the *male* model soldier." As he said this he clicked away at the computer, and an MP3 started playing loudly. I recognized the hip-hop as one of the tracks off Ethan's *NBA 2K* game.

I frowned at Ethan as if to say, "What the fuck," and he shrugged his shoulders. He was far more amused by Tuy than I was. I wanted to dismiss the guy as just some random army fuckup, but the problem was he didn't look like it . . . at all. Fixing people's computers, king shit poker player, Mr. Go-To, everybody knows his ass. *Whatever, who fucking cares?* I thought. *This guy probably just wants attention.*

A woman's echoing voice rose alongside the pulsing static of a drum machine. Ethan turned to Tuy. "Uh, turn that down, please."

"Don't be hatin' on Goapele. She's coolio, yo!" Tuy said mockingly, like he'd gotten his feelings hurt. But the music got quieter.

"Anyway," I continued, "the whole thing is fucked up, dude."

"What is?" Ethan said.

"Soldiers laughing, not taking this shit seriously, not understanding fuck-all about our purpose here—missions, Sunni Awakening, shit like that."

Ethan raised his eyebrows again. "There you go again, getting worked up over what these snickering morons think or don't think. You think any of these drooling idiots are capable of understanding our mission here?"

"That's just it. Shouldn't we all know why we're here?"

Ethan laughed. "Oh, and you are here to tell us."

Again I got a complex, like I was a complete idiot but had something incredibly profound to tell the world. "Well, shit, *somebody* needs to figure it out."

Ethan grabbed the sports chair leaning against the wall and opened it up in front of me. He let out a long breath as he sat down.

"You gotta . . . look, dude," he said, looking back at Tuy, who was still clicking away at the keyboard. "When you talked me into this shit—uh, right after 9/11—you seemed pretty messed up. Which, don't get me wrong, I totally understand. I mean, damn, I can't imagine actually witnessing . . ."

Ethan trailed off, obviously not sure what or how to say it. I immediately felt it, that same explosive cocktail of emotions—KZ syndrome, as my stupid therapist had called it, concentration camp syndrome, survivor guilt. But I had yelled at her that I was never fucking in Auschwitz. Well, Ethan had said the magic words, and *poof,* there it was again.

"Oh, right, *I* was messed up?" I said sarcastically. "I told you before, who cares what happened to me!"

Ethan stared at me sympathetically. I looked away; I couldn't stand it. But of course the poster was right there, as always.

"You know who's *not* messed up?" I said, pointing above my bed. "Mercer. He'd *love* to be messed up. He'd be *lucky* to be messed up, 'cause he's fucking dead right now."

I stopped there, knowing if I continued it would just get worse. And I had been through it so many times before, it was the same useless soap opera over and over: I get pissed, people look at me with those stupid cliché consoling eyes, I yell and scream about God never taking any action, never doing anything. They sit and listen, blah blah blah. I was so fucking over it; I was so done with that shit.

"No, I just mean . . . the reasons why . . . *why* you wanted to join up . . ."

"Fuck the reasons, Ethan!" I said, glancing over at Tuy and trying to subdue my voice. I didn't really care what he thought, but at the same time I didn't want people talking about me like I was going psycho.

"Point is, the shit happened that day, period. And I knew someone, okay? But so fucking what? It happened to lots of people. Thousands. All way worse than me. And where was God for them, huh?" I looked at Ethan as if he should answer, but he was silent. "You really asking me, why did I join? If nobody else was going to do anything, then what the fuck, dude?"

Ethan just sat there, hand on his chin, looking at me. I wiped my forehead, staring down at the camo pattern on my legs.

"Think about it, dude. Would our parents do this shit?" I said, waving my hands around the hooch. "Would they join up to go save a bunch of hajjis six thousand miles away? Fuuuck no!"

Ethan chuckled a little.

"Do you think my mom—Miss 'Oh, those poor kids in Africa, let's feel bad for ten minutes, then not send them a fucking dime'—do you think *she'd* ever do this shit? Did she ever do anything about 9/11? Little Miss All Talk, No Action?"

Ethan gave me a moment, as if making sure I had time to let everything out before he offered anything conciliatory. "Well," he said, "I don't think our parents' generation had half the shit going on we do now. All they had was the Abadan Crisis, a couple hijackings here and there, an embassy bombing . . . let's see, there was the '72 Olympics, Black September, the Beirut embassy, the hostage crisis in Iran . . ."

I didn't know what to say to that. Ethan knew all the history—dates, events, names, the PLO and Arafat, Mossadegh and Pahlavi. All that shit. I couldn't even say which country they were from. But I knew some things. I knew what mattered.

"So maybe if our parents had done something back then, we wouldn't have this shit to deal with," I said.

Ethan burst into laughter, as if he were spitting up water. "Dude, my dad's solution to the Iran hostage crisis was to march down to their embassy in DC and start hurling bodies out the third-floor window until they released our people."

"Nice," I said. "Well, at least your dad *had* an opinion. My dad . . . I never heard my dad say a goddamned thing about one single thing going on in the world. One time I asked him what he was doing during the sixties—civil rights, Martin Luther King, Bobby. He gets all defensive, glaring at me, lashes out with 'Son, I was in military school! I had my head in the books, *that's* what I was doing!' Jesus Christ, Dad. Sorry I fucking asked!"

I started unlacing my boots. Tuy called Ethan over to the computer for something. I lay back on the bed, thinking about the time Mercer flew me up to New York to see his company. He gave me a tour and explained what an internship was, and we talked about NYU over sushi. There was this cute admin girl, Bryn, who was busting on him for never having sticky notes at his desk. When we came back from lunch, there was a stack of hot pink ones on his chair, with a smiley face scribbled on top. Three weeks later she was dead.

I flinched and broke my stare at the ceiling, turning on my side to grab an Oxy. Ethan walked back over to my area. "Oh, come on! You back on that shit again?"

"You don't understand," I said, holding the pill bottle unopened.

"I can't stop. Ever since Bryan . . ." I felt my lips quiver as I said his name, and I couldn't control my face. I looked up at Ethan apologetically. "Jesus! What the fuck is my problem?"

"It's okay, man. He was a great guy. We all hated to lose him."

"How can you . . ." I sat up and rubbed my face. "Okay, fuck it, we have a job to do. I'm gonna put this shit behind me." I tossed the bottle absently in my MOLLE pack.

"Yeah, dude, try not to think so . . . I mean, although I can appreciate your, uh, noble cause, this shit has been around for a long, long time, and it ain't going away anytime soon."

I heard the words clearly, and I easily could have exploded. But Ethan was just trying to help, and I didn't want to stop him. "Ethan, I keep thinking about Dr. Geisler."

He sat down again, trying to look attentive. But I could tell it was wearing on him. "Oh, dude, don't be doin' that."

"Can't help it. Remember when I was watching all those videos, people jumping from Tower Two?"

"Yeah, of course."

"I saw this one guy jump, and I swear it looked just like Mercer. I tried to research and confirm it was him . . ."

Ethan looked confused. "Dude, I know. I vividly remember how you were printing out images of the building, pasting them together, counting windows, counting down from the one hundred and tenth floor to see which one he'd . . ."

I inhaled sharply. "Which floor he jumped from. Yeah. Well, I think I blanked out some of it. I know we took a train to New York, stayed with your sister and Tony, and they took us down to Ground Zero so I could take all those pics."

"That's right," he reassured me. "You took like ten terabytes of photos. And remember the memorial fence at St. Paul's Chapel? You hung a little white bear or something, holding an American flag?"

"Yeah, kind of. The fence was completely covered in handwritten notes and photos, or maybe I just saw it on TV later. I'm worried I forgot something; that I won't remember."

Ethan shook his head. "Dude, hello? Can you say alcohol-induced amnesia? When we hung out at Debra's, drinking their entire liquor cabinet . . . I have, to this day, *never* seen you so fucking wasted. You were drunk as fuuuck. Ran us all over the city to get that tattoo."

"Oh yeah," I said, glancing down at my biceps. "At like four in the morning. I was extremely messed up."

"Okay, so . . ." Ethan started to say something, but Tuy blurted out another quip as he stood up to stretch.

"New York City? Le's go, beyatches!"

Ethan and I looked over at him. He had seemed totally oblivious, tuned out to our conversation, yet somehow he'd picked up on the general topic.

Ethan stood up and did his Chris Rock imitation. "Who you callin' 'bitches,' bizach? Did you fix my damn laptop, nigga?"

"Uh, your registry had garbage in it, you had an email virus, and looks like your machine was being used as a slave at some point."

"Well, fuck me." Ethan lit up with his classic dry sarcasm: "Well, I'm glad you enjoyed your evening with Windows XP. Care for an after-dinner mint?"

Tuy looked up at Ethan with an exaggerated Confucius face, then whipped his head around at me. "I solly. I no undastan'. Redneck speak in code."

"It's an obscure as fuck *Three Stooges* reference that maybe three people on the planet would get," I said, trying to force myself to refocus.

"From the 1930s," Ethan said. "Sorry, man, we watched waaay too many TBS reruns growing up."

Tuy looked all deadpan. "That show pre–banana boat. Me no in USA. Me still gook."

I couldn't help but smile a little. *This guy is fucking out there*, I thought. I'd never seen anything like it. *Very odd individual.*

Tuy started showing Ethan various things to do to keep his computer healthy. I lay back on my bed and thought about the trip to New York, trying not to replay the horrific memories. Ethan walked over and put a sheet of paper on my chest. "The poem you wrote, hanging out with Walker," he said. I sat up. The paper was thick and textured, and the lettering was in dark-blue ink, written in script.

Ethan raised his eyebrows. "I saved it to show you once you, shall we say, became more cogent. And I know you wrote it—I recognize the handwriting—but if I'm interpreting it correctly, then it is totally different from everything you've been saying about 9/11. You should read it."

I looked up at him. "Oh, really?"

He turned back around to Tuy. "Yeah, dude. Like I said before. It's some pretty trippy shit."

I began to read.

To the 19 hijackers

forget about virgins, get ready for fire
as hot as the burning bush, or should I say oven?
see, you may think of yourselves as david
and us goliath, but sorry, *we* pick the stories

so here's the new best seller: Hate us for our Freedoms
which soccer moms buy, because serving the country is shopping,
patriotism is wetting the bed, fretting over mushroom clouds
and then phoning in airstrikes. who's the target? everyone

so get ready, the hurt's coming, whoever you are
we'll crush your qur'an underfoot, right, jesus?
like concrete slabs did to those in the towers
sipping coffee one morning, blinking their eyes

we will throw new bodies onto old bodies
ah, the pit, god's landfill, mesopotamia,
where blood has passed through so many hands
you can see history through a glass of it

and then we'll slip away, come home and clean weapons
telling ourselves, as we look in the mirror mirror
that we're the fairest, still—a shining example
and *you* are the world's fire starters, not us.

The words were at first completely foreign to me, then certain phrases struck a chord, like I had read them somewhere before, or someone else had said them to me. But when I got to the part about the towers and concrete slabs, I knew where it had come from.

"I wrote this before, but . . . it's different," I said.

Ethan looked over at me. "What do you mean?"

"I wrote this. I wrote this originally right after 9/11. But now it's . . . revised, like I turned it into something different."

"Yeah, dude. You do not sound yourself."

"I don't even recognize some of it. I know that before, it was just about getting back at the terrorists, pure anger. I remember I wrote it as an exercise in my therapy. But now it's like I took the whole idea and . . . I don't know."

"You totally flipped it on its head. It's like you led the reader down one path, then *bam!*" Ethan said.

I frowned, looking down at the paper again. "Oh, I did?"

"You don't see that?"

I reread the last few lines aloud, repeating some of the phrases: "'history through a glass of it'? . . . And 'you are the world's fire starters, not us.' Do you get that?"

"Oh, totally," Ethan said, "but I don't want to bias you. You should come up with your own interpretation."

I started at the beginning again, reading carefully. Tuy finished with Ethan's computer, and they stepped outside. I mulled it over for a few minutes, then put the poem away.

T he next few weeks were mostly uneventful, at least for our squad. We went out on a few of the escorts, in order to—in the words of the assistant S2—pay off terrorists. But all it was, really, was driving a few Humvees to a secluded house somewhere outside the city; rolling down a dirt road past a few mud houses, maybe a junkyard or storage building; and providing an armed escort to the guy with the money. He'd walk in and meet with the Sunni leader, they'd have tea and talk for a few hours, and then we'd jump back in and drive back to the FOB.

One morning four or five of us were leaning against the vehicles, smoking and playing cards. We were in the middle of nowhere, so there wasn't much security to pull. Ethan and this one guy I didn't know started talking about the Sons of Iraq and what was behind this type of mission. I had just gotten back from using their god-awful, nasty bathroom inside.

"Yeah, Maliki just tells American commanders what they want to hear, but he's fucking us big time," said the guy I didn't know.

Ethan looked appalled. "You gotta be shittin' me. We're tossing hundred-dollar bills at these fuckers, and Maliki's not even backing us up?" Ethan motioned toward the building where the officer was meeting with the sheikh.

The guy talking to Ethan looked like he was on a roll. *Oh God, here we go again, another weak link*, I thought, rolling my eyes. I leaned over to get a look at his face to see if he was one of those guys who are completely full of shit.

"Oh, hell yeah! Dude, the last guy I interviewed said he tells the Americans all the time Maliki is tricking us. He's working all the time with the Iranians." He pivoted around to stand in front of Ethan, instructing with his hands. "Dude, think about it. We're paying ex-Baathists—you know, as in Saddam's boys?" he said, butchering the pronunciation of "Saddam" to imitate Bush Senior. *This punk's starting to sound like a goddamned smart-ass*, I thought.

"So?" Ethan frowned. He took a drag off his cigarette. "I mean, it sucks to have to pay off the bad guys, but in the end they'll be on *our* side, right?" He seemed to be deferring to the fucker with all the answers.

"What are you, some kind of journalist?" I said without looking at the guy, then gave Ethan a "what the fuck" sneer. The other soldiers had walked closer to the building, having their own conversation.

The guy turned directly toward me and rattled off, "I'm a journalism major. When I get out of here, I'll be professionally war blogging."

He sounds so fucking chipper and self-assured, I thought. *I mean, who the hell knows for sure they'll be offered a job when they get out? So stupid.*

"Mmkay," I said. "So just a *wannabe* reporter. Gotcha."

"Dude, so what?" Ethan said, turning to me for a second. "Give the dude a break. This shit is interesting."

"Yeah, okay, whatever," I said. I reached into my sleeve pocket for my cigarettes.

"But no, paying them off's not the problem," the guy continued. "The problem is, Maliki—the government—is Shiite, right? Sons of Iraq are Sunni. Maliki doesn't trust these fellas, like *at all*. And guess what's gonna happen when we leave? Maliki is gonna take over the entire little project we have going here."

Ethan shook his head. "Well, that's speculation. He might try, but does he have the support to pull it off? Especially if more insurgents start pouring across his borders after we're gone?"

"No, actually, it's happening right now. The Awakening movement is being transferred to the government, and they're not happy campers."

Ethan gave the guy that stupid "ya don't say" nod with pursed lips. That was it for me. I breathed in deeply and turned around, walking over to the side of the Humvee and lighting up. I could still hear them talking, but they didn't know that. I couldn't believe Ethan was getting his information from that idiot. Misha. That was his name. Punk-ass car salesman. He was the type of guy who could step in dog shit, and next thing you know, he's telling the story like he's Captain Jack Sparrow, and a hundred people are gathered around with dumbass enthralled looks on their faces.

Finally the officer came out of the meeting, and we got back in the vehicles and left, thank God. On the way back Ethan made some lukewarm comment about how Misha could make a decent journalist, as long as he double-checked his references and didn't just take people's word for it.

"Misha? What the fuck kind of pussy name is that?" I said. Ethan didn't respond. *Whatever, dude*, I thought, staring out the window at the storefronts going by. I imagined having a chat with the company commander, discussing such misinformation. He seemed cool. Not like that dick McLoughlin. Giving him a knowing smile, I would shake my head in disbelief: "Sir, I'm sure you agree; people's wild imaginations can really be dangerous in this situation." He would nod, totally getting what I was saying: "Son, I appreciate the intel. You better believe I'm going to call a huddle and clear this damn thing up post-haste."

The radio crackled, and voices came on talking about a roadside bomb on the south side of the city. Ethan gripped the top of the wheel firmly with both hands and turned sharp right as we pulled up to the FOB entrance. For a split second it occurred to me that what I had just been thinking was incredibly childish. I immediately dismissed the thought, however, and it pissed me off that I always had to doubt myself. *Thanks, Mom. Thanks for being such a shitty example for me, never showing self-confidence.* I decided I would try to call my dad.

I dumped my gear at the hooch and headed for the poker tables. I was in luck. Tuy was there, and he had his SAT phone available.

"Dad?"

"Well, hello there, son!" He lit up, cheery and animated, sounding slightly patronizing. His southern drawl stood out a little more than I'd remembered.

"Is now an okay time?" I said. "I know it's a little early over there, but . . . I just needed someone to—"

"Oh, it's a fine time," he cut in, not aware of the couple-second delay of the satellite phone. "We *were* heading out the door to go to Cracker Barrel, but I saw the number on the caller ID began with the numbers one nine nine. That is one of the standard prefixes for calls from Iraq."

I waited to make sure he was done. "These phones have a couple-second delay, Dad. You probably noticed." I got onto the gravel path and started walking toward the chow tent.

"Why, yes, I *did* notice the delay. You must be on a SAT phone," he said, with lots of emphasis on the word "SAT," like he wanted me to notice he knew the word.

"Wow, that's right. I borrowed my friend's satellite phone. And how'd you know about the prefixes?" I asked, impressed he knew but careful to make sure I *sounded* impressed.

"Oh!" he exclaimed, like he was completely thrilled I'd asked. "Well, there are a few specific companies that servicemen commonly use for what they call morale calls." Slight pause. "Have you heard that term before?"

"Uh, yeah, it's a pretty common term, Dad."

"Oh, okay. You're familiar with the term. Well, what you may not have heard is that they use a handful of numbers—I learned this on *60 Minutes*, why, I believe it was just last week—and I decided to keep a list handy . . . in case m' boy called!"

He relayed this to me with an almost overacted enthusiasm, the last phrase sounding slightly off, as if it were something he normally genuinely felt but at that moment was reciting for a play about fathers proud of their children.

"That was a good idea," I said impassively. I was not quite sure how to segue to the real reason I had called. The conversation was already too upbeat.

"So, the Corps treatin' ya A-OK over there, son? Sergeant treatin' ya fair?" he said with obvious facetiousness. I had a hard time appreciating the humor. It was funny, I guess, in a way. Just seemed a little off to be so jovial. Me being in the middle of a complete shithole, friends getting killed, losing my fucking mind.

"Dad, I'm not doing so good." I went ahead and said it, already feeling like it was a mistake. There was a long pause, and with the long distance and delay, I had to wonder if he'd even heard what I said.

"How's that, son?" The words finally arrived, and with them came that tone. That phony, disingenuous "oooh, I'm so confused" tone. Both my parents understood me right away—pretty much effortlessly. This was him pretending not to.

"Well . . ." I paused, wondering how to phrase it perfectly, unassailably. "It's not that I didn't expect this place to be a hellhole. I knew I'd see horrific things. Death, all that. I knew I'd be mentally, physically stressed. It's just . . ."

He didn't say anything, letting me finish. I sensed he was taking notes, forming an impression in real time with each word I spoke.

I found it hard to say what I meant, just like when I was younger. "I take this mission very seriously, as you probably know—I'm a serious person—and people here just . . . they just aren't proactive. That's what really concerns me. They don't want to solve the real issues."

He cleared his throat, then echoed back what I had just said: "'Don't want to solve the real issues.'" I immediately felt a sense of dread. *Yeah, this was a mistake.*

"That is a little vague; can you be a little more specific?"

"Well, I mean why we're here—freeing the Iraqis, rebuilding, establishing the peace. You know, all those things we're trying to do over here, the big-picture stuff. Making friends, not enemies, right? That kind of thing."

He should be able to follow that, I thought. *Pretty simple; obvious, really.*

Dad let out a short, sarcastic chuckle. "Well, Gandhi, how long you been in Iraq?"

"Come on, Dad, you know what I mean. I'm not trying to save the world, just trying to be a team player, trying to keep the overall mission in mind. This shit is pretty important."

I could visualize it; I could see him taking down my words, snipping them into little pieces, and pasting them together to shove back into my mouth.

"Well, what does your commander say?"

I paused for a long time, not sure what he was trying to do. I paced around the back of the DFAC as I held the phone to my ear, back and forth, steering clear of anyone walking around. No one needed to hear my conversation.

"What does my commander say? What do you mean?"

"Well, how many friend-making missions have you been on?"

I felt my face flush. I held the phone out in front of me and flipped him off with my other hand, waving my middle finger violently. "Come on, Dad, you serious? Friend-making missions?"

"I serious!" he said with mocking laughter.

I couldn't let that jab go. "Look, that's the way we talk, okay? It's the younger generation. Shoot me."

"Hey, I'm just tryin' to be hip like you, dawg! I can talk like Randy too!"

An incredulous smile crept onto my face. *Oh my God,* I thought. *Was that his attempt at a Black accent? And did he just make an* American Idol *reference?* It was so laughable I couldn't even make fun of him. I had to let it go, or he would have made me the a-hole.

"Cute," I said, "but look, there *are* no missions like that. That's not how it works. It's not like we go door to door asking, 'Will you be my Valentine?'"

He roared with laughter. "Well, I see you haven't lost your sense of humor, son!"

"Whoever said I did?" I yelled. *What a fucker.*

"That is what I just said, son!" he said. His tone said I was being completely unreasonable, that nothing whatsoever had provoked me to lash out. A few moments passed, and he responded before I could, meaning he had the upper hand.

"Those were *your* words, son. You said, 'Making friends.' I'm simply asking what orders you have been given by your superiors in that regard."

I shook my head. "Look, as I said, it doesn't work like that. Sometimes we hand out candy or toys. Our squad hasn't per se, but we probably will. But that's not the point I'm trying to make."

"Okay, that's not your point."

"It's pretty simple, Dad. You can't just bust down the door, Shock and Awe, kick ass, drop a bunch of bombs, and suddenly the war's over and peace and harmony and no more 9/11. We have to work with these people, build their trust, rebuild, help them with security. They have to trust us and we have to get along, don't you see that?"

He did his classic deep inhale, always through his nose, and I knew what to expect. I'd been down this twisted road so many times.

"Son, what I see . . . is that you are struggling with some very . . . serious issues."

"Goddamn it, Dad! Can't you just accept my premise for once? Can't you just indulge my argument, just one time? It's not like I am spouting some crazy, wacko 9/11 truther bullshit. Jesus! It's a fact. We actually *do* hand out candy, you know."

"Who hands out candy?"

"Pfft, gee, Dad, let's think about that. Who is it that hands out candy? Duh, I wonder!"

"Well, son, you just said you *didn't* hand out candy."

"Goddamn it! You know what I mean. Us American soldiers hand out candy!"

"Well, now we're getting somewhere. You answered my question."

Sarcastic asshole. He's actually enjoying this shit. I kicked some gravel against the metal siding of the building, wiping the sweat off my forehead.

"Okay, so do you know *why* they hand out candy, son?"

"That is what I am asking *you*!" I screamed.

He seemed oddly immune to how fucking livid I had become. Almost like he was more comfortable with it.

"You really want to know? Are you ready for the answer?" he said smugly.

"Yeah. Sure, Dad. Tell me the answer." *Yes, bestow upon me the answer, oh mighty god of fucking knowledge.*

"The soldiers hand out candy"—he paused for effect, then ever so calmly said in a lilting staccato voice—"because those are their orders." As he finished, he drew out the *s* sound at the end.

I had to sit down. The sun was just vicious. I found a small spot of shade on the side of the storage facility and sat right on the gravel, clearing away the ants and other insects.

"Are you still there?" he asked. Just another statement that implied he had the upper hand.

"Hang on," I said, raking my bare hand across the dirt and grass and rocks in one violent motion, "just grabbing a seat in the shade."

Suddenly he decided acting chitchatty was appropriate. "Oh, I bet it is hot as hell over there."

I breathed out loudly, trying to give him an obvious message. "Yep. Iraq is hot. So back to my question . . ."

"Yeah, you sound a little winded," he said. *Fucking smart-ass. He knows exactly what I was insinuating.* My hand was stinging.

I swapped the phone to the other ear and examined my palm. Blood mixed with dirt. The skin was scraped off in places. I continued talking. "Since obviously these toys and candy missions are something we've been doing, tell me why we do it. If building trust isn't the reason, then what *is* the reason, huh, Dad?"

He erupted in another sarcastic chuckle, but more vicious this time. Like he had tolerated me questioning him long enough, and his patience had worn thin.

"Son, that is out of the purview of this discussion!" he yelled, his accent now in full bore, the vowels drawn out in diphthong. "I'm not having a discussion with Secretary of Defense Rumsfeld! I'm not talking policy with your battalion commander!"

"Oh, I see, so I am just a lowly grunt, is that it?"

He let out an exasperated breath. "I am not disparaging your rank, son!"

"Wow, really? Funny, 'cause it totally sounded like that just now." This time it was me being a smart-ass, but of course he didn't get it.

"Well, you fail to understand what I'm saying."

"Oh, really. I do, do I?" *I fail. Funny how it's always something* I'm *doing.*

"Yes, you do. I look at all ranking positions equally; they all have their place. Oh, from the private cooking beans all the way up to the general."

I had to laugh. "Our cooks are foreign nationals, Dad, defense contractors."

"Uh-huh," he said, somehow conveying that he wouldn't admit even the tiniest error.

I took a deep breath, wiped my face. I felt the heat of the metal siding through the back of my shirt. "So, just to be clear, you're saying you will not even discuss this."

"No, son. I think you are having some issues, and I would be more than happy to discuss those issues."

"Oh Jesus fucking Christ!" I jumped to my feet, my boots crunching in the gravel. "You are un-fucking-believable." I took a few steps, then turned around and stopped. Everything I could say to him jumbled together, and I stood there motionless, holding the phone to my ear.

"Son," he said slowly, trying to sound sympathetic, "you sound really angry right now."

I closed my eyes and moved my hand up to my forehead, then began bearing down and pressing my skin and rubbing it raw. My neck muscles strained against the force, pressing back, shaking. There was nothing else to do. He said something while I was doing this, something about being concerned about me. Sweet words, consoling words, like I had just lost the game, and better luck next time, champ. It came to me from somewhere—how he understood my anger, how he wanted to help me with my problem. It kept going, and I kept pressing, straining, pushing all the blood to my face. Finally I let out a guttural sound of despair.

"Oh, you wanna help me? Start with this! Bryan's dead, Dad! He's fucking dead." I slammed my fist into the metal siding.

There was silence on the line, then Dad's voice, genuinely sympathetic. "Oh gosh. Bryan . . . is this someone in your platoon?"

"He was a friend," I corrected him.

"Well, I am truly sorry, son. How did it happen?"

I felt like saying, "Fuck off, what do you care?" But oh no, as usual I took the bait and fell right back into the same old role: me on the damn couch, with him listening charitably and taking notes. I recounted the events: our squad took fire on a rooftop, Bryan fell and broke his neck, he was in recovery and got electrocuted. When he asked how it had affected me, I opened up, maybe because in some sick way I needed him to make it all go away, yet at the same time I wanted to show him he couldn't.

But in the middle of telling him, I got stuck, like I didn't know how to phrase the part about the neck brace. I got to the word and felt a sense of worry, even guilt, like I was about to hurt my father's feelings. I stopped. In that split second I could not believe how I could go from almost sheer hatred to feeling completely sorry for him. *Fuck this*, I thought.

"Bryan was wearing a neck . . . uh . . . a neck brace, Dad. And for obvious reasons, seeing that was . . . pretty difficult for me." *There. That was safe. I didn't accuse him of anything, just stated a fact.*

"How was that difficult for you?" he said, sounding like Dr. Phil spouting off the stock duh questions. Especially with the accent.

"It brought back bad memories, Dad."

"Memories? How so?" he asked.

I exhaled. "Gee, do I have to spell it out?"

"Yes, please," he said.

"*Mom*, Dad. It brought back memories of seeing Mom . . . in a neck brace."

"Oh, I see, of your mother," he said, waxing even more clinical. "Well, so this is what's called psychological baggage. Your challenge will then be having more of this to deal with than most soldiers."

"Oh, here we go," I said. *I'm such an idiot. I protect him; he's condescending.*

He chuckled. "Yeah, man! Here we go! Let's face these issues head-on!"

"What?" I yelled. Now I was pissed. I wanted to just hang up on his ass, but no way in hell was I letting that go.

"There are trained professionals over there who can help with issues like yours—loss, grief . . . anger."

"Ah. The problem is *not* caused by me and *not* my fault. But if I fix myself . . . you call that facing the issue head-on?"

His voice turned caustic. "It's called personal responsibility, son."

Oh, holy shit. "Let me get this straight, Dad." I stood up and started pacing. "I perceive what is causing the violence, and I go and try to fix it. But in your mind I should shut my mouth and accept violence, but instead go fix *myself*? Fix *my* anger problem? That is fucked up."

There was a slight pause. Then he said calmly, "Son, who was it that chose to join up and go to war?"

That did it for me. I threw the phone as hard as I could and screamed at the top of my lungs. The phone sailed about thirty meters, skipped off the edge of the gravel path, and tumbled into the grass. I walked over and picked it up, flipping it over to make sure the call was ended. I had an urge to cry in frustration but checked myself. *Don't give him the satisfaction.*

E arly the next morning Huey called a quick meeting. I'd skipped chow, slept in. I was hoping it was about some bullshit policy change, so I could go back to bed. I was in no mood to hear it wasn't, and it didn't help having to stand in the huddle and appear to be listening as Huey droned on, while all I could think about was that phone call with my dad.

"Another goddamned cordon and search?" I said, stepping inside the hooch behind Ethan.

He turned and looked at me with a little confusion. "Uh, yeah, and that's surprising . . . why?"

"What the fuck for, is why!" I said, waiting to close the door first so no one would hear. "Cordons are fucking useless. Bust into some haj—some Iraqi's place, riffle through their shit, find nothing, say sorry, leave."

Ethan walked over to his locker. "I know, dude, but you just gotta . . ."

I waved my hands, miming it out. "It's like, bust the door down, wife screams and drops her plate of kebabs—crash!—kids run cowering in the corner, crying. Not even one male in the entire fucking house. Or wait, maybe Grandpa comes out, yeah. 'Freeze, motherfucker!' Hell, maybe he's got a hearing aid bomb. Shoot him!"

"I know, dude. It's stupid."

"Goddamned waste of time," I said, yanking my rucksack off the wall and throwing it on the bed. I got my gear together—Handi Wipes, snack bars, bottled water, shades—but I was tossing them randomly inside. I opened up the cabinet to grab a handful for the day. "Oh, fuck me!" I said out loud. The box was empty. I checked the other shelves, pulling shit out and dropping it on the floor. Ethan asked me what was wrong. I poked my head around the locker.

"Where are my fucking pills?"

He scowled. "How should I know? I don't care much for opiates."

"Well, the shit's gone," I said, slamming the door shut. Ethan had all his gear together and was standing near the door.

"You ready?"

I grabbed my stuff off the bed. "Goddamn it!" I shouted, slamming the cabinet shut. The door crashed and swung back open, vibrating. "Ready for what, another fucking *Groundhog Day*?"

I worked silently at the motor pool, checking gear and readying the Humvee, not talking to the others, then stood leaning against the front grille, smoking, until Ethan got back from the mission briefing. The sun was coming up, bright and unobstructed in the blue sky. It felt like the temperature might be cool, unlike the past few weeks. I stared off in the distance toward the city center, thinking the day might actually be bearable. As Ethan came around the corner, I stepped on my cigarette and got in the passenger side. Ethan climbed in and started doing his checks: rearview mirrors, fuel levels, radio. He cranked the engine and waited for the other two vehicles to go ahead of us, then pulled in behind.

The chatter started up on the radio: "We're heading north on Highway 9 for about thirty minutes, should be smooth sail . . . activity near Abu Ghraib . . ." The voice trailed off. I took a swig of Vitaminwater, staring out the window, only halfway listening.

Ethan leaned over to turn up the radio. "Excuse me?" he said.

"What?" I asked, looking over to him.

"That's not what they said in the briefing."

A few seconds passed, and someone in vehicle two came on: "Say again, last transmission? Didn't copy."

". . . FRAGO. Heading north twenty-two klicks," the other guy began. "We're going to go past Abu Ghraib, then we'll keep . . ." Then all we heard was static and his voice all chopped up.

"Oh, just fucking great!" Ethan said. "The nuclear launch codes are A, B, C, and most importantly . . . garble, garble, *sssss.*"

"What the fuck? We just fucking left!" I said, reaching for the map.

Ethan seemed unnerved. "Dude, if we get separated from the group, be ready to climb up there and get on the fitty, shoot up some shit."

"Gladly," I said.

We rolled past a marketplace, got behind some cars lined up to get onto the highway. The lead Humvee pulled up over the median and got on the wrong side of the road as the radio crackled: ". . . the fuck out of the way, hajji!" Ethan followed cautiously, minding the oncoming cars that were slowing down and pulling over to avoid us. Once we got onto the on-ramp, we roared up to about seventy. I looked out the window across the landscape: stretches of fields that looked like dust, an occasional mud-colored farmhouse. After a few minutes it all seemed the same. Hardly any trees, just barren, depressing nothingness. I put my elbow up against the window to prop my head up, and closed my eyes. The roaring, whining sound of the engine, the vibrating and jolting of the vehicle, the noise of the radio cutting in and out—I just wanted those things to stop, or at least not affect me. *If I could only do that,* I thought, *be one of those people who can sleep through a train wreck.* Without nightmares. No meds, and no nightmares. My head kept bobbing back and forth, but I had no energy to fight it. I was exhausted. I became aware of the radio going silent, the lulling sound of the tires as they thumped rhythmically over the separations in the pavement, and my breathing getting deeper and more tranquil. Moments passed, and I slid into REM, my hearing cutting out before my other senses. I don't remember anything else, but what I missed was apparently horrific.

D ude, you didn't, like, die on us, did you?"
I heard the voice and knew it was Ethan's, but something had me in this weird state—meds, but way stronger than the stuff I'd been

taking. It was like I was monitoring myself giving knee-jerk reactions to a predefined event, in this case finding myself in a hospital ward. The metal railing of the bed, the TV mounted in the corner, the blue cloth dividers. Before anyone came in I had been staring at this stuff for half an hour, knowing where I was, knowing I must have been in some kind of accident or got shot or something, but everything was so trippy. I was trying to think normal thoughts like *Okay, what happened to me? Do I have critical injuries?* But the thoughts kept dancing away from me like they didn't want me to catch them, and then I'd doze off, and then I'd wake again, straining to focus.

"Hey, Ethan," I heard myself say. "Thanks for coming."

Ethan busted out laughing. "Well, gee, truth be told, I wasn't really stopping by. I just happened to be down this hall . . ." He was obviously fucking around. I smiled. He shook his head mockingly. "Yup, best vending machine's in this building. Damnedest thing, can't find Funyuns anywhere else on post."

"You fucker," I said, noticing there was less delay in my reaction.

I rolled to my side to look at the tube sticking out of my wrist, then propped myself up in the bed. I noticed there was something hanging down from my forehead across my left eye. I reached up and touched some kind of soft cloth, then checked my forehead. *I must look like an idiot*, I thought, *'cause I know I already talked to the medic, but I can't remember a damn thing, except I definitely talked to the medic, I think.*

"They told me you'll be fine. Minor head injury. Like a concussion, except one where you check out for a while."

"What do you mean?"

"Dude, I don't know quite how to tell you this. You've been in a coma for . . . the year is . . . 2069."

For a split second I actually hesitated and had to think about it. But sitting up, I was becoming much less out of it.

"Cute," I said. "Nice touch, too, with the sixty-nine. Just some number that happened to pop into your head, huh?"

"H'yeah, spent some time with a nurse on the way up here," he said, stretching his arms to totally overact his coyness. "It's kind of a shout-out to her."

I busted out laughing. "Wow, that is so convincing! You should go into acting, really."

We clowned around for a few minutes until the doctor walked in—female, captain. Ethan immediately got up and suggested he take off to give me a little privacy, which seemed silly to me.

"Dude, it's not like I'm getting a bris here."

He chuckled. "Jesus! Yeah, I think I'd pass on a bris."

The doctor looked at her chart and said, "I do have you down for a triple vasectomy . . ." That sounded just like my dad's humor, all dry and slightly off-color.

"Okay, I'm out. I'll stop by tomorrow," Ethan said, walking toward the door.

"Wait!" I paused, looking at the doctor. Suddenly I felt paranoid having to ask the obvious question. "You're gonna . . . tell me what happened, right?"

Ethan's face had a slightly odd look to it. "I'll fill you in, tell you all about it," he said, turning back around.

"Yeah, that'd be nice!" I said loudly as the door closed behind him.

The doctor seemed uninterested in getting into that conversation. She began asking questions, mainly about my memory: did I know basic things about who I was, my rank, MOS, why I was in Iraq, and so on. She seemed unconcerned as she did this, mainly focusing on changing the dressing on my head and checking for any bruising or swelling around my forehead.

She left for a few minutes to talk to the corpsman in the hall, who looked like he had been tasked to go do something. Then she walked back in. "Okay, your head is fine. I don't see any signs of a traumatic brain injury, but I'm going to order an MRI and have you take a cognitive functional assessment test. I'd like to keep you here for a few days, just to be on the safe side, make sure there aren't any hidden issues going on."

I wanted to be nice but was also a little annoyed. "Is anyone going to tell me what happened?"

She looked confused for a moment, then glanced down at her chart and read some notes. "Wow, definitely some retrograde going on." She approached the bed again, appearing much more attentive this time. "Well, you came in yesterday, having suffered from an IED explosion. We checked you out, and you seemed fine. In fact, your buddy, uh, the specialist who just left?"

"Ethan," I said.

"Ethan. He gave a play-by-play of everything that happened. I also went over the medical aspects with you. You don't remember any of this?"

I sat there for a moment, staring up at her. "Not really. I mean, I remember . . . it's weird, I remember the *fact* that it happened, but I don't remember it happening. I mean, I can't remember a single detail. Any casualties?"

"No, no. You were the only one they brought in."

I thought for a moment. "Okay," I said.

She put her hand on my shoulder. "Nothing to worry about just yet. It's only mild retrograde amnesia. Sometimes certain parts of the brain are more affected than others. Quite common. We'll run some tests to be sure, but you are young and in good health. You should be fine."

I looked up at her smile. She seemed pretty cool, not the type of person who would bullshit me or hide anything. I just had to deal with the freakiness. Having an entire day blanked out, especially having a huge event completely erased from my mind. *Holy fucking shit! I got blown up by an IED? Jesus.*

"Okay," I said.

The next day Ethan stopped by again. He said there was nothing going on with the squad; things were pretty quiet, so he had plenty of time. He wheeled me over to the cafeteria. They were serving green bean casserole and some nasty burrito-taco concoction, and it all looked just as gross as the hospitals back home. We passed it all up and grabbed some fruit and a few sodas from the machines. When we got situated at the table, Ethan seemed to know there was only one thing I wanted to talk about.

"So, dude, I understand you have a few corrupted sectors on the old hard drive, so I'm going to go over what happened with you again."

"Cool," I said.

Then he added, with his signature wry humor, "With any luck, I won't have to keep repeating the same exact story verbatim every single day for ten weeks, but hey, man, whatever it takes, I'm here for ya."

I smiled. "Thanks, dude."

Ethan breathed in and made a motion with his hands that signaled "Okay, listen up." He was an expert at recounting events, like he was leading you by the hand to knowledge. It didn't matter if he had to use crayons or a quantum physics book. He'd walk you through it.

"So how far back do you remember? Taking fire? Passing Abu Ghraib?" He judged the look on my face. "Okay, let's start when we got on the highway. You remember that, right? We passed the market, got on the on-ramp . . ."

I nodded. "Yeah, we were on the wrong side of the road."

"Right, we were in total *Grand Theft Auto* mode for a minute. That was before. Okay, and the radio transmissions kept breaking up, remember? We were joking about it?"

I lit up. "Oh yeah! Dumbasses. They were telling us the route—pfft, while en route."

"Well, we got a FRAGO. But the platoon net was fucked. Anyway, we got on the highway, heading north. Went for about twenty kilometers, all quiet. You fell asleep at some point. So we passed the prison shortly after, the convoy slowed down, and I heard more crackling on the radio. Couldn't make out shit what they were saying. Next thing you know, an IED goes off next to the lead vehicle, just to the right. I swear to God, the pavement rose up like a huge bubble—like a big-ass wave of dirt and asphalt coming up out of the ground."

"Holy shit, dude."

"Scared the ever-loving shit outta me. You woke up, of course. I yelled for you to get on the .50, and you scrambled up there. We'd come to a stop by that time. Smoke every goddamn where. I heard more crackling on the radio, said they were taking small arms. You yelled down that you couldn't see a thing. The convoy started backing up. Walker almost ran his Humvee right into me. I threw it in reverse, backed up going ninety, seemed like. When we cleared the dust and could see what the fuck was going on, you started unloading with the Deuce. Not sure what you were shooting at."

"Jesus, really?" I said.

"I know, right?" he said, pausing to take a sip of his soda. "I kinda figured you might remember that part, since it really isn't like you to cut loose on the .50-cal with no clear target in sight. I mean, we all know how you feel about collateral damage."

All I could do was stare back at him in disbelief, even though I somehow knew he was telling me the truth.

Ethan swallowed and cleared his throat. "So next thing you know, they're giving the command to move forward again, and this time we drive across the median to avoid the debris and dust cloud. We crept up past where the IED went off, and got back on the right side of the road. Then I knew for sure none of the vehicles or our guys had been hit—thank God—but we were still taking fire from one of the buildings to the right of us. Couldn't tell where, exactly. So we were going about twenty and had just crossed back to the right lanes, when all of a sudden they stomped on the gas and got way ahead of us. I immediately tried to speed up and had pretty much caught up with them, when I looked to the right and saw a muj running out of the building. He wasn't holding a weapon, but I swear I saw him holding a cell phone or something, some kind of detonator or some shit. Then . . . boom! Our Humvee seemed like it went ass over end, careening through the air. Seemed like a hundred fucking feet. I swear, one second I was looking out the windshield at the back of Walker's truck, the next second all I saw was pavement, looking straight down. It was intense. We landed upright, but the steering was all fucked up. Plus, there was no acceleration, just a nasty clanking noise from the rear. I was fine, ears ringing like hell, but I was okay. I turned around to see where we got hit and saw a big, gaping fucking hole on the side of the Humvee."

Ethan laughed at this point, like he still could not believe it.

"Goddamn, dude. Where was I?"

"Dude, you were still up there on the fucking .50!" he said excitedly. "Well, I take that back. You were up there when the IED went off. Get this. Here's the weird part. When the goddamned thing exploded, there is no way you could've been anywhere else, except for maybe thrown out of the vehicle, but . . . Jesus, and I don't see how the fuck this happened, but when I looked up there, the fucking turret seat was all mangled, you know, from the blast underneath. There was no way you could have been sitting in it without"—he laughed again—"getting fucking chunks taken out of your ass."

I realized I hadn't been eating at all. I absently took a sip of my drink and started to peel my orange, not looking away from Ethan. Of course, true to form, Ethan was not going to spoil the suspense and just blurt out where he ended up finding me. He saw far more important things going on.

"Dude, I consider myself a rational human being. You know me, I am all about explaining things in terms of logic, science, physics. *Ghost Hunters* on the sci-fi channel? Fuck no! Area 51? Aliens? Just *try* and show me some hokey paranormal bullshit. I will fucking embarrass your ass. But I'm telling you, I am at a total loss trying to explain what happened next. It just makes no fucking sense." Ethan paused for a moment, looking almost embarrassed to continue. I was impressed by how serious or concerned he sounded, but I didn't think it would be that big of a deal.

"For God's sake, just get on with it, Coffelt!"

He took a deep breath and looked me in the eye. "Okay, so you were not in the turret, thank God, and I was looking around in the back to see where you were. Now, keep in mind this is literally seconds after the blast. At the most, let's say a minute. Sixty seconds, and that's reeeally pushing it. So I turn in the chair, look around, nothing. I'm thinking, of course, you must have gotten thrown out, or worse, *blown* out of the fucking Humvee, so I open my door, step out, and walk—actually, kind of run—to the back of the vehicle. Nothing. So I keep going around to the other side. I see the big, huge hole in the side. I come around, all the way to the front. I'm even checking underneath."

"Maybe I was thrown further away?"

Ethan nodded. "Exactly. So I looked again, this time ten, twenty feet away from the vehicle. There was some smoke, but I could see okay. Honestly, dude, by this point I was fully expecting to only find parts of you with smoke still coming off them. I mean, shit, somewhere in the back of my mind I was already imagining how I was gonna tell Sandy, and worrying that she was going to hate me forever for having to tell her you were . . . ya know, not coming home."

I was kind of startled by that comment. I had never really thought about that before. Not the dying part—we all thought about dying—but I had never really stopped to consider the details. Of course it would be Ethan who called Mom to give her the news. I'd never thought about how difficult that would be for him. Sure, I would do the same thing for his mom if the shit were the other way around, but he would have to go over the details with my mom and all my sisters, and my dad. Holy shit, it would be like the fucking Spanish Inquisition. I suddenly had newfound respect for my friend.

Ethan continued, "So I'm totally starting to freak out. I couldn't find you any fuckin' where, so I doubled back, went around to the rear again, and came all the way around to the driver's side door. I opened the door, about to sit down, gonna radio in for help. But something caught my eye, and I looked over at the shotgun seat . . . and that was when I almost dropped a log in my boxers."

Ethan shook his head, visibly upset. I just looked over the table and waited for him. He always did this thing when he was dumbfounded or baffled by something—well, usually some*body*—doing something utterly, inanely stupid. He'd repeat the first word three or four times, like a deliberate stutter. "I . . . I . . . I . . . have no logical explanation for this, but . . . *you* were sitting there in the shotgun seat, completely soaking wet, like you'd been dunked in water, and just staring off into space."

"What?" I said.

"Yeah, you had this creepy-as-hell look on your face. Well, I mean, it wasn't like what you see on TV, like *Medium* or anything. It was just like a pleasant look, but so goddamned inappropriate, like nothing had happened. That's the best way to describe it."

"Wow, did I say anything?"

"No, didn't say a word. You just sat there. I tried to ask you what the fuck, how the hell did you get back in the seat. You just sat there and didn't respond."

"That's fucked up, man."

"Ya think? Hells yeah, it was fucked up. I was out of that vehicle maybe twenty seconds—at the most. There is no goddamned way . . . and it's not like you were there the whole time and I didn't notice. Oh, no. It's like you just fucking—*poof*—appeared out of thin fucking air. Totally freaked me out."

"Hmm," I said. "Maybe I was thrown out and walked around and got in."

This got Ethan all excited. "H'yeah, if only that were possible! But guess what. When we went to help you out of the vehicle, you know what? The fucking door wouldn't open! The fucker was jammed shut by the explosion."

I raised my eyebrows. Wasn't sure how to respond.

"But I did try to dismiss it; I mean, at least *your* weirdness. I figured you'd most likely had some head trauma, so I chalked it up to that. But goddamn, the other shit? Believe me when I say I've been over it again and again in my head, but I just can't wrap my brain around it. You're like a fucking bona fide miracle with a bad memory."

I looked down at my tray. I'd hardly touched my food.

A fter I'd been there a week, they released me. They'd run all sorts of tests. MRIs, angiograms, problem solving, cognitive skills, you name it. They couldn't find anything wrong with me. And I was so bored. All day watching CNN's thirty-minute rotation of news loop over and over, seeing the same staff walk the same path into my hospital ward to do the same routine to me. Every day the same food, the same three choices: bland, dry, or rubbery. All the lying around was starting to make me feel flabby. I actually missed PT and wanted to hit the workout hut as soon as they would let me. I did feel a little better mentally. Felt like I myself had kind of been in a loop, and all I'd needed was a big jolt, something to break me free. Getting blown up may have been drastic, but maybe that's what it took sometimes. At least that's what I thought, anyways.

Ethan came to the CSH one last time to help with my stuff, and together we walked back to the hooch.

"Still not much goin' on with the platoon," he said. "Just sitting around playing chess. And ain't *nobody* beat me yet . . . 'cause I am da man!" He made a slam motion with his arm.

The sun was in my eyes, but I looked over and smiled.

"We do have the village assessment coming up, for what it's worth. That might break the frickin' monotony a little."

I got all happy. "Oh yeah! I *do* remember that. We're taking the helos again, right?"

"Yep, it's like an hour or two by air, middle of fucking nowhere."

We got up to the little wooden stoop in front of our place and set the bags down.

"You got a smoke?" I said, standing on the top step.

He grabbed a pack from his sleeve pocket, squinting up at me. "Dude, can ya ease up on the hillbilly heroin this time?"

"Pfft," I said, lighting up, "I'm so over that shit."

Ethan didn't say anything. I knew what he was thinking, though: *Sure ya are.* I looked away from him, blowing out some smoke, and we stood there for a minute.

"Whatever," I said, stepping on my cigarette, then turned around and opened the door.

"Want your gear?" Ethan asked.

"Leave it there," I said, and walked inside.

All my stuff was just as I had left it. I sat down on my bed, pulled one of my boots off. I noticed a weird red tint on one side and turned it over; all the treads looked like they'd been stained. I took the other boot off, and it had the same thing. Perfectly clean, other than a little dirt from the walk back, but completely stained through, kind of like red food coloring. I placed them under the bed and put the rest of my stuff away. The empty box where I'd kept my OxyContin was back on the shelf. I didn't bother asking Ethan about it, just assumed he had put it back for me. He was at his desk booting up his laptop. I sifted through my pile of magazines and letters from home and came across my journal. For a second I wanted to find Walker, get maybe one or two just to relax me. It didn't last long, though. Ethan blurted out a sarcastic tirade about how Windows can't just do what you say without turning it into some goddamned cluster fuck: "'You just clicked OK when I asked if you wanted to cancel; did you mean OK as in *don't* cancel? Please click either OK or cancel.'"

I looked over and gave a short sniff to acknowledge the satire, then sat on the bed and opened up my journal, wondering what other weird stuff I'd written besides that poem. I thumbed through it backward to find the first page with anything coherent on it. Mostly crossed-out lines, rewrites, words scribbled through. Sand particles were stuck between the pages. I brushed off one side and began to read, and for the first time in months I actually nodded off on my own without taking anything.

Note to self

we've got guys in the ER, pushing the
spilled guts back into their sockets
while you just spray your bullets, like you're
some kind of Santa Claus handing out chocolates
wake up you sick savior
get your ass to school
the world is sick of you
the whole world
is sick of you

We had a week or so before we were to fly out on the village assessment, and we spent the time wisely: we fucked around. Tuy was hanging out with us outside the hooch, playing poker, and happened to mention something about his Xbox 360. Soon as Ethan and I found out he had *Call of Duty 2*, we just about got down on our hands and knees and begged him to bring that shit over and set it up at our place. Tuy didn't look up from his hand, just mumbled indifferently that the FedEx box hadn't even been opened, and he'd been using it as a monitor stand for six months. Tuy was a freak. He seemed like he had every cool tech gadget that came out, and he could talk about the shit like he'd been an Apple tech for twenty years. Yet he couldn't care less about all of it. Almost like he just toyed around with stuff, learned how it worked, and moved on to the next thing. Weirdo.

But anyway, we got him to set up the console with a piece-of-shit old monitor, and Ethan and I got our game on for the entire week. Omaha Beach, trying to take out Germans up on the cliffs; Stalingrad, fighting in close quarters through buildings or up on the roof as snipers; and bombing runs in Tunisia. The game play was awesome. Fantastic dynamic lighting, shadowing effects, and sound effects, and realistic enemy dialogue.

Tuy stopped by the hooch a few days later to see how we were enjoying the setup. He came up and stood behind us. We barely noticed, completely engrossed in the action.

"Y'all is some dumb mudda fuggahs," Tuy muttered in his tongue-in-cheek tone of utter disdain.

"Hey, wassup, Chino Loco!" Ethan said. "Muchos thankos for the Xbox, dude."

I looked up at Tuy. He was standing next to my chair, watching the action on the screen. His eyelids were half closed, so I could tell he was going to say something smart-ass. I had learned by now he put on this little role-playing thing, halfway between Spock and someone out of *Goodfellas* about to whack somebody.

"I can feel myself getting stupider just watching this shit," he said.

"Come on, dude, this is awesome!" Ethan protested, laughing.

I cracked a smile as I lined up a guy in the sights of my MP-44. A German soldier jumped out from behind a tank just as a grenade dropped on the sand in front of me. As it exploded, my half of the screen fogged over with red. I hid in a foxhole until I recovered, then mowed the German guy down.

"Hmm, so when shot, the human body recovers to one hundred percent within four seconds. Wow, did not know that!" Tuy said.

Ethan giggled. "Hey, it could happen!" Just then I got pegged by some guys in one of the gun emplacements. My screen turned red again.

"Again?" Ethan yelled. "I just rescued your ass! Now I'm in the trenches, and I got Wehrmacht all around me!"

Tuy watched as Ethan somehow made his way back down to the beach to help me. Five minutes later we got separated in the tunnels, and I got ambushed.

"What the hell, dude? I told you don't go left, you'll be slaughtered," Ethan said.

"I know, but I thought—"

"We don't pay you to think, soldier!" he yelled in a gruff voice, totally over the top.

I giggled. "Sir, yessir, sir!" I looked up at Tuy, who smirked and shook his head, then walked out.

I remember that particular night, not just because we were able to get away from the war and play some kick-ass video game, but because of what Tuy said to me later. Not sure why he didn't tell Ethan the same thing. Maybe he thought I was more approachable. Or was it more impressionable, in which case he'd be dead on. Ethan once told me a story about standing in line outside smoking, and some lady behind him asked him to put his cigarette out. He turned to her and said, "Absolutely not," and turned back around and kept smoking. I, on the other hand, would never have the wherewithal to do any such thing. My parents had brainwashed me into thinking everyone else's rights trumped any of my own, and I wouldn't have told that lady— or anyone, for that matter—to fuck off even if they'd walked up to my car and told me to hand over the keys, title, and ten bucks for gas.

"You do realize playing that shit makes you less effective as a soldier," Tuy began, glancing at me, throwing a handful of chips into the pot. I'd stepped outside for a cigarette. Tuy was playing Texas hold'em with a couple of noobs.

He looked playfully at one guy, with a Padres ball cap. "Not bad, Catracho Uno, but I call and raise you cinco."

I'm beginning to understand this guy, I thought. *This isn't some dumb shtick, saying shit just to shock people, for the attention. No, he doesn't even seem aware of how much attention he's getting. Look at him, he absolutely could not care less.* But apathetic or not, nonchalant as it was, his comment couldn't just sit there. It had to be answered.

I chuckled. "Oh, really? Playing a first-person shooter makes me less effective."

"Yep. It's like anti-training."

I paused for a second, chewing on that odd little morsel. "Uh, oookay!"

He threw in more chips. "Call . . . Hey, whatever, man. I thought you took battle preparedness seriously. Guess I was wrong." He sighed.

What? What does this fucker know? How could he tell that? I thought. But he didn't seem malicious about it.

"Taking it seriously? I don't get it. Of course real battle is nothing like *Call of Duty*. No shit."

"Okay," Tuy said, nodding to acknowledge my agreeing with him so far, "so you want to stay as sharp as possible, maximize your reaction times in battle, right?"

"Oh, really? Wow," I said, overdoing the sarcasm. Tuy's face didn't move. He had the exact same focused look, staring at me. He got what I was saying. Definitely. But he had absolutely zero reaction. That really struck me.

The guy across the table from Tuy laid another card down on the table. "There's your river. What are you gonna do now, bitch?"

"Take your money . . . again. All in." Tuy pushed his stack of chips toward the center of the table. The other guy grinned.

"Not this time, bitch. I rivered my straight. I call." The guy turned over two cards in triumph, slamming them down on the table. Instantly Tuy flipped his own two cards at the guy.

"Boat. You lose . . . again. Count 'em up." With deft hands Tuy began gathering the large mass of chips into stacks. I got the feeling this was the way things usually went at this table. Tuy stepped right back into our conversation like he'd never left.

"So to maximize your reaction time in situation A—real combat— you do exercises in situation B, i.e., inaccurate simulations of combat. Gotcha."

I paused for a second. "Oh, so you're saying I'm throwing off the calibration of my motor skills by playing a first-person shooter."

"Not motor skills. More than that," he said, taking an odd-looking pack of cigarettes out of his leg pocket. The bright-red box said "Gauloises." He looked up at one of the rookies. "Hey, Cripple, deal me out. I'm on smoke break." He lit his cigarette, standing up to walk over to the steps next to me. I watched him. It was like he'd been completely engrossed in something, but then something else slightly more interesting came up, so he just dropped the first one like it never existed.

"Think of it like this," he said, exhaling smoke. "What's the name of that old World War II documentary series?"

"Oh, *Band of Brothers?*"

"No, that was a drama. This was a television documentary, British . . . from the seventies?"

I nodded. "Oh yeah, Ethan was obsessed with watching those. I've seen parts of them. *The World at War*, I think."

"So, which is more accurate, that documentary or *Saving Private Ryan?*"

"Pfft, well, duh."

"Okay, better question: how many people watched *Saving Private Ryan* versus that series?"

"Well, damn, dude, have you seen *Private Ryan?* The shit kicked ass!"

Tuy smiled. "Right, kicked ass . . . for you."

I lit up another cigarette, watching as Barco and Thiessen came around the corner. The rookies were calling them over to play cards. Tuy leaned back and propped his foot up against the sandbags.

"Aw, come on," I said, smiling a little sheepishly. "There are some facts in there! Omaha Beach scene? That shit was messed up, dude! No sugarcoating there."

"It's not about sugarcoated, it's about what's missing. It's not what you do see, it's what's left out."

"Such as?"

He thought for a moment, then gestured with his hands. "It's like this. Say you date some girl. After a few months you find out she's psycho. But you don't break up . . . 'cause she's super-hot, smart, whatever . . . but she picks damn fights like every day. She's insane, and after a couple of years you get tired and dump her."

"Okay, yeah, fuck dat bitch."

"So I come over one day—say I don't know you—and open up the photo album of you two," he said, pausing for effect. "What do I see? You two on the beach, smiling, birthday party, whatever—and it's all true, all one hundred percent accurate. But would I really know you or her? You can say the things I do know are true, but there are so little of them compared to unknowns, that anything I say will probably be wrong."

"So few of them," I said.

"So few of them. But it's like if I have a bag of ten different-colored marbles, and you reach in and pick a couple blue ones, then you assume—no, let's say you get the impression—that most are blue. Chances are you're wrong."

"'Course," I said.

"If you pick nine blue marbles and guess blue, then chances are you're right."

"Or you can pick just one or two as long as you pick the average."

"But here's the problem: no one puts average shit in a photo album or in a movie."

"I think you're about three levels deep in your analogies," I said.

"Fuggit," he said, flicking his cigarette butt out toward the card table. It bounced off one of the Red Bull cans and landed almost perfectly inside ball cap guy's shirt pocket, right in the crease.

"Fucking assbag!" the guy shouted, jumping up and looking down at the front of his shirt.

Tuy giggled, hurrying down the steps. "Hey, thoopid," he said, "you just knocked it inside."

The guy looked both disoriented and completely pissed off. Tuy grabbed a bottled water and turned it upside down, filling the guy's pocket and drenching the front of his shirt.

"Holy mother of—" he said, backing up, glaring wide-eyed at Tuy with his arms open in the "what the fuck" gesture.

"I had to. It would have burned through, you dorkus maximus," Tuy said, pulling the drenched butt out of the guy's pocket with two fingers. Everyone was howling with laughter, myself included. The guy just stood there, holding his shirt away from his chest. Tuy sat down to play another hand of poker. I was watching the whole thing, still chuckling, but wondering to myself, *How does this guy get away with this shit?*

"*No te preocupes*, Catracho Uno. If there's a hole, I'll trade shirts with you. Looks like you're a little porkier than me, but hey, we can try."

The other guys laughed and they got back to playing, almost like nothing had happened. I smiled, opening the door. "That fucker is crazy," I said, directed more at the two guys I didn't even know.

Tuy's head snapped dramatically toward me. He made a goofy face like the bad guy in an old martial arts movie who can't act—half-closed eyelids, no smile at all.

"You just sign you own death contrac'," he grumbled.

I laughed and walked inside.

S o the day finally arrived. They had our asses scheduled to be out there at oh-dark-stupid, waiting for helo pickup. But we showed them. Me, Ethan, and Barco stayed up all night playing Texas hold'em and drinking some of that nasty Iraqi hooch Ethan had scored through Tuy. Sergeant Huey wasn't too happy about it, but overall he was pretty cool, really. When he came by the trailer to make sure we were ready to roll, Ethan had just woken up and I was still dead asleep. His way of rousing us was to bust in the door and shout at the top of his lungs, "Wakey, wakey, eggs 'n' fuckin' bakey, boys! We need help unloading *illegal* alcohol off the Black Hawk!" Luckily I had my shit ready; they had come by the day before with a checklist, and we were in good shape.

A few minutes later Ethan and I walked out of the hooch, threw our gear in the Humvee, and were at the helo pad in ten minutes. Everyone else was already there in a huddle, getting briefed. I felt woozy—not just sleep deprived, but still a little drunk. Ethan and

I stood in the back of the group almost intuitively, just like in high school when you don't want the coach to smell anything or notice how you look like complete and utter dog shit. And it was totally dark out there. We just stood there, feeling the chill of the morning and craning our necks to hear about our mission. Provincial Reconstruction Team, blah blah. Captain So-and-So, heading up the team—great guy, but these damn Iraqis need to step up, uh-huh. Interpreter assigned to each group, yada yada. *Let's just get the fuck in the damn Black Hawk, it's frickin' freezing out here*, I thought. I was suddenly reminded of something, and I almost fucked up and laughed out loud: *"I've been frozen for thirty years, okay?"* My dad used to quote that line from *Austin Powers*. Before the divorce he'd let us do kids' pick movie night, and he absolutely loved that one. So whenever he was in a good mood and my sisters and I teased him about not knowing some hip term, he'd rattle off that line to us, messing it up, which made it even more hysterical: "I've been frozen for fifty years, okay, kids? I need the info here, people."

I let out a quick snort and felt Ethan look over at me. I coughed to cover it up and tried to focus back on the briefing. Village was called Hamza. Very rural, population of a few thousand, mostly expected to be friendly to us. There'd been no combat in the area since the war began. I felt kind of excited about the mission—something new, interesting, change of pace. The last thing the commander mentioned was that we'd be pulling hearts and minds activities, handing out candy and school supplies to kids. I remembered the conversation with my dad. *Ah, maybe this is where I will make a difference, do something meaningful. See, Dad? Idealists are the ones who change the world.*

As the Black Hawk rose slowly up above the dimly lit buildings, I pressed my head against the window, trying to see as much as I could. A taxi standing at an intersection, a shopkeeper opening up his street stand, a cluster of bright lights off to the north I assumed was the FOB. We made a slow turn and headed across farmland, and the view below turned dark. I looked over at Ethan. He was already out, his helmet bumping against the aluminum frame of the seat. I remember thinking there was no way I could fall asleep like that, not with the high-pitched whine of the engine. Next thing I knew, I was waking up to obnoxious slapping on the top of my head. I looked up to see the copilot looking back at us like a bug with his big dark shades, pointing toward the ground to signal our descent.

It took a minute to register what was going on; I was in a different world, lost in some serious REM. It was the Wild West, and me and some posse were riding into town. We came upon Stuart—aka Big Country—standing feet spread out, blocking the road. He was holding a dozen roses he was going to give his girlfriend, and then suddenly he was beating me over the head with them, scolding me, saying, "What'd I tell ya about choosin' the right lie to believe?" That's when I woke to the guy slapping me on the head.

I checked my cell phone. Zero seven thirty. I looked out the window and saw us descending. Sand kicking up from the road, curious locals starting to gather around. The sun was breaking over the mountains. It was a gorgeous sight.

"If they don't eat ham, then why they call it Hamza?" the guy next to Ethan said, glancing at us like he wanted everyone to think he was clever.

I looked at Ethan, and he rolled his eyes. "Uh, pronounced 'Hahm-za,' not 'Ham-za,'" he shouted.

"Oh, okay," the guy said, suddenly all self-conscious.

"What are you, twelve?" Ethan asked him.

"Sorry. Stupid joke," he said.

Ethan shook his head. "No, I'm really asking. How old are you?"

"Nineteen," the guy said.

Ethan shook his head again. "Don't look a day over twelve."

A few minutes later we had filed out of the helo and formed into three five-man teams to begin our first mission—talk to the locals, ask about living conditions and political activities, find out if they had running water and if any facilities needed repair. It was as simple as that, and a half hour later we were walking down the main drag, stopping and talking with dudes in man-dresses; me and Ethan, Lieutenant Jacobs—our team leader—and the twelve-year-old recruit and his buddy, who were pulling security, plus our interpreter, "Bob." When I heard that name I immediately knew what was up. His real name had to be something that wouldn't go over well with Americans. *Probably Osama*, I thought.

The surrounding shops looked like ones I'd seen once in Manaus, cinder blocks slapped together, some piece-of-shit metal door, open windows with bars over them. We went into one little convenience store, and this young guy was nailing up a piece of cardboard to use as his counter. He was very friendly. He offered us tea and showed us some of the merchandise. I felt like I wanted to buy something, help the poor guy out. Ethan and I browsed around, politely picking up books we couldn't read to save our lives and packages of food with God knows what in them. Then Ethan found a box full of DVDs, each stuffed inside a plastic sleeve. "*Fahrenheit 9/11?*" he said, pulling one out. He snorted sarcastically. "Distributed in Iraq illegally. Oh, the irony!"

"Ha ha, can you say bootleg?" I said.

"This is like breaking fifteen international copyright laws," Ethan said, picking out several more. "I just gotta get me a few of these."

The owner walked over, all excited about Ethan's interest. He wrapped the movies in handmade paper and even put tape on it. I was happy we could give the guy some business. I don't know if it was my imagination, but I got the impression all the shopkeepers were one sale away from closing down for good.

"I understand the Sons of Iraq visited here a few months ago," Jacobs said. The terp translated. I listened, recognizing the phrase "Abna al-Iraq." The store owner stood behind that pathetic cardboard counter, still smiling.

"Amreekee good, good," he said, looking at each of us. I smiled back. Then he rattled off a long sentence in Arabic.

"He says the Sons of Iraq, yes, they came, but he did not talk with them," said Bob.

Jacobs stayed facing the store owner, looking through his dark tactical eyewear. "Were they able to help the community? What did they do?" He turned to Bob. "Ask him what people think of Abna al-Iraq."

Ethan walked outside for a smoke. I stayed inside. I wanted to see what the guy said, get a feel for what they thought of us being there. I listened for the entire thirty minutes. They joked about how shitty the crops were this year, talked about how water is a huge big deal way out here. The guy seemed pretty honest and open. And Jacobs seemed to buy it. At least he acted like he did. At one point he motioned to a poster of Bob Marley on the wall.

"You a Marley fan?" he asked, but didn't wait for an answer. "Don't care much for his politics, but his music's good," Jacobs said. *What the hell?* I thought.

"*Shukran,*" Jacobs finally said, and we were on our way down the dirt road into the residential section.

A rivulet of nasty yellow water ran down the side of the street, spilling onto the sidewalk in some spots. It wasn't like back home, with mailboxes beside each driveway, a plush green front yard, rhododendrons or whatever. The houses were all enclosed in a concrete wall running along the sidewalk. At each residence there'd be some type of gate—usually rusted-out metal—painted some ugly blue or something, adorned with decorative metalwork. Just high enough so you could barely see into the courtyards. They were all the same, except some might have a palm tree; some, a small patch of grass.

Ethan turned around toward the recruits. "Rooks, tighten it up." They trotted up closer to us. Jacobs held a small map in front of him—a composite of satellite imagery and graphics—with all the streets labeled with sports names. So we were walking down Favre Avenue and turning left on Kobe Street. I saw a man in a long white robe standing in front of his gate smoking a cigarette, looking to his side at us. He looked serious and mistrusting. *Smile, dude,* I thought, remembering Ethan's little tirade. But when we waved and shouted hello to him, he waved back before he walked inside. A dog lapped at the water for a second, then scurried away from us.

The sun was bright, and the air was growing warmer. After we passed a few houses, Jacobs stopped. We rapped politely on the gate, looking through the holes into what I guessed was the kitchen window. Jacobs said to wait for a minute or so, which we did, then he opened the gate and walked into the courtyard just as the owner opened his door.

"*Salaam,*" Jacobs said, with no apparent attempt at the right pronunciation. It sounded more like "slam." Ethan elbowed me, and I had to cover my mouth not to laugh.

"*Sabah al-Khair,*" the man said. "Good morning."

He stepped aside, holding the door. I guess inviting us to come in would have been redundant. He put a pot of water on the stove while Jacobs sat down at a wobbly kitchen table, barely able to fit with all his body armor and gear hanging off him. The two rookies started to follow us inside; Jacobs told them to stay and pull security, then had Ethan and me search the house. The living room behind the kitchen had a concrete floor and a couple of pictures without frames tacked to the walls. I opened the drawers of an old wooden dresser; clothes in one, old books and papers in another. Ethan checked under the sofa and behind the drapes.

"Ain't shit here," Ethan said facetiously. We brushed past the curtain into a decent-sized bedroom with furniture stuck in every spot possible. "Oh God, this'll take a while," I said. Ethan laughed as he began opening drawers. I started with the armoire. Tons of shit, but I noticed how organized it all was. Shirts, magazines, curios—everything had its own little place, nice and neat. Even the socks were folded and stacked. I didn't want to just throw shit everywhere. Ethan seemed to think the same thing, as he looked through each drawer and then carefully slid them back into place. As I got near the bed, I happened to look up high enough to notice a fluffy white cat perched on a shelf in the corner, nonchalantly watching us.

"Holy shit. Check it out!" I said.

Ethan walked over and looked up. "How the fuck does it get up there?"

I laughed. "Yeah, exactly! Nothing to jump up there from."

We stared for a few seconds as it stood up to stretch, at which point I got a much better look.

"Wow, that is weird," I said. "Ethan, this cat looks exactly like

Edelweiss, the cat I had when I was growing up." I kept staring at her. So enigmatic, looking down at me with those light-blue eyes.

I was almost eleven when my sister Kelly had her ninth birthday. After opening up the usual metric ton of gifts we were always showered with, my sister looked up to see my mom walk in with the coup de grace: Edelweiss, wrapped in a cashmere baby blanket. I don't know exactly what it was about that kitten, but I immediately became obsessed with making Edelweiss belong to me. I fed her by hand with those ridiculous little gourmet cans, I brushed her, I even got her to start sleeping in my bed, curled around my neck. Finally Kelly caught on to what was happening and told on me. But it didn't matter that my parents got royally pissed, sat me down with some lecture on ownership and, as if it had just occurred to them that we went to church, what it meant to covet. No, that didn't matter. And it didn't matter that Edelweiss would be around me just as much regardless of whose cat she was. It wasn't enough for me just to be in her presence. I had to know she was my cat, and I wanted others to know she was my cat. Including poor Kelly, who must have felt totally cheated. But I didn't care; I was a selfish little shit.

By the fall of the next year, when my parents' fighting had escalated to its worst and they were about to divorce, Edelweiss was more or less considered my cat, so I had gotten what I wanted. But somehow it no longer mattered to me. I had already begun to get messed up from the violence, the fighting, the horrific screams at night reverberating through the walls. Something was threatening me, poking at me with a stick, aggravating me. That thing was about to take our huge dream house and turn it upside down, and we'd all come pouring out. So I could not have given a shit about losing a pet at that point; I was too worried about drowning in the family drama.

"What in the fuck is taking so long?" Jacobs came barreling into the room. Ethan and I looked over at him. Jacobs stopped for a moment, looking at Ethan neatly stacking clothes back in the drawer.

"This ain't goddamn *Extreme Home Makeover*, guys!" Jacobs pulled a drawer out and dumped it upside down. A small glass box came tumbling out and broke on the cement floor. I looked up and saw the owner standing in the doorway. I tried to give him an apologetic look, but he just turned and walked out. "There. This room should be cleared in ten minutes, no more," Jacobs said, and followed the man.

I bent over to start dumping shit onto the floor, mumbling to Ethan, "Nice . . ." Then I heard a growling coming from the cat on the perch. I looked up and saw her still lying there staring at us, same impassive look on her face, but then she hissed loudly.

"Geez, sorry, cat!" I said. "Just following orders."

A round noon the team met up at an outdoor restaurant, and I ate some of the best kebabs I have ever tasted. The owner kept coming out to the patio, saying, "You like lamb? Best in all Iraq!" His *r*'s smacked the back of his teeth, almost like a *d* sound.

One of the rookies responded with his mouth full—"Shit is kickass"—and giggled.

The owner looked all serious, trying to learn a new phrase. "Kickazz . . . good?" Of course everyone fell all over the tables, so I had to try to tell the guy those weren't exactly nice words. The rookies just kept it going, one of them saying slowly, "This motherfucking shit kicks fucking ass!" They all roared with laughter. I felt a little of my old self again—on my guard, watching the guy's face for signs he thought we were a bunch of disrespecting American assbags who didn't give a fuck about anyone. I was trying to relax a little, not take it too seriously. They were just being idiots, yukking it up. But then the owner walked over to the server and said a few words under his breath. I kept my eye on them and listened. I heard the word "Amree-kee" and saw the flat expression on the server's face.

Next thing you know, Jacobs announces it's Easter and pulls out a Bible, calling for everyone to bow their heads while he reads a passage. *Oh, just fucking perfect.* I got up and went out to the street for a smoke. I sat on a wall near the street, watching the people across the way picking fruit in the market, old, beat-up cars driving by, boys with no shoes kicking a soccer ball in the alleyway. I got through almost four cigarettes.

"There you are," Ethan said, coming out of the front of the restaurant toward me.

I looked over my shoulder. "Hey, man, what's up?"

"What's going on?" he asked. I could tell he knew I was pissed.

"Have they offended the *entire* restaurant yet, or still working on it?"

He gave a quick laugh. "Lieutenant Jacobs is holding an impromptu briefing. There's been a change of plans."

"What, handing out Jesus T-shirts outside the mosque?"

"No, we're being called to visit a collateral damage site. It's a grammar school that got accidentally hit by a missile."

I raised my eyebrows. "Really? Shit."

"Yeah, so come on. They're paying the bill so we can head out. It's a little ways from here. Edge of town."

"Okay," I said, grabbing my rifle.

Lieutenant Jacobs was still talking when we got back to the patio. More about provincial reconstruction, talking to folks about repairs and rebuilding—in Jacobs's words, "to teach them how to be civilized." Meanwhile, our real mission was threat assessment. "Fuck hearts and minds, handing out candy and shit," he said. "And now we've got this goddamned school issue. PRT's job, as far as I'm concerned." Jacobs called out names and what each of us would be doing: rookies pulling security outside, and Ethan and I escorting the engineer and going inside the buildings to assess damage.

"Are we clear on our mission?" Jacobs finally barked out.

"Hooah!"

"Are you well aware of your surroundings?"

"Hooah!"

"Are you expecting the unexpected?"

"Hooah!"

"Then let's do this thing!"

The day had turned into an oven by the time we left the restaurant and began walking down the main drag away from town. Jacobs had his map out again, stopping every so often to have an exchange with the interpreter, motioning toward a mosque or other landmark and pointing back at the map. Ethan and I were pulling up the rear, tipping up our water bottles every five minutes, wiping sweat off our faces, squinting to try to see ahead.

"This heat is fuckin' brutal," I said, turning to Ethan.

"Yeah," he said, taking a breath. "Hotter 'n a June bride in a feather bed!"

We stopped at an Iraqi police station surrounded by a wall with barbed wire across the top. Jacobs waited for his engineer to show, then brought him inside with the terp while we took seats outside beneath a palm tree. I finished off my water and opened my ruck to grab another bottle. I noticed a wad of paper sticking out of one of the inside pockets. I unfolded it and saw there were several sheets of blue paper—nice quality, handmade, textured with random pieces of gray woven into the sheet. I didn't recognize it right away, except for my own handwriting. It was a letter to my family I had written when I was hanging with Walker. Ethan went to ask about using the bathroom, so I started reading.

Death Letter

Dear family,

Sorry for your loss. Oh god, how cliché. No, but I do mean that sincerely. I'm sure it is hard to deal with, and probably trippy to hear me writing to you, like a ghost or something. Well, I don't have a lot of time, haha, so I will get to the point. I was no rock star. You always fawned over me like I was some Olympic Gold Medal winning son/brother. That was b.s. and you know it. You were just too busy saying 'I love you' to tell me what you really thought. Be honest, you all found God and I didn't. So by your own definition I was lost. So let me just confirm it: I *was* lost. Completely lost, the entire time I was here. Mom, I was on a mission to save people's lives and all I accomplished was killing. Killin' in the name of—! Sorry, my friend's playing that song right now. I'm also kinda high. Model son, I know. My friend also died when I was here and I failed to protect him. Just like the time Kelly and I heard Mom screaming and I went and grabbed Dad's .45 thinking I could save our family from him. No fucking chance. Dad was the Alpha Male, I was the runt. He was the World Superpower, I was piece of shit Grenada. Okay, that was off the wall. Sorry, I took a lot of Oxy's tonight. Yeah, that's right, I did drugs, because I could not handle the war. So Maddie, I'm not your ideal war hero brother, sorry. I'm just an empty shell desperate to be filled with something. I'm no different than when I was five, Sarah, when Mom dressed you up in a frilly, fuchsia onesie and Mrs. Willingham got so excited and called you a "cute little rosebud." Mom, hope I'm telling it right. I think I stood there for a second then blurted out: "I'm a little rosebud too." So desperate for attention, that's me.

"Ready, man? We're heading to the school." Ethan tapped me on the shoulder. I stood up and followed him, holding the letter in front of me as I walked down the street.

So desperate for attention, that's me. I wanted to save the world by myself and have everyone give me a parade. I wanted to be the one kicking the door down, pointing the gun at Dad saying "leave us the fuck alone," and all I became was the guy kicking the door down while kids look at me and say "leave us the fuck alone." Dad, I know in your heart of hearts that is not what you wanted to be and neither did I. I'm gunna go. You all probably won't need to read this letter and I'm glad cos it's hard core. It's just that Walker's opened my eyes and things are so much clearer to me and I wish I could write down everything I see before I forget tomorrow. Or die, haha. Oops, sorry, too soon?

"All right, stay alert, guys!" Lieutenant Jacobs had spun around toward us, motioning to some graffiti on the side of an apartment building. It was a stencil of that famous Vietnamese girl running naked, screaming, but she had Ronald McDonald and Mickey Mouse on either side of her, holding her hands and waving. "Not all of 'em want us here."

"Gee, can't imagine why," Ethan muttered.

I was sticking the letter into my bag but looked up at him. "What do you mean?"

"Oh, I dunno, say one of our Predator drones fucks up and hits a school?"

"What?" I said. "I thought UAVs were only for aerial surveillance. Reconnaissance and shit."

"Nope. The Predator has mounted Hellfire missiles, and the Reaper has like fifteen times the munitions as the Predator. Hellfires, Sidewinders—"

"Wait, so this school was targeted by a drone?"

"Yeah. At least Jacobs kind of hinted at that."

I stopped walking. "What the fuck? When did he say that?"

"After lunch. I walked up and asked him straight up. He didn't come right out and say it or anything, but I could tell. Yeah, it was probably a UAV—surgical strike, except . . . none too surgical. Probably took out a lot of kids." He sounded so nonchalant about it, even for Ethan.

As we rounded the corner I could hear the noises of children playing. It was the school. It stood on top of a small hill, surrounded by a short wall that ran down the sides of the slope to join at the entrance on the street. A few men were standing in front of the gate, waiting for us. Jacobs shouted out to the men, "Zahid Mohammed al-Rawi?"—again completely butchering the pronunciation.

The taller one began walking toward Jacobs, said something in Arabic. The terp translated: "This man was sent by al-Rawi to meet us."

"That's fine," Jacobs said. "Ask who the other fuckers are."

More Arabic. "They were there when the school was attacked," the terp said.

"'School attacked,' my ass," Jacobs mumbled. "Tell them move away from the fucking gate!" he said, waving his arm.

Jacobs shook the tall guy's hand and began asking about meeting with al-Rawi. We stood around Jacobs just to be safe, scanning the surrounding houses. Kids started gathering across the street, staring at us. One of them tried to say something in English slang; sounded like he was trying to say hi. We waved and smiled. It didn't take long before four or five of them came up to us. First they were giggling and trying to shove each other toward us. Then one got bold and just walked right over, and the rest followed. Ethan practiced his Arabic with them, bending down on one knee. "*Shuku maku?*" he said. "What's up?" They giggled and echoed it to each other. He told them our names and tried to ask if this was their school. A kid in a soccer T-shirt got all animated and blurted out in English, "No school— bomb," making an explosion sound.

"Hey, rook," Ethan said, turning to one of the new guys, "this kid's almost the same age as you!"

Jacobs overheard the kid and turned his head toward us. "Yeah, 'kaboom' is right, kid. Probably just what the little fucker learns in these *madrasas.*" He turned back around and continued talking to the tall guy.

The kid kept smiling, clueless, gesturing to Ethan to show them his rifle. He pulled the strap off his shoulder and let the kid touch it, careful to keep the barrel pointed at the sky. A group of women in black walked up, stopping short on the other side of the road. They began waving their arms, calling the kids over.

"It's okay, they're fine," Ethan shouted out to them, smiling, all friendly.

The women didn't even acknowledge he'd said anything. The kids went running to them, and they all stood there watching us for a minute, and then the mothers herded them away.

Jacobs stepped through the gate and signaled us to come closer. "Rawi is going to meet us over here. Meanwhile, we'll take a look around, assess the damage."

As we passed through, Ethan pointed to the Arabic lettering on the gate, turning to the interpreter. "The name of the school, I'm guessing?"

"Yes. It says 'Amiriyah 1991,' the name of this school and year it is built," he said.

We walked up the hill and into the playground area. Jacobs and the tall guy faced the main school building, pointing and talking through the interpreter. The windows were shattered, but otherwise the entire wall seemed to be intact. The adjacent building in front of us had a large tarp covering what was apparently the impact area. Pieces of glass and debris lay on the ground beside a wooden jungle gym.

"Jesus, when did this happen?" Ethan said.

"That's the theater," Jacobs answered. "They covered it with that tarp to keep it exactly as-is so we could see the damage . . . they *said*, anyways." He began stepping over broken glass toward the impact area, looking up at the wall. He turned to the terp again.

"Ask him how many missiles. I wanna see what he says." Jacobs continued over the broken concrete in his heavy boots.

"Yeah, just one. Same like what report says," the interpreter said.

Jacobs pulled up the tarp and checked out the window frame, then turned back to us, squinting. "Not that bad, actually, for a Hellfire. They were lucky."

Like he'd fucking know, I thought.

We went inside the main building and assessed the damage there, which wasn't much. The first room looked like a teacher's lounge or meeting room. The engineer took some notes and measurements, rapped his knuckles on a few walls—whatever the hell *that* was supposed to do—and Jacobs rambled on about what type of stuff they wanted to see in our report. I stood at the door smoking, looking at some men walking across the street toward the gate.

"Hey, hey, hey!" Jacobs shouted to the engineer, who was holding his flip phone in front of him. "No pics. I told you."

The engineer guy looked confused. "None at all, Lieutenant? I thought you just said none that make it look worse than it is."

Jacobs shook his head. "Look, it's real simple. We're here to do a CDA, a collateral damage assessment. We decide what goes into that report. It's what *we* see, *our* words. Not photos some chickenshit like Keith Olbermann can show on TV, and suddenly everyone does their own assessment. This is *my* fucking assessment."

The engineer didn't say anything. He had a little twitch on the side of his mouth, and he just looked at Jacobs, who was sticking his head into the next room. I turned back toward the men, who were now entering through the gate.

"Sir, I think the tribal leaders are here," I said to Jacobs.

watched as they walked methodically up the hill, taking slow, almost reluctant steps. *The old guy with the checkered keffiyeh and the clunky seventies glasses must be the head honcho*, I thought. His eyebrows were bushy and white. He wore a slim dishdasha that brushed the ground as he walked. I could tell he had to put more effort into making his steps look effortless and austere. The second one was middle-aged. He reached down and brushed a smudge of dirt off his shoes. I was guessing he was some kind of official—clean shaven, business suit, watch with a thick band. *Yeah, lawyer, maybe.* The third guy walked behind the other two, looking at the ground. Baggy polyester slacks, dress shoes that looked like Salvation Army, and one of those tan safari shirts everyone wears untucked. *This one's country*, I thought. *Country folk.* Maybe I was reading too much into it, but I thought he walked pathetically. Like he felt less important in this world than the other two, or maybe *they* thought he was. Total extreme opposite from that blowhard commander who dressed me down at the CLC briefing, taking those huge, clomping goose steps, practically shouting every word he said, while idiots like us listened in total awe. *As if his existence even fucking matters.* I took one last drag and put my cigarette out in the dirt. *Ah, mankind*, I thought. *What a fucking joke.*

When they met with Jacobs, I got to find out if my impressions were correct. We collected a few chairs that weren't busted and set them up on the patio just outside the main building. Another guy in a dishdasha showed up with tea, and we found plastic crates to place next to each chair.

Jacobs sat there in full gear, his legs spread wide, looking totally out of place holding his scalding-hot cylindrical glass of tea with his gloves, while the tribal elders sat in their chairs all formal and spouted "We love Amreekee" bullshit for the first ten minutes. Ethan and I stood close by, looking out toward the city. I was right; the old man was the clan chief. The well-dressed guy was a respected doctor in the village. The poor man hadn't spoken yet.

After ten more minutes I was tired of it. *Let's just scope out the school, people, see what we can do to repair it.* But they had certain ways of doing things. *Whatever.*

Just as I was glancing over at Ethan to roll my eyes as if to say, "Jesus, get on with it," a group of little kids came around the corner of the school and stood politely next to the chief. The doctor stood up, apparently to introduce them. The children smiled, at least the ones who could—because each one had what looked like severe injuries to the face and limbs, probably from fragmentation or burn blast or both. My first reaction was to look away. But Jacobs caught my attention, saying, "What the fuck's *this* noise?" half under his breath. The chief said something to the interpreter, who turned to Jacobs.

"On the day the attack came, the school have a theater day. The girls and boys, some of them part of . . . theater, and some only watch," he said, struggling with the words.

Jacobs seemed impatient. "It's called a play. So the kids put on a play. Got it."

"Yes, play . . . and then the missile came in the middle of the play."

The doctor leaned down, putting his hand on the shoulder of one little girl, who peered at us from underneath her blue scarf. She was holding herself up by leaning on the girl next to her.

"Yara," she said.

"They bring that day Yara to me first," the doctor said. I was surprised he spoke English. "She had a broken arm and damage quite terrible on her leg. It had to be cut."

I glanced down and saw—one little brown foot in a sandal, toenails painted, the pant leg next to it hanging loose.

The doctor took a step to the right and put his hand on the next girl's shoulder. Her face was severely burned, and one eye was shut. To me the skin looked like melted plastic, or wet clay someone had smoothed out with their thumb. I let out a long breath and reached for another cigarette. I noticed Ethan had already left and walked to the side of the building near the playground.

"Narjis," she said nervously, trying to keep her one eye pointed at us. Her hair was combed over her head but was obviously half gone.

The doctor asked her something in Arabic and listened for her response. He translated: "Narjis was on the stage. The explosion threw her against the other children and burned her face."

Narjis looked up at him and added something. He put his arm on her shoulder. "*La la*," he said, shaking his head. "No, no." He looked up at us. "She thinks her body killed Dalia." He bent down and said something to her in a soft tone; I assumed it was "Don't think that" or something.

The little girl didn't appear to be upset, just politely stood there with that little eye dancing back and forth. The doctor moved on to the next kid, a little boy.

"My name is Zahir," he said, taking a step forward, all formal. The boy had a bandage around his head, and his hand was wrapped in thick gauze that went up to his shoulder.

"Zahir was also horribly burned on his arm," the doctor said, and then looked down at the boy, who rattled off something. The doctor continued, translating: "He was found under debris the next morning. His mother found him. He will not use his arm again."

And on it went. Azhar, Warda, Yasmin. Jacobs just sat there putting spoonfuls of sugar into his glass of tea and stirring it. His eyes barely left the glass. When he did look up, it was as if to give the obligatory "No, no, keep going. I'm listening."

When the doctor finished with the last kid, there wasn't a millisecond of silence before Jacobs stood up and began blurting out the "Thank you *so* much for coming" bullshit, trying to shake hands with the doctor and pat the kids on the head: *Run along, now. Time for grown-up talk—things like war you children wouldn't understand.*

But then the old man reached up and put his hand on Jacobs's shoulder, saying, "Please, please," motioning to the chair. Jacobs sat again, glancing quickly at his watch.

"We have a special one to show you," the doctor said, turning to the man in the tan shirt. "Mahmoud will now bring his daughter, who is now the story everyone knows in the whole province."

The man in the tan safari shirt stood up and walked past the group of kids and around the corner. I could hear his voice speaking softly. A few moments later he came back into view, a little bushy-haired girl standing chest high in front of him, more or less being nudged along. She didn't appear so much reluctant as distracted. She held an odd-looking green tube in her mouth, kind of like a plant stem, and was blowing a soap bubble, staring into space like babies sometimes do with a pacifier. She had mesmerizing deep-brown eyes. Her father leaned down to her and said something, obviously coaxing her, and when they were standing in front of the group, facing us, he took the thing out of her mouth and said something to her firmly. She straightened her body rigid, mocking standing at attention for us. I was struck by how adorable she was. Ferrari red pants, matching blouse with ruffled sleeves and a bear on the front. Dark, bowl-cut hair, all thick and mussed and flipped up at the edges. Looked like a mushroom overshadowing that tiny face. But very cool, very French. And it seemed like I'd seen it once before, a long time ago. Like if I'd been to Paris or maybe out in the countryside I would have seen some girl with that hairstyle, biking thirty miles to go to the university or something. *Maybe I saw it in a movie,* I thought.

She took a deep breath and launched into a soliloquy, blasting out what must have been four or five sentences before her father jumped in to tell her to wait for the interpreter. Her voice, rhythmic and lilting, stopped midsentence, and she looked up at him. I turned to Ethan, who had walked back over next to me. We stood there to listen.

"My name is Abeer. I am seven. I have nothing wrong with me," the translator began. "Other children and parents were hurt during the play. Some of them are even killed. But I was not."

The little girl continued, but this time it sounded like no more than three words before she stopped and motioned with her hand to the interpreter, like suddenly she was running the show.

Ethan leaned over to me and whispered, "So I think if you look up *adorable* in the dictionary, they have this kid's picture."

"I know, right?" I said.

The little girl's father smiled politely and prompted her to say a little more. At this point she caught on and said just the right amount before pausing.

"I and Yara—yes, my sister Yara—we were in the play. Also many other girls, and boys also. We were in the play, on the stage, when the . . . rocket thing came through the window."

Her eyes shifted around to each of us, locking on each person's gaze for a few seconds before moving on to the next one. Even Jacobs sat attentively, like he was at a kindergartener's recital.

"The rocket thing, most did not see it coming. Some who were watching the play said after, yes, they saw a flash, but the children were acting in the play and did not see. But I did. I know exactly where . . ."

At this point the little girl scuttled across the patio, past Ethan and me to the front of the school and pointed to the sky above the mosque, then rushed back to her spot like a ball girl at Wimbledon and continued. This time her tone changed.

"Because before it flew through the window, that is when everything turned strange. I saw everything for longer, because . . . because my eyes were going fast, very fast . . . my eyes were running."

"Uh, question!" Jacobs said, clearing his throat. "Eyes were running? What's that mean?"

Ethan spoke up. "Probably the rush of adrenaline, sir. You know, time appears to slow down, vision is more acute, senses seem sharper."

Jacobs gave him a dumb stare. "Mmkay," he said sarcastically.

The interpreter asked the girl. She responded quickly, matter-of-factly.

"She says it is easy. Once she was in a car and passed a horse, and the horse was going slow, but really it was going fast. Sounds also. All of them slower, like thunder."

Ethan turned to me and bobbed his head, widening his eyes at me. I nodded in agreement. She looked way too young to say something that technical. The girl continued for a while without stopping, as the interpreter tried to keep up.

"I have many pictures in my head, pictures of everything: Leilah, how she first flies toward the big boom and then flies away from the big boom. Her face was pushed in like a doll, like dough. Then her eye comes out. The seats, I see them break, I see wood pieces drift away together. Every small piece of glass, I see it floating through the air. The fire is chasing it. Baqat's father is pushed by the wind to the ceiling. He hits his head on it, makes a hole." The interpreter turned to us. "She said we can go see. She can show us where is the hole. She said her eyes were fast; she has many, many images."

The group fell silent for a few seconds, then a few more. After a minute had passed, the silence seemed to grow heavier and heavier, harder for anyone to break. I looked around at some of the tribal leaders. They had their arms crossed, mouths pursed, staring at the ground. The children stood still behind the girl, facing forward, so respectful and polite. *They should be playing right now*, I thought. *Laughing, climbing trees.* My nose began to tingle as I looked at each of their faces—the way they just . . . existed. Faces deformed, burns, legs missing. How could it be? They were supposed to get the first few years of their lives for free, like we did, like a fairy tale, but instead they were already paying dearly, crawling along. Not living, but struggling to exist.

The girl blurted out one more thing, which the interpreter translated.

"She's telling me the words also, on the missile, they are not Arabic letters, what is printed on the side, but she can write them all exactly, no problem at all for her."

Ethan and I looked at each other. "Uh, how old is this girl?" he said, frowning.

I raised my eyebrows. "Seven, she said. Hey, it sounds like she could ID the missile."

Jacobs slurped his tea and set it down, breathing in sharply through his teeth. "I said, goddamn, that's hot! Um, so, uh, wow. That is some story there, little girl. You got a good memory, huh?"

He pointed to his eyes and then gestured like he was turning a key against his temple, as if that was supposed to translate. *What a fucking moron*, I thought, wiping the side of my eye. The girl looked confused and waited for the interpreter, then burst out in excitement when she found out what he was asking. Her hands waved, and she moved her body as she spoke.

"I always have bad grades in school because I cannot remember what I read. Also stories I do not remember . . . my father punished me for this many, many times. But no. Not this time. This time I remember everything."

As she talked she nodded her head like an adult, raising her eyebrows to emphasize certain points. She would stop and reach her arm out to cue the translator, too. A thought popped into my head: *Maybe she has some special ability.*

"Yes, I remember everything," she continued. "Even you can make a hard, hard test about this, and I answer every question, easy. You ask me to make drawings, I make it perfectly. Ask me what colors, any color. The fire. It was orange like the sun, with silver and white around it. The smell was of the polish my mom uses on her fingernails . . . but also a little cinnamon too."

She paused again, lifting her hands up to her ears and grimacing.

"The sound was like Allah was whistling from the sky, going to kill all of the world! And then I saw it. It came through the window, turning around slowly. Words like in TV from USA, I could see them easily. Black letters on white, but some numbers too."

A boy in the group of kids stepped forward and tapped the girl on the shoulder, then held up a sheet of paper for us to see. It looked like a laser-printed photo. The girl continued.

"Here is one. I have only a box of pencil colors, but if I have every color made in all the entire world, I can make it exactly. This you see is just one picture in my head."

The little boy handed the photo to the old man, who handed it to Jacobs. The interpreter continued translating: "This is just one picture. There are many others. They are all in my head, very neat and put away—like when my mother places little things in drawers."

Jacobs held it in front of him, took another sip of tea, and passed the paper back to Ethan and me. We stared at it for a few seconds, and a chill came over me. What I was looking at was not a photograph at all. It was a drawing on a sheet of plain paper, but the realism was shocking. There it was, a clear side view of a Hellfire missile poking its nose through the theater window, halfway through detonation, glass fanning out, some shards even clearly bent back. People in the audience sat in their seats, looking forward, unaware. One kid in the third row was sitting on her dad's lap, rubbing one of her eyes. The shadow of her arm fell on her mother's abaya. I recognized the girl. She had been the last one to speak before Jacobs tried to wrap up the meeting.

"How the fuck?" Ethan said. I kept staring. The detail. It didn't seem possible, even if she had painted it with oil. *It's not even blurred,* I thought. *There's no fucking way.*

Ethan wet his finger and wiped it on the corner of the drawing. The color smudged. I turned the drawing over, felt the material.

"It's just colored pencil," I said.

"Jesus Christ," Ethan said. At first I thought he was just blown away by how good it was, but then I saw his face. Eyebrows furrowed, mouth half open. Just shy of furious. I recognized that look—when something defied all logic, could not possibly be true, and had no explanation whatsoever, yet there it was.

I handed the drawing back to the old man. Jacobs began his wrap-up talk again but was interrupted midsentence. One of the rookies pulling security stood up on top of the wall and shouted over to us.

"Sir, looks like an angry mob coming this way!"

We walked over to the playground and looked down the hill. Twenty or thirty people dressed in black gowns were walking up the street toward us, holding posters and handmade signs. Each of them wore a white mask.

"Fucking great," Jacobs said, standing next to me. We watched them cross the traffic circle and begin heading toward the hill. Several of the kids ran past us and stopped together, looking down at the people approaching the gate. I had the feeling they'd known about the protest ahead of time. I looked to my left; the tribal leaders strolled over and stood beside us, not alarmed one bit. *Yeah*, I thought, *these guys knew about it.* Jacobs was fidgeting, then craned his neck, looking around behind us.

"Where's the terp? Fuck! Coffelt! Where's Bob?"

"I dunno, sir, back inside, maybe?" Ethan said.

Jacobs scrambled back toward the building. The protesters were slowly making their way along the path, trying not to slip in their long robes. By the shape of their heads I thought some of them were probably women. I could now see their signs more clearly—photographs of children, handwritten words in Arabic. Quotes with the word *Allah* in them.

"March of the dead," Ethan said. Something caught my eye, and I glanced at the group of kids standing with their backs to us. On the far left was the little girl in the red pants, facing the exact opposite direction of the others, staring at me instead. She was blowing bubbles again. I smiled at her, but she just stood there expressionless, with those dark eyes. I didn't think much about it. I turned to Ethan. "What'd you say? What's it called?"

"March of the dead," he said. "Dressed in all black like that, with the white masks."

The protesters opened the gate and filed in, gathering just inside. Jacobs came out of the school with the interpreter. He paused next to Ethan and me. "This shit wasn't in the goddamned manual," he mumbled, then stormed off past the kids and double-timed it down to the group. The interpreter followed like a small dog.

One of the protesters stepped forward to talk with Jacobs, who stood there, arms crossed, asking questions, wearing those ridiculous *Top Gun* shades. He'd stick one arm out and point at the protesters, say something, and then fold his arms again. His chin was stuck out the whole time. The gaggle of children began whispering to each other for some reason. Then they started chanting some two-syllable word, quietly at first, increasing in intensity. It didn't last long, though. The old man walked down to them, clapping his hands sharply, and they stopped.

I turned to Ethan. "Wonder what that meant."

He looked at me disgustedly. "Probably like 'Asshole! Asshole! Asshole!'" he said, with the same cadence.

I chuckled. "Yeah, really."

Jacobs began leading the group up toward the school. I realized I hadn't gotten pics of any of it, so I started fishing through my pockets for my cell. I looked down, and the little girl was right next to my leg, staring up at me.

"Holy shit!" I shouted, followed by a surprised laugh a couple milliseconds later. The girl took a quick step back but walked back toward me. "Damn, little girl, you scared the shit out of me!" But I made sure to smile so she'd feel at ease. She put the pipe in her mouth and blew another bubble, staring at me silently again. I turned to Ethan, bewildered. "Did *you* see her walk over here?"

"No, dude. Two seconds ago she was over there," he said, pointing at the kids. "She is seriously starting to creep me out!"

I knelt to her level, putting my rifle down on the ground. "Cool, huh?" I said, pointing to her pipe. I made motions with my hand to imitate bubbles and made a few popping sounds.

Ethan looked over. "Already making little explosions? They sure start 'em young, boy, I tell ya," he said with a wry smile.

I turned to him. "Cute, Coffelt."

"Why, thank you," Ethan said with his patented "damn, am I clever" smirk, taking a long draw off his cigarette.

I turned back to the little girl. She handed me the bubble pipe. "*Shukran*," I said, and started to blow on it, but she grabbed my hand and guided it to the bottle of liquid. "*Shoof shoof*," she said—"Look"— and dipped the end into the soapy liquid. I blew on the pipe, and bubbles shot out. She smiled for the first time and said something else. I looked up to see Jacobs bounding toward us. He took long, forceful steps, making eye contact with me as he passed.

"Where the fuck's PRT when you need 'em? They should be doing this shit."

"What's going on?" I asked.

He blew past me, waving his hand dismissively. "What's it fucking look like?" he said out of the side of his mouth. "I'm meeting with the goddamned hajji protesters."

I didn't bother asking for more. He obviously was pissed. I handed the pipe back to the girl and stood up. The group of kids were falling in line behind the protesters walking toward the main building. Ethan finished his smoke, and we walked up to the building, standing by the doorway watching all the black robes shuffle into the meeting room and stop just inside. I was close enough to see their eyeballs sunk deep behind the holes cut in the white masks. They had drawn black teardrops underneath, running down their plastic cheeks. I smelled incense. I noticed their hands; they had dipped them in paint to make them look bloody. I looked silently over at Ethan and then peered inside.

Jacobs had set up the folding chairs inside and now stood in the front with the interpreter as if they were hosting a seminar. Except no one sat down. The protesters lined up along the back wall and held their signs by their sides like it was order arms.

The girl was next to me again. I looked down at her, and she had her little round face turned up at me, holding the pipe up to her mouth.

"What is her deal?" Ethan said.

I shook my head. "Dunno. Kind of weird, huh?"

Jacobs's voice bellowed loudly against the concrete walls. We stepped inside the doorway to listen.

"My name is Lieutenant Karl Jacobs. I am heading up one of the teams here in Hamza performing a village assessment, which includes estimating damage at this school." He paused for the interpreter.

The protester he had been talking to down at the gate stepped forward and said a couple of words quickly.

"Not only damage. Severe damage and death," the interpreter said.

Jacobs nodded to acknowledge him. You could tell he was trying to act sympathetic. Not *be* sympathetic or anything. Just act it. He took a few paces to the right and pivoted back toward the audience, placing his hands on his hips.

"If I had my druthers, I would take full responsibility for the injuries and property damage that was done here. I would—"

"Sir," the interpreter interrupted him, "I do not know this word *mydruders.*"

Ethan slapped my side with the back of his hand. I turned to him, rolling my eyes. "Really? Using slang to talk to Iraqis? Really?" I whispered. Ethan shook his head.

Jacobs stopped and faced forward, hands still on his hips, feet spread apart. He looked like a pair of ridiculous scissors. "My. Druthers. Two words. It means 'preference.' If I had my choice," Jacobs said, taking another few steps, "but I don't. I *cannot* take responsibility, because it is not under my control." Again he paused for the translation.

"I have no knowledge of who fired the missile. No knowledge of what the target was or what the objective was. For all I know, it wasn't even ours."

As soon as that was translated, I heard rumblings in the back of the room. One of the protesters held up a placard with a photo of a child and yelled something in Arabic. All I could make out was the "Amreekee" part. But it didn't sound good. A few others started chiming in. Jacobs immediately raised his voice and waved his hand in a downward motion.

"Hold on!" he said, turning to the interpreter. "Tell them to shut up and list—tell them . . . please hold their questions until I'm done."

The interpreter managed to quiet them down. Jacobs put his fist up to his mouth. I thought he looked like a prick. *Oh God, he is horrible. Let me up there, for God's sake,* I thought.

Jacobs began pacing again, hands on his hips, doing the Fiskars routine. Ethan leaned in near my shoulder. "He thinks he's fucking Patton."

"I know. And you see the looks on their faces?" I whispered back, nodding toward the tribal leaders.

"Yeah. I can't listen to this shit. I'll be outside," Ethan said, reaching in his sleeve pocket.

"Okay, I'll be right there."

"Folks, *we* are not the enemy," Jacobs was saying, pausing for effect. "We are the good guys. We are here with the PRT—Provincial Reconstruction Team—to take notes on what you people need . . . and to fix it . . . We are the good guys." He went on, listing specific efforts—pumps for clean water, power stations, hydraulics, and so forth. "Again, we're the good guys."

I felt a faint tug on my pant leg. Abeer was staring up at me, specifically at my left shoulder. I glanced down to see if I had an insect crawling on me. No, it was just the bottom edge of my 9/11 tat sticking out from underneath my shirtsleeve. She said something excitedly and jumped up on my arm, trying to grab it, but she couldn't reach. She bounced back up again, sweeping her hand upward frantically to try to push my sleeve over my biceps. Finally I knelt down and pulled my sleeve up to show her. She stared at it, rubbing her fingers on the Twin Towers. She looked at me and smiled broadly. "*Al-humdullelah*"—"Thanks be to God." Then she grabbed my arm and pulled on me to go outside.

"*Thanks be to God*"? I thought. *What the fuck? That is so messed up, teaching little kids that shit.* But I let her drag me along anyway. She was probably just echoing what adults had told her. At least, I assumed so. She tugged as hard as she could, pulling me past Ethan, who let out a breath of smoke and started to say something. But before he knew it, she had grabbed his wrist too and was dragging us both across the playground toward the blown-out part of the school.

"What do you need, kid?" Ethan said, stopping. She pointed at me, then toward the theater, where the tarp covered the impact area. Then she grabbed us again and pulled. I glanced back at the rookies, who were looking down toward the road and taking pictures.

"Whatever it is," I said, "she seems pretty concerned. Dead body, maybe?"

"No way, they'd have found a body already. Maybe it's her dog or something."

"Yeah. We got a few minutes. Won't hurt to check it out."

When we got up to the wall of the building, she let go of our wrists, lifted the tarp, and disappeared underneath. We heard her call out for us from inside the building. We adjusted our rifle slings so our weapons were against our chests and peeled the bottom of the tarp back. The little mouse hole she'd scurried through looked too small for Ethan and me, so we scoped out the blast area above to see how we might clamber up into the opening. I stepped onto some rubble and began to pull myself up.

"So we're climbing over, I assume?" Ethan said dryly.

"Sure."

Ethan looked back toward the other building. "Why not; Jacobs is busy anyhow. We'll only be gone a few minutes."

"Maybe we can check out the damage," I said, finding a good handhold to pull myself up.

When I got to where I could see inside, I saw Abeer watching us from below. Looking around, I could tell it was a pretty decent auditorium. I could make out dozens of chairs scattered all over the floor. Broken glass and tables. And about twenty rows down to the left was a stage. Hardwood surface, little stairsteps to the right and left. A white curtain tied up on each side with ropes. Seemed pretty nice for such a small school. It looked a lot like the auditorium at my elementary school.

I hopped down onto a small pile of rubble, and a piece of wood tumbled onto the floor. The sound echoed against the concrete walls. The little girl waved in front of my face and pointed up toward the top of the front wall, to the left of the stage. It was one of those round metal clocks. I looked down at her. She blurted something out and pointed at my wrist and back at the clock, motioning for me to bring it to her. She grabbed my hand and tugged at me.

"Jesus! Hold up, little girl!" I looked back at Ethan. "Dude, for some reason she wants that clock."

Ethan was positioning himself, about to let go and drop the rest of the way down, but he stopped, looking up to where I was pointing. He studied the inside wall for a few moments. "No problem. I'll get it," he said.

"Uh, wait, are you kidding?"

"Nah, I could use a challenge."

"You're gonna free-climb that entire wall just for—"

"Sure. Why not?"

He turned to the wall, finding his first handhold, and began pulling himself up. He had his hands inside a crack in the wall so he could lean back and walk up the surface.

I shook my head. "Okay, but make it quick."

"Pfft, two minutes, tops," Ethan said.

The little girl seemed anxious and pulled me by the arm down the aisle to the side of the stage. She scampered up the steps on all fours, then turned to make sure I'd followed. Sunlight shone through the ceiling where a few roof boards were missing. The entire back of the stage was a mess of splintered wood, mangled pieces of metal, and concrete debris. I took a few steps. A small bulb popped under my boot. I looked over to make sure the little girl wasn't falling in one of the holes or touching any wires or anything.

She was okay. She stood front stage, facing an imaginary crowd, took a bow, and began rattling off a bunch of stuff in Arabic, like she was making an announcement. Her voice was loud and animated and seemed to have a friendly tone. She waved her arms about and flitted from one side of the stage to the other, bending down to touch or smell imaginary objects and reacting delightfully. She then stopped and exclaimed something urgent, rushed over to me and grabbed my hand, rotating it and bending my fingers so that I was pointing at her, and dropped my arm. She turned to the imaginary crowd and clapped, as if by doing that I had won an Oscar or something. I smiled and just enjoyed her vivid imagination. I guessed the things she was interacting with were actors in the play. *Probably introducing each one,* I thought. I glanced up at Ethan hanging from some kind of wooden molding, edging his way closer to the clock.

The little girl waved her arms at me, saying something excitedly, grabbed my hand again, and led me to the curtain. She motioned for me to grasp it and pointed above me, then ran over to the other side of the stage and acted like she was reading something. She then ran back to me, grabbed the curtain—"Blah blah"—and jumped into the middle of the stage, turning to me as if I was supposed to follow her lead. I hopped next to her, and then she ran to the front of the stage and began reciting some lines: "Blah blah blah . . . Abeer." She moved my hand again to point it at herself. She turned to me and said, *"Radid badi"*—"repeat," a term I had heard quite a bit. So I said her line, or tried, rather; I thought I was at least saying her name right.

"La la!" she said in Arabic, shaking her head. "Blah blah blah Abeer."

I tried it again, and this time she got very excited and said the word for "good" a lot.

She had me do this several times until I understood that my part was to leap onto the stage, run to the front, and say the first few words, and when I got to her name, to point to her. Next she added another phrase, which was short and easy to remember, and at the end of it I was supposed to point to myself this time. Once I got that, she had me repeat both phrases together until I'd pronounced it all correctly and gotten all the choreography down.

I peered up at Ethan, who was high in the corner of the room, straddling the two walls, stretching his hand out inches from the clock.

"Ethan, she is seriously into this play."

"I know, man. I can hear her."

"Hurry up, dude."

"Hang on! I'm about to be a hero here."

"Okay, you can toss the clock down to me, then go back the way you came."

"There's a lot of clutter," he said, "but I'll see if I can—"

But Abeer was tugging on my shirt, apparently saying a third phrase. I smiled and clapped. "Bravo!" But she shook her head and repeated the words slowly, reaching up to touch my lips. "Okay, okay!" I said. "Help! Ethan, I'm getting roped into acting here."

He laughed. "Well, she picked the right guy to memorize lines."

She had me repeat the last part, which was longer, and had me point to the broken window and make an explosion sound. At one point during this rehearsal I thought I heard a sound outside.

"Blah blah," she said, walking to the front of the stage again. She stopped and repeated the same lines she'd said before. She turned back to me and motioned for me to come to her. I could now hear Ethan thumping around above.

"Dude!" I said, looking up into the rafters. "What the hell are you doing?"

"Hang on. Trying to find a way down," he said.

I flipped my Maglite on and scanned the structure hanging above me. "Uh, no, dude, there's no way. I told you. Just climb back the way you came."

I stood there for a few moments as he rustled around above me. I heard sounds again—people yelling from the playground or maybe down the hill. Sounded odd. Not like calling out to someone. More like crowd sounds from a concert. I kept listening, but that was it.

"Dude," Ethan said, "there's a stool, a can of soda, a theater program. There has got to be a way for people to get up here."

I shined the light to where he was poking his head out.

"Here, take the clock," he said, and dropped it down to me.

Abeer turned to me, her face lighting up.

"*Shukran,*" she said. She grabbed it from me. She moved the little hand of the clock straight up to twelve and rotated the big hand carefully to quarter of. She paused and stared off, squinting, then moved it back five minutes, then up slightly. 12:41.

I saw Ethan out of the corner of my eye, climbing along the wall back toward the tarp. I fished through my pockets for my cell. *Shit!* Twenty-five minutes already.

I turned to Abeer. "Okay, go now," I said in Arabic, motioning to the exit.

"Blah blah," she said, pointing to the clock and nodding at me, and she took off down the stairs and then up the aisle.

I laughed. "She keeps doing that!"

"What?" Ethan said, jumping down to the floor. Abeer flipped the tarp up and scurried through her little mouse hole.

"Rattling off shit. Like we're fluent in Arabic."

"Where is she going?" he said.

"No clue," I said. Suddenly I heard yelling again outside. This time it was definitely urgent, sounded like one of our guys. I looked at Ethan. "Uh, what was that?"

The tarp slapped open, and the little girl came bursting out from underneath.

"*Urkuth!*" she yelled, waving her hands at us frantically with a pushing motion.

We heard gunfire in the direction of the school office.

"Oh, fuck!" Ethan said.

"*INHEHZIM!*" she screamed again, more upset. I'd heard this expression used by insurgents in battle.

"She's telling us to run," I said.

"Fuck that," he said, and threw the tarp open. The hole was barely big enough for us to fit through. Ethan decided it was worth trying.

"Stay here. I'll check the area," he said.

"Okay . . ."

The little girl tugged at my arm, screaming in a high pitch.

"Gimme status soon as you're outside," I said loudly.

"Roger that," he said, sliding on his stomach. He had to squeeze through the hole, then maneuver his body around a wooden support structure. That was as much as I could see. I knelt down to Abeer and tried to calm her, but she was completely panicked. I heard yelling in English outside, followed by a huge burst of gunfire.

"Ethan!" I shouted, peering into the hole. I looked over at the stage, wondering if there was an exit through the back. The little girl put her palms on my stomach and put all of her body weight into shoving me toward the stage. "Goddamn!" I swiped her arms away. "Hold the fuck on a second!" I knelt down to look through the hole. I saw the fingers of Ethan's glove grip the edge of the wood, and his body whipped around it violently. I saw his temple scrape hard against the concrete.

"Contact!" His voice shook. I saw his face and the look of sheer panic. "Fuck-ton of hajjis. We're getting overrun," he said. I grabbed his arm and helped pull him through, and we all ran down to the stage. Ethan and I had started up the steps when the girl stopped us, pointing. There was a wooden panel door leading underneath the stage. I pulled it open and we crawled inside, shutting the door behind us.

At first I thought I'd left my Maglite on the stage. "Hang on," I whispered, patting my belt blindly. I could sense Ethan next to me, kneeling down in the dirt, but the girl took off like a mole, feeling her way underneath the stage. I could hear her sliding her feet.

"Abeer!" Ethan said in a hushed voice.

"Come, come," she called out in Arabic.

I checked my belt again, feeling all the way around. Nothing. "Fuck it," I said, "let's go." I nudged Ethan forward with my hand on his shoulder. I thought I heard a noise from inside the theater, and my legs shook with adrenaline. We duckwalked a few steps, following the girl's voice.

We continued in the dark, hearing sounds behind us coming from the theater. There were footsteps that I estimated were at the front of the stage, and then I heard them clomp up the stairs.

"Fuck," I whispered to Ethan, pressing on his back.

"Slow and steady. Too fast, and we'll knock our helmets," he said back to me.

I felt my legs wobble, like I had glucose deprivation. We came upon a stack of crates or boxes and moved to the right around them. Abeer called out again in a subdued tone. Her voice was to our left, emanating from the other side of the crates. Now I could hear footsteps directly above us on the stage. *Fuck*, I thought, *how many are there?* My calves and Achilles tendons began to burn, and it was awkward with one hand on Ethan's back and one following the contour of the support beams. As we got to the edge of the stack of crates, the footsteps continued overhead; I heard several others clomping down the steps in front of the stage.

"Get down!" was all I had time to say. The panel door opened, and light seemed to fill the entire crawl space. I saw the red color of the dirt floor; I saw Abeer next to a panel door at the rear, just as she squatted and made herself into a little ball. We ducked down in a single, quick movement and froze, but I rotated my helmet slowly to look to the left.

I could see the heads of three men over the top of the crates. *At least one AK*, I thought, hearing a rattling sound. A flashlight waved around the crawl space. Ethan was on his knees, weight forward, tilted on his right elbow and looking back at me. He was completely motionless, staring. He looked like a street performer. The light swept over our heads and stopped, illuminating the top of Abeer's head and part of her back. One of the men said something. To me it sounded like a suspicious tone, but I was hoping it was just paranoia. The light stayed on Abeer. *Don't panic, little girl*, I thought. *They'll go away, you just cannot fucking move.* She was doing well, all balled up, head tucked inside her arms.

So we stayed still and waited.

In the darkness I could smell the wooden beams above us, thick and sweet, like vanilla mixed with tar. I recognized it right away: creosote, used as a preservative. *God, that's weird*, I thought, *how that triggers such a vivid memory. Creosote. Dad taking me and Karen to*

Six Flags. I could picture it exactly, the three of us waiting in line as the looming, thundering roller coaster swept back and forth above us. The elaborate latticework of pitch-black railroad ties vibrating all around us in low, growling tones. And that smell. For years afterward I would come across it, and everything would come back to me like I was eleven again: how it started pouring down rain and the park nearly emptied out; how the three of us literally ran from one thrill ride to the next, zigzagging through the maze of ropes, through the turnstiles, and straight into the very front seats; and how Dad was so fun, in such a good mood, an entire day of not getting mad or anything. That smell meant a strange thing to me: a memory of happiness, relief, of not having to worry. But also a reminder, a nagging suspicion that this was my future, being with Dad and not Mom, or Mom and not Dad. It's what they wanted, ultimately, even if it meant the worst thing imaginable: separation, divorce, never having to be around each other again. It was the inevitable, their only answer, the non-solution. A resolution to address nothing. They were two archenemies who wânted a wall between themselves. That was their ticket to peace. Note: doesn't apply to children.

Finally the men moved the light away from us and pointed it to the ground below them. One of them, a guy with a beard, moved back outside the panel door. The other two continued talking and pointing to things on the ground. I heard the word "Amreekee." I felt my pulse surge in my eardrums as I realized they could see our footprints. There would be no mistaking our type of boot. One of the men knelt down in his robe and began crawling in our direction, rifle in hand. In that split second I had no idea whatsoever what to do. I looked at Ethan as if to ask him, and he just held out his hand flat and stared at me. The guy with the beard came back inside and handed an AK to the one standing there. He took the weapon, shined the flashlight in our direction, and started crawling.

All of a sudden the door at the back swung wide open, and I heard the little girl shout "Amreekee" something. I glanced back toward her. She had stood up and was walking hurriedly toward the men, pointing at the door in the back. "Amreekee blah blah. Amreekee blah blah," she repeated, approaching them. They blurted out some questions to her, and she answered, sweeping her hand and pointing to the back again. My first thought was that she was telling them where we were. But then the man with the flashlight waved it around, and she acted annoyed and shouted, "No, no" something, and pointed away from Ethan and me. I realized what she was doing. She had opened the door so it looked like she had come in through the back door, and she was saying something about having seen Americans come through. *Holy shit*, I thought. *I remember that trick. I used to pull it on kids during recess.*

I watched as the little girl talked to them, and the man with the flashlight and the man with the robe crawled back toward the entrance, stood up, and ducked their heads under the panel door. The girl followed, and they shut the door. Ethan and I waited for a minute until we could hear their voices way inside the theater, and then we scrambled to the rear door. When we got to the outside, we were careful to check the area behind the building. Then we shut the door.

There was a small field in the back, overgrown. A rusted-out vehicle lay off to the side. To the left, the wall surrounding the school grounds butted up against the corner of the building. It looked like people rarely went back there, though I noticed a few items lying in the gravel that looked like props for a play. There was an oversized teacup and spoon, wooden cutouts of a mosque, and a dark-gray raincloud. Ethan picked up an empty drink bottle, looked at the label, and then scanned the area as though he'd lost something.

"We need to fucking hide, dude," I said.

He leaned back, squinting, peering up at the roof. Above the crawl space door a small metal ladder ran up the side of the building. He grabbed the bottom rung and began tugging on it.

"I think I know exactly where," he said, prying the ladder away from the building. It was held from the top and had a few flimsy brackets about halfway up.

"What are you doing?" I asked him.

"We'll climb up there, then tear the ladder down."

He tugged again, loosening the brackets some more, then put a boot up and started to climb.

"Okay," I said. I took off my boots and used my hand to sweep our tracks off the ground, then put my laces in my teeth and climbed up in my socks. Ethan reached the top and peered over.

"Always knew you was part Injun," he whispered in an over-the-top hayseed drawl. It caught me so off guard, I had to suppress a giggle. I lost muscle strength in my mouth and almost dropped my boots. I got to the top and laid them on the roof.

"Fucker," I said. Ethan sniffed an acknowledgment but quickly reached over the edge and tried to pull up on the ladder.

"Here. Pull on that side," he said. I gripped a couple of rungs down and pulled hard. One of the brackets bent up toward us. Ethan started to push down on the ladder.

I paused for a second. "Wait, hold on," I said. "Maybe we shouldn't take it off." Ethan looked at me. "'Cause if they see it's missing, they'll know we're up here," I said.

"And you suggest?" Ethan said.

"Well, unhook it but leave it hanging," I said, thinking. I gripped the edge of the hook and tried to pry it with my hand. "We can bend the hooks up, make it look like it slipped off."

"Okay," Ethan said, trying to bend the metal.

"Shit. Aluminum," I said, pressing the edge into my fingers.

"Wait, I know." Ethan stood. He positioned the hooks on the top edge of the roof and stepped one foot onto the first rung.

"Hang on to my ass so I don't fall."

I held him under one arm and steadied my stance. He put all his weight on his leg, and the hooks bent a little, slipping toward the edge. He took his weight off and moved the hooks back into position. I held on to him again as he put more weight on the ladder. This time the aluminum flexed and slid off the edge, and Ethan dropped over the side, slamming against his chest.

"Fuck me," he said, frantically feeling for a handhold.

"I got ya," I said, grabbing under his arm. I started to pull him up.

"Hang on," he said. He let go with his left hand and reached underneath. "I'm good, just grab the ladder."

I reached over the edge. He had caught the top rung with the toe of his boot and was now hanging on to one hook with his fingers.

"Go ahead. I got it." I let him crawl up and then pulled the ladder up and set the hooks back on top again.

"Well, that worked . . . not so much," he said, rubbing his chin. I walked to the rear wall to check for anyone coming.

"Okay, fuck it," I said. "We'll just leave it hanging on the edge, and if they try to use it, it'll slip off."

Ethan stood up and brushed his chest off. "See anyone?"

"No, just a field back there."

He pointed to a rectangular metal cover in the middle of the roof. "So here it is, dude, just like I figured."

"What?"

"This leads to the area above the stage."

I bent down and put my fingers underneath the edge and lifted it up. In the sunlight I could see inside: dust-covered wooden rafters, various ropes and wires, stage props, and a few empty water bottles.

Ethan looked at me. "This is our hiding place."

We were at the far end of a large, flat roof that spanned the length of the theater. The air felt thick and hot on the surface. I began imagining it carried our voices down below, like insurgents were crouching everywhere around the base of the building, heads cocked, fixated on the roof, listening.

"I'll check the north," I mouthed, pointing.

"What?" Ethan said. I shook my head and waved him off. *Never mind.* I got as low as I could, eased up to the edge of the roof, and peered over slowly, looking down onto the playground area surrounded by the stone wall. A man in a yellowish-white dishdasha rushed through the gate, holding an AK, and walked rapidly up the hill toward the meeting room. The rookies had been pulling security right in front of the meeting room. Now that area was empty.

Someone inside a window yelled to the man with the AK. I couldn't see him, but his voice was crystal clear, echoing off the stone wall. I ducked down and waited a few seconds, then peered over again slowly. The dishdasha guy had gone inside, but moments later both men appeared, dragging a body. It was one of our guys; I saw the brown-and-beige camo, the dark glasses. And there was blood all over the face and chest area. His gloved hands dragged on the ground. I inhaled sharply like a reflex, realizing it was Jacobs or one of the rookies. But I couldn't tell exactly who it was from that distance. Ethan's vision was much better. I reached behind me and snapped my fingers. I felt him crawl up next to me.

"They got one of our guys," I whispered. "Can you tell who?" I pulled back from the edge as Ethan took my place.

"Jacobs," he said right away.

"You sure?"

Ethan kept his eyes fixed on the men. "Yeah, pretty sure."

"Fuckers," I said, louder than I wanted. I began shaking again with adrenaline. I heard something like a voice and glanced over at the ladder to check for any movement. It was nothing.

Ethan backed away from the edge. "Yeah, it's Jacobs." He blew air slowly out of his mouth, his face pointed down at the roof surface. "I recognize the Wiley X goggles."

I crawled to the ladder and checked below for insurgents. Ethan crossed over to the south wall.

"Clear," he said softly.

"Clear," I said, relaxing my volume a little. We walked to the center and sat on the roof access cover.

"Okay, so assuming we're safe up here—for now, at least—do we stay here or . . ."

"We wait," he said firmly.

I peered over the edge again and scanned the area. I could see a group gathered in the street. It looked like the same protesters from before, dressed in black, with white masks. The area at the bottom of the hill was clear, and the gate was left open. Below I could see the jungle gym. The tarp had been pulled down and was draped over the kiddie slide. I crawled back to the roof cover.

"So tell me what happened before," I said.

He paused for a second. "Not much to tell, really. Fuckers just came running up the hill, shooting. I saw Jacobs and the rookies take cover inside that meeting room."

"So was it the protesters?"

"Yeah, plus some muj-looking guys. Like the ones down there now."

"I know. That's what I was thinking, that they looked mujahideen, with the red-and-white turbans and the beards," I said.

"Twenty to thirty men. I think they started engaging from the street. Jacobs was probably pinned down inside. Then they advanced. By the time I'd taken cover on the playground, they'd topped the hill, storming the building."

"Did they see you?"

"No, but almost."

I paused for a second. "You see any of ours get hit?"

He took a deep breath and exhaled, rubbing his forehead. "Not exactly."

I wasn't going to ask him any more. At least not right then. We sat there for a few minutes, not saying anything. The image of Jacobs getting dragged away was flashing on my eyelids every time I blinked. I looked up at the sky and tried to just not close them at all. *I wonder if it'll happen again*, I thought. *This could make me go psychotic, just like before.* Not because I'd liked Jacobs, but because I hadn't. I'd thought he was a dick. And then—*poof!*—he was magically taken care of, and it was cosmically my fault. These thoughts could have started a loop through my brain any second. The only way to stop them was to stop thinking. Stop thinking and talk.

"So, dude, do we know what we're doing?" I said, turning to Ethan.

He was lying back on the roof cover, motionless. His cheeks were getting red below his sunglasses.

"Waiting it out," he mumbled.

"Right, but then what? We need a plan."

"Yeah, wait 'til dusk, then bounce the fuck outta here."

"Well, regroup first, if the others are even still alive," I said. "Fuck. No radio headsets. Who made *that* call?"

"Doesn't matter. We check the meeting room, surrounding area. If they are gone, there ain't shit we can do. We roll out, get to a rural area."

"Try to make it all the way back through the city? At night?"

Ethan tilted his face to me. "Gee, ya think?"

This was how he reacted in these situations. So used to immediately knowing the right answer, making snap decisions that were dead on, Ethan hated it when there *were* no good options, and pointing it out pissed him off to no end.

I turned my head toward the city. The buildings were illuminated in the earthy yellow of the sun, yet shadows had begun to form. I checked my cell: eighteen hundred. We had a couple more hours to wait. I checked the sides again, then rested my chin on the edge and listened. Nothing but the sound of a barn swallow perched on the wall behind the building. A few minutes later I rolled over and felt something in my leg pocket. I reached inside and pulled it out. It was the phone I'd used to call my dad.

"Well, ho-lee shit," I said as Ethan turned toward me. "Tuy's SAT phone."

"Are you serious? We can probably call the FOB on that bitch."

I pushed power. "Yeah. That crazy fucker. I can't believe he didn't even miss this."

"If we can reach someone, we can call for an evac."

I thought about it for a few seconds. "So . . . okay, we'd have to make the phone call short. Plus, we can't give away our location."

"Dude, they're not like the NSA, wiretapping us and triangulating our position."

"Fuck, dude, I don't know. Just to be careful."

Ethan took the phone and studied the display. "Well, reception sucks, of course. But at least there's a bar or two."

"Power?"

"Yeah, we're good there."

"Hey, wait a second. Maybe Tuy called some guy on the FOB. Give me that thing." I scrolled through the calls made. All appeared to be stateside. I kept pressing rapidly and went back too far, and the numbers looped around.

"Shit. Must've been deleted."

I went through them again, a bit slower. Then I went through other categories.

"Check incoming calls," Ethan said.

"Did that already . . . wait, let me see one more thing." I went to the messages.

"Man, he was a texting motherfucker," I said, scrolling through. I finally came upon an outgoing text with a label instead of a long international number. The label was simply "me."

I laughed. "What the fuck? Who stores a number and calls it 'me'?" I showed Ethan.

"964. That's Iraq," he said. "He must have gotten an Iraqi cell phone."

I looked at the sun again. "Good. We should go ahead and make the call so they have time to get here before dark."

I pushed call and watched while it attempted to connect. It felt strange, the concept—out in the middle of nowhere, and in a war, yet only a few buttons away from talking to anyone on base. Or anywhere, actually. I could have called home and said, "Hey, Mom, me and Ethan just on a rooftop waiting for the muj-looking guys with AK-47s to go away, so I had a few minutes."

The first thing I heard was a huge, long, extended burp, then "Yeah?" I recognized the voice right away.

"Tuy? Is this Tuy?"

"Well, you dialed 'me,' didn't you?" He let out the same giggle as before, the sinister SpongeBob. I heard other noises in the background, like a TV playing and people interrupting him, telling him to lift his arm. It was so off the wall I couldn't help but smile. Except this was pretty damned serious, so I tried to get his attention. "Tuy, this is—"

"'Sup, Forrest? You enjoying my phone? Kicks ass, doesn't it?"

"Yeah, look, I need your help. We need an emergency evac. We were on a village assessment and came under attack. Now we're—"

His tone instantly changed. "You serious?"

"Uh, yeah, we're stuck on top of a—"

"Don't tell me over the phone. I don't need to know anyway," he said. I was a little stunned.

"Right, can you get in touch with—"

"No, listen. Who's the CO for the mission you are on? That's all I need to know."

"Jacobs. Lieutenant Karl Jacobs. It was a village assessment," I said.

"I'll call you back in ten minutes. Turn the phone off 'til then."

"Okay, so . . ." I hesitated, trying to think what else I needed to relay to him. But he'd already hung up. I pulled the phone away from my ear and glared at Ethan. "Fucker hangs up!"

"What's the deal?"

"He's gonna track down our location and call back in ten minutes." I pushed the power button.

"Yeah, he's right. No sense using up batteries."

I put the phone in my pocket and lay back on the roof cover again. The metal surface was almost too warm against my back. I felt grains of sand caught in my shirt pressing against me. Warm, gritty, salty dried sweat. But I was so tired, I didn't care. A minute later I felt myself drifting toward sleep.

"I just need five minutes, that's all. You got phone duty?"

"Yeah," Ethan said. "I'll wake you for the call."

W hen Tuy called back, I was dead to the world. Ethan had taken the phone out of my pocket. I woke to the grayish outline of him sitting on the corner of the roof cover, whispering simple yes or no answers. I wasn't sure how long I'd been out. Seemed like over an hour. I crouched and made my way around the perimeter, trying to adjust to the light level. The drone of sunset prayers seemed to echo from all sides of the building. The front of the school was clear. The shops across the street were all closed, except one. Two or three men stood outside smoking, watching a mini TV through the store window. The playground and other buildings looked empty. I checked the rear of the building, which was darker still. I had to prop my chin on the edge and stare for a minute before I could make out anything. I got up and moved to the rear near the ladder just as Ethan got off the phone. Then I heard it.

Something shutting, like a car door. Plus a voice, or voices—at least that's what I thought. Whispers, maybe. I froze, turning wide-eyed to Ethan as he snapped the antenna down. I knelt down and crawled toward the edge near the back corner, holding my rifle. I hadn't thought about how the black roof would be an issue at night. It wasn't exactly littered with debris, but I remembered seeing metal clips and small nails here and there. *Jesus, don't let me hit one of those*, I thought, watching the weight I put on my knees. I got up to the edge and began to peer over but froze again. I heard footsteps directly below, coming around the corner from the back. Faint voices, speaking Arabic. A soft beep sounded from the phone as Ethan powered it off. I jerked my head around at him. *Holy fucking shit, dude!* He stared back at me as if to say, "I know, I know."

I turned back and looked over the roof's edge, at the treetops in the background, trying to picture the men. I heard the crunch of footsteps in gravel, so they had probably stopped in front of the ladder. I held my breath to hear better, feeling my body wobble with my pulse. I tried to tell by the frequencies whether they were looking up at the roof as they spoke. Maybe I could glance down there. No, not yet. I sensed Ethan approaching behind me, crawling in slow motion like a sloth. Then voices again, this time much clearer.

I turned to Ethan and held out two fingers. He pulled in close and cupped his hand on my ear. "See any lights?"

"What?" I mouthed.

"Do they have flashlights?"

I shook my head. He was probably hinting that it was safe to peer over if they didn't. I had a vision of me peeking over the edge of the roof and suddenly getting lit up with a big prison spotlight as I stared down at the insurgents. Like something out of *The Three Stooges*—me smiling sheepishly and waving absently with my fingers. I caught myself on that thought. *How the hell can I think of that shit at a time like this?* I gripped my weapon and leaned my head over the edge. Slowly.

The men below actually did have a light, but just a small lantern, which ended up being a good thing. When I looked down, one of them was holding it up to light his cigarette. I could make out his dark beard, his ragged collar, and a red-and-white-checked keffiyeh. He replaced the glass case and handed it to the other man, who was holding two AKs. I noticed how out of shape they were, especially the older one. His belly jutted out of his button-down shirt. He looked very out of place, in a way. But with the weapons there was no question. He wasn't one of those fat guys I'd seen sitting outside a shop in Baghdad, drinking chai and watching soccer, bursting out in celebratory excitement at every goal. His features lit up as he held the flame to his cigarette. No, this was the face of a man whose little daughter had probably died for no reason whatsoever, except she had practiced hard and was chosen for a part in the school play. Maybe it was their only child, and now there was nothing. The wife would be at home, sitting in a window, staring out at emptiness through a sheer curtain, knowing her husband had lost his mind and made a phone call: he didn't care about his life anymore, and he wanted to kill the Americans.

Ethan came up next to me and peered over, barely enough to see. We stayed in that position, watching the men like two cats, motionless, vigilant. They smoked and talked in serious tones, leaning against their rifles and pointing to places around the school.

I t was daybreak by the time they finally left. Ethan and I had taken turns napping, lying on our sides on the roof next to the one keeping watch. We were paranoid of making even the slightest snoring sound, so whoever wasn't sleeping made sure the other kept his head elevated and didn't roll over.

I was on watch, just feeling myself drift off into microsleep, when one of the men made a sound, standing up to stretch and brush himself off. He exchanged a few words with the other one, and they walked back to their vehicles. I nudged Ethan and looked out over the mosque, dimly lit by the sun coming up over the ridge behind us. A single bird began chirping with long pauses in between. I heard the men's car doors slam and the engines roar to a start. Ethan crawled over and watched as the men drove off. We stood up and checked the perimeter. The area around the school seemed safe.

"Jesus, I thought those fuckers would never leave," Ethan said, pulling the phone out of his pocket.

"Yeah, give Tuy a call, see what he found out."

"Prob'ly have missed calls," he said, powering the phone on.

He pressed a button and then held the phone to his ear. He listened for several seconds, then looked at me with surprise. "They're coming. They sent a helo for us."

"Holy shit!" I exclaimed, trying to keep my voice down. I held out my arm. Ethan met mine to do a fist bump as he pushed a button to listen to the next message. He suddenly looked at the face of the phone.

"Fuck! What time is it?" He paused the playback to look. "Oh, great, they tried to call us to get—"

"What's happening?" I said.

"Shh." He fumbled for the volume buttons and continued listening. He quickly rattled off some numbers: "One, nine, six, seven— remember that." He began dialing. "Four, seven, plus one, nine . . ."

"Six, seven," I said.

"Six, seven," he echoed. He held the phone to his ear. "So they sent the helo to the village. ETA was oh five hundred, but they needed our exact location."

"What time is it now?" I asked.

"Like fucking six, almost."

I looked out toward the village. Not like I knew they'd be coming from that direction, but that was where we had walked into the city, and to my mind that meant our way out.

"Hello? Yeah, this is Specialist Coffelt, Second Platoon, Bravo Company, Second of the Tenth . . . Yeah . . . Roger . . . Roger that, just west of there, I think. Do you know the grammar school we were sent to? . . . Right, that's the one."

He listened for a minute, nodding his head.

"Just the two of us, far as we know. No confirmed casualties. Insurgents took one of ours. Two, no, three more are missing . . . Yeah, our CO, Lieutenant Jacobs . . . Roger . . . Roger that."

Ethan ended the call. "Okay, so here's the deal: they got delayed, they're en route now, ETA less than thirty minutes. Coming from the northeast."

My first thought was *Thank fucking God.* But it wasn't that simple. "So what about Jacobs, the rooks. We can't leave 'em."

"Yeah," Ethan said, rubbing his forehead, "they sounded like they're working on an action plan. Not sure what it will be, though."

I walked to the north edge and peered down at the jungle gym. "If they're planning a *Saving Private Ryan*, we should check our weps, be ready for some action when they get here."

Ethan exhaled loudly. "Yeah, good call."

He bent down to lift the roof cover.

"Hang on," I said softly, holding out my hand. I turned toward the ladder. "I heard something."

I knelt down again and crawled to the edge of the roof, trying to locate the sound before peering over. But that was it. I waited but couldn't hear anything, just the bird again. For those few seconds I thought maybe it had been from farther away, sound that had somehow traveled. Maybe women talking on their patios a few blocks away. I slowly began peering over, when the hooks of the ladder made a nasty grinding sound next to my ear.

I turned to Ethan, thinking how petrified I must look. He pointed to the roof cover. *Fuck*, I thought, *we didn't plan out what to do if someone started up the ladder.* My face became flushed as the thought made my panic worse. I held out my index finger. *Wait, let's be sure they're really trying to get up here.* He seemed to understand. The metal scraped again on the cement, like it was being positioned. Then the bracket flexed as someone put their weight on the ladder. Ethan was crawling toward me. I stared at the ends of the hooks, watching them flex, bouncing slightly. *Yeah, those are steps. They're coming up here.* My next thought was that I needed to look down there sooner rather than later. See if they have weapons. See how many. See the faces of the men who wanted to end my life. But it wasn't needed. Next thing I knew, a whisper emanated from just below us—one I not only recognized but one that was calling out to us, speaking English.

"Hey, it is me, Bob," a voice said in an Arabic accent, "and the little girl."

I turned to see Ethan had already stood up. He peered over the edge. "Holy shit, it's the terp!"

The interpreter ascended the rest of the ladder and crawled onto the roof, brushing himself off. I held the top of the ladder steady while the little girl climbed up. She came bounding up the rungs as if it were routine.

"Jesus, where were you, we've . . . ," Ethan said, smiling.

"Yes. They came with weapons . . . we saw this, Jacobs and I. So we were starting to go to hide. But Jacobs was still at the window, so was hit by bullets. I ran, and they did not see me. And so I just was hiding . . . for a very long time, hiding."

Ethan glanced at the girl and back to the terp. "So . . . she told you where we were?"

"Yes, she came and find me. Very smart. Yes, very brave," he said, smiling down at the little girl.

I stepped toward her. "Hell yeah, she is! Saved our frickin' lives." I bent down to be at her level. "You," I said, pointing to her, "are a little savior," and gave her a hug.

"Gimme some skin, little savior," Ethan said to her, holding his hand out. She slapped him five. Ethan turned back to us. "Okay, how about the others? Do you know where they are?"

Bob stared blankly at Ethan for several seconds. His beard quivered around his lip. Finally he inhaled sharply. "It wasn't good for them . . . they . . . Jacobs was—"

"I know, we saw them from up here," Ethan said, cutting him off.

I chimed in too. "Yeah, they took him, kidnapping, probably." I was trying to ease the poor guy's discomfort. He seemed very disturbed.

He lowered his head and shook it back and forth. "No, no, no. Not kidnapping. Jacobs . . ." He looked up at Ethan. "He is not okay. No one are okay."

Ethan looked at him sternly. "So they're all casualties?"

It took a second for him to confirm, but I saw his face and knew that he knew and that there was no question. Finally he nodded.

The little girl was staring up at us as if she were putting it together just from our expressions and tone of voice. I noticed she had a backpack on. Looked like she was ready for school. *School where?* I thought. I put my hand on her shoulder, bending down. "Hey, where are the men with the . . . guns?" I looked up at Bob to prompt him to interpret.

"*Wain il musallahin?*" he asked her.

"*Rahu,*" she said, "*rahu ila el mosjud.*"

"Gone, she says. Gone to the mosque. Probably where they have a meeting."

"How do you know?" I asked her. "Did you hear them say that? Which mosque?"

Bob translated my question.

"*Ila el madina. Ana samiatohom,*" she replied.

"In the city, she heard them say," he said.

"Ask her if she could show us where it is," Ethan said.

Bob exchanged a few quick phrases with the girl and then turned to us. "No, I won't."

"Excuse me?" I said. "Did she say no, she *can't* or no, she *won't*?"

He asked her. She seemed to answer in one word without thinking. He turned to Ethan. "The word she used translates to 'won't.'"

Ethan's demeanor changed quickly. He reached into his biceps pocket and took out the phone. "We'll just have to fucking see about that, you little shit."

He punched redial and held the phone to his ear, turning away from us. I heard him relaying our new situation and that we might have some intel on where the rest of them were located. He talked for a few minutes, pacing up and down the south edge of the roof. Then he ended the call and walked over to me.

"Okay, here is the deal. It's just after six. They'll be here in about half an hour. When they arrive, we're going to be taking the little girl so she can show us where the insurgents are."

"Uh, okay," I said, "and if she doesn't want to fly in a helo 'cause it's loud and scary as shit and has Amreekees with guns?"

"We fucking make her," he said, glancing quickly at the little girl. She stared at him, frowning, like she was straining to understand. Ethan walked away from us. I figured his idea was not to tell her until the last minute. Just grab her and go. I pictured her screaming bloody murder, kicking and clawing while four soldiers tried to get her on board. She looked up at me inquisitively.

"You bring your little pipe?"

She smiled at me. Bob wasn't paying attention, so he didn't translate. I looked out over the city, which was still mostly in darkness but with a faint blue light growing behind it. The helo would be flying in low, lights off, using night vision. *Thank God*, I thought, *thank God they're finally coming for us.* For a second it felt great, like the end of a horrible nightmare, except it wasn't the end at all. We were about to go after the fuckers who killed Jacobs and the rooks 'cause we shot a Hellfire into their school—which wasn't even us, it was a fucking drone—but we'd kill those fuckers, maybe. Or maybe not. Maybe one or two would survive, and then they'd regroup, recruit, and next month hit us with an IED. I knew what it was. Fucking *Groundhog Day*.

I walked over to Ethan. He was checking for text messages.

"I'll do another perimeter check," I said.

"Okay."

I'd gotten used to us being well hidden in the dark, and now the area around us was starting to get too visible. I went back to crawling up to the edges and peering over. Bob and the little girl sat and waited on the roof cover. I leaned over Ethan to check the time on the phone, then crawled to another side and scanned. It was the longest thirty minutes. But finally they came.

"Praise Jebus!" Ethan said. I looked up at him.

He was pointing out over the city. The helo was approaching from over the minaret. I could see the dark exhaust swirling off the back. I could hear the low-pitched flutter of the rotors. I smiled and watched it come toward us. As it got closer it looked like an insect—bulging windshields, one on each side; big, rounded nose with no mouth.

"Oh, fucking great!" Ethan said. I turned to him. He had a huge grin. "A Black Hawk. They send a fucking Black Hawk to rescue us?"

I chuckled. "Hey, don't worry, Mogadishu happened already . . . and we all know history never repeats itself," I said, all smart-ass.

He laughed. We stood there for a few seconds, almost unbelieving, as if to be sure it really was happening—we really were being rescued.

"Hey, that's not even a UH-60," he said. I noticed the bubble-style glass canopy, the tiny landing skids, and the simple T-shaped tail. And there was a pair of feet dangling off one side, just above the skids.

"Holy shit, that's one of those MH-6 Little Birds."

"Yeah, I think so," he said. As the forms became more defined, I could see the soldier hanging off the side, sitting on a kind of metal bench. No seat belts, no straps, nothing—nonchalantly gripping a support bar in one hand and his rifle in the other.

As the helicopter descended over the school grounds, we cleared away from the landing area. I grabbed the little girl's hand and ducked down behind the roof cover, covering her ears and face as the flutter of the engine got louder and sand began blowing to the sides. We waited as the pilot touched down on the roof surface and reduced power. The guy who was perched on the bench hopped off and stepped toward me, motioning us over. I put an arm around the little girl and guided her, ducking under the rotors. She seemed nervous but not resistant at all. The soldier tapped her head and pointed to the compartment behind the pilot and copilot. I lifted her with one arm, stepping up on the landing skid, then saw what little there was back there.

"No seats?" I shouted.

"What?" he yelled back.

"She's got to be strapped in!"

He shook his head. "Not needed," he said, and circled around to the other side. There were no doors, just simple cutouts in the skin of the aircraft. I stooped down and put her inside. She just held on, shielding her face from the debris, until I set her down in the compartment. There was what looked like a rappelling rope tucked halfway under the seat, so I scooted it back and formed it into a makeshift seat for her. Then I sat down on the bench outside the opening, assuring her I'd stay right there, close, that she was safe inside. Ethan sat down next to me, to the rear. The soldier and the interpreter took seats on the opposite bench on the port side of the helo. I motioned to the little girl and pointed to the terp, showing her that between him and me, there was no way she could fall out. The engine revved to full throttle, and we lifted off the roof, doors wide open. The little girl slapped her hands over her ears and clenched her teeth. I smiled. The noise was hardly deafening, but I imagined for her it wasn't too fun. I looked down at the theater building as we rose above the school grounds. As we rotated slowly I strained my neck to catch a glimpse of the entire area below.

Ethan elbowed me, pointing at the gash in the side of the theater. The tarp had been pulled down and now revealed the extent of the missile blast.

"Goddamn," I said, shaking my head. I thought about the school kids, seeing them standing there all solemn and polite, telling their stories. I remembered the trauma I saw in their faces. Not just from the explosion, the schoolmates who got killed, but from what had happened to the school itself. It was obvious that for whatever reason, they really, truly liked school. It was important to them. Not like back home, parents yelling, "Wake up, you're late again." They really cared about it.

I looked back at the girl. She was staring up at me pathetically, almost asking me to reassure her she was safe. I grabbed her little hand between my thumb and two fingers and squeezed.

I looked down, beyond my boots dangling above the landing skids. The roofs and terraces of the beige and brown houses passed underneath. I caught a glimpse of an old woman as she looked up at us, holding a basket of clothes. A few houses passed. A yapper dog was going crazy on an outside patio, barking at something. Smoke rose from a street vendor's open grill.

The copilot turned around to Ethan and me. "We'll keep it fast and low to the river," he said, yelling above the whine of the rotors. The soldier and the terp on the other side shifted their bodies around to check on the little girl. She sat there with her feet propped against the two seat backs, her arms bracing herself on either side.

I tapped the copilot's shoulder. "So where we headed? Since we gotta get intel from the girl first?"

"FOB Scania!" he said. "There we'll switch to a bigger helo. Black Hawk. More firepower."

"Gotcha," I said, turning to Ethan.

He rolled his eyes sarcastically. "Black Hawk. Just fucking great."

"Plus, we'll want to pick up more troops," the copilot added.

"Okay."

"So that little girl, she can give us a target?"

"Yeah. Supposed to, anyways," I said. He nodded.

I felt my body press down into the bench as the helicopter banked to the left.

"Jesus!" Ethan snapped, tightening his grip. "A little warning, people?"

Out the left side I could see we were leaving the town. What had been houses and streets scrolling by below us were now fields and groves of trees. The helicopter leveled off slowly. I looked around and saw we had reached the river. The banks rose just above the water and were lined with reeds and tall grass. I figured it was about forty meters wide. In some spots streaks of oil ran along the surface, contrasting with its light-beige hue.

"Tigris River," the copilot shouted back to us.

Ethan gave me an exaggerated confused look. "*This* is the cradle of civilization?"

I laughed. "Mesopotamia, baby—the *real* Bible Belt! Now, is this worth occupying, or what?"

The pilot banked to the right and left, obviously trying to show off a bit, making turns that weren't really needed. The copilot let out a few whoops, like it was the Grand Canyon whirlwind tour or something, looking back at us for validation. Ethan and I smiled politely. *Really?* I thought. *A muddy, oily piece-of-shit river lined with dirty weeds, running through the desert?* And we weren't even going that fast.

We passed over a fisherman standing up in his motorboat in a black skirt, dragging in a net. In the distance, along the horizon, huge plumes of smoke rose into the air. I motioned to Ethan and pointed.

"Oil pipelines," he said.

"Yeah."

I strained my eyes and could make out small areas of bright orange in the center. From command I knew this to be sabotage by rebels, but of course "rebels" could mean anything. "Hey, so what did gas cost before Saddam?"

He raised his eyebrows. "In Iraq? Like a nickel a gallon!"

"Really."

I turned around to check on the little girl. The terp and the other guy were leaning over, trying to talk to her. She had her hand cupped to her ear and was grimacing. The terp said something, and she shook her head. He leaned in closer and yelled in her ear. She shook her head again. This continued as I watched for a minute. Since I couldn't hear much and it was in Arabic anyway, I turned back around. Besides, they knew what they needed; they didn't need any help from me. I did feel a little protective of the little girl, getting essentially abducted and thrown onto a helicopter, then drilled with questions. But I figured it was pretty harmless; they were just asking her where some men were.

Turned out I was very wrong.

I looked out across the river for a while at the small inlets and tributaries, the tall reeds along the shoreline, the cranes and egrets taking off from the marshy areas. It was almost hypnotic, with the whine of the rotors and the pilot's swaying us back and forth. I relaxed my grip on the support bar slightly, my other hand planted flat on the bench. I looked straight down and watched the tops of trees pass underneath us. Ethan nudged my shoulder and pointed up ahead. We were approaching a small town, or at least what looked like small apartment buildings along the river. It didn't take any time at all to get up to them. We swerved to the east, following a bend in the river and putting the glaring sun exactly in our eyes, then swooped back left, away from the sun, and the buildings were right there.

What happened next was something so bizarre and out of context, I initially rejected it; there was no way it was real. Out of nowhere came an ear-splitting sound, accompanied by the helo being jolted violently. It was like a sound bite of an explosion, except sped up twenty times. I turned toward the cabin to check the pilots' reactions, but as I did I saw the girl over me. She had somehow managed to stand up, had grabbed the back of the copilot's seat, pulling herself sideways to stick her head out the doorway, and was leaning over my shoulder to try to see something behind the helo.

In that split second my mind could not justify this. Something had just happened, yet she was already investigating it. It was immediately disorienting. Meanwhile, I had an overwhelming sensation like vertigo; I felt weightless, and my body seemed sluggish. I tried to adjust my position so I could free up a hand to grasp the little girl. But as I rotated around and tried to move my hand to another position, I felt myself going even slower. It was the most bizarre thing. I was turning my body, same as I always did, but the effect was different. Everything became drawn out, protracted. My head, arms, legs. Decelerating, as if floating through space. The cuffs of my shirt flapped gently against my wrists. Ethan's mouth was opening; a drop of saliva clinging to his upper lip stretched, bent in an arc, and drifted off behind us. The background below us swept past like a ceiling fan on low speed.

In a way, I knew things were occurring normally, and I wanted to believe my mind was just fucking with me; yet at the same time it was so convincing, so real. I was observing a world moving in slow motion—expanded, pulled, stretched out. Not slow-mo like in the movies, where everything is being played back at one-eighth speed. Vin Diesel reaching his hand out, yelling, "Nnnnoooooooo!" in a deep baritone. It was about my awareness, like there was a huge difference in sharpness. My mind was spun up, had instantly doubled its processing speed or something; I was recording faster, taking in tons of data. Like a high-speed camera.

So as I continued to rotate, trying to reach out to Abeer, something to my right caught my eye, below and to the rear of the helo. It was a small green tube with a black bulb, streaking past us, ejecting a thin, gray stream of smoke. It looked like one of those ergo pens with a gel grip on the front. And I could clearly see the tube rotate, even the lettering. Flat metal fins spun around in the rear, bent back from the air resistance. And I knew what it was. *Missile. Oh, thank God, it's going past us*, I thought, when a piercing sound registered in my ear. It was the little girl, screaming right next to me. The frequency of her voice was so shrill, it was like the ringing after a flash bang goes off. And I realized it had been there all along. It had been part of the same moment things had switched to slow motion.

When I had fully rotated my body around, I could see the girl was moving back into the cabin. Strangely, she moved fluidly, not quite at normal speed but like half speed. Her actions were methodical, unhurried.

All the while, the helicopter slid through the air, puttering like a blimp over the top of the apartment building below us. Abeer leaned over the seats to the pilot and copilot, feeling around on their bodies, looking for something. She bent down, ran her hand underneath the copilot's seat, stood up, walked over, peered over my shoulder again, looked back past Ethan. She pulled herself up again to look over my shoulder toward the missile. Her face was right in front of me, with little emotion. She glanced at me clinically—no puzzlement at all, as if people around her moved like molasses all the time. As she looked past me in the direction of the missile, her eyes moved around, scanning the sky. Then they stopped, squinting, and finally opened wide. Another piercing scream erupted from her mouth. She looked at me desperately, yelling something at me. But it was nothing but shrill high frequencies. She pushed on my shoulder for a few seconds, putting her entire body into it, but my body barely moved. It slowly drifted away from her. She reached over me, trying to push on Ethan, away from the helo. *What the hell? Is she trying to push us off the bench, to fall to our deaths?* She couldn't get a good grip on Ethan's ACU, so she stopped trying and turned around to the cabin. She looked around, took a step toward the terp—whose hand was extended, inching toward her animatronically—and felt around on his clothes, not finding what she needed. She then knelt down and grabbed the rope she'd been sitting on. She uncoiled the rope in front of her face, trying to measure its length. She held one end against my shoulder and pushed the rest across the cabin. It twisted and floated slowly in the air. It reminded me of videos of astronauts doing experiments on the space shuttle.

The next instant the entire scene was engulfed in a blinding light, just for a split second—the little girl, the cabin of the helicopter, the sky in the background, everything—washed out in a yellowish-white flash. But it was weird. I could also see through every object, as if their forms were negatives or images on an x-ray. And then it was gone, but I now heard a low rumbling tone with a wavering frequency, growing louder. The little girl rushed over to me on her tiptoes, looking behind me again. Her mouth opened; more piercing screams.

She turned back to the coil of rope that was still falling toward the floorboard, and snatched it out of the air. She took one end and threaded it underneath one shoulder strap of my ACU vest. I wanted to turn my head, but I might as well have been under a hundred feet of water, trying to react. I could feel her pull the rope across the back of my neck and feed it through the strap on the other side. She then pulled the end through and tied a knot in the rope halfway between each shoulder strap, almost like a leash.

She turned to Ethan, who had barely moved toward her. His expression was the same. She fed the rope through her hands and it floated in space again, out away from the helo. She found the other end and made the same type of leash on Ethan's vest. My hand had reached my collar by this time, but I knew it would take forever to undo. At one point she noticed this and quickly took my wrist and pulled with all her weight to move it down to my side.

As she finished up with Ethan, I looked past her and below the helo and noticed we had turned sideways. The force was strange, like

I felt my insides inching their way to one side ever so subtly. The little girl turned around, rushed up between the cockpit seats again, and came back. She then paused, looking at me for a long moment. Her eyes were wide and distressed. Her nostrils flared as she took quick, deep breaths. She held out her index finger as if asking me to wait a second, then turned around to the cabin, knelt down at her backpack, and unzipped one of the pockets. She reached in and pulled out an empty DVD case. Then she felt around some of the other pockets and finally turned the backpack upside down. Things spilled out slowly and spun around their axis—little pieces of orange candy, pens with erasers shaped like hearts, colorful plastic jewelry. A shiny, unlabeled DVD flipped head over heels and hit the back of the pilot's seat. She reached both hands out delicately with palms open and clamped the disc between them. My hands were around the rope again in a futile attempt to untie it. She came back to me and pushed my wrists down again. But this time she looked at me, holding the DVD in front of my face, and then pointed at me, looking into my eyes. She opened her mouth to say something, but shrieking came out. She seemed to catch herself and tried again, slowing it down as much as she could. It still sounded high pitched, but at least I could hear something intelligible. Whatever it was it didn't sound Arabic. "*Le sabre*," maybe? She pointed to the DVD and back at me and said it again, even slower. *Oh*, I thought, *that's what she's saying: "Little savior."*

She then leaned over my shoulder and riffled through my vest, opening up magazine pouches and trying to fit the DVD inside. She looked behind her and turned to me again, feeling my shirt and the pockets of my pants. She finally stuck her hand down the front of my vest, felt around, and opened the Velcro of the map pouch. She took her other hand with the DVD, slipped the disc inside, and closed the pouch back up. She pulled at the rope and found the spot halfway between Ethan and me. She looped it around her waist several times, making sure there were equal lengths from her to me and to Ethan. She pointed to my combat vest, looking in my eyes, and said, "Savior" one last time. Then she threw her arms around my neck and squeezed hard. And with that, she stood on the edge of the bench like an Olympic diver, clenched her eyes shut, and jumped.

I watched as her body fell away from us, descending toward the water—hair flowing, arms extended, little legs making back-and-forth motions as if she were running through the air. The rope followed her, rapidly uncoiling from where it had gathered between Ethan and me. I saw the surface of the river scrolling past as her figure fell away, getting smaller. For a second it seemed she was just about to strike the water, but then I saw the last part of the rope fly past my head and go taut against my jacket, and my upper body was jolted forward. I slid off the bench and rolled slowly, falling, then into a nosedive. I could see Ethan in my periphery, his arms flailing as he rotated forward. I could see the little girl's body below, yanked upward like a rag doll, spinning around the axis of her waist, the rope going slack, then tightening again as she fell back toward the water.

I continued to rotate, and as I flipped completely over I saw a glimpse of the helo; then a bright flash of light engulfed it as a second RPG struck just below the engine on the side. I felt a wave of sound come at me, increasing in frequency, growing louder and louder until it stung my eardrums. Then I was flipped over again, and I saw the little girl had hit the water, and again I was jerked down and back away from the explosion. Ethan was ahead of me now, somehow lower. I could see the bottom of his boots as they rotated around. A wave of heat rushed over me from the back, seeming to double in intensity, until I felt the back of my neck flash-burn, like someone had pressed down on it with a hot iron. I flipped over again and felt it on my pant legs, even through my boots. Only when I rotated around again for the last time did it stop. I hardly had time to see anything as I plunged headfirst into the water. I remember the coolness, the relief, but also the surge of pressure as my head was slapped violently, snapped forward by the impact, and then it all went dark.

I am not sure what age I was the first time I had to go to the hospital. I did a lot of crazy shit growing up: running around barefoot all day and stepping on broken glass, doing insane jumps on my skateboard and splitting my elbow open, and of course plowing into that SUV while riding my bicycle.

Probably when I was in first grade. We had a miniature merry-go-round my sister and I called the Forty because that number sounded huge to us. It was a little metal contraption with four seats facing the center axis. You sat and rowed with your arms and legs to make it spin around. But not me, of course; instead of sitting in the seat like normal, I had to stand up and straddle two of the seats, gripping the middle frame while pumping the handles with my bare feet. The Forty would spin around wildly, its legs lurching up off the ground, while my sister did nothing but hold on for frickin' dear life.

By some miracle I actually never hurt myself riding the Forty. But I did fuck myself up pretty bad once on my way to ride it. My sister and I used to get all crazy, pumped up, maniacally insane when one of us would say something about going to ride the Forty, and we'd scream and tear out of the front door and run around to the backyard and jump on. So one time I blasted around the corner of the house, near Mom's little garden with its cement frogs and fairies. I tripped, did a serious face-plant, and busted the shit out of my eyebrow. Dad sewed me up, just like a bunch of times before. Except this time he was out of iodine solution, so he drove me down to Erlanger, carried me into the ER, scrubbed up, and did his thing. A quick four stitches over my left eye as he joked with the staff, and we were back home by dinner. But at school I got tired of answering all the people who would stare at my bandage and ask what happened, and I started interrupting them midsentence: "I tripped on a rock and fell on a rock," I'd say. "What happened to your—" "Tripped on a rock and fell on a rock." I got to where I'd rattle it off so fast, I smashed it all into one phrase: "Trippedonarock, fellonarock."

This memory must have been jolted free somehow, bubbling up from the depths of my consciousness, like the impact of my head hitting the water had sent me into la-la land and I'd woken up with my brain's clock turned back a decade. Because apparently, from what they told me, when they brought me into the combat support hospital, I was completely knocked out, nonresponsive. But then out of the blue, I started repeating, clearly, coherently, "Yeah, just trippedonarock." I was making expressions and hand motions like a kid would do. "Trippedonarock, but Dad's a doctor," I said, shrugging. "No big deal, just trippedonarock. Dad'll fix it."

Finally, as I was coming out of it and stopped babbling, I heard a voice: "Whatever they've got you on, I want double the dose." Then I heard someone giggle mischievously. I opened my eyes, but something was hanging down from my forehead—some kind of soft white material stuck to my skin. I reached up and tried to peel it up over the crust of blood above my eyebrows. This sent a nasty sharp, stinging pain into my skull.

"Ahhhh!"

"Don't fuck with it, dude," the guy said. I turned my head and opened one eye. He was next to me in a bed with metal rails, sitting up, wearing a blue hospital gown.

"You have a huge gash. I saw them bring you in, blood everywhere. Looked like the prom scene from *Carrie*."

"Uh," I mumbled, turning my head slowly to look around the room. At first the surroundings meant little to me. A room constructed of plywood and paneling, with a row of three or four beds on one side, each with unused curtain dividers; a machine on rollers, with an LED display and tubes and wires hanging off it; a TV hung above the wooden double doors. My bed was on the end, next to a window. I noticed a cubbyhole stuffed with boots and combat uniforms, and a rifle leaning against the wall. I closed my eyes again. As the guy next to me continued talking, the meaning of his words drifted in and out. Something told me it was familiar, someone I knew. It was hard to listen and think about where I was, but the frequencies were familiar. Especially the laugh. I had a disoriented sense of numbness, like my body was floating. A couple of minutes later I was fading off to sleep, feeling as if I were slowly but perpetually sinking. At one point my hearing cut out, which was a weird sensation, so I started to come back up, but then I eased to a stop and descended again. And then I was out.

I woke to the sound of a TV. A nurse was just walking in through the double doors.

"How's your new neighbor, still groggy?" she said to the guy next to me, coming around to lean over my bed.

"Dayum, girl!" he exclaimed, "what's this, Halloween, and you dressed up as Sergeant Major Hottie?"

She seemed to smile despite trying not to. "It's called 'laundry service still has my uniforms,'" she said, giving him the raised-eyebrow, nonplussed look. Everything came to me more clearly, less confusing now. Words were making sense.

"Hi, I'm Rachel," she said to me. "I'm one of the CSH nurses."

"Don't let her fool you," the guy blurted out. "It's not pronounced 'Rachel,' it's 'Ratchel,' as in 'Nurse Ratchel,'" he said, followed by more mischievous giggling.

She tried to suppress a smile again. "Okay, let's see how we look here." She began lightly dabbing places on my head. I could feel the entire top of it was wrapped in bandages. A tiny ceramic figurine dangled from her neck over my chest. She wore the same brown cotton tee they gave us but had on an olive-and-tan-patterned skirt that perfectly matched.

"Hold still, this may hurt a little," she said.

"That's what *she* said" came the voice in the bed next to me. *Wait*, I thought, *I know him*. I started to turn my head.

"Hey, you need to keep your head still, unless you're into pain."

The guy purred a lewd yum sound. "Nurse Ratchel, *I'm* into pain," he said, giggling like a motorboat again.

"Uh, that's Tuy"—she gave me a confiding look—"one of our, ahem, favorites around here." She rolled her eyes and turned to glare at him playfully.

"Yeah, riiiight," he said, then glanced at me. "You know how at hospitals they try desperately to keep patients alive? Well, with me it's the opposite."

This time she couldn't help herself. She let out a laugh, even while starting to peel the gauze from my forehead. She pressed gently on my skin, pulling slowly. A faint waft of perfume emanated from her. I liked her eyes: a sunburst of fine green lines shooting out of a small, dark center. They were iridescent, calm. I kept staring at them while she worked. At one point she noticed and looked back at me and paused for a moment. "Any headache or dizziness?" It seemed like she was just trying to say something professional.

"No," I said, still staring. I looked closer and noticed hints of brown and beige. I looked at her dark hair pinned neatly on top of her head. She turned to the table and picked up a bottle of surgical soap. She poured the red-orange liquid on a piece of gauze and cleaned the area delicately. She twisted something next to my arm. I felt coolness surge into my wrist and reached over to feel the tube with my other hand. I looked up at the bag hanging above me.

"That's a strong narcotic. For pain." She continued removing the bandage. I stared for a minute or two until the world became different.

"It's making me . . . ," I said slowly. She placed the strips in a blue hazard container. It seemed like a long delay before I heard myself say the rest of it: "Affectionate. I feel like I love everybody." I stared at her. I'd known what I was saying was totally out there, but I'd wanted to say it anyway. She smiled at me.

I heard the guy next to me mumble in an over-the-top disgusted tone, "If *that* ain't gay, I don't know what is."

"Let's let the stitched-up area breathe for a bit."

I reached up clumsily to feel the top of my head. She grabbed my wrist. "Whoa, whoa! You have to keep your hands away from it, okay? You can infect the area."

I brought my arm down and looked up at her. "How could I bust my head open falling in water?"

She shook her head and adjusted my pillow. "Look, you just need some rest. Things are probably a little fuzzy right now." She rubbed my forearm lightly. Suddenly I had no concerns but to look at her, and then I laughed at myself out loud for being such a typical guy. But two seconds later there were tears coming out of my eyes, and my nose was stinging.

"What is wrong with me?" I said, staring at her for answers.

She raised her eyebrows and pouted her lips slightly. "Oh, poor thing. It's just the morphine," she said. "Narcotics can make you—"

"Gay?" the voice from the other bed chimed in.

She shook her head. "Tuy," she scolded him.

I sniffed and squinted. I suddenly didn't feel whatever had made me upset. My mind had recognized the name and was now refocused. I looked over to the bed beside mine. An Asian guy was sitting up in bed, shirtless, looking down at a laptop propped up on his legs. *What the hell?*

"Tuy?"

He let out a long baritone burp and looked over at me.

"Dat's what they calls me!"

Someone poked their head inside the door and motioned for the nurse. She walked over to talk to them. I felt another wave of dizziness as my eyelids drooped. I just stared at her, trancelike, watching her move her hands, trying to follow their conversation. But the words flew off in different directions, away from my grasp. Eventually everything grew dark again.

I woke the next morning to the glare of sunlight coming through the window. It had already gotten uncomfortably warm. Tuy got up and walked over to shut the blinds, then disappeared into the bathroom. I heard what sounded like him moving a chair, then running a shower. Finally he emerged with a towel around his waist, just as the nurse was tapping on the door and walking in.

Tuy covered his chest with one arm. "Nurse Ratchel! I know I have a sexy body, but puh-leeeese!"

She smiled reluctantly, blushing. "Cute," she said, speeding her step. "Sorry, boys, just dropping off breakfast for you all."

She set a tray down on the over-bed table and rolled it toward me. Tuy had walked over to his cabinet and was putting his boxers on underneath his towel.

"Tuy, I'll leave this here for when you're ready. And . . . liquids. Make sure you drink *everything*," she said. At the door she glanced back at both of us. "Okay, so we all set?"

"Yes, Miss Ratchel!" Tuy said, mimicking a chorus of grade school kids.

I opened my plastic bottle of juice and began picking at the eggs. I looked over at Tuy. He was on his laptop again.

"Tuy, how'd you end up in here?"

"Burn pits," he said. He seemed matter of fact.

"Burn pits?"

"Yeah, toxic fumes. Fuck-tard contractors put them right next to our sleep trailers. Gave me insane headaches, stomach pain."

"Damn, dude, that sucks."

"No matter," he said dismissively. "They're getting a big fat lawsuit. If I end up with cancer or lung disease, I'll document every minute and post it. They'll pay for it."

I sat for a moment, thinking about his response. His tone sounded like he was refusing to be affected, like he didn't want me to think he needed sympathy.

"Hey, your buddy stopped by," he said, changing the subject.

"Who?"

"That guy from the party? H.I. from *Raising Arizona*," he said.

"Ethan? He stopped by?"

"Yeah. You were sleeping. They told him come back."

"So he wasn't admitted?"

Tuy gave me a look. "Uh, whatchu talkin' 'bout, Willis?"

"To the hospital. He didn't have any injuries?"

"Eh, looked perfectly fine to me," he said.

"Oh," I said finally. "Well, damn. He's lucky." *Wow*, I thought. *I get my head busted open, and he walks away, not a scratch.*

My head was throbbing and stung in places. I reached up and felt along the edge of the incision, moving lightly over the tender, puffy skin where they'd shaved my hair.

"Fuck," I said, wincing.

Tuy looked up from his laptop and saw what I was doing. "Okay, idiot, just let me show you what it looks like." He stood up and removed a camera from a rucksack at the foot of the bed.

I put my hand down. "Okay."

He messed with the settings, then pushed record and waved it across my head for a few seconds. Then he pushed another button and took some regular pictures.

"Here," he said, showing me the playback button.

I was stunned. There was a long, narrow bald patch all the way across my skull. A purplish-red-and-black line ran down the middle, with wads of skin gathered up on each side of the thick dark-blue thread. I played the video a few times, then scrolled through the still shots. One of them was close up, and I could have counted the stitches. They went all the way across the top of my head. Tuy was back to his laptop.

"Shit, that is a huge gash," I said.

"*Sí, señor*," he said, like Speedy Gonzales. He was watching a news video or something on YouTube.

"I don't even remember hitting anything," I said.

"Pfft, 'course not, dumbass, you hit your head. That's like"—he paused for a second—"it's like saying you were recording with a microphone and took an axe to the microphone cord, and then asking why didn't it record the chopping sound."

"No shit. I know. Retrograde amnesia."

He didn't seem to even notice he'd annoyed me. He was focused back on the video.

"It's just weird, 'cause I remember landing in the water," I said, a little louder, "not on some rock or anything."

"What water?" he said, half paying attention.

"The river," I said. It seemed to take a few seconds for him to process. He finally answered absently, "You dumb fucks. Who drives a Humvee into a river?"

"No, we were in a helo," I said. He didn't answer. I turned to the window. *Weird*, I thought. *He just says shit so freely. Says and does whatever.* I looked over at him again, remembering him from before, playing poker and messing with the rookies. *It's like he doesn't have to answer to the world, or doesn't know he's supposed to.*

I felt my scalp stinging, starting to throb in places. The meds had almost worn off. I closed my eyes and tried to ignore it, focusing on the relative quiet filled only with the soft clicks of Tuy's typing. Every once in a while I could hear a bed being rushed down the hall, the hurried footsteps, the beeping of machines, the muffled tones of a doctor barking orders to support staff. I felt another cold rush of liquid in my wrist, and soon I was drifting off again, wondering about Tuy.

I had a dream that was like a Salvador Dalí—random shit was morphed together, like someone I knew, and their face was clearly them, but they were from my trip to Brazil, and there was a building falling down from an earthquake, and my boss called to tell me that because of the recent events I didn't have to come to work anymore, so just relax. I woke up hearing a loud boom that scared the shit out of me. Tuy was rushing over to the window.

"What the hell was that?"

"Mortar round. Those fuggers. Every damn day. At least two or three."

He put his face against the glass to try to see.

"Shit," I said. "How close does it get?"

"One hit the building the other day." He pointed outside. "Well, actually right out there, but still. This hospital's nothing but wood and aluminum 'n' shit. We'd be done if it hits us."

"Jesus."

Tuy let out another deep belch, walking back to his side of the room. The nurse was just coming in. Tuy smiled overly sheepishly.

"Oops, pardon my *français*," he said with a sarcastic, exaggerated accent.

She smiled and rolled her eyes. "I just came to check on you guys. They told us one shell hit the helipad; apparently there is damage."

"Where is that?" I said.

"Next building over."

"Fuck," I said. I got a weird look from Rachel, but she didn't say anything. I looked over at Tuy.

"Oooh," he said, giving me a ridiculous wince, like I'd just accidentally insulted the Queen or something. "Uh, you'll find the staff is kind of, uh . . . religious here." He snickered subtly.

I looked at Rachel. "Oh, my bad."

"That's okay. She doesn't know what *fuck* means, not 'til she's married," Tuy said, giggling.

"Tuy!" I couldn't help but laugh, though.

Rachel shook her head, smiling slightly. "Okay, so stay away from the windows until this is over," she said, and started to walk out.

"Until it's over?" I asked.

She paused. "Well, it usually lasts about an hour."

Tuy played off what I was saying. "Basically stay away from the windows until the war's over," he said.

Rachel closed the door behind her.

"We're scared, can we sleep with you?" Tuy shouted. No reply from Rachel, but he didn't care. He was already on to the next thing, rummaging through his rucksack for who knows what.

It went on like that for the next few days. Lying in bed, getting juiced up with meds, listening to Tuy banter with the hospital staff. Rachel mainly, but there were other nurses who came by here and there. One of them was bullshitting with Tuy and mentioned viruses on his laptop. Next thing you know, he's bringing it in and sitting on the bed like a student while Tuy walks him through how to fix it. He tried desperately to pay Tuy but got nowhere. Since he was from Afghanistan, Tuy told him to bring in a goat karahi recipe. "Just make sure it's good, no shitty country cooking," Tuy said.

A doctor came by to check on me, to ask about my pain, which was way better. Said he'd probably schedule me for a CT scan. I asked him casually if it was really needed, since I had no symptoms of brain injury. He gave me the quick "let *us* handle the thinking" answer, then turned around and chatted with Tuy for ten minutes.

I got word from Ethan that he was caught up doing patrols and would stop by as soon as he could. They assured me my CO knew what had happened, and I didn't need to worry about reporting in or anything else. Just rest up and get healed, they said.

I began to notice the God talk from the staff here and there. It was subtle at first, then grew more frequent and overt. A chaplain came by, rattling off some shit about how God's hand had been placed on the vehicle I was in. I listened politely, wanting to ask if God's hand was too busy working a slot machine in Vegas the day the little goat girls got smashed under truck tires. But I just told him I was not religious. Tuy made some crack about how he needed to stop giving me hope and just give me my last rites. The chaplain smiled, placed a pocket-sized Bible on the table, and left.

Another time two jumbo linebacker types came in to change the linens. First they worked silently. They lifted me up like I was nothing, and removed the sheets. But then they opened their mouths, and I couldn't believe my ears—the most effeminate, lispy voices I'd ever heard. And they were talking about when to meet for Bible study, and they hoped Levi could make it. Of course when they left, Tuy wasn't going to miss an opportunity. He looked at me straight-faced and said in his disdain voice, "There ain't no praying *that* gay away." I laughed so hard the skin on the top of my head stung.

A couple days later Rachel was leaning over me again with her figurine dangling in front of my face. Of course, I was focused on the tops of her breasts, not her dumb necklace, but when she caught me looking I blurted out some nonsense like "Where'd you get that ornament? It's really cute."

"Oh, no," she said, "this is Precious Moments." She looked down. "I got it at Jesus camp. Graduation gift from my God partner."

"Oh," I said. I wasn't about to ask her to elaborate. I rolled my eyes to myself and breathed in deeply. *Just fucking great. She's one too.* I realized she might notice my annoyance, but I didn't really care. *I go two goddamned years without sex, and this is what I get?* I thought. And just to make it more torturous, she turned around and bent over, letting her hair fall away from her neck so she could feel for the clasp of her necklace.

"This thing is a pain. It gets tangled in my hair all the time," she said. I rubbed my forehead. I almost didn't want to look at her ass. I had checked her out plenty of other times, from every angle, every chance I got. But for her to be so blatant, so naïve? *What the fuck is she doing? How could she not know?* She stood back up, holding the necklace out to me, all smiling, completely clueless.

"But I wear it every day, every single day. It's saved me. Saves me from terrorism . . . I believe that."

I held the figurine in front of me. It looked like an adorable little toddler but was dressed in armor, holding a shield and a sword. On the back was engraved "Rachel 2005—Onward Christian Soldier." I wanted to hand it right back to her but held it for the obligatory few seconds to pretend I gave two shits. She stood there like an idiot, beaming like she was letting me hold her Olympic gold medal.

"Good for you," I said, handing it back.

In the next few days Rachel and the rest of them stepped up their game, predictably, sneaky little references to Jesus turning into pointed questions. One day it was "What church do you go to?" A couple days later: "So I guess you're just a nonpracticing Christian?" And then: "Now, if you don't mind me asking, do you at least believe in God?" I'd seen this all before. Patronizing evangelism thinly veiled in curiosity. It was so obvious what they were doing. I pictured them all huddled together in the hospital break room, with their Bibles full of colored bookmark tabs, scheming what angles to work on me, who they'd send in next, what they'd say. Same exact shit I'd seen growing up on the mountain. It happened all the time, at random. I'd watch my mom stop her cart in the produce section because some lady with big poufy hair and blue eye shadow had said hello with such absurd excitement you'd think her life was finally complete now that she'd run into my mom. I'd smile and say hi. The lady seemed so friendly, I didn't know any better. But then I'd see my mom's expression and how she gave short, quick one-word responses. Barely even polite. The moment would always come when suddenly Mom would raise her eyebrows and say something like "Kitty, a person's faith is their own business." And she'd coolly pick up an apple as the lady stumbled through a response and walked away. "You have a blessed day too," Mom would say with a funny tone.

And I'd seen it later, when Joshua started asking me to his church.

He and I were inseparable in grammar school; same clothes, same music, same tennis coach at the same country club. Both our dads were big, important doctors. Joshua and I mimicked each other, talked like each other, wanted to *be* each other. But thrust in the midst of that Presbyterian congregation, I saw very quickly something . . . different. *I* was different. I could not be Joshua, 'cause I was not like them. I was not quite right. I was one of the "other" guys—the Episcopalians, the "wayward" Christians. So they'd ask me questions, questions that weren't questions. They'd act chummy and pry, try to get info on my mom. They'd pray for me, never mind I had told them already I was saved. So I didn't see their warm southern smiles with the sugary-sweet welcoming voices. All I saw was a private party, with people dressed up all perfect, and my friend Joshua inside, mingling, getting patted on the back, fitting in. So of course I joined Teen Missions with him. I went to Brazil to spread the word, to join the "better" party.

S o yeah, I totally saw it coming. When the hospital staff made their next move, I so called it I almost laughed.

"Uh, would it be okay if we said a prayer for you before you eat?"

They didn't hit me with this right off. First they'd come in, put my food tray down and pause, closing their eyes for a second and then walking away. But after they pulled this a few times, I started telling Tuy what was going to happen. I thought he'd chime in and start taking bets, or at least we could laugh at their dumb asses, but he didn't seem into it. They weren't bothering him anyway, which pissed me off even more.

One thing I did get wrong. I expected them to send Rachel in for the final kill—to work the old sex angle. I tried to impress Tuy with this prediction: "And watch, she'll fuckin' ask me to pray with her." But as it turned out, they sent in some big-ass loudmouth chaplain and her mousy sidekick.

"Good morning, how you doin'? . . . My name's Hilda. Blah blah . . ."

I glanced quickly at Tuy. He put his hand over his mouth and faked like he was unable to contain his laughter. *Smart-ass.*

"Make sho' you eat everthang now, you need that energy . . . Mind if we pray wit chu first?" she said, finally stopping her chatter.

"Knock yourselves out," I said.

She planted herself down on the poor plastic chair next to the bed and looked at me. "Now, how 'bout we just hold our hands together, sugar?" she said in full voice, reaching out to me. *Ah, here we go.*

"See, this is how *we* did thangs, growin' up. Er'body be singin', shoutin', joinin' hands. We was *all* kinds o' friendly. See, y'all folks missed out," she said with a chuckle.

I looked at her. *Oh Jesus, seriously? "Y'all folks"?*

"Now, don't worry, baby, you don't have to say nuttin'—unless, of course, you want to," she said, winking at me like she and I had some secret. Her nasty floral perfume wafted over me. I glanced at the assistant. *That other one*, I thought, *ain't she homely as a stuffed pheasant.* But just as I was about to say no thanks, she grabbed my hand, smooth as shit, turning her head to the side toward her little friend standing there like a dumbass.

"Sit on down now, Gina," she bellowed. "Come on in close and let us pray, nkay?" Her eyes closed as she tilted her head up to the ceiling with a ridiculous pained look on her face. "Dear, sweet Jesus, most heavenly fahthuh . . ."

As I sat there, eyes open, with the tips of my fingers pinched tight in their hands, I remember thinking there needed to be a new word invented for what they'd just done to me. *Look at this shit*, I thought. *I just got fucking chumped. They know full well I'm not into this religious shit. But do they care? Fuck no! Oh, look! A poor lost soul! Let's do our duty and save him. Oh, never mind he didn't ask for it. Yeah, we have all the answers, so let's just smile and talk loud and fast, and he won't even get the chance to say no. Condescending, self-serving, arrogant jerks.*

I stared out the window, motionless, feeling like a total assbag. I was completely pissed off I had let it happen, but I couldn't act like it. I didn't even look at Tuy, who I pictured had some moronic expression, all giggling at my plight. I had to play it off. Show my humiliation, and I'd look like they just played me; get offended, and I'd look like a whiny little bitch—all of which pissed me off even more. *Yep*, I thought, *there needs to be a word for this.*

When they left the room, she spouted off some more sugary bullshit. "God bless you" or something. All I could do was give them silence and hope they got the hint. Of course she had a counterattack for that too, like she probably did everything. She stopped short, patting her pockets and glancing at her sidekick. "Gina! Girl, did I forget my treats . . . *again?*" She shook her head at herself—"Hilda, Hilda, Hilda"—then turned to me. "Baby, remind me. I will make sho' I come back here, bring you a little sump'n." She continued to fish through her pockets.

I looked up from my food. "No biggie, it's okay, really."

"Oh, you just gotta try one of Hilda's famous pink divinity!"

Before I could intentionally say nothing, she pulled her hand out of her purse. "Now, here we go!" She waddled over to the bed and plopped down two of the nastiest-looking neon blobs of crap I had ever laid eyes on.

I began to wonder where Ethan was. I'd expected him to come by after a few days, and it seemed like well over a week at that point. I wasn't sure.

"How long have we been here?" I asked Tuy.

"You or me? . . . I've been here two weeks. So you, a couple of days less."

"Seems like ten weeks. So where the hell are my guys? What's the deal, they don't allow people to call into the damn hospital? This is ridiculous."

Tuy raised his eyebrows. "Dude, what are you worried about? You that anxious to get back to the war?" He sniffed out a laugh. "You *do* need a CT scan."

"No, I know, it's just . . . we got missions to do, my unit needs me, that's all."

Tuy looked at me with eyelids half closed. "Oh . . . my . . . GAWD," he said sarcastically, a one-second pause between each word.

I didn't know what he meant. "What?"

"You think you're important out there! That you're . . . vital to operations." The last part he tried to pronounce with a choppy drawl like George Bush.

"Not really," I said dismissively. "No more important than other soldiers."

But Tuy seemed to latch on to this, like he'd found something interesting to toy with and bat around. He did his little sinister giggle. "Okay, so there's what? A hundred-something thousand troops in Iraq, and as you say, they're all equally important. But somehow it actually matters you're not out there."

"Every little bit helps, dickhead."

"Uh, oookay!" he said, all sarcastic. "Hello! I think somebody's got a little Gandhi complex!" His voice was high pitched and cutesy. Sounded like a mother correcting a toddler. He opened up his laptop and started untangling some ear buds. He seemed not to give a shit whether I wanted to keep talking or not.

Oh Jesus Christ, I thought. *This again?* I wasn't about to tell him everyone kept telling me the same thing. I forced a laugh. "Gandhi complex? What the fuck's that?"

Tuy took his time. I wasn't even sure he'd heard me. He finished putting his ear buds in. "Or Jesus complex. Messiah complex. Whatever it's called."

"Pfft, I don't think I'm Jesus, dumbass."

"Doesn't have to be that you literally think you're Jesus. You just have to think you have some important high purpose, like you're destined to be here or something."

I paused for a second. He talked with such simplicity yet such matter-of-fact authority. Almost like he knew all about the subject and was dumbing it down for me.

"Well, don't we all kind of have a purpose? I mean—"

"Uh, no," he snapped back condescendingly. "Fool, how could everyone have a purpose?"

"I don't know, I mean—"

"Does someone who is comatose have one? How about . . . how about those kids born into Cambodian brothels? I saw a documentary on it. Do they have a purpose? The little girls start having sex at like eleven or twelve. They're sold as virgins to some businessman, passed around like property, end up at some brothel where they basically have the little girls as slaves. You seen it?"

"No, I haven't."

"It's pretty fucking . . ." He trailed off, stopping to click something on the screen. I waited, finding myself wanting to hear his thoughts, tactless or not. It was just nice to hear someone who'd actually pondered things that mattered in this world.

"Here it is. It's called *Holly*. Pretty fucking messed up, dude." He turned to me, looking truly, genuinely disturbed.

"Jesus, eleven years old? That is horrible," I said.

"Yeah. Sick motherfuckers."

"So . . . I don't get it. What's wrong with seeing something like that and wanting to do something about it?"

"Nothing. I just doubt that's what you're doing."

I sat up in the bed, feeling the blood rush to my neck.

"Oh, really? Well, that's *exactly* what I'm doing, dick. And by the way, so should everyone." I tapped on the plastic bedrail.

Tuy seemed amused he'd gotten to me. "Don't get your panty in a bunch. I'm just saying—"

"Pant*ies* in a bunch. Plural."

"Fine, pant-eez," he echoed back sarcastically. "Gee, how am I supposed to know you're wearing more than one?"

I tried to smile. Somehow, in his presence, getting mad just felt like it would come off as being weak.

"But no, it's all good, holmes," he said. "You're not the only one doing it. I've never seen anyone *not* do it."

"Do what?" I asked.

"Not have an ulterior motive."

I laughed impulsively. "You say 'ulterior motive' perfectly but fuck up your plurals left and right?"

He lowered his eyelids halfway at me. "Fuck plural. It's a waste of time."

I chuckled. "So anyway, what'd you mean? What ulterior motive?"

Tuy held out his hand to illustrate. He seemed to speak with such confidence and yet such apathy. "No, think about it. These Jesus freak hospital staff, for example. The only reason they do good things is to get into heaven or inherit the kingdom—how's the Bible verse go? 'I shall separate the sheep over here, goats over there,' or something?"

Sadly, I could still remember this quote verbatim. "It goes 'Before him all the nations will be gathered, and he will separate them one from another, as a shepherd separates the sheep from the goats,'" I said. "'Sheep on his right hand, but the goats on the left.'"

"Yeah, whatever," he said. "Point is, they believe Jesus says whoever does good things in life, like sees someone hungry and feeds him, sees someone naked and gives him clothes, etc., those people are the ones getting into heaven."

I added, "Plus, there's that part about 'Whatever you did for the least of my brethren, you have also done for me.'"

Tuy rolled his eyes humorously. "Well, *ob*viously. Otherwise you could just kiss up to rich guys and be an asshole to everyone else." He paused for a second. "Point is, the only reason they do good things is to get into the sheep group and make sure they're not a goat."

I nodded. "Yep, 'cause the poor goats get cast into everlasting fire . . . Hey, how come you know so much about this Christian shit? I thought you were born in Vietnam."

"Thoopid. I still lived in the US since 1995."

"Oh yeah. I guess so."

He shook his head. "Plus, Christians were in Vietnam too, dumbass."

"So you're saying it doesn't count because what? 'Cause it's for a different reason?"

"No, it's not that it doesn't count. It just can't be called doing good for others. It's not being the good Samaritan, it's the opposite. It's looking out for number one."

"Oh, so I'm selfish?"

He looked slightly annoyed. "No, idiot, not everyone has the same real reason. Yours might be selfish, might not. But I just doubt it's what you think it is."

I picked at a crease in the sheets. Someone dropped a metal bowl in the hall, and I looked up. Tuy clicked something on the laptop.

"Have you heard this song? Gorillaz. Freaking awesome!" he said, turning it up. I heard a catchy hip-hop beat with a prominent dub bass as the singer said, "Feel good" like a malfunctioning robot over and over, then started singing the verse through an electronic megaphone. I listened for a minute. He was right, it was cool as hell. Stylish, creative. Tuy started bobbing his head. Then it reached the chorus, repeating something about windmills and falling down. Very ethereal and melodic.

He looked at me playfully. "Hey, they talkin' 'bout windmills, homey. Like what's his name. It's your theme song, loooser!"

"Fucker," I said. I couldn't help but laugh out loud, although I was still thinking about what Tuy had said before. *What is it with him? If anyone else had said what he did, I'd want to kick their ass. But somehow he gets away with it.* I was actually intrigued, even. I'd met people who were blunt and insensitive. I'd known others who took absolutely nothing seriously. And I'd seen characters on TV who instantly got the big picture, solved the crime, knew the answer, and could even explain it all to you in three words or less. But I'd never seen all of these things at once. He sat cross-legged watching the video, giggling.

I raised my voice and tried to sound sarcastic. "So, Dr. Phil. Why'd *you* join up?"

"Had to," he shot back.

I waited for more, but that was it. I chuckled. "Uh, you 'had to'? What the fuck's that mean? Recruiter held a gun to your head?"

Again he responded right away, raising his eyebrows "get with the program" style. "No, 'had to' as in 'do it or face charges.'"

I burst out laughing, and it took me a second to realize he wasn't playing. "Holy cheeholies, dude," I said, still smiling. "You? What the hell, what'd you do?"

"Cybercrime. Fuckers had no valid proof either, but the judge was old. She didn't know shit about IT, much less internet security."

"Damn, so she ordered you to join the army?"

"No, they can't do that anymore. But I basically convinced her the evidence for malicious intent was weak and suggested if I could prove I was already joining the military, the charges could be dropped."

"Damn, dude . . . so . . . wow, that sucks ass. Which ended you up in this hellhole, and you were completely innocent."

"You f-tard," he snapped impatiently. "I was not completely innocent." By then I knew this about him: he didn't give two shits about you supporting his point, but he couldn't stand inaccurate statements.

"Oh, really? So what did you do? I'm just curious. I mean, you don't have to—"

"Don't be a pussy." He shook his head with a disapproving smirk. "You ain't gonna offend Chino Loco."

"Ha ha ha. Okay then, what'd you do, create a computer virus?"

"No. I kind of . . . uh, collected, shall we say, personal metadata."

"Oh, like socials?"

"Not just socials. DOBs, addresses. Mostly phone records. Shit-loads of phone records."

"Damn. I guess that's pretty serious."

"Yeah, it is if you take the data off-site, use it for personal gain, sell it—that type of shit. But I didn't do that. Basically what I did was . . . okay, it's kind of technical. I took a terabyte of data and transferred it across the internal network in little pieces which I encrypted myself. So no one's information ever left the building."

"What company was this?"

Tuy paused for effect. "Uh, if I told you, I'd have to kill you. In fact, it's so secret I have to kick your ass for asking."

I laughed. "Ha ha. Cute. So I take it this was a gub'mint agency."

"Yep, and I'm sure you could guess which one . . . but anyways. Point is, I never stole any data, the 'tards." He laughed mockingly. "Only reason they even found out I was doing it was I went to them and told them they had fucked up their records."

"Holy shit, you brought it up to them? So wait," I said, then paused. "How'd you know there was an issue?"

"So, okay, all this personal information, it's gathered from external sources—in this case, phone companies. But their code that reads it in was broken, and they didn't know how long ago it broke, so I wrote a program that figured out—using probability methods—what data was most likely bad. Which they were happy I could do for them, but problem is, I found like five hundred thousand records that were fucked up." He snickered. "I, uh, don't think they likey dat too much."

I looked up. Rachel was coming through the door.

"Oh, hot dayum!" Tuy blurted out, then gave her a mischievous look. "Here for my sponge bath already?"

Rachel smiled and rolled her eyes at me, same as before. "No, just checking on you guys. Anything I can get for you?" She swung her head around to Tuy. "Anything reasonable, that is?"

"No, we all good," Tuy said.

"Okay, well, let us know. Hey, Tuy, we're getting a blue death screen with one of the desktops. Do you think you can take a look?" Rachel bared her teeth, looking slightly guilty for asking.

Tuy burst out in laughter. "Uh, I think you mean 'blue screen of death.'" He shook his head at me, smiling, and stood up next to the bed. "She's sooo damn sexy, it almost makes up for her dumbness. Oops, I mean, uh . . . blondness."

"Hush!" Rachel said, taking Tuy's arm and guiding him out of the room.

Tuy looked over his shoulder at me. "How can I be so popular around here, yet they all want me dead?"

I laughed. Then he let one fly before he walked out. Rachel slapped his shoulder playfully. As the door closed I heard him say, "Oops, sowwy, Nurse Ratchel" in a little kid's voice. I sat for a moment, smiling. *Yeah, exactly. How is that?* I thought. *How is it you're so popular? How do you not give a flying fuck about anything or anybody, and people just flock around you like you're the damn pope?*

I reached over and grabbed the controller and turned the TV on. Stephen Colbert was on C-SPAN, speaking at a podium at some formal dinner. He was in a black tux and wearing nerdy rimless glasses, and was gesturing to President Bush at the panel table, then pointing his finger at his stomach. I unmuted it to see what he was saying. Colbert spoke in a loud, grandstanding voice, talking about what a privilege it was to celebrate the president, because they were alike; they both "got it." They weren't nerds who relied on dumb old facts, they used their guts. He turned to the president and asked, "Isn't that right, sir?"

His parched-dry deadpan delivery was just barely discernible from complete seriousness. I remembered one guy back in basic who didn't get Colbert at all. Ethan told him he was a spoof of Bill O'Reilly, and the guy almost lost it. He literally pointed at Ethan, laughing—first I thought he was kidding—and called him a typical pathetic loser desperate for some liberal comedian to compete with Fox News. "Hey, news flash, motherfucker," he sneered, "no one can touch Fox!"

Colbert waved his arm toward Bush again like an illusionist, saying how he and the president didn't need all that stuff; they didn't listen to polls, 'cause polls were nothing more than statistics that scientifically reflect what people think in reality, and as we all know, reality has a liberal bias.

I burst into laughter. "Holy shit," I said out loud. I could not believe they were letting him keep talking. I turned up the volume. I noticed how quiet the audience was, awkward giggles here and there. As C-SPAN panned around the room, people were doing that thing where they almost spit up their drink, cover their mouth, and turn to someone they know, like, "Oh my God, did he really just say that?" I listened for a minute. Colbert continued, setting up jokes like he was fawning over Bush, only to flip them around at the last second into a full-on body slam. He got more and more sarcastic and brutal, saying how great it was we knew where the president stood, because Dubya believed the same thing Wednesday he believed on Monday, no matter what happened on Tuesday.

He had just started in on Fox News, and I was laughing so hard my forehead hurt, when the screen went black, then turned to snow.

"Fucker!" I reached for the controller, going up a couple channels and back down. "Oh, come on!" I said. A few seconds later I stopped on the channel again. The picture was back, except now it was some televangelist waving a Bible around on stage at a megachurch. I sat there in shock. "Oh, you have *got* to be shitting me," I said, looking out the glass panes of the door toward the main hallway, as if any of the hospital staff could do anything. I flipped around for another minute, then turned the TV off and flung the controller to the foot of the bed. It hit the rail and tumbled to the floor. I sat there staring, watching people moving at the end of the hallway, wondering which of those fuckers cut the C-SPAN feed. I felt it, the urge to tense up, squeeze the muscles in my face as hard as I could until the blood burst and everyone knew it was the worst fucking mistake of their lives to fuck with me.

Jesus, I thought, *what the hell is wrong with me?* I rubbed my head and breathed in deeply, trying to stop my mind, not make a big deal out of it. But the fact was, just three seconds ago I had been completely okay—laughing, calm, watching TV—and just like that I had lost it, and I was well aware, and it freaked me out. I wondered about the meds they'd given me, if maybe I was having a reaction. *Maybe I should ask for Oxy*, I thought. *Yeah, OxyContin. I could use a handful of that shit right now.*

The door opened and Hilda waddled in full speed, a big smile on her face, all animated and cheery. "Now, is this a beautiful day the Lord has made? Mmm, mmm!" she said, stopping at the window to adjust the blinds. That was it for me. I just went off.

"Hey, eighty-six the Jesus shit, okay. Who's fucking with the TV channels?"

Her whole body froze; her eyes bugged out at me. "Excuuuse me?"

"The te-le-vision," I said, pointing, talking loudly and slowly. "Some-bo-dy is fuck-ing with it."

"Chile, you bes' watch yo'self!"

I still could not believe how cliché she sounded. She even had a little action with the neck moving back and forth, which had gone out like five years before.

"Watch *my*self? How 'bout you go tell them quit cutting the C-SPAN feeds, and then guess what I *will* watch? The goddamned channel I was watching!"

Well, that was the end of that exchange. She winced visibly when she heard "goddamned," and just walked out. Muttered something religious to herself on the way out, asking God to give her strength or some stupid nonsense like that. I didn't give a fuck. I was glad I'd unloaded on her. *Maybe she'll go tell her buddies, and they'll stop coming in here trying to snare me like sticky-sweet God flypaper,* I thought. I spotted the edge of the remote next to the leg of the bed. I bent forward and stretched my free arm out as far as I could without pulling the IV out of my arm, but it was just out of reach.

"Fuck me," I said.

I eased my head back on the pillow and closed my eyes. Breathing, filling my chest, exhaling. A smell wafted in from the kitchen, triggering a memory: Crazy Bread from Little Caesars, the time Dad and I got carryout right after I'd been kicked out of one of my classes for doodling a swastika. I hadn't even known what it meant. A fucking idiot at world history, I'd been guilty of that, but I'd intended no malice. But they didn't care. They dropped me from the course and gave me a failing grade. Dad didn't care, either. He took their side, told me I was a fucked-up person. "You're just like your mom," he said. I knew he was just pissed off, trying to shake sense into me, but the words had stuck with me, like a whisper of a voice in my head, because I knew what was behind it. I was too much like Mom; I was a victim, thrown in jail without a trial but ready to fight for justice. I was standing up for myself, thinking independently. This was my mom— the bleeding heart, entitlement, buck the system. Everything that was wrong with America these days.

So whenever I felt cheated, fucked over, someone had gotten the best of me, those words would whisper in my head. And every time, without fail, I would flip my dad the mental finger: *This shit's not over yet, asshole.* I'd be driving in the car and start talking aloud, acting out an imaginary trial—Father vs. Son—presenting my case to the judge, God himself. I'd picture a huge library cart overflowing with evidence—high school and college diplomas, affidavits of women who adored me, bosses' recommendations, raises and salary figures, hugely successful marriage, kids, grandkids—all spilling off the cart and onto the floor in front of the judge. And these episodes would build to a frenzy: throwing things in the car, shrieking in rage, laughing, mocking, sneering. I always won these imaginary trials, explosively, dramatically, like Tom Cruise kicking Nicholson's ass in *A Few Good Men*: "I want the truth!" "Your son's not a loser. His mom is not a loser. They'll do something important one day. Say it!"

But sitting in that hospital bed, for the first time I could remember, I was actually considering that Dad was right. I was my mom. I was a poor, pathetic dreamer with delusions of grandeur. I'd accomplished nothing. And I was my dad—nothing but rage, lashing out at anyone who got in my way. I inhaled sharply at that thought, felt my face flush and contort, and I shook uncontrollably, letting the air out. Tears ran down my face as I felt the unbearable helplessness.

"Luuuuucy, I'm home!" came a voice out of the blue—Tuy busting through the door, sporting a Puerto Rican accent.

"Took you long enough," I said, wiping my forehead with the sheet to shield my face.

"I was, ahem, a little distracted," Tuy said in a weird tone. It was enough to make me wonder what he was referring to. He walked over to the bathroom sink and held his whole head under the faucet.

"So? Did you fix it?" I said.

"What?" he said. He turned the water off and shook his head like a dog.

"Did you fix her computer?"

Rachel was walking in from the hallway just as Tuy came out of the bathroom. He looked at me with a stupid grin, biting his bottom lip. "Oh yeah! Dude, you are *not* going to believe what just happened."

"Seriously?" Rachel said, stopping to glare at Tuy.

"Ah!" he blurted out. "Dayum, girl! You scared me!"

Rachel turned to me, obviously trying to play something off. "Do you need anything or . . . anything?" she said. I could tell she knew how stupid this sounded. She blushed, then whipped around, her back toward me, facing Tuy. After a few seconds Tuy giggled. She slapped him on the shoulder much less playfully than before. Tuy was attempting, very unsuccessfully, to hold back something he apparently thought was oh-so fucking hilarious.

Of course with all this, I knew right away what was going on, especially from the dumbass look on Tuy's face. Guys only looked like that for one reason.

"Hey!" I shouted out at them. They turned to me. I motioned to each of them with my hand. "Are you fucking serious?"

Rachel turned back around and slapped Tuy again.

"Come on!" he said, full-on laughing. "It was just a little kiss!"

Then he added, "Eh, mostly." He was trying to be cute. Rachel raised her arm over his head, and Tuy shielded himself.

"Wow! I'm so glad for you both. Makes my fucking goddamned day!" I said.

They both looked at me again. Rachel reached for the door handle, mumbling some bullshit about checking on the ICU, and thanks, Tuy, for helping with the green screen.

"Blue screen!" I snapped. "It's blue screen, you know, like blue screen of fucking death?"

She pulled the door open to leave.

"Oh, and by the way, I want my fucking friend on the phone, like right fucking now," I called out.

The door swung shut behind her. Tuy was on his laptop again. He didn't say anything to me.

All I could think of was how in the fuck he'd managed to bang her. *Or whatever he got her to do. Fuck! She's a born-again Christian, for God's sake! It makes absolutely no goddamned sense that she would even . . . Jesus! Even if he just got her to make out, that's still . . . it's fucking bullshit.*

I sat there clutching the sheets until my arm hurt where the IV was stuck in me, staring at the TV I wanted back on, but of course the remote was still on the floor. Tuy clicked away on his computer, *tap, tap.* The sound of a video playing in his headphones, followed by an abbreviated snicker from Tuy. More *tap, tap.*

Fucker, I thought. I knew it was unfair for me to think this. It wasn't like he'd done anything. *Who cares? This is bullshit.* I clenched my other hand. Finally I let out a deep breath, and he must have noticed.

"So, uh, obviously you're pissed."

I hesitated for a second, thrown off by his tone. He sounded like he almost felt guilty or something. Tuy clicked pause on the laptop and tugged his headphones loose.

"Nah man," I said. "Good for you, you deflowered her. Round of applause."

"Oh God, dude, we didn't have sex. All we did was—"

"Hey, whatever, kissed her, felt her, licked her. Whatever it was, you cracked the code." I laughed sarcastically. "Hey, ya picked the lock on the old chastity belt. Bra-vo!"

He slapped the laptop shut and stuffed it in his bag. "Not exactly."

I turned to my side, moving the sheets away to face him more directly. "Come on, give us your secret. How do you do it? I mean, look, you walk around joking about everything, you don't give a flying fuck about anything or anybody, and people fall all over themselves to hang out with Tuy. You rattle off shit to women off the top of your head—most of which, by the fucking way, is kind of rude, tactless, insulting, etc.—and they sleep with you. Dude! What the fuck?"

Tuy looked at me with his classic deadpan. I wasn't sure he was planning on answering at all. And that only made it worse for me. *Always in complete goddamned control. The fucker is not fazed by anything. It's like he's fucking immune to life.*

"I think you just *think* I don't work for anything. Actually, I work harder than other people. Much harder."

That set me off. "Goddamn it! I have heard you say with my own ears you have no clue why people think you're so great. Don't give me that bullshit!"

Tuy laughed sheepishly. He knew he couldn't say shit to me.

"You fucking kill me! You don't give a goddamn about why we're here, what the fucking war is about. Hey, casualties? Who cares! Gee, maybe on the way out of the hospital we'll accidentally run over two more little girls, but, pfft, that's inconsequential in Tuy's book, isn't it?"

Without thinking I waved my right arm wildly, yanking the IV cord, which knocked the drip stand into the monitor, which started chirping obnoxiously. "Fuuuuuck!" I yelled at the top of my lungs.

I jumped out of the bed, frenetically grabbing at shit to put it back in place. The stand was caught on something. But I was just going to yank it back into place no matter what, 'cause the shit was not about to fuck with me. Well, out popped the IV from my wrist, a piece of plastic molding snapped off, the monitor slipped off its little cart, head-first, of course, cracking the screen casing, and the drip bag burst open and dumped liquid all over the floor.

I sat back down on the bed and held my wrist. There wasn't blood squirting out or anything, just a little trickle. Tuy's reaction was his usual goofy sarcasm: "Holy mother of God!"

He walked over nonchalantly, stared sympathetically at the mess at my feet, and then stepped outside into the hall and motioned for the hospital staff.

I sat on the edge of the bed, pressing my wrist with two fingers. A few minutes later Rachel rushed in and started picking things up. Tuy stayed outside, talking to one of the doctors. Rachel lifted my legs back onto the bed and pulled the sheets straight, then began refitting my IV tube. I was hoping she wouldn't talk to me, that Tuy wouldn't talk to me, that no one would, ever. Except for one thing.

"More morphine," I said as Rachel leaned over me. Then I added, "Please," and looked at her. She paused, blinked, and said nothing, then turned away and continued putting the drip stand upright and hooked up another bag. She bent over to wipe the floor. I noticed this time she bent her knees and rotated her torso sideways. I got the hint. The subtle body language. *Bitch. Like I was even interested in checking out your ass anyways. Just get me my goddamn drugs.* I closed my eyes and plopped my head back, biting the inside of my lip, waiting for her to finish and get out.

I opened them for a second when I heard her walk out of the room. But she came back in and continued, first lowering my bed, then messing with the IV. Moments later I felt the rush of coolness through my wrist. I stared at the divider bars of the window, breathing slowly, deeply, until they spun me around like the Forty, lifted me up like a helo, took me out of this realm, like a fever.

saw Rachel leaning over me. I wasn't sure how much time had passed. She stood watching with little expression, like she was seeing how fucked up I was. But the effects had mostly worn off.

"I want you to know it is normal to feel like you do."

I sat up. "Oh yeah?" I said dismissively. "How is that? How do I feel?"

"Well, probably agitated, angry, easily, uh—"

"Easily? Seriously?" I snapped. "Gee, ya got me, doc. I got an anger problem. *Anger Management.* Pfft, yeah, that's me. 'Calm down, sir! Sir! Calm down!'"

She sat down, laughing nervously. "Oh! I saw that movie, that was funn—"

"Well, this isn't fucking funny. This is a goddamned war."

"You don't need to take the Lord's name—"

"Fuck that! What's he done for me? Oh, that's right. How could I forget? Fucking my life up royally on 9/11. Thanks for the monkey wrench, bitch! Hey! Next time I have plans for my life I need put through the fucking shredder, I'll just say a prayer or two, and Allah can send another fucking plane my way!"

Rachel sat in her chair, turned sideways, looking all sympathetic for me. "Look, IED attacks are known to cause these kinds of—"

"For the last time, I was not in a goddamned IED attack. It was a helicopter crash!"

Finally she paused and actually took a moment to think. She pursed her lips slightly. "Hmm, well, I guess maybe there was a mix-up. But that's what I was told, and Tuy said the same thing, so—"

"No, 'cause Ethan shoulda been brought here too. He was with me. He fell out of the helicopter into the river. Five feet from me." I motioned emphatically with my hands.

Again she looked at me, considering what I'd said.

"Look," I said, "I remember every detail. The firefight in Hamza. Our squad took casualties. Someone will be writing an AAR, and I need to contact them to provide info for the report. This shit's important."

"So how'd you get out?" she asked halfheartedly.

"Ethan and I were on a roof. We called for evac. We basically hid until our guys came and—wait. Holy shit!" I said as something hit me. I pointed to the cubby and my ACUs. "The SAT phone! It's gotta be in there."

She stood up.

"One of the cargo pockets. Pants, probably."

She riffled through my clothes and couldn't find anything, then reached and pulled a box out of the top cubby. "They empty everything out of . . . okay, here it is," she said, handing a phone to me. But it was the wrong color.

"No, no, not this one. This is my Nokia. It's black, has a short, fat antenna."

"I thought you said yours."

"No, it's actually Tuy's. I borrowed it."

She looked in the box again and went back through the pockets. She turned around to me. "That's the only phone."

"Tuy probably grabbed it. See if he's still outside," I said, motioning to the hallway. Rachel pushed the door open and pulled Tuy into the room.

"Hey, man, did you grab your phone back from me? The SAT?"

He made an aha expression. "Oh, so *you're* the fucker who stole it!"

I rolled my eyes. "No, dumbass. You loaned it to me."

He thought for a second. "Oh, that's right, you had to call home or something."

"So are you sure you don't have it?"

"No, *idiota*, I been looking all over for it."

"Oh, and I don't suppose you remember us calling you? For evac?"

Tuy gave me a dumb look. I rolled my eyes. *Why'd I even ask?*

Rachel turned to me. "Well. Maybe you just forgot which one you used?"

"No, goddamn it, I know which phone I used. It looks different, more expensive. Somebody here probably ripped it off. Hand me the box."

The box had all the rest of my shit: Godzilla lighter, smokes, wallet, including a wad of twenties, and a couple rings—all of which had stayed dry, even the pack of cigarettes. I put the wallet next to me and handed the box back to her.

"Can you please go and check hospital records, find out where the hell Ethan is?"

Rachel paused, pursing her lips again. "But do you think . . . could this all be . . . just a memory thing?"

"Oh Jesus Christ! I told you no. Could you please just go? Pull the records, talk to some people. I promise you. Specialist Ethan Coffelt. He was at least airlifted with me, if not checked in, and released or something. Someone saw him."

"Okay," she said, "if it will help you sort this out."

"Yes," I said, "it will."

B ut sorting out was not at all what I got. The person at the medical records office was off the next day, so the following morning Rachel stopped by first thing, telling me she was headed over there again. She came back, and she had checked the records. In fact, she not only did what I asked her, she apparently put considerable effort into it and did a little gumshoe work. She was gone forever. She got ahold of the records, tracked down who was on duty that day and talked to them, found out details, brought back notes. But what she came back with was something I wasn't ready for.

"Okay," she said, standing at the foot of the bed, holding one of those little spiral notepads. She glanced momentarily over at Tuy, who was sound asleep. "March 22. Thirteen hundred. Medevac called out to Highway 9, just north of Abu Ghraib prison. Small convoy of three Humvees hit by roadside bomb." She paused, flipping a few pages, but I exploded in a short burst of laughter.

"Dude! Hello? That's the IED attack I was in before! That was a fucking month ago!" I waved my arms around. "Does this *look* like the same CSH?"

Just then a short coffee-skinned woman walked in, apologizing to Rachel for getting delayed. Rachel appeared relieved.

"Oh, there you are!" she said, before turning back to me. "Okay, this is Safaa. She was on duty when you were admitted. She works with Captain Mullein, who was the trauma team leader that afternoon."

I was barely listening. I put my head down, rubbing my forehead and biting the side of my lip.

"He's off base until the end of Holy Week, but Safaa can answer any—"

I jerked my head up. "Whoa, whoa. What did you say?"

Safaa answered, "Yes, he is away. Making Catholic service at Haditha."

"Sorry, the captain is also a priest," Rachel said.

"No, no. I mean Holy Week. That's *before* Easter," I said.

"Yes, Holy Week is the week before Easter," Rachel said.

I rolled my eyes at her. "Uh, no shit! But are you telling me we haven't had Easter yet this year?"

Rachel shook her head, with her eyebrows raised and that smirky pursed lip.

Safaa pulled her sleeve up and held her watch out to me. "No, five of April."

I wasn't sure what to do with that. I sat there looking back and forth between their dumb stares. Something was fucked up. Something. Either someone was wrong, telling me wrong, lying, or whatever.

"Why? What's the matter?" said Rachel.

I glared at her. "What's the matter? Easter was two fucking weeks ago, that's what! We were at the village, about to do our assessment, and Lieutenant Jacobs said a prayer. An Easter prayer, okay? Easter! No, I am not insane, and no, I didn't imagine this shit 'cause I hit my head. So hey, either bring Ashton Kutcher in, let's see the hidden cameras, we'll all have a few laughs, or how about you just quit the bullshit and stop fucking with me."

They both stood there awkwardly. Tuy rolled over and sat up in bed, wiping the edges of his eyes. "What's with the yelling?" he said dryly. "We better have won the war, or I'm gonna kick someone's ass."

I ignored his little quip, snapping my fingers. "Dude, what's the date? Check your computer."

Tuy opened his laptop. "The fifth."

"Of?"

"Uh, April?" he said.

"Okay," I said, "then our squad must have . . ." I looked at Rachel. *It's total bullshit that* she *has to be the official judge of my mental competence,* I thought. "Simple. Jacobs must have just gotten the date wrong, that's all. And no one noticed, including me."

Rachel came over to my bed, putting a hand on my shoulder. "I also checked the AKO white pages and sent him an email."

I looked up at her, wide-eyed. "Wow, you found another soldier named Jacobs. Somebody call CSI!"

"Well, only one Lieutenant Karl Jacobs was listed," she said, "but he replied to the email, saying he heard about the IED attack a couple weeks ago but does not know you or your friend . . . but your CO contacted the hospital and he's sending Specialist Coffelt back here tomorrow." With that she added a click of her mouth: *You poor, delusional bastard.*

I burst into laughter. "Rrrright, you got an email from a ghost, but he has amnesia. Good job! But hey, I don't care if the bitch from *The Ring* crawls through the fuckin' TV and hands you an email. Long as Ethan shows up, I'm golden."

Rachel left the room. After a few seconds of relative quiet, with only the soft beeping sound of the monitor every few seconds, Tuy cleared his throat. "Uh, how exactly do you hand someone an email?"

I turned my head toward him. "Cute. Real cute."

He burst into his motorboat giggling, ridiculously, overly pleased with himself. It seemed like it was more that he'd been able to lighten me up, even if just a little. I couldn't help myself, seeing his obnoxious display; a grin spread over my face. I frowned and shook my head. "You okay? Kinda crackin' yourself up over there."

He ignored my comment as usual, jumping to the next neural firing in his brain. "Hey, tonight's movie night, yo."

"Uh, okay?" I said, like, what the hell's that supposed to mean?

"Movie night! Somebody's gonna bring us a DVD player and a few movies."

"Oh, oookay."

"Yeah," he said, nodding his head gangster style, "Uncle Tuy takes care of his peeps."

"Ha ha. Uncle Tuy? Gimme a break." I tried not to smile, but it was just so dumb.

Awhile later a guy dressed in scrubs with a stethoscope around his neck came in, holding a DVD player under his arm and gripping a stack of movies in his hands. Tuy looked up from his laptop. "What the hell? You didn't send a hot nurse to hook it up for us?"

The guy laughed. "Nah, sorry. You're stuck with my ugly butt."

Tuy shuddered sarcastically. "Ew, like, plumber crack is, uh, *not* what the doctor ordered, know what'm sayin', yo?"

More laughter. The guy connected everything, then turned to us. "Okay, here are the choices," he said, flipping the first DVD case up for us to see. "*Lord of War*. Nic Cage movie. He's an illegal arms dealer, international weapons thug. Excellent. Lotta action, chase scenes, people getting shot, blown up, run over. Cage is awesome. Kind of liberal for me, though. Supposedly based on real events, talks about there's one gun for every twelve people on earth"—he chuckled— "just let me watch the darn movie, okay? Anyway, oh, skip the ending, too. It's some kind of follow-up documentary. Hello? Borr-ring!" He laughed again.

He held up the next DVD case. It showed George Clooney dressed in a suit and tie, gagged and blindfolded. The blindfold was made of the lettering of the movie title, *Syriana*, and the words over his mouth read "Everything is connected."

"This is a CIA-slash-espionage political thriller. Matt Damon, Amanda Peet—she's hot. It's kinda slow, parts of it . . . uh, cool missile strike, though. Come git sum, Saudi prince!"

Tuy snorted at him. "Uh, dude, I think we're friends with the Saudis."

"Well, it was *one* of those Arab leaders; some bad guy in a black SUV. Awesome graphics! I loved that scene." He turned the DVD over, reading the back. "I'm not usually a Clooney fan. Kinda artsy-fartsy for my taste . . . oh yeah, that's right, this is about the Middle East oil. Based on some dude's memoir."

He handed the DVD to Tuy. "Oh well, sorry, guys. This one's kind of leftie political too. But hey, it's still pretty good action."

By this time Tuy had reached up and grabbed a couple more cases and was reading them, half listening to the guy. Tuy held up one called *Munich*, with a fiery scene of the top apartment of a three-story building exploding over the street, and a shot of two guys walking with handguns, wearing tight seventies dress shirts and big Ray-Ban sunglasses, superimposed over it.

"Hey, T, just curious," Tuy said, chuckling, "do you have a single movie *not* about the Middle East?"

The guy gave Tuy a confused half smile, half frown, and shuffled through the other DVDs. "Are they? Hey, I just look at the cover. If it's a cool, professional shot, say of an explosion, a hottie with a gun, martial arts dude kicking butt, something like that, it's usually a sign of a good film."

Tuy looked sideways at me and talked out of the side of his mouth. "Did he really just say 'kicking butt'?"

"Hush," the guy said to Tuy. "I don't swear. Oh, hey, here is one," he said, holding up a dark-bluish-black image of a Halloween mask. Looked like a possessed serial killer rabbit. "Good old *Donnie Darko*."

"What the hell's that?" I asked.

Tuy did a Conan O'Brien double take. "Huh-whaaa? Dude! You never seen *Donnie Darko*? Are you fweaking seewious?"

"'Twenty-eight days . . . ,'" the guy said real deep, like a robot whose voice was being cloaked.

"'Six hours,'" Tuy joined in, and they spoke in unison: "'Forty-two minutes, twelve seconds.'"

They got increasingly louder with each word, finally ending with "'That is when the world will end!'" They laughed.

"Oh, how about that lady who kept walking across the street to open her empty mailbox?" Tuy said.

"Grandma Death!" the guy answered. "Man, that Frank dude creeped me out."

"I know, right? Donnie says, 'What are you doing in that stupid bunny suit?'"

"Oh yeah!" The guy laughed. "'What are *you* doing in that stupid man suit?'"

They continued this exchange until I told them to shut the hell up before I felt like I'd watched the entire damn movie scene for scene. They threw the other movies in the box. There was no question which one we were watching. Tuy's buddy grabbed one of the chairs from next door and sat between us. He even went and commandeered some popcorn, nuked it, and brought it back with a few sodas. It was nice to kick back and get lost in a movie. Reminded me of back in Dalton, renting movies with my mom and Glenn late on a Sunday night. Back then it seemed each of us wanted to escape, to forget something that was looming. For me it was forgetting 9/11 and waiting for the therapist to say I was right in the head again; for Glenn it was forgetting his job, which he hated like *Death of a Salesman* but refused to leave; and for Mom it was emptiness, I guess. The absence, the fact that she had nothing she had set out to conquer, nothing she'd have to survive, nothing to get her out of bed early each morning. Sunday nights were pure escapism for us. We knew it was fleeting, but we could feel good for a couple more hours, squirrel away some contentment while we still had the chance.

D ude, you didn't, like, die on us, did you?" Ethan blurted out, walking through the door early the next morning. Rachel trailed behind him, smiling.

I was still a little groggy, but I perked up immediately. "Eeth! Well, it's about damn time!" I said, holding my arm up.

He shook my hand, then leaned down to give me a quick hug. "Sorry. Hitched a ride with a FUBAR convoy. Don't *even* get me started."

"Thanks for coming for me, man."

"No worries, I'm just glad you're okay. Jesus."

Rachel lingered in the background. Kind of looked like she was waiting to see Tuy, who was in the bathroom.

"How you doing?" Ethan said. He pointed to the bandage around my head, smiling. "You look like fucking Axl Rose."

I laughed. "Ah, I'm good. Probably just a concussion. They're gonna do an MRI or something just to be sure."

"CT scan," Rachel said.

"Oh, okay," I said.

"I've got you scheduled for tomorrow morning."

"Okay, cool." I turned to Ethan and rolled my eyes. "Once they get a clue I'm perfectly sane, thank you very much"—I opened my eyes wide at Rachel—"and not imagining entire episodes of my life, they'll let me out of here and I can get back to the suck."

"Yup," he said, nodding his head, his lips pursed. He stood there for a few seconds with an odd expression. There was something there. I could sense it.

"So, dude!" I said. "What the hell happened to you at the river? Last thing I remember was we fell in the water."

Ethan bit his lip and glanced quickly at Rachel and back. Brilliant as he was, he had *the* worst poker face. Rachel stepped over toward us almost on cue, as if to rescue him.

"Yeah, uh, well, dude," he said, "about this whole . . . helicopter crash . . ."

The blood had rushed to my face already. I glared at him, unsympathetic to whatever the fuck he was uncomfortable about.

"Oh Jesus, don't tell me—"

He came right out with it. "Think about it, man. You had a head injury," he said, defensive and almost pleading with me. "Trauma to your fucking head! Do you know what kind of weird shit can happen to the brain?"

"Oh my fucking God," I said, sitting upright in the bed.

Rachel put her hand on my shoulder. "Ethan's right," she said, "but this can be treated, you understand?"

"Okay, you know what?" I gestured with my hands for them to back off. "Now I *am* going fucking insane!"

After a few seconds of silence, a clicking sound emanated from the bathroom door lock. Tuy cracked the bathroom door, letting it creak open slowly about an inch. He stuck his nose out, and one eye blinked cautiously above it.

"Mommy," he said in a baby voice, "I'm scarwd."

"Tuy, shut the fuck up!" I yelled.

Rachel walked over to the door and said something to Tuy in a hushed tone. He opened the door, and she motioned him out of the room like a kid. Then she followed.

"Ethan," I said, trying to calm down and show some reason, "are you telling me you have no recollection of being in a helicopter crash? With me? The little girl?"

He shook his head sympathetically.

I opened my eyes wide. "Really. You and I, dug in on the roof of the school. We called for evac—with the SAT phone I'd borrowed from Tuy. And they picked us up in an MH-6, with the little girl dressed in red pants and a ruffled shirt? Dude! I have a crystal-clear memory of all this shit."

"I'm not saying you don't. I believe you. You *do* have the memory. But look, I was not on a village assessment. You say I was? Fine, but guess what. I did not get hit in the head. *You* did."

I rubbed my face. "This is just so fucked up."

Ethan turned to the side and looked up at the TV. He folded his arms and let out a deep breath. "I guess this is not like the movies," he mumbled. "Shit's always so cool and interesting in movies. Like *Memento*, remember that? Trippy!"

"Oh, thanks. Now I have no short-term memory?" I snapped.

"No—I'm sorry—I just meant . . . okay, I'm making things worse here. Maybe you just need to be left alone for a while." He made his way to the door.

I wanted to tell him, "Yeah, go fuck yourself," but I didn't. I had no one else to help figure this shit out. *Well,* I thought, *there's Tuy. But some help he'd be.*

After Ethan left I sat there, monitor beeping softly, and could hear the blood rush through my temples. And I thought about it. Poring over the events I knew had happened, goddamn it. Trying to think of the one thing that I could say, or something I could produce, to prove it. *Where is that goddamned phone? When the hell was Easter? How can I prove this? Because "It's all in your head" is complete bullshit.*

But there was nothing. Only what I said versus what they said. No proof, just numbers. Strength in numbers. And they win, of course, 'cause I say the sky is blue and they all line up and say nope, we all see red; you're the one who's crazy. *Fuck.* I went in circles like that for what seemed like an hour, obsessing, rubbing my temples, until the worst headache came on. It felt like the pressure underneath my eyebrow was so explosive, it was forcing my left eye shut. Finally, after I pushed the blue button a dozen times, the door swung open. I looked up. It was Tuy.

"Where the hell are the nurses?" I said. "I need meds in a big fucking way."

"What's wrong?" he said tonelessly.

I took my hand away from my face. "What's wrong? Wow. And I could have sworn you've been in the same room for the last few weeks."

"Uh, well, I heard a bunch of yelling awhile ago. Didn't know what the hell for, though."

I just stared at him for a few seconds until he looked at me. "Wow. I mean, wow. You have got to be the most immune person on this fucking planet."

"What do you mean, 'immune'?"

"I mean I have never in my life seen someone so goddamned un-affected, so oblivious to everything." I waved my hands around in the air. "Hey, Tuy, there's a war going on. Did ya even notice?"

His expression didn't change one bit. Cool and deadpan. "What is your definition of 'notice'? You mean, am I staring at it completely paralyzed?"

I was stunned. "What? You think I'm paralyzed?"

He raised his eyebrows. "By what you've told me, you don't seem to be making much progress so far or accomplishing what you said you'd like to."

"Holy shit, are you serious?" I looked frantically for words. "I—do you . . . have any fucking idea what kinds of things . . . the magnitude of what I am trying to do?"

"Saving the world?" he said.

Hearing him say those words, I felt like a fucking idiot. *But why should I?* I thought. *This is bullshit. I should be proud.*

"You know what? Yes. That is exactly what I am doing. What the fuck are you doing? Besides nothing."

"A lot, actually," he said, staring at me blankly.

I laughed. "Oh, really? How'd you make a single impact, I'd just love to hear."

He motioned with his thumb toward the hospital. "Actually, they just thanked me a few minutes ago for fixing their laptop, 'cause they were able to locate a squad that was missing."

"You? . . . You fixed their computer," I said.

"Yeah, don't you remember Rachel asked me—"

"What? I thought you were banging her!"

"Dude, I told you. We didn't have sex. I just helped her, uh . . . manually." He smiled briefly, then seemed to try to erase it. A sheepish little smirk still lingered.

I shook my head and exhaled deeply. "Gee, but of course! He does both!" I mumbled to myself, laughing sarcastically.

"Both?"

I ignored his question. I sat there rubbing my forehead, looking over at him while he waited for me to say something. I couldn't help but note he now seemed well aware of the seriousness of my state of mind.

"Okay," I said, almost in a whisper. "I give up."

"What do you mean?"

"Fuck it, I give up. Tell me your secret. Tell me how you do it."

"Oh no," he said, "we gonna have *this* conversation again?"

"No. I'm serious. I just want to know. I'm done with being pissed off. I won't be knocking shit over."

Tuy paused. "What secret? I don't really—"

"No, no. Yes, you do. I want to know how you skate through, no effort at all, no concerns, no worries, don't give a flying fuck, and, gee, apparently get to accomplish more than I do, without even trying."

"Uh, well . . . I'm not trying to save the world like you, but you can't do it the way you're going about it."

"Why?"

"Because you joined up. You're part of this whole thing. This war. The entire thing is a . . . net loss. And you, me, every one of us here, we're all part of it."

"You saying we're going to lose the war?"

"No, I'm saying it is a net loss, even if we win. We kill Saddam, kill Osama, al-Zarqawi, whoever. Doesn't matter. We'll do more negative than positive. This is not World War II, where we swoop in and save the day, defeat Hitler, and rebuild roads and schools, and the Germans all love us forever. This—"

"Don't you think our commanders have thought of all this?"

"Who, you mean Rumsfeld? He and Cheney? They're the ones who did all this. They *have* no plan. All they planned was the invasion, Shock and Awe, which killed a shitload of civilians, for starters. Then they did zero rebuilding and fired all the Ba'ath leadership, turned them into insurgents—good job, fuck-tards—oh, which also caused a civil war, by the way. And now there are tons more Muslims in the world who hate us."

Tuy looked pissed at this point. "I thought you didn't care about any of this," I said.

"Of course I do, dumbass. I read everything."

"Is that what you're always doing on your computer?"

"Yeah. In between porn, yeah."

I laughed. To me he was switching gears instantly, smoothly. One second dead serious about a subject, the next second fucking around and laughing at it all.

"So you're saying there is nothing that can be done. That's pretty depressing."

"No, I'm not. Just nothing *you* can do from where you are."

"Uh, okay . . ." I wasn't sure what he meant.

"It's like you're in the Twin Towers on 9/11, rushing up the stairs to see if anyone is trapped. You think you're helping, but the entire building is going to fall, so you're just killing one more person, yourself."

These words seemed to pierce me and push on my lungs. At the same time, I sucked in with short, labored breaths. My face flushed red and hot, and an uncontrolled groan left my throat. I don't know if it was the effect of coming off the morphine, but my emotions took over, and it was like I was watching my own body as I convulsed. Tuy's voice came through to me, and I realized he was standing next to me.

"Dude, you okay?"

I could only manage a few words. "What you said . . ."

"Uh, what I said? You mean 9/11?"

Forever seemed to pass. I tried to stop my body from heaving but couldn't. My thoughts were abstract and undefined, yet thick, black, and desolate. My face must have been a contorted mess for Tuy to look at. He put his hand on my shoulder. Even in my state I noted this as unusual for him, showing compassion like that.

"It was just like Brazil," I sobbed, squeezing my eyes shut. My lips were trembling as I spoke.

"What was?" he asked calmly.

"9/11, man! I'm useless. Fucking useless!" I cried.

Tuy stood there, hand on my shoulder. "I'm confused," he finally said.

"Too hard to explain. I'm just worthless. That's all."

"Hey, aren't we all! But, like, how does it help to think that?"

"It doesn't! See? There's the proof! Nothing I do helps." I was almost wailing at this point. "I can't save anyone. I can't fix anything. Can't save a single life. Can't rescue anyone. It's just like Brazil."

"What happened in Brazil, dude?"

Somehow the effort of explaining it for him calmed me down, at least for the moment. I wiped my face with the sheet, and Tuy pulled a bag of Skittles out of his pocket.

"Here," he said, waving it at me. "Believe the rainbow. Taste the rainbow."

I shook my head. "No, thanks."

"Okay, you were saying?"

"My parents. I was thirteen. I was in Manaus on some dumbass evangelical mission, saving the poor 'godless' Brazilians. And I got a letter from my mom. She said Dad was moving out, and they were getting divorced. I was so devastated and messed up over it. I told Joshua, my best friend who I went with. I told him about it. And he tells me—no, scratch that—he *promises*, and makes a huge fucking deal out of it too. He says we can pray about it, and God will fix it; Mom and Dad will get back together. So I prayed. I prayed like fucking crazy."

"Well, there's the problem. Fucker set you up, holmes." Tuy's levity didn't register with me.

"Dude, you don't even know. I prayed constantly. Every breakfast, every devotional, every rally and prayer dinner for like weeks, until the next letter came from my mom."

Tuy plopped down in the chair and exhaled. "Okay, I understand. That was pretty traumatic, but how does this relate to 9/11?"

"'Cause I . . . 'cause I didn't do anything. God didn't do anything. He didn't do shit, so somebody had to, and I failed. I fucking failed."

"I thought you didn't believe in God."

"Well, if he exists, then he's an asshole," I said.

Tuy winced comically. "Well, all righty then! What do ya call that, an Assiest? Asstostic?"

His goofiness finally got to me. "Ha ha ha," I said.

Tuy stood up and walked around the front of my bed. "Okay, so what do we have here? Your parents got divorced—ahem, like half of America—and you felt responsible. Gee, if you saw a shrink, then that fugger's an idiot, 'cause I can solve this shit in two seconds."

"No, not responsible, just . . ."

Tuy paced the floor like he was working a problem, but impatiently. "Okay, I don't need detail. Just give me simple answers off the top of your head. Was the divorce your fault?"

"My fault? No."

"And you were in Brazil, no phone, in the Amazon with a bunch of religious freak who didn't fly you back home, so there was nothing in your power to stop it."

"'Freaks,' yeah."

"Whatever. Who's the therapist here, bitch?" he said, total deadpan. I knew he was kidding, and this made me smile. "And one of these religious freakzzzz, which was your dumbass friend—probably in the closet, too, I bet—he promised you shit he had no evidence to back up. Said God would come fix everything."

"Yeah."

"Okay, so . . . what *did* cause your parents' divorce? Fifteen words or less."

"Uh . . ." I thought for a moment. "Dad and Mom, oil and water . . . no. Dad was potassium, Mom was water. Huge explosion. Domestic violence."

"So, what? He hit your mom?"

"Yeah."

Tuy paused. "So did you ever do anything about it?"

"Uh, no. Nothing *to* do. I was a kid."

"How about sneak out a window, get the cops, throw his ass in jail?"

His answer totally threw me off. "Uh . . . yeah, I guess that—"

But Tuy just moved on. "Okay, so what about 9/11? Same thing, I assume; God sat on his ass, didn't come fix anything, and you couldn't do anything?"

"But it's—you make it sound so simple," I said.

"It *is* simple! Most things are trivially simple. It's only complicated in people's mind."

I shook my head. "See, you weren't there, so you cannot even imagine—"

"It doesn't matter," he said.

I felt it coming over me again. Like a shell, closing around me, darkening. Without even realizing it, I'd let Tuy lead me back into that place. "Doesn't matter? Our friend fucking died, Tuy. Everyone in his company died, his boss, interns, the hot admin I met, everybody."

"Of course it matters people died. That's not what I meant. For me to help you, it doesn't matter that I wasn't there."

"Yes, it does! You can never know what it was like. You can never understand because you were not there."

"Wrong," he said. "*You* can't understand because you *were* there."

His response stunned me. A deep, percussive vibration swept through the building as a helo flew over, making its approach to the landing pad in the back. We both paused and looked toward the window for a moment until the shaking stopped. "And if I *had* been there, I could *not* help you. Because I'd be cripple like you, mentally."

"Well, I wasn't there, either. I just witnessed it."

"What do you mean?"

"I was on the phone with someone. He was in Tower One."

"Okay, well, then you *were* there. Go on," he said.

"It was a family friend. M-Mercer. Really close, like a . . ." I took a deep breath. "That morning he could not get in touch with his wife, so he called my dad's house in Tennessee. I answered; I was sick that day. I yelled for Dad, who ran downstairs. We put the phone on speaker. This was right after the first plane."

"Damn, dude."

"Mercer told us a plane had struck the building—we could hear all sorts of horrible noises on the other end—and they needed help opening the door to the stairwell, so he said, 'Let me call you back.' And then Dad said we"—I started losing it at that point—"said we needed my mom, we needed her . . . expertise." My chin bunched up, and my bottom lip quivered. I looked at Tuy almost pleadingly. "Even the very day he died, he was still bringing my parents together."

"It's okay, man," Tuy said, but I felt like I needed to get it all out. I wiped my face and took a deep breath.

"When Mom got to Dad's, Mercer had just called back. They had moved the door, and Mercer and this guy Khalid were talking about trying to get upstairs to clear the way so others could make their way down, and then . . ." My voice cracked.

"It's okay, I understand," he said, sounding uncomfortable.

"No, goddamn it! I am not going to tell some poor, pitiful Tower

One story! I have always told the entire fucking story, and I'm going to now!"

Tuy shut up for once.

"My mom started to tell Mercer, do what's in your heart, she's very proud of him, and stay focused, be smart." I started losing it again. I couldn't stop. I thought of how incredibly strong my mom could be in these types of moments—real crises, the ones where most people buckled emotionally. She would be energized, cool, almost playful, while simultaneously making tough decisions and dispatching orders. My mother, who I'd always thought was spineless. She sure as hell wasn't a basket case that day.

I took my thousandth deep breath. "But my dad spoke up. He pretty much ordered Mercer to leave. Mercer said he was scared shitless. He wanted to. But he also wanted to help. Said, tell Dreda and the kids he loved them and . . . but then Dad cut in and blurted out, 'Mercer, don't be a fucking hero.' And he almost never swears. When Mercer said he felt he had to do something, Dad started yelling and said, 'It's no time for your—'" I choked on the words, and tears came again. "'It's no time for your liberal save-the-world bullshit!'"

It seemed I would have kept sobbing endlessly, but Tuy said something that turned everything for me a sharp ninety degrees.

"Good. He was right. 'Cause those guys saved no one and ended up dying, and it could have been one more. Your dad was right."

I grabbed the sides of my face with my hands and pressed as hard as I could, tensing the muscles in my neck and letting out a muffled cry: "Fuuuuuuuuuuck!"

I began breathing heavily, like a slow, painful hyperventilation. "He's always right. I'm always wrong. Zero sum. Fuck. He wins. I lose. Every fucking time. I am useless!"

"Dude, try to calm down a little," Tuy said softly.

I tried, but there was so much energy. Everything seemed to be spinning madly in my head, imploding. I looked up at Tuy.

"Well, if he's right, then I guess we need to call up Mrs. Beamer, tell her her husband was *not* a hero on 9/11 for rushing the terrorists on that flight. He was a fucking loser!"

Tuy fluffed up his pillow, then stretched out, putting his arms behind his head. I expected him to come back with something, at least react to my rampage.

"Ah," he said, nodding in satisfaction. "How come real therapists don't do it this way? I mean, why should the patient be the only one who gets to lie down?"

In a way his stupid comment left me all alone, like there was no one. Tuy wasn't going to help me, and I was stupid for hoping he could. "Pfft, you're no fucking therapist."

"Whaaaat?" he said, mocking offense. "I take that, kind sir, as both an insult *and* a challenge!"

I tried to ignore him but couldn't help calming down ever so slightly.

"Tuy, when that book came out, *Let's Roll*, about Flight 93, all I could think about was buying a copy and waving it in front of my dad, saying, 'See, Dad? This is what heroes do. They sacrifice. They change things.'"

"Mmkay."

"I mean, what the fuck, Tuy? How am I supposed to live my useless life now?"

Tuy leaned forward, wrapping his arms around his knees, and turned to me. "I don't know, but I *did* tell you, didn't I? Dr. Tuy was right."

"Told me what?"

"I told you you're trying to relive this shit. That's why you have the Gandhi complex." He pursed his lips and nodded, all self-satisfied.

"No, I don't want to be Gandhi. I . . . just want to help save . . . or, I mean, help. Just help someone for once. That's all."

"Exactly. That is what you need to stop doing."

"Oh, stop trying to help? Fucking brilliant!"

"No, that is what you are repeating." He got up and walked to the bathroom. "The scenario you are playing out again and"—he paused while he ran water in the sink, then walked out, drying off his face with a towel—"and again and again." He made a circular motion with his hand. "I'm just curious: has anyone ever told you to get over it?"

"Oh Jesus fucking—you telling me I need to move on to the next stage of anger? Acceptance stage? Gee, never heard that one before."

"No. I'm asking 'cause that is the *worst* advice they could give you. You can't get over this thing. It's like energy. You have it inside you for a reason, and it's not going away. You have to transform it into something else. Like mass to energy or energy to mass. You know, E = mc² shit. You have to convert it into something you can use."

I sat for a second, biting my bottom lip. For once I'd heard something that didn't sound like bullshit. It was classic Tuy: off the wall, atypical, antithetical. He wasn't trying to act like some PhD in psychology. He really seemed like he could see what they didn't, even if it was something so basic, everyone should.

"How? I mean, I'm trying, believe me," I said.

"No. You're trying to *be* Gandhi, not do what he did."

"Oh, right."

He stepped around to his bed, motioning toward the TV. "No, really. It's like . . . you know Lendl? You ever notice how he never celebrated a single tennis shot? You know why?"

"He wasn't emotional."

"No. More than that, dude. He knew it was a waste of time. Watch him. He is one hundred percent focused. Total concentration. He is Zen, dude. He knows getting pissed off or getting excited does nothing to advance his position. He takes the mental shortest distance."

"What about whatshisname—the Superbrat—from New York?" I said.

"Oh, McEnroe. Well, shit, dude, he is the perfect example. He plays better when he's pissed, that's *why* he gets pissed. He channels the energy. For him this is the shortest distance."

"Oh."

"Damn straight, holmes. You listen to psychotherapist Tuy. He da most psycho therapist there is. Hee hee hee hee."

I laughed.

"No, but seriously, dude," he said, stretching out on the bed again, "it's really simple. I told you. Almost everything has a simple solution. But it's like a puzzle. You can't just do random things and expect results. It won't be solved just because you felt you put all that effort into it. It has to be very specific things, following logical rules. I'm not sure what you want to do, but if you really want to do it, you have to figure out the puzzle. That is what Gandhi did, and MLK and whoever. And guess what? So did Cheney and Karl Rove, tricking us into this shit. You may think they are evil assholes, but it doesn't matter. They found the magic formula."

"Well, hopefully, if they are trying to do good for the world, then hopefully they'll, uh, get a little help from above, you know?"

"Ugh," Tuy said, shaking his head. "Dude, you need to make up your fucking mind. No wonder you are so confused!"

"Huh? What do you mean?"

"You believe in God or not?"

"Of course I don't, I was just—"

"Then what you said makes no sense. Quit clouding up your own mind. I don't give a fuck one way or another, but don't be mentally sloppy. I hate that shit. Don't say you or anyone else is saving the world and then turn around and make a casual comment about God helping out." He paused and looked over at me.

"Okay, sor-ree," I said.

He seemed annoyed. It was a strange feeling for me. Like shame, almost—like I should already understand this metaphysical shit or at least be working like hell to figure it out. Not challenging myself was unacceptable. It reminded me of my band teacher in seventh grade. Mr. Davis. He'd yell at us in class, and his face would turn blood red. He'd call us stupid idiots when we missed a note: "How could your parents raise such morons?" He'd get so physically upset he would go into the bathroom and vomit. But in the end he expected us to excel, and it worked; it pushed me. I proved to him I could do it. It was the year I got first chair.

The next day I finally got the CT scan. Rachel woke me early, pushing a wheelchair up to the bed, and rolled me down to the end of the hall and out to a mobile unit sitting outside the CSH building. I had to walk across the gravel. I looked around quickly at the palms, the light of the sun coming over the hills, and a couple soldiers at the main entrance putting out their cigarettes. I was in and out in about ten minutes. The tech had me lie down on a table with rollers that lifted me and slid me headfirst into the center of a big plastic doughnut. The thing beeped and whined, shifted me back and forth a little, and it was done. When the guy came back with Rachel, I made some crack about how the images would show nothing wrong with me whatsoever except that teeny trace amount of cancer commonly seen in people who get CT scans. Neither one laughed. Rachel wheeled me back to the room, and that was that. As she helped me into the bed, I couldn't resist.

"So what do ya say? Ten bucks says they don't find shit."

She only gave me a polite smile and leaned over to unwrap my bandage. "Your forehead is looking very good." Her necklace dangled over my shoulder.

"Hey, better yet, your pendant. Perfect! If they don't find anything wrong with my brain, you give me your little necklace there. But if they *do* find something wrong with my brain, I'll accept Jayzus." I surprised myself with the way the last part came out, and laughed.

"Thanks, but no thanks," she said, discarding the strip of gauze in the biohazard waste bin.

"Oh, come on! This is your chance to convert somebody. I mean, risking a cheapo piece of jewelry to save an entire soul?" I smiled, thinking of what Tuy had said. *All they want is to feel like they're in the God club.* No way in hell was she going to take me up on it. *These people wouldn't risk a morsel of that feeling to actually help someone.*

"They should have the results in a few hours," she said, collapsing the wheelchair. She rolled it to the door and turned around. "We'll let you know."

"Where is Specialist Coffelt?" I asked.

"He said he's going to wait for the results and see if you're released."

"Not if, when," I said, and she walked out.

I sat there for a few seconds, reveling in how bad I had balled her up, then glanced over at Tuy, who was still sleeping. *God, and he missed it!* I thought. *'Cause that shit was funny.*

A couple of figures walked by the window. I heard their footsteps in the gravel, and they stopped, still talking, just out of view. Then there was a pinging sound like something striking a long metal pole. I tilted forward but couldn't see them. So I crawled toward the end of the bed, wheeling the IV stand along, and leaned out as far as I could, balancing myself on the plastic footboard. Turned out there was a flagpole outside, and two soldiers were lowering it to half-mast.

That night Tuy disappeared for a few hours, who knew where. One of the staffers came by, bullshitted with him, talking about somewhere that had excellent kebabs. Then they left. I remember I'd seen the guy come by before. Young Iraqi. Black beard and hip nerd glasses. He had a T-shirt with a picture of a kid running screaming away from the explosions of an airstrike. Across the top it read "I can see those fighter planes."

When they left, I flipped through the channels with the remote, now with one button missing and white surgical tape wrapped around it. I chuckled to myself. By coincidence, a tennis match from back home was showing on TV. Nadal was playing some guy named Djokovic, from Serbia. Nadal was looking way better, but he was grunting like an idiot and taking an annoyingly long time between serves, going through what looked like a twenty-step OCD ritual every time. I immediately wanted Djokovic to kick his ass. I watched for a while and fell asleep, then caught the end of the match.

Sometime during the night, Tuy came back in. I woke to the sound of whispering and rolled over.

"Damn, you a light sleeper, yo," Tuy said. His speech was slurred slightly. The Iraqi guy was standing there. Tuy was pulling a portable hard drive and cables out of his laptop bag to hand to the guy.

"Thanks, Tuy," he said.

"It's a terabyte. It should hold all of your porn. Hee hee hee."

The guy laughed embarrassedly. "No, no! My religion is against this!"

"Whatever, man, tell it to Mohammed, I don't give a damn," Tuy said.

The guy giggled, trying to be quiet, then stuck out his hand toward Tuy. "Okay, *salaam*."

"*Allah yasalmik, kalbouz*," Tuy said, slapping his hand.

"Okay, fool," the guy said, smiling. They hugged, and he left. Tuy flipped on the bathroom light.

I sat up. "So where'd you guys go?" I said.

"Kebab place. Kind of a restaurant-slash-nightclub. Hazim's uncle owns it." He turned on the water in the sink.

I raised my eyebrows and shook my head. It was hopeless to be shocked anymore. I just resorted to sarcasm. "Nice. So you sashayed off base and went strolling into the city."

"No, fool, just a couple kilometers from here."

I didn't even bother asking further. Tuy splashed water on his face, then stepped out of the bathroom.

"Guess what was on TV tonight?" I said.

"Uh, I dunno, *Gandhi*, the movie?"

I laughed. "Cute. But no. Tennis. Nadal and some guy named Djokovic."

"Oh yeah, my boy Novak! Kicks ass, yo." He rubbed his face briskly with a towel.

"Well, Rafa won. Sorry."

"Motherf'er and a heffer!" he said mockingly. He went back into the bathroom and closed the door. I fluffed up my pillows and lay back, closing my eyes in the dark. I wasn't really sleepy, though. A few minutes later the door opened. Tuy pulled his shirt off and stuffed it into his cubby.

"I used to play a lot, you know," I said, staring at the ceiling.

"What, tennis?"

"Yeah. It was big where I grew up. Country clubs, private school. Everybody played."

"Oh, so you a spoiled little rich kid."

I laughed. "Yeah, I guess. Lookout Mountain. Bunch of upper-class family money. Everybody had maids. Very old south. But anyway, I was thinking about what we were talking about before, about Lendl, the mental aspect of playing. I . . . I had a lot of issues with tennis. I was always struggling with it, constantly. It was pretty horrible for me, actually."

Tuy seemed confused. "Why?"

"Well, everything you said about not being emotional? Uh, I was pretty much the complete opposite of that. My dad had this book, I remember. *The Inner Game of Tennis*. It was like his bible. I read it too. It told you how to overcome self-doubt, not psych yourself out, deal with nervousness, lack of confidence, all that shit. But every time I played, it was like a fucking train wreck. I'd be up an entire set, feeling great. Then I'd miss a shot or two and everything would start to shake and crumble. I'd go from 40–love to losing the game, then two, then the entire match. This one time—"

"It was the book, you idiot!" Tuy blurted out.

"Wait, one time my best friend Joshua found out I was taking lessons and asked to play. He'd never even been on the court. Oh, in fact, he held the racquet like halfway up the fucking handle. Total douche. And he swatted at the ball like it was ping-pong."

"And he beat you," Tuy said, nonplussed.

"No. Not just beat me. He balled me up. The little shit. Kicked my ass all over the place. It was fucking embarrassing."

"Makes complete sense," Tuy said. Again, unimpressed. "He didn't give a fuck. That book is why you lost. It should have been one page." He gestured with his hands. "You look at the cover. 'Hmm, *Internal Game of Tennis*. Sounds interesting.' You open it up. It's one page. It says 'DON'T THINK.'"

I continued staring at the ceiling, my eyes beginning to adjust. "Yeah, I guess," I said.

"No. That is exactly it. Don't think. From now on your only thoughts should be about form, footwork, keeping your eye on the ball, all that shit. No other thoughts should enter your mind. Period."

He opened up his laptop, and the ceiling lit dimly. "Next?" he said, like a surly clerk at the DMV. I smiled, disarmed once again. The thought of not having to deal with all that excess bullshit, the overthinking, the struggle that never ended, dragging me down—it seemed too good to be true, and yet there it was, right in front of me. Proof that it could work. No, that it *was* working, just in someone else's head, not mine.

"Oh, by the way," Tuy said, "you said after 9/11 you wanted to do something about it, right?"

"Yeah."

"Me and Hazim's family were talking about it tonight. Here's what the US should have done if they really wanted to help: built a mosque in the middle of Ground Zero."

I burst out laughing. "Oh, right! Let me just call up the mayor. People of New York would love that idea, especially the victims' families!"

He snapped, "No, dick shit for brains. I didn't say anyone *would* actually do it. Of course they wouldn't. I said that is what they *should* have done."

"What would that have accomplished?"

"Simple math, fool. How many died in 9/11? Like three thousand? So from that point forward, count the number of lives lost, only counting the so-called good people—innocent civilians, soldiers, Americans, people from friendly nations, whatever. Let's call them good lives lost," he said, using quote fingers. "Count the number. How many good lives lost since 9/11 so far?"

"I don't know," I said.

"Hundreds of thousands in Shock and Awe, for one. A couple thousand US troops, plus other country troops. Then there's future terrorist attacks 'cause of vengeance, more hatred for the West, etc., etc."

"Okay, a lot of people," I said.

"A shitload of other people, and that's so-called good people, which is subjective. But look. Say instead we don't invade Iraq. No Afghanistan. Instead, we build the mosque. And what the hell, let's go completely insane and make a big-ass marble plaque that says 'Our apologies for whatever caused this. Let us make amends.'"

I laughed. "Oh God, dude, a memorial? Now you're fucking nuts."

"Am I? 'Cause that is exactly my point. *Don't* go insane. *Don't* go into a fit of rage. Do the exact opposite. The so-called bad guys start a fire, but instead of throwing gas on it, you should throw water."

"Well, it's never been done before, I give you that," I said.

"Exactly. And why not? You ever thought about that? Here, I'll ask you one question that will prove my point to you. Say you are—

let's say you are Bush, standing on the pile of rubble at Ground Zero. With the bullhorn, talking to the American people. And you shout out to everybody, you will do everything in your power to protect American lives so that this never, ever happens again."

"Okay, so? He pretty much said that."

"Did he? Did he say he would do everything in his power? Did he say he would do *anything*?"

"Sure. I'm sure that's what he meant."

"Nope. He meant he would only do *some* things. 'Cause there are certain things he would never do—no president would ever do. Things that might solve the problem, but they would just never try. That's what Bush should have said: 'The whole world is gonna hear from us, blah blah, and oh, by the way, if you think I'd do anything in the world to protect America, you're dead wrong. Let's be very clear. I am not open to *all* ideas.'"

"Well, not your crazy ideas."

Tuy shut his laptop and ruffled the sheets, slapping the pillow a few times. "Nope. Not my crazy ideas."

A few moments of silence filled the room. I sensed he was annoyed. I stared at the ceiling, thinking he was done talking.

"Except one thing, you dumbass. Ideas like mine—exactly like that—were shared with us right after 9/11 and came from possibly *the* most credible source on the subject. But they were completely ignored."

"What credible source?" I said.

"Think about it. Who would have the best access to knowledge about why 9/11 happened, what led to the attacks? Think of the simplest answer."

"Oh, please tell me you're not talking about '9/11 was an inside job.'"

"No, idiot, that would be *more* complicated, not less," he said.

"Well, it's a complex issue. You can't just give some simple—"

"Wrong! The answer could be complex. That doesn't mean it *is* complex. That's the problem with people. If they're in some big complicated mess, they assume it has to be caused by something big and complicated. That dumb-shit idea that Cheney and Rumsfeld planned

9/11? Do you realize how impossible it would be to pull that off, all the people who would have to be in on it? Hundreds, maybe thousands of people. Agencies who don't even work together to begin with, all perfectly coordinated. And not one of them leaking it. That conspiracy theory is just fucking stupid."

"I know, I know. So you gonna tell me or not?" I said.

"Nope. Try to guess. If you don't figure it out, you won't really know the answer."

"What is this, Confucius shit?"

Tuy laughed. "You racist motherf'er!" he said, pretending to be outraged. "No, but it's true. It's like you can . . . like if you read a book about who shot JFK, all you end up knowing is really the author. But if you do the research yourself, analyze the Zapruder tapes, construct it from scratch in your head, then you might actually know who shot him."

I laughed. "Man, you really are full of yourself, aren't you?"

"You f-tard. If someone has the answer to a question this important, why do you give a fuck if they are full of themself? See how you're focusing on other things that have nothing to do with the problem?" He gave me a playful smirk. "You just flunked the Lendl test, loser!"

I smiled. *Full of themselves*, I thought, tempted to correct him. But this time I didn't.

Rachel walked in, all business. She checked my IV and gave me a bigger dose of painkillers since I hadn't had any all day. I smiled to myself mischievously; I hadn't had any pain since early the day before. I started to drift off as Tuy bantered with her, but when she left I rolled over on my side, still half conscious, staring at the window and corner of the room. My mind seemed to casually tinker with Tuy's riddle, imagining a smooth box with no lid, turning it over, looking for a seam. Like the bizarre blue box in *Mulholland Drive*—mysterious, profoundly symbolic, but almost impossible to decipher. Then I was in deep sleep, images of the box fading, mixing with their representations in my head: a puzzle, a mystery of the universe, saving the world. It must not have been long. I slipped right into REM. And the dream I had was like none I'd ever had. It was lucid, vibrant, and unfaded. As clear as waking life.

We were standing at parade rest, Ethan and I, in the playground outside the theater at the school in Hamza. The kids played on the slide and chased after a soccer ball rolling away toward the gate by the road. I had just put on my combat vest and neatly secured the Velcro pockets. In front of us about ten meters stood the little Iraqi girl. Her arm was stretched out forcefully, pointing at me. She kept saying, "*Hinak!*"—"There!" None of this was choppy or blurred. It was no different from being awake, yet I knew it was a dream, and I was actually trying to figure out what she was pointing to. Ethan looked at me, wondering the same, but snapped back into position. I snuck my hand out and pointed to myself as if to ask, "You mean me?" and she jabbed her arm out in frustration, pointing more specifically at my upper chest. I got back to parade rest, eyes forward, looking at the little girl. She stomped her feet and thrust her arm out again, and I finally had to look down at the front of my vest. At that point I woke up abruptly.

Moonlight shone in through the window and lit up the corner of the ward. The cabinet and cubby shelves were in plain view, and the cabinet door stood wide open. There I could see my combat vest hanging by itself among a bunch of coat hangers. The shadow of the flag fell onto the inside of the door, swaying toward the open cabinet, then away. Toward, then away. Outside the window, the metal clips clanked against the flagpole, keeping time with the shadow's swaying. That is when it hit me. I threw the blanket off, jumped out of bed, and rushed over there. "No fucking way!" I said. My IV tube pulled taut, and the stand almost tipped over again. I grasped the pole and rolled it over with me to the cabinet and yanked the vest off its hanger. *I can't believe I forgot about it*, I thought. *All this time it's been here, and it never once occurred to me.* I flipped the vest over and tore open the inside pouch and stuck my fingers inside. I pinched the thin plastic edge and slid it out. There it was, the DVD, the same one the little girl had given me in the helo. "Holy fucking shit!"

Tuy!" I yelled. He didn't rouse. I rolled the IV over beside his bed and shook his shoulder. "Hey!" He groaned and cracked his eyes open. "Where's your laptop?" I said.

He frowned. "What the fuck?"

"Sorry, man, can I borrow your computer?"

He sat up and pointed to his computer bag. I tore open the Velcro and grabbed his laptop and ear buds. "Thanks. Go back to sleep."

I stuck the ear buds in and inserted the DVD, and it began to play. The first thing I saw was the back of a chair, someone's head. It was someone's personal video. The picture wobbled and fell to the floor. A young girl holding the camera giggled and whispered a question in Arabic. I adjusted the volume. Another girl's voice answered, and the camera swung back up above the chair and showed two or three rows of people. It then panned momentarily up and to the left, where the bottom edge of a clock was visible. A woman off camera said something about the date. I understood that much. Then the camera swung back to the right to reveal a stage, where an elfish boy stood in front of a curtain, holding a placard. The girls were in the third or fourth row of a small auditorium filled with mostly children.

The boy mumbled something quickly, then darted down the steps and to his mother in the front row. The curtain rose, and what I saw crashed into me on a wave of emotion. Relief and redemption, yet so overwhelming. It was Abeer, the little girl we'd seen, with the Ferrari red pants and bubble pipe. She was standing in front of a large wooden container like an oversized sandbox, dressed up like a flower. I wiped my eyes. *Oh my God*, I thought, *this is the same stage. We were there. This is where the little girl led us.*

She wore a bonnet. Bright yellow-and-blue petals surrounded her face. She began speaking, narrating a story to the audience in loud, staccato sentences. She stepped away from the box, waving her hand like a magician, and heads started popping up from inside the box, all with multicolored flower bonnets. The audience laughed. Abeer continued the story with a couple of short sentences, stopping nervously to repeat a word she seemed to mispronounce. A tall boy dressed in colorful linen and wearing a gold headdress walked onto the stage, holding a cloth bag. He approached the flower box and dipped his hand inside and sprinkled bits of sparkly paper over the heads of the children. They craned their necks out and opened their mouths, eagerly miming lapping up the drops. One kid accidentally caught a piece in his mouth and spit it out violently, disrupting the play momentarily. He grinned at the audience and bowed theatrically. They burst into laughter. The girl with the camera focused on Abeer again, who had waited patiently and now continued the story.

At this point I had to force myself to pause the DVD. I looked over at Tuy, who was rolled over, half underneath the pillow. "Tuy!" I said. I put the laptop down and nudged his shoulder again. "Yo! Where's Ethan?"

"Holy mother of—" he said, swatting the pillow away.

"Sorry, man, just tell me where Ethan is."

He sat up to look around the room and saw how dark it was. "Isn't it the middle of the night?" he said.

"About four. Did they put him up in an empty room or something?" Tuy groaned. "He's outside, in a trailer."

"Okay. In front, to the right?" I said. I knew it wasn't the one with the CT scan equipment.

He sat up, eyes half closed, obviously annoyed. "You can't just walk out of here, dumbass." He pointed. "Go to the end of the hall. That is the entrance. There is a guard's desk. Hazim is there tonight. Tell him you know me. Also mention you are an idiot." He plopped down on the pillow.

I chuckled. "Thanks, man."

I unhooked the IV catheter tube and pushed the door open to the dark hallway. Dim lights emanated from some of the rooms, and I could hear low beeping noises. A TV was turned down low somewhere. I felt the adrenaline. Shaky, but at the same time, giddy. *Look at me*, I thought. *Hospital gown, tiptoeing around, peering into these rooms. I'm like an escaped mental case.* I snickered. *Nurse Ratchel's probably gonna come around the corner and strap me down and give me electroshock.* I walked past the rooms unseen and found the guard desk positioned to face the glass-door entrance, but no guard. Just a clip-board sign-in sheet. I looked around. Another hallway went off to the left, where Rachel had wheeled me down for the brain scan. I started to call out, "Hello?" but noticed there was no lock or alarm on the glass doors. "Ah, fuggit," I said, pushed it open, and stepped outside.

I took a quick survey of the front area. In the dim light I could make out two trailers, one to the left, which I knew was the CT scan trailer, and one in front of the CSH to the right. A gravel path led to that one as well. "Shit," I said, "crunchy frickin' gravel." But there were raised wooden blocks lining the path. I stepped up on the first one and hopped to the next, careful not to miss since I could barely see. I gained my balance and jumped to the next, and the next, until I made it to the steps of the trailer. I paused there, wondering if the se-curity guard was out patrolling the grounds.

The hospital sat quiet, lit up by a few security lights. Only the dis-tant sound of a dog barking, the hum of a generator somewhere, and the soft clanking of the flagpole, which I could see along the left side of the building, lit up by a spotlight. "F it," I said, and rapped on the metal door. "Eeth!" I whisper-shouted. I looked around again. "Open up!" I knocked harder and waited. Finally the door opened. Ethan stood there in his boxers.

"What's going on?" he said.

I rushed inside and shut the door. I opened the laptop in front of him. "You gotta fucking see this."

He cleared his throat. "You don't have to whisper," he said. "There were KBR contractors here, but they went on vacation."

I looked at him. "Vacation?"

He shrugged. "Yeah, Dubai. Must be nice, huh?" He pointed to my catheter and gave me a funny look.

I hit play. "Take a look. F-ing unbelievable." The video continued, showing a yellow cardboard sun rising up from behind a backdrop of hills, and the little flowers all reveling in its warmth. A boy dressed as a king walked on stage and began talking to the other one, motion-ing to the flowers.

Ethan folded his arms across his bare chest. "Some kind of play, I'm guessing?"

"Yeah, it's a school play," I said, finally pulling my catheter out and wrapping the tape back around my wrist. The voice of the little girl came on again, and the camera panned back to where she was standing politely on the side, holding the book up. "There!" I said. "That's the little girl. That is Abeer."

Ethan looked at me dumbly. It was so hard for me to fathom that he had no recognition of any of it. I let him watch, looking for any reaction, but there was nothing. I paused the video. "Dude, I found this video in my combat vest, exactly where she put it when we were in the helo."

"Uh, when *you* were in the helo," he said.

"No, we were both there, goddamn it! This is the"—I pointed to the screen—"that is the stage in the theater! The little girl led you and me there, she showed us the stage, then saved us. I swear to God!"

He gave me another dumb stare. I took a deep breath and set the laptop on the table. "Okay, this means nothing to you. You weren't there, don't remember, whatever. But just watch, okay? Maybe something will trigger—"

He rolled his eyes and began to turn around.

"No, no," I corrected myself, "or maybe it's me. Maybe I'll wake up and realize I dreamed it or I'm fucking insane."

He took a few steps and opened his rucksack. "Well, I'll watch it if it'll make ya happy, but not in my damned skivvies."

"Sure, dude, no problem," I said, hitting play again. He stepped into some shorts and pulled a T-shirt over his head. "Okay, so." I paused it again. "So, big picture here. We went to the village, did an assessment, met with the town leaders, blah blah. I can tell you details later. But while you and I were pulling security during their meeting, this little girl, Abeer, she grabs our hands and leads us to the theater to show us something on the stage." I paused for a second, thinking. *Jesus! So many things happened*, I said to myself.

Ethan watched for a few minutes. I could tell it was doing nothing for him. The play continued, but it was in Arabic, of course, so that made it even worse. All either of us could make of it was that the king and maybe a prince—"sultan," Ethan corrected me—were in a heated discussion about the flowers. I kept my fingers on the mouse, ready to pause it or back up if anything significant came into view. I glanced at Ethan. He wasn't exactly engaged. He stood there, arms crossed, eyebrows raised.

"Dude! It's a grammar school play," he said.

"No shit!" I snapped. "I'm telling you, the little girl—that one right there—she told us about this very play."

Ethan threw his hands up. "Oh, so you weren't even at this play? Wow."

"No, dumbass. I told you. She told everyone about it at the meeting. This video was taken before the explosion. See? The stage is not damaged. This play happened before we even got to the village."

"Before you *dreamed* we went to the village," Ethan said under his breath.

I just about threw the laptop down on the table but turned around to face him. "Oh my fucking God!" I said, pointing to the video still playing. "Look, dickhead, this shit happened. I was there. There is no fucking way, even if I hallucinated this shit, that I could make up a story that fits perfectly into this play, the stage—"

"The play you've never seen."

"Jesus! The stage? Didn't I say the girl led us to a stage? How could I—"

"Well, unless you'd already seen this video."

"What?" I lost my mind at that point. "Ethan, are you insane? So I made up a memory based on a DVD I saw and then forgot I watched it? Gee, let's call Oliver Sacks up, 'cause this is *the* most elaborate neurological disorder known to fucking man. Oh, and my CT is clean too, by the way. I mean, goddamn, my brain cells must be good! They're misfiring like crazy, then flipping back to normal when shot with a magnet!"

Ethan chuckled briefly but restrained it. He knew I was pissed.

"Right," I said. "I made up the entire mission to Hamza, down to the tiniest little detail. I imagined—I dreamed up—us going to the theater, the little girl rescuing us, taking a metal ladder to the roof, witnessing Jacobs getting killed, the helo evac . . . right. My fucking ass."

I turned around to close the laptop. I was furious. I just wanted to leave.

"What did you say?" Ethan said, grabbing my shoulder.

I glared at him. "What."

"No, say that last part."

"We got evac'd."

"No. Before that," he said. For once his face looked attentive.

"Uh, went on the roof? We saw Jacobs get shot."

Ethan paused. He put his hand to his mouth, staring at me like studying a mental patient.

"Who is Jacobs?" he asked.

"He was our squad leader."

He got that look again, the one where he was annoyed and defiant over something he witnessed that had no logical explanation.

"What about it?" I said.

He paused for another second, the color in his face changing dramatically. "I . . . I never told you his name. Holy shit, dude. I never said his name!"

I felt a huge relief. "Good. You didn't have to, 'cause I know who he is."

"Okay, wait, hang on." He turned and scrambled around the room. He picked up an envelope and a short pencil, scratched something down, and then came back and put it facedown on the table. "Okay, what's he look like? Describe him."

"Uh," I said, "he's . . . tall, narrow face, curly hair. He reminded me of the food guy on Travel Channel's *No Reservations*."

Ethan picked up the envelope and held it in front of me. It read "Elliott Gould."

"Right, yeah, like him," I said.

"Holy shit." Ethan stared at me, looking almost sick. "Jacobs was just assigned to our squad the day before I left to come get you."

closed the laptop and tucked it under my arm. "Finally. So can we go now?" I said.

Ethan stared for a few seconds, then took a deep breath. "Sure, roger that." He spun around, scanning the room, snapping his fingers a few times. "Uh, what do I need, where are we going?"

"Nothing. We'll go ask Tuy if he knows someone who can translate the video."

*B*am! The metal screen door rattled against its frame. Ethan and I looked at the door. "Who the fuck?" Ethan said. He leaned over to the window and squinted, trying to see to the side. "Security guy," he said. He opened the door, and I saw who it was. Young guy with a dark beard and glasses. His uniform seemed out of place, but I recognized him: Tuy's buddy Hazim.

"Hey, man, what's up?" I said, trying to be friendly.

At first he seemed not to know who I was. "You didn't see me before, but yes, I saw you!" he said, all smug, pointing toward the main building.

"Yeah, I'm . . . I had to talk to my friend here. I had something very important to show—"

"IDs, please," he said. He studied them closely.

"I'm in the same room as Tuy—your friend?" He looked up at my stitches, then nodded. "Oh yes! 'Jesus guy,' he calls you! You were hit with IED?"

I shook my head. "Oh God, here we go. Yeah. I'm Jesus. IED. Whatever. Look, we have something important—"

"No one is allowed outside hospital after twelve," he said.

"Understood. But can you help us? It'll take five minutes . . . please. Very important." He hesitated. I opened the laptop. "Just translate some of this Arabic." I replayed it from the beginning, sliding the volume up. Hazim watched for a second and stepped inside toward the table as if curious, but then seemed dismissive.

"What is it?"

"It's a home video. Shot—made—at a school in Hamza," I said.

"Oh, Amiriyah. I know this. Very nice school."

Of course, in the first minute or two of the video, nothing important was happening whatsoever. Hazim started to leave.

"It is late. Tomorrow I translate, no problem."

"Hang on. Just watch for a minute," I said. The girl holding the camera panned up toward the clock. Hazim listened as the woman said something off camera.

I turned to him. "That's a date, right?"

"Yes, she says it is twenty-two of March," he said.

I looked at him, confused. "Twenty-second of March? Are you sure?"

"Yes, it is what she says."

What the hell? I thought, *same date as the IED?* I looked at Ethan. He didn't seem weirded out by it.

"Must be the . . . practicing for tomorrow," Hazim said.

"Oh, a rehearsal?" Ethan said.

Hazim nodded.

I looked at him. "Sure doesn't look like a rehearsal. Wait, did you say tomorrow?"

"Yes."

"Where?"

Hazim frowned. "There also, at the school. Amiriyah."

"How do you know that?" I said.

"I was there yesterday evening, for a soccer game. They say it." He began leaving again.

"Oh God, wait!" I said. "Please, just—here, I know you have to get back to making rounds."

"We can do in morning. No problem," he said.

I picked up the laptop. "How about this: Ethan has to stay here, and I need to go back to my room. So let's go. You take the laptop and watch the DVD."

"No, you can't leave. The other guard is outside. He is . . . not so nice." He gave Ethan and me a knowing smile.

"You're kidding me," I said.

"No, not kidding," he said.

"Here," I said, "then take the laptop."

He raised his eyebrows. "But you must stay, okay?"

"No, no. Absolutely. I won't move. Just, please, will you watch the—"

"Yes. Right now."

I patted him on the shoulder. "Awesome. Thanks, Hazim." He opened the door and stepped out on the stoop. "Hey, just write down anything important. Like weird stuff, especially the little girl."

He looked up at me.

"There's a little girl. Her name is Abeer. She is the one reading for the play."

He looked confused. "Play?"

"Yes, a play." I motioned with my hands. "It's a story? With actors . . ."

"Oh yes, play, I know." He nodded, starting down the steps. "'The Killing Flower.'" He stepped onto the gravel. I started to stop him but didn't. I shut the door and turned to Ethan. "Did he say 'Killing Flower'?"

"Sounded like it," Ethan said.

I t's really absurd how life presents these pivotal, climactic moments where one little random choice we make can change the course of everything, yet in hindsight we like to glamorize it as the proverbial fork in the road, marked "high road" and "low road" in big, bold letters. Truth is, these moments are more like walking aimlessly along, right past a tiny little footpath off to the side, completely obscured by undergrowth—of course that'd be the one you're supposed to take— or it's like you're doing ninety down a road and come across a huge tangled mess of intersecting highways, off ramps, bridges, and tunnels, all with confusing signs and arrows pointing everywhere, and you have five seconds to pick one.

I'd love to say I heard what Hazim said, made the connection to Stuart's vision, put it all together with the DVD and the helo, and figured the whole thing out. In fact, there wasn't nearly enough time to process such a complicated and bizarre series of events. There Ethan and I were, talking through this Hamza thing into the wee hours of the morning, completely confused, with only a vague notion of what we thought we could do, and no idea of the how. And I knew it was my moment; I had the benefit of big neon lights that said "problem." All I needed was to come up with a theory—quickly—calculate the odds, and then go all in. So if I had figured anything out, it was how to do what Tuy had talked about; if there was an answer, it might be simple, not complex, so get unconfused, stick with the math, be logical enough to consider even crazy ideas.

Ethan was totally convinced of my story at that point. He told me to recount the entire thing and asked me detailed questions, especially about things moving in slow motion, the distorted frequencies of the girl's voice, her tying ropes to us and jumping. He must have said "holy shit" a dozen times. There was no denying some bizarre stuff was going on. I also told him about Stuart and his vision of the girl and me falling. His eyes widened, and he got up from the couch. "Jesus! Are you serious?"

"Yeah, it was pretty freaky."

"We gotta find out what all this means."

"I know. Like, what's with the March twenty-second thing? What the fuck? Same date as the IED explosion!"

"Well, coincidence, maybe, or the woman got the date wrong. But what I don't get is, Hazim says the play is tomorrow . . ."

"Which it could be. Let's say the video *was* of a rehearsal."

"Right, forget the DVD. But tomorrow is the eighth, and you— we—were at the school on the eighth, and the missile had hit some time before that, you said. Like not days—weeks, probably."

"And holy shit," I said, "it can't be before, if Hazim was there just yesterday. Dude, the school is not that big. The only place for a soccer game is the playground, which is right in front of the theater."

Ethan smiled. "I feel really stupid saying this, but . . . I think you . . . I think your little trip to Hamza, I think it, uh, maybe hasn't happened yet."

"I know. It's fucking out there, dude. Or maybe all these things *have* happened, but I've just jumped back to a different, I don't know, version or something? Maybe when I fell out of the helo I . . ."

Ethan stepped toward the back. I heard the toilet lid go up. "Go on," he said as he began peeing.

"But where the hell'd the little girl go?"

He chuckled. "And if I was in the helo, where did I go? And wait, holy shit. What about when the IED went off and you seemed to just appear in the seat. Where did you come from?"

I sat for a minute, lost in thought, until Ethan walked back into the room. "I don't know, dude," I said. "It's trippy."

Bam, bam, bam! The door frame rattled again. This time it was in rapid succession, hard pounding.

"Jesus!" Ethan said; his whole body jumped.

"Open the door!" came a muffled voice from outside. It was Hazim. Ethan reached for the handle and almost got his fingers jammed as Hazim came blasting through the door. His face had a panic that reminded me of the soldiers that day the mortar round exploded in the chow tent. He held the laptop under his arm as he waved the DVD at my face. "Where you get this sick shit?"

"What?" I said.

He pointed his finger at me. "You make this? This video? Iraqi children? Horrible killing?" He threw the DVD at my chest, and it bounced onto the table. I backed up.

"Hey!" Ethan stepped forward and blocked him with his hand. "We don't know what you're talking about!"

Hazim stood glaring at me.

"We barely watched the DVD," I said. "A little girl gave it to me. An Iraqi girl!"

Hazim studied our faces. "You did not video it?"

"Absolutely not. Hey, you saw the first part. A couple of girls filmed it, right?"

He paused, then seemed to surge in anger. "Well, do you know what I saw? You have an idea? My cousin dies. I see him die!" His face contorted. "Children all dies!" He wiped his eyes.

I took a few seconds to process everything. "Wait, what do you mean? You mean everyone in the play? All the kids?"

"No. More. Kids, also men, women. Mothers and fathers. A big explosion. The whole room is—"

I looked at Ethan. "The missile. It's the missile." I grabbed Hazim's shoulders. "Did you see anything like a rocket? RPG? Coming through the window, from the left?"

He shook his head. "No. I didn't see. I mean, it was so quick. The camera fell on the floor."

I stepped to the table and opened the disc drive of the laptop.

"Here," Ethan said, handing me the DVD.

"Oh yeah." I turned to Hazim. "Listen. This is going to sound fucked up—"

"I don't want to see it," Hazim said.

"That's okay. Not asking you to," I said. "Ethan and I can watch. I'll mute it."

I dragged the slider almost to the end, where the camera showed a sideways image of chairs and debris on the floor. Then I moved it backward through the explosion. Most of it was blurred and only took a few frames. It very quickly jumped to images of the play. I slid it forward but went too far and saw the chairs again.

"Just play it from here," Ethan said, pointing, "around 10:17."

"Okay." I moved the slider. Hazim sat down on the couch, rubbing his face. Ethan and I watched closely. The camera showed the stage from a wide angle, including the tops of heads in the audience, and the window on the left wall, the one Ethan had climbed. I could see Abeer on the right, narrating.

"I guess they don't know what a zoom button is," Ethan said sarcastically.

"Well, they're kids," I said, turning to make sure Hazim was not watching.

"What was *that*?" Ethan said. I turned back around. The video had already reached the explosion. Ethan grabbed the slider and moved it back a few seconds.

"You missed it," he said, and played it back in slow motion.

Abeer was narrating again, her arm slowly stretching out toward the audience. And then I saw it, what would have been a split second on the video, right before the explosion. The image switched abruptly to two separate ones, overlaid on top of each other—Abeer, the stage, the audience still visible, but mixed with what looked like a crowd of people gathered outside, moving in one direction. The figures were clearer on the left, where the original image had nothing but the blank wall next to the stage. But what I saw next was so shocking, I just said, "What?" and stared at the screen.

It was the kid from the meeting, the one whose face had been burned and looked like melted plastic. But there she was, looking into the camera, her face filling the frame, making a goofy expression for her friend. And it was fine. Her face was perfectly fine. I moved the slider back and replayed it, hitting pause when it got to her face again. "Oh my God, oh my God, oh my God," I said, standing up and holding my forehead.

"What, dude?"

I pointed to the screen. "That girl, oh my God . . ." I thought for a second. "That's . . ." I said, "that girl, I saw her before. She should have burns, Ethan."

Hazim came over to take a look. "That's her," I said. "She had fucking burns all over her face, eye. Holy shit." I walked over to the couch and sat down, rubbing my forehead.

"Are you sure?" Ethan said. I just sat there, rubbing, shaking my head, until finally I stood up, looking at him.

"This is it, man, we gotta go there."

"What?" he said.

"We've got to. We've got to prevent it."

"Whoa, whoa, hold on!" he said. "So suddenly you got everything figured out? All these events? All this space-time shit?"

"Don't need to. That explosion hasn't happened yet. It's going to tomorrow . . ." I looked at Hazim. "Save those kids? We gotta go, guys. We've got to go there and prevent it."

He just stared at me blankly, rubbing his beard.

"Hazim, how far is the village from here?"

"Dude, are you serious? Really?" Ethan said, shaking his head.

I stepped over to Hazim.

"Village?" he said.

"Hamza."

"It is . . . three hours, or four, going up the river."

"Can you get us there?"

"I don't know, I mean . . ."

"What's this 'us' shit?" Ethan said.

I turned to him. "Well, *I'm* going . . . if he can take me. I'm fucking going. This is it, man."

"How the fuck?" he said, motioning with his hands that I was insane.

"Look. Hazim's cousin and all those kids? They're still alive! Ethan, you know this. Hazim, just . . . you have to trust me; they're not dead. But they will be. We've gotta fucking go there."

I opened the door and peered out toward the CSH. A hint of light was beginning to illuminate the sky.

"And do what?" Ethan nearly shrieked.

I held the door open and stepped through.

"Wait!" they both shouted simultaneously.

"Where the fuck are you going?" Ethan said.

"To grab my shit while it's still dark out."

Hazim stood up. "I go with you . . . the guard."

"Oh yeah, you'd better." I stuck my head inside the door. I'd never seen Ethan so fazed, so out of sorts. "You don't have to go. But . . . I could use your help . . . planning this shit."

He raised his eyebrows and chuckled sarcastically. "Rrrrright. Hey! I just love a good AWOL planning party!"

I gave him a half smile. I knew what he thought. There was no logic to what I was doing. None whatsoever. "Okay," I said, "well, back in ten minutes." I followed Hazim out and let the door slam behind me.

I t took longer than that. At least it felt that way. Hazim and I had to circle all the way around the CSH and enter through the door in front of the CT scan trailer. We were trying to go through the main entrance, but the guard surprised us, coming out the front doors and turning right, facing us directly. There was no way to hide and let him pass, so we scurried around the corner and double-timed it along the left side of the building ahead of him.

As we passed the flagpole, I took a couple of seconds to check the window, see if it happened to be unlocked. No luck. I cupped my face against the glass, but it was too dark to see anything. Hazim pulled at my arm, and we continued to the rear of the building, across the helo pad, past the refuse bins, and back up the other side. We peered around the corner, and the fucker was coming right toward us again. The CT scan trailer was to our left, the side entrance right next to us. We ducked down, but I impulsively made a move toward the door.

"Tsch, tsch." Hazim grabbed my arm and whispered, "You go in; I cover," and he stood up and opened the door, frantically waving me in. I rushed inside before it dawned on me what he had planned. But it was genius.

Just before the door shut, I heard Hazim: "Jim! You out here?" As far as I could tell, it worked perfectly. I heard the guard start to ask where the hell Hazim had been, then the door shut. I knew I didn't have long to grab my things and get out. I hoofed it to the reception desk, down the long, dark hallway, and into the ward. I threw on my clothes, emptied my box of stuff into the laptop case, and grabbed my rifle. Tuy was dead asleep. I wanted to tell him good-bye. *Thanks, dude*, I thought. *You're right, I do have a Jesus complex.* I unlatched the window and cracked it open. It made a god-awful sound as the frame scraped against the metal. I heard Tuy roll over as I stepped one leg outside.

"Hmm?" he said. "You done gone completely nuts, boy?"—his usual wry voice. I looked over in the direction of his bed. *Oh God, please don't ask for your laptop back.* Tuy's dim figure lay silhouetted against the wall.

I hopped up and pulled the bag through. "Just need some air," I said, and shut the window.

I had no idea if Hazim and I were thinking the same thing. He might have been waiting for me to come back through the building; he could have been trying some crazy scheme to distract the other guy, Jim. I had no idea. Get back to the trailer—that's all I knew. I ran up to the corner, peered around front, and scurried toward the gravel path. I could hear the birds starting their morning calls. It wouldn't be long before sunrise.

I wasn't sure what to expect when I got up to the stoop and opened that door. I guess I expected no one. Ethan would be in bed, ready with a quip for me when I woke him up to ask one more time, "Dude, you sure you don't wanna—" He'd cut me off: "Nah, my fat ass would just slow ya down." "Nah, I'm not much for adventure." "Nah, AWOL's not my bag." It could be any of these. And Hazim. He wouldn't be there either. He'd helped enough, even risked his job already. And come on, I was a complete stranger to him.

But none of that was waiting for me. I literally flinched when I stepped inside and saw them standing there—both of them, Ethan and Hazim, grinning at me. "'Bout time, lard-ass," Ethan said, zipping his bag shut. I just laughed and shook my head.

The next few minutes were a complete blur, a barrage of rapid questions back and forth, a flurry of ideas: "What's the plan?" "How far's this place?" "We'll need food, flashlights . . ." "What about weapons?" "Hazim, do you know the area?" We all talked over each other.

Ethan rummaged through an empty file cabinet and came up with a blank sheet of printer paper. "Let's be methodical about this shit," he said, slapping it down on the table.

"Good idea," I said, setting my rifle down.

"Okay, here's what I'm thinking."

I took a quick look out the window. "We've got like zero time before it's light outside."

"Yeah, fuck it, we gotta get going," Ethan said.

I looked at Hazim. "Okay. First we take, say, five minutes and grab every fucking thing we might possibly need."

Ethan patted his ruck. "I gots all my shit, holmes."

"Weapons?" Hazim said.

I looked at him. "Uh . . ."

"Oooh. Bad idea," Ethan said. "Going outside the wire, into the population? Bad."

I thought for a second. "Yeah, maybe we need to blend in, kind of."

Ethan laughed. "Pfft, right, blend in! Two pasty white boys."

"Well, as much as possible," I said.

"What else?"

"Uh, laptop, DVD . . . oh, right, food. We have no idea how long it'll end up taking. Hazim?"

Hazim took the pencil and started sketching a map. "Okay, we are here now. We go to here, at the river. My uncle has his boat we use for fishing." He marked another spot a few streets away. "Here I get drinks, bread, kebab maybe, gas for boat."

My eyes widened. "Really?" He nodded. I looked at Ethan and back at Hazim. "What's there?"

"My uncle. His restaurant."

"Holy shit. Dude, your uncle is fucking genius," Ethan said.

I grabbed the laptop and shoved it into the bag. The three of us stood there for a few seconds.

"Okay, so we're good, right?" I said.

"Wait." Ethan slapped Hazim's shoulder. "How do we get outside the wire?"

"I know. Easy," he said, and we left.

There were three trailers set up next to Ethan's, lining the road from the CSH to the main gate. Hazim led us down the steps and to the right, away from the hospital, each of us with a bag over the shoulder, to the back of the first trailer. It was easy to get around quietly—dirt and sand beneath our boots, plenty of clearance between the back windows and the fence. Hazim shielded the lens of his Maglite in his palm and let the light spill out just enough for us to avoid scraping our gear against the siding or the fence. He stopped at the corner, cutting the light out.

The next trailer, which angled in toward the fence, had lights on in the bathroom and the back bedroom. Ethereal, haunting music played inside. I recognized it immediately: "Airbag" by Radiohead. Rapid, spacey guitar trills, siren noises, vocals droning with reverberation like in a music hall: "In the neon sign, scrolling up and down, I am born again . . ."

Hazim leaned into my ear, pointing. "We go to the end," he whispered. I peered around to see. The corner was pitch black. Impossible to tell if there was a way around it. We'd have to do the proverbial crouch and tiptoe underneath the windows to get by. I looked at the two of them, barely able to make out their faces. Ethan shrugged as if to say, "Just go." We crossed the gap to the edge of the second trailer and bent down as much as possible underneath the light. I couldn't see shit where I was stepping. I grabbed Hazim's shirttail. *Jesus*, I thought, *if there's a plastic bottle back here, it'll crunch loud as shit.* I began to barely lift my feet off the ground so I'd at least move any obstacles out of the way. I had to carry the laptop bag in my hands to keep it from dragging on the ground. I was paranoid the strap would slip off my shoulder and I'd trip and bang into the side of the trailer. I ducked my head underneath the bathroom window. The bass pulsed louder as Thom Yorke's wailing voice drew out a long, reverberating note.

Hazim was tiptoeing so slowly in front of me. My back ached. *All those dumbass exercises in basic, and they never had us practice sneaking around a fucking building?* Hazim stopped and clicked his flashlight on. There was a small gap between the corner of the trailer and the fence. Each of us squeezed through sideways. The last trailer was set right up against the fence, no lights on. "We go in front," Hazim whispered. "This one is empty."

I looked out at the road. Seemed risky. Up the road, vehicles entering the complex would have to stop at the gate, giving us time, but not those headed out. Hazim walked cautiously to the front of the trailer, then stepped over the path to avoid the gravel. I could see the main gate fifty meters ahead. A Humvee was parked up there, and two guards were smoking, leaning on the hood. Hazim stopped. The open area on that side of the trailer was lit up by a big-ass lamp hanging above the storage containers in the back.

Hazim crouched and motioned us to get down. "We must get there," he said softly, and pointed. There was a break in the fence underneath the light, and a path was visible between the containers.

"Those fuckers are facing this way. They'll definitely see us," I said.

Hazim looked around quickly, taking a deep breath and blowing it out. We sat there for a second. I bit my lip and glanced over at the guards.

"Okay, here's the deal," Ethan said. "We're hospital staff fucking around. Follow my lead."

"What about curfew?" I said.

He shook his head. "They're fuckin' guards, dude. They don't give a shit."

I turned to Hazim. He nodded, and said, "Not their responsibility. *We* enforce."

"Okay," I said, "let's go." We stood up and walked into the open.

"An entire month of leave? You lucky bastard!" Ethan shouted.

I jumped up off the ground and pointed down at Ethan with devil horns. "Dass right, nigga! You know it!"

We didn't overdo it. We strolled casually toward the path, acting like we were just meandering around the base. I resisted the urge to look back at the guards. But they didn't do a thing. We got under the light, and Ethan jumped up and smacked the metal cowling. "Ixnay, Coffelt," I said with clenched teeth, scooting past him, head down.

We were now between the storage containers, hidden from view. Hazim got in front and switched the Maglite on again. "Straight across this way," he said. We made our way past pallet racks, generators, and wheelchairs. It wasn't an area where we were likely to be seen that time of night, but I was still nervous. It was dark; all we could see was what was lit up by Hazim's Maglite, but that also included us, three dickheads out wandering around at the crack of dawn with bags over our shoulders.

"Oh, we don't look suspicious at all!" Ethan said with his classic sarcasm.

I chuckled. "I know, right?"

"The outside wall is not far," Hazim said. He stopped for a moment to shine the light ahead. More shipping containers. Looked like a dozen or so side by side. He cut to the left. Our boots crunched in thick gravel. I switched the laptop strap to my other shoulder. We seemed to be near the corner of the base. Once we got past the last container, Hazim led us around the side, where a ten-foot retaining wall towered above us. He stopped there and shined the light along the top edge.

Ethan made a sarcastic nasal sound. "Now, how in the fuuuck . . ."

"But there was always a vehicle!" Hazim said, pointing to his feet. "Right here!" He waved the Maglite around, perplexed.

"Well, it ain't here now, fool!" Ethan said.

I followed Hazim as he looked around with the light. No vehicle. Just an empty patch of gravel. He shined the light onto the wall again. The long side of the end container came into view until he turned around again. "We have to find something," he said.

"Hang on," Ethan said. He took the Maglite and stood between the corner of the container and the wall, shining it upward. "I can jump that," he said. "Question is . . . okay, let me up there." He motioned for me to give him a boost. There was a hollow sound as his boot struck the side of the container, then he was on top. We looked on as Ethan studied the distance and angle. He turned to us, leaning down with the flashlight. "Shine this on the wall," he said, then turned back around.

"Hang on a second, dude," I said.

"D'oh!" he said. "Now I can't see my damn feet!"

"Dude, what are you doing?"

Next thing we knew, Ethan was taking a few clomping steps across the top of the container and sailing across the gap to slam onto the top edge of the retaining wall. "Oof!" I heard the air slap out of his lungs. His arms were stretched across the top, grasping the far edge.

"Holy shit!" I said.

Ethan scrambled, then pulled himself up into a sitting position, taking a deep breath.

"You okay?" Hazim said.

"Well, I fucked *that* up!" he said, shining the flashlight down below him. Turning himself around, he gripped the edge with both hands and hung there for a few seconds, then dropped to the ground next to us.

"Well," he said, brushing off his ACUs, "it ain't fun, but . . . it's doable."

"I don't see what else we can do," I said, turning to Hazim.

"It is the only place we can cross the wall," he said.

I shook my head. "Fuck it."

I boosted Hazim, then Ethan boosted me. Hazim and I each gave an arm to Ethan to lift him up.

"Okay, Mr. Parkour," I said, "show us how it's done."

I held the flashlight as Ethan said, "Take two or three steps, bend your knees, push off with your strongest leg, but swing your arms and throw them in front of you right when you spring off the ground."

Hazim went first. I took his bags while Ethan choreographed the steps for him. "So it's one . . . two . . . three steps. That's really all the room you have up here. Do not, I repeat, do *not* take any more than that. Unless you want to pull a nasty major-fail face-plant into the retaining wall. Okay?"

Hazim nodded and walked it out a couple of times. Then he stood and focused for a few seconds, shaking his hands out to his sides.

"You got this, bro," Ethan said to him, and he went. I followed his feet as he ran.

The container echoed as his boots struck the surface. He jumped across, smacking the top of the wall and almost slipping off. "*Khara!*" he said. He hung awkwardly on to the edge with the side of one arm.

Ethan chuckled. "Oooh, Hazim! You came in a little low, son!"

Hazim pulled himself up enough to get a leg across.

"You good?" Ethan said.

"Yes, okay," Hazim said.

Ethan turned to me. "You next."

I handed him the light and laptop bag. "This fucker's heavy," I said. I walked forward and back, through the steps.

"Remember, just three steps, and throw your arms way out." Ethan shined the light on Hazim, who slid himself back out of the way, straddling the wall. "Ready, man?"

"Okay," he said.

I took off. Three quick steps and into the air. *Bam!* I landed hard on my upper chest, arms across the top of the retaining wall. "Fuuuck," I groaned. I barely had air in my lungs.

Ethan laughed. "Kinda hurts, don't she?" he said with a drawl.

"A-hole," I said, trying not to laugh. I lifted my leg up and over. Ethan stood on the edge of the container, ready to throw the flashlight.

"Now, drop this and we're seriously fucked," he said.

"Understood," I said.

He threw it perfectly into my lap. I shined it on him as he carefully tossed the bags to Hazim, one by one. He then took a few steps back, and I scooted myself backward away from Hazim to leave room, then turned the light on Ethan again.

"Not in my eyes, you stooge!" he said.

"Sorry." I lowered the light to his feet. He paused, then adjusted his stance and ran full speed and jumped. Boom. Just like that, he was perched on the top of the wall.

"You showoff motherfucker!" I said. He'd bent down, almost fully touching his knees, sprung up, arms toward the sky, and sailed through the air like it was nothing. And he'd landed in a perfect squat, feet squarely on the edge. No wobble or anything.

"Okay, that time was better," Ethan said.

Hazim was smiling. "Cool, man!" he said.

Ethan pointed to the Maglite. "Okay, turn that fucker off."

I clicked it off, and we sat there, resting for a moment. The air was cool now, and there were almost no sounds. In the distance just a few vehicles on a highway, some insects in the grass outside the retaining wall. The quiet glow of sunrise lined the very edge of a city three or four klicks away. "Pretty nice up here," Ethan said.

I looked back toward the hospital. "Yeah, it is."

Hazim led us along the wall, tromping through thick grass and brush, until we reached the edge of a field. There we followed a narrow dirt road to a bridge. I could see the town to the right of us. The river was shallow but lined with thick mud, Hazim told us. We'd have to use the bridge to cross, which was risky.

A car approached from the long stretch of road behind us. We crouched down beside the culvert and let it pass, then ran across. From there we kept jogging. For the kilometer or so remaining, we continued without stopping, except twice, when we had to duck down in the grass as a vehicle drove by.

"Not too far," Hazim said, out of breath. His feet dragged on the sandy pavement, bag slapping against his side with each trotting step. As we reached the edge of town, the sunlight began to seep over the hills. Their great shadow receded over us like a tide. The houses were still dark, thankfully, but not for much longer. I was nervous as hell.

"Where's the . . ." I paused to swallow. My throat was completely dry.

Hazim turned his head to the side. "The next street."

We crossed, went down a narrow alley, and paused at the corner in front of a major street. No one anywhere. Just a gangly dog sniffing at something in the drain. "It's that restaurant there." Hazim pointed to a small restaurant with outdoor seating. The dog ran off as we crossed the street. Hazim had us duck down behind the plastic tables while he snuck down the alley to the back. We heard the metal door click, and he cracked it open enough for us to squeeze inside.

"We pack a few things," he said, "then go outside from the back."

Hazim led us to the kitchen. We passed a small cooler and grabbed some sodas and water bottles.

"Here, take some of this," he said, pointing to a storage shelf next to the sink, and disappeared in the back. We found plastic bags of pita and some cookies shaped like crescent rolls. "Oooh, those look good," Ethan said. He unzipped his ruck. "Some kind of date filling." We stuffed them inside. Hazim came around the corner just as a car drove by. Arabic dance music blared through the windows, then faded quickly. Hazim had a tall gas container, straining to hold it with one arm.

"Shit, do we need that much?" Ethan asked.

"Three or four hours. Yes."

Ethan looked around the room. "What else? How about an extra baggie—poor man's dry pack."

"Okay, and one of these small knives, maybe," I said. We grabbed what we could think of. Hazim found a portable gas generator.

"Oh, thank God!" I said. "I forgot all about that; laptop's probably low on power." We stuffed it in a bag and left.

Hazim took us a few blocks behind the main street and back toward the river. There was way too much light. Shopkeepers would be opening up; people would be driving to work. We could be discovered at any moment. Around the corner we saw an open market. They were busy setting up, and none of them looked over at us. "Normal pace," Ethan whispered. "Just a morning walk here, people. Nothing to see."

Hazim took us down an alleyway to get behind and around the market. My hands were shaking, and I could feel my heart thumping. Finally we reached the south edge of the town and the river. A half-dozen long wooden boats lay on their sides on the grass and stones. Hazim stopped in front of one that had an outboard trolling motor. He scanned the area, then bent down to grab the front. "We pull in the water, and you two get in," he said.

We dragged the wood along the ground. "Shit," I said as it made a scraping sound against the rocks. I lifted higher, and the boat slapped onto the water. Hazim waded in, setting the gas can in the rear.

"Okay, now," he said to us. Ethan and I tossed our bags over the side and climbed in. Hazim pushed off, jumping into the back as we drifted away through the sparse reeds poking out of the water.

Ethan and I instinctively kept low, looking to Hazim for direction. He checked behind us, then pulled on the motor cord a few times. The engine finally sputtered and started up. It sounded like a light-duty lawn mower. Hazim lowered the prop into the water, and we headed downstream.

"What time is it?" I said, turning the laptop bag over to find the zipper.

Ethan checked his watch. "Oh seven thirty," he said.

Hazim adjusted his position on the rear seat, one hand on the tiller and the other leaning on the side railing. He looked exhausted. I opened the laptop and held down the power button. As it booted I checked out the river ahead. We were gliding along, making our way through a narrow passageway with walls of towering reed beds on either side. As we rounded a bend, a long riverbank came into view, fully illuminated. The mirror image of the thin grass stretched out toward us along the surface.

"Come sit back here, dude," I said to Ethan. He stood up, balanced himself, and took carefully placed steps down the middle of the boat. I watched as the screen lit up. "Shit!" I said.

Ethan sat down beside me. "What?"

"Fucker's really low on power. Twenty percent."

Ethan spun his head around to Hazim. "How much gas we got in the tank?"

Hazim chuckled. "We know when it stops," he said.

Ethan turned back toward the screen. "Greeeeeat," he said.

I played the video from the beginning. "We'll watch as much as we can," I said. Ethan rested his chin on his palm and watched intently. The little girls wobbled the camera around, they giggled, the audience began milling into the theater and taking their seats in front of the camera. Not much going on in the first few minutes, as far as I could tell. Of course, the Arabic was mostly gibberish to us. I turned to Hazim. "You're listening to this, right?"

"Yes. I hear it," he said.

I clicked the pause button. "Hold on," I said. "So what exactly are we looking for here? I know we want to confirm the play is actually planned for today, but anything else?"

"The target. The bad guy," Ethan said. "If we can tell who the missile is—was—trying to take out . . . I mean, there probably ain't shit chance we'll find any clues, but we should still look for 'em."

"Yeah," I said. "Okay, Hazim, can you make sure you listen closely? Translate anything you think is critical? I mean, obviously ignore the bullshit unimportant parts, but . . . you know what I mean."

"No problem. Now they are just talking about buttons and holding the camera."

"Cool," I said. We continued watching. The camera panned from left to right, stopping on certain people taking their seats. "They are saying, 'Look, there is my friend's parents,'" Hazim said.

The girl with the camera shouted a name excitedly, and the mother turned and waved. The next few minutes, all we could see were the backs of people's heads, the stage, and a portion of the wall to the left.

But suddenly I remembered something. "Hey, the clock," I said, and pointed.

"What clock?" Ethan said. I paused the video.

"Shit!" I pointed again. "It's out of the frame, but it's like right up there on the wall. Upper left." I quickly explained how he'd climbed up there before, noticing his affect. I couldn't help feeling like he really knew what I was talking about. I just continued playing the video. The camera stayed at the same level, panning back and forth to focus on certain people. We got a good look at the window where Ethan and I had crawled through the blast hole.

It got to the point where the woman said the date. "That's the date, what about the time?" I said.

"She does not say it," Hazim said.

We watched closely. The damned camera kept wobbling around but never panned upward far enough. The audience settled in, and the curtain rose. Abeer stepped onto the stage and started reciting her lines.

"Shit," I said, "the play's not going to tell us anything."

But I kept watching. We'd already seen the end, where the explosion happened. Might as well make sure we saw the entire thing. The kids, all dressed as vibrant flowers, popped up from inside the big box; the tall boy came out and watered them. Abeer continued her narrative. Suddenly the computer made a *tonk* sound, and a pop-up appeared on the screen: "Running low on power."

"Fuckin' great," Ethan said.

"Okay, close all the apps," I said, reaching for Hazim's bag and the gas container.

"Oh, you couldn't have done that before or anything," Ethan said.

"Hey, I'm working off of like zero sleep here." I stuck the tube from the generator into the gas can and started it up. "Cool, it's charging," I said.

"Maybe half hour is good," Hazim said.

There was an old canvas tarp under our feet. I pulled it up and draped it over the generator to muffle the sound. Ethan lit up a cigarette and propped himself against the side of the boat. I glared at him. "Brilliant. All these gas fumes, and you light up a match."

He blew out a puff of smoke at my face.

"Ah, fuggit," I said. "Gimme one of thems."

We looked out on the water. A man stood on the bank, holding a fishing line. Hazim waved. A crane flew in low and landed behind the reeds. And I saw just how tranquil and undisturbed it was there—nature, moving slow and quiet. No bombs or explosions to rip out its insides or send it screaming for dear life. We came upon a break in the vegetation, where a patch of sand lay against a backdrop of bright-green grass. A herd of sheep were stepping apprehensively through the sand, making their way toward the water. A thin man in a beige dishdasha guided them from the back. I motioned to Ethan. "Check it out, dude."

He turned around. "Damn. Well, that's picturesque as hell," he said. We watched the scene ease by us.

"Yeah. I'm expecting to see Jesus any minute now," I said.

Ethan chuckled. "I know, right? I think I see baby Moses over there in the reeds, floating in a basket."

I turned around to Hazim. "Sorry about all the Christian references, dude."

"We also believe in Jesus. Moses too," he said.

Ethan made a nasal sound like poorly suppressed laughter. "Pardon my friend, Hazim, he flunked World Religions."

"Smart-ass," I said. I settled back into my seat.

Ethan pulled the package of cookies out of the bag, and we passed it around. They tasted incredible. "Hazim," Ethan yelled, his eyes all wide, "what are these?"

Hazim looked closely. "Oh, they are called *klaicha*. It is our nation's cookie of Iraq. You like it?" he said, turning to me.

"Yeah," I said, nodding my head. "Kinda like a gourmet Fig Newton."

We finished the bag and brushed our hands off. For a few minutes we sat quietly, watching the scenery. Ethan finally tilted his head back and closed his eyes. I lit up another cig and checked on the lap-top. Still a ways to go. The video stayed on my mind. There had to be something there, some kind of clue. Well, no, I corrected myself, there didn't *have* to be. But what if there was? What if it was so obvi-ous and I couldn't see it? What the hell had she given me this DVD for? I remembered what Tuy had said about complex problems and not assuming they have complex answers. I took a deep breath and looked over at Ethan—stretched out on the bottom of the boat, his arms folded, resting his eyes. I turned around to Hazim. He was clenching his eyes tightly, then opening them wide.

"Want me to steer?"

We switched places. He sat close, making sure I stayed away from the shallow areas. It seemed to wake him up for the time being.

Again I thought about what Tuy had said. *Is this complex? Really? We're just assuming it is. So either way, the solution could be simple. Or complex, even. You can't assume anything. I guess that is the point. Can't assume anything.* "Hmm," I said aloud. Hazim turned to me. "You know what?" I said. "It's really the assumptions. They are what get in the way, probably."

"Assumptions?" he said.

"No, I mean this thing we're trying to figure out. It's like an optical illusion. Better yet, it's like a magic trick. Hard to understand because it's based on your assumptions, which are wrong. We ignore certain things just naturally. And it's like these things are in your way, block-ing your view."

I moved the tiller a little to round a bend. "So the question is, what assumptions are we making?" I said.

"I don't know," he said, "the DVD is true?"

"Well, okay, yeah. We're assuming I'm not fricking insane and made a fake video, but I mean specifically, about the DVD, what we see in it."

"Yes, what we think we see."

I thought aloud for a moment. "The school kids are putting on a play, a couple girls make a home video, halfway through the thing a missile comes through the window—"

"And that happens today," Hazim said, "in the afternoon . . . we think."

"Right." I exhaled and shook my head. "And based on nothing, essentially. Just someone saying a damned date that could be totally wrong."

"Yes, except my cousin. He is going there today. I know this."

"Jesus!" I said. "I fucking forgot. Call his ass. We gotta confirm this shit."

Hazim reached in his pocket. "No connection here."

"Goddamn it. No service," I said. "This sucks."

I wondered if I'd fucked up royally. *Maybe if we'd stayed back, we could have kept trying his cousin. Watch us go all the way there and the play was fucking yesterday.*

Hazim interrupted my thoughts. "What about the little girl? You talked to her?"

"Yeah, we both did, Ethan and I. First she told us—the elders and our squad leader—about the missile and the explosion. Then a little later she led us to the theater, I guess to show us. I don't know."

I pushed the tiller to one side to avoid a big branch in the water. "You assume," he said.

I looked at him "Yeah, I assume. Shit, man, she was speaking Arabic. What the F do I know? I . . . I guess she must have wanted us there to help her rehearse. She had me say some lines."

"Hmm," Hazim said. "It seems strange for her to do that. After her friends died."

"Yeah, it was strange. I'm telling you, that little girl was completely unafraid of us, grabbed us by the hand, had us do some acting—you know, typical seven-year-olds—and then, when they came after us, she fucking rescued us." I thought about the events in the helo and all the slow motion and her tying ropes around us and jumping. I looked at Hazim. "Dude, you have no idea."

For a while we sat in silence, looking out on the river. I stared at fishermen on the bank as we drifted by. I shifted my hands on the tiller to light a cigarette. A shiver came over me from the cool morning air. Hazim let his eyes fall shut here and there.

"Better stay alert, man," I said. "I don't know where to go when these splits come up." I motioned ahead of us. He rubbed his eyes.

"Go left here." He pointed. More moments of silence. I tried to think of what it was about the school I might be missing. The girl, how she saved us. The tribal leaders and townspeople, how they turned on us. *What was it? The place was a target, so there must be a person of interest attending the play . . . Assumptions. What are the assumptions? Who the hell knows?* The lines the girl had me memorize popped into my head. I began mouthing them to myself.

I turned to Hazim.

"So, Hazim, what is this play about?" I said.

Hazim was staring ahead at the water. He looked at me, totally out of it. "What is what?"

"The kids' play. What's it about?"

"It is . . . well, it is a very old story in Mesopotamia; we were all told this as children."

"Oh, like a fairy tale," I said.

"Yes, for kids when they go to bed."

"Oh, okay. So what's it about?"

"It's . . . I guess to translate to English you will say, 'The Story of the Killing Flower.'" He smiled. "Strange to hear someone ask what this is; everyone always just knows it." He paused, then asked, "So what do you call *malek* in English? Like Tutankhamun?"

"King?" I said.

"Yes, king. It is the story of a king and his three sons, and a beautiful flower they find from a different land. And it turns into lions and snakes and kills all the people."

"Oh, nice wholesome children's bedtime story."

Hazim smiled. "Yes, well, the first son takes the flower and tries to keep it, and it turns to lions. Then the second goes to fight the people and take more flowers, and this time the snakes come."

"Hmm, sounds like the Israelis and Palestinians," I said.

Ethan made a sound, then sat up, semidelirious. "What about Israelis and Palestinians?"

"Hazim was telling me about the play," I said.

"Oh, the kids' play? It's about two of the worst enemies on this frickin' planet? How depressing is that?"

"Well, yes, it is about Palestine, but also every similar thing in the world. Shia and Sunni in Iraq, South Africa, even your Irish and British. It is about everyone," Hazim said.

"Oh, like mankind," I said.

Hazim nodded. "Yes, happy, but also a sad story."

"But there's a message of peace on earth and everything, right?"

"Well, yes, of course, like all stories, when the third son is king. But it is always told to be sad, because it will never become true," Hazim said. "We even have a saying: 'The third son is never king.'"

"Ah, don't feel bad, dude," Ethan said. "It's the same with stories in the Bible. Have we ever actually *done* what God said? Fuck no." He chuckled. "Hey, just look at us now! 'Vengeance is mine.' Pfft, my ass!"

I turned to Hazim. "So anyway, what's the ending?"

He looked at me for what seemed like a minute, then shook his head. "If I tell you, it will ruin the story. You need to hear the whole thing."

"Oh, come on!" I said. "I don't even speak Arabic. When am I going to even—"

"I promise I will tell you, or I will have someone translate it, after all this."

"Yeah, dude, we got shit to take care of," Ethan said, reaching for the laptop under the tarp.

"Fine," I said. I wasn't happy with the cliffhanger, but I tried to put it out of my mind. Ethan handed me the laptop, and I opened it up.

"Cool. We're almost back to full charge," I said.

Hazim and I switched seats again, and I cut the generator. Ethan and I continued watching the DVD. The little kids with the flower bonnets popped up and down in the garden; the tall kid sprinkled them with colored paper out of his watering can. They stood up and stretched toward the bright, glowing sun that hung from a rope above them. Abeer continued her determined and precocious narration. The girls holding the camera giggled as certain kids stumbled through their lines or did something random or unscripted. I watched intently, forgetting for the moment that we were looking for clues. The children were adorable, and it touched me in a strange way, knowing the horrific tragedy that was about to happen, and that at the same time had *already* happened. It was surreal, and confusing, and hard to take, and heart-warming. All of these things.

I watched the crowd as they burst into suppressed laughter, trying not to disrupt too much. A woman in the front row, cloaked head to toe in black, turned to whisper a quick word to her friend next to her. *No doubt one of the mothers,* I thought, *all proud and excited. It's just like back home.* And it occurred to me just then that I was no longer there as the visitor, the invader I'd been when I first arrived. I was no longer peering through the glass at some exotic thing—these people— observing or watching or poking at them. I was completely inside now, mixed in with them, immersed.

Hazim snapped me out of my thoughts. "Right there! Stop it!" he shouted.

Ethan and I turned to him.

"Go back! Reverse it." He looked at the screen.

I hit pause and moved the slider backward.

Hazim leaned over my shoulder, standing, almost losing his balance. "Okay, good. There."

I pushed play.

The camera had lowered abruptly and angled sideways, and stayed there for a few seconds. In plain view was the dress of the woman sitting next to the little girls. Her hand was resting on her knee, palm facing up, but then turned over momentarily. There, on the back of her hand, was what looked like a few words scribbled in ink, like a note she'd written to herself. Hazim squinted at the screen. Ethan and I looked at him anxiously.

"What? Pick up a jug of milk on the way home?" I asked.

"Move it back," he said.

I held down the rewind button and let it play again. It seemed a little blurred to me. Hazim frowned, turning his head sideways.

"Again," he said, waving his finger to the left. I backed up the video and replayed it.

"Would slow-mo help?" I started to say.

But before I could finish, Hazim exclaimed, "*Ithna'ash wa nus!* Twelve thirty."

I paused it again. "You sure?"

"Yes, she writes, 'School play. Twelve thirty.'" He tapped the screen.

Ethan widened his eyes and moved his face up close. "Oh my God, dude. How the hell can you read that?" he said.

I checked my phone. "Okay, so that's an hour and a half. Can we make it?"

"Ah, it will be close," Hazim said.

I turned to the motor putting along. "Can't this fucker go any faster?"

"No, sorry, I don't think it can go more."

"Great," I said.

"It couldn't be easy or anything," Ethan said sarcastically.

I wiped my forehead. The sun was almost directly above us, not quite baking, but it would be soon. I shed my vest and let it drop to the floor of the boat.

"Hazim," I said.

"Yes."

"Check your cell signal." I yanked the power cord of the laptop and slammed it shut. "Fucking great," I mumbled, wrapping the cord around the computer.

"What?" Ethan said.

I glanced at him. "We wasted gas, that's what. Charging this piece of shit." I tossed it on top of my vest.

"But we had to find out what we could," he said.

I ignored him, turning to Hazim, who was staring at the screen of his phone. "Here," I said. I grabbed it out of his hand.

"Try turning it off and on again," Ethan said.

"What'll that do?"

"Forces it to search for the closest tower."

I tried it. As we waited for the phone to power back up, Hazim gave me a sympathetic look. Finally the signal icon appeared. I shook my head and rolled my eyes. "Fucking unbelievable."

"Well, look at it this way, dude," Ethan said, shrugging his shoulders. I could tell what was coming. I'd seen that expression before.

"What," I said, inhaling deeply. This didn't stop him.

"The worst that can happen is what's already happened anyway."

"Well, holy fucking shit, man!" I yelled, glaring at him. "You just solved the mystery of mankind! All we've ever needed is a big fucking dose of fatalism!"

Ethan's face changed. He said nothing, just giggled, embarrassed, and made a gesture of surrender with his hands. "Sorry, man, I can be that way sometimes."

I reached down for the cigarettes in my vest, trying to do something, or maybe to shut myself up before I made him feel like shit. I was so incredibly pissed, yet I somehow felt such . . . I guess it was sympathy. *As fucking smart as he is,* I thought, *this seems like such trivial no-brainer common sense, yet he doesn't get it; sometimes you have to say fuck it and go all in.*

The next thing that happened was even worse than the phone not working. But as it turned out, it was what got Ethan fired up. The motor, which up to that point was emanating a steady, continuous purr, suddenly skipped a beat, revved high, and then growled as it bogged down and slowed until it cut out. Hazim checked the fuel, then examined the engine. He pulled on the cord a couple of times. "Oh," he said, putting his weight on the tiller to rotate the motor out of the water. I saw it. A nasty, wet algae-covered cord or something had wrapped itself around the propeller shaft.

"We have to cut," Hazim said.

I turned to Ethan. "Grab that knife." Ethan started going through the bags we'd brought, unzipping and tearing open Velcro pockets. I ran my hand around the rope to find the end, but it must have been wedged underneath.

"It's a slimy piece of net, I think," I said to Ethan. "Wrapped tight as shit around . . . it's stuck between the prop and the stationary part of the shaft."

"Here," Ethan finally said, handing me the knife. It took about five minutes, but I was able to cut enough to pull and unwind the pieces. Pretty easy. What wasn't, though, and what made no sense whatsoever was that the engine would not start. Hazim cranked and cranked, adjusted the throttle, checked the gas again. Nothing. We even lifted the prop out of the water and made sure there wasn't any more shit wrapped around the thing. No. The propeller spun around smoothly, no problem. I watched as he tried everything, and finally he just looked at me helplessly.

"Oh, okay, I see. I get it!" I yelled, slapping the side of the engine. "So for no fucking reason—whatsoever!—this goddamned piece-of-shit engine is just not going to start. Boy, God's got a sick sense of humor, huh?"

Hazim went back to pulling on the cords and messing with the throttle setting. "But I thought you didn't believe in God," he said, giving me a knowing look. I wanted to glare at him, but he'd already turned back to what he was doing. I was in no fucking mood to get called out on anything. I just wanted to say something to shut his ass down.

Too late, though. Ethan had already jumped in: "He's complicated."

"No! I'm not fucking 'complicated'!" I snapped. "I just want God to know—in the off chance he is up there, which I'm sure he fucking isn't—that he's a . . . whatever. Who cares."

Ethan's response was to take a long, deep breath and start rummaging around the bottom of the boat. Hazim kept trying with the motor. We now floated uselessly in the water. Finally Ethan dropped a corner of the tarp over the generator, flipped a latch, and pulled a long wooden paddle out toward himself.

"What are you doing?" I said.

He gave me one of his knowing, matter-of-fact looks. "Well," he said, handing me the paddle, "in the absence of God, let's get to rowing."

That brought a huge smile to my face.

I stood up and steadied myself, then stepped carefully to where Ethan was. He slid the second paddle out. We positioned ourselves at the bow, on either side, dipped the paddles in the water, and moved ourselves forward.

"Hazim, just tell us the turns," Ethan said.

"It is a long way, though," Hazim said.

"Fuck it!" Ethan said, breathing hard.

I laughed quickly. "Don't kill yourself, just a smooth, steady pace."

Hazim kept messing around, trying different things. He tilted the prop out of the water, which was smart. Less drag. I kept my strokes in sync with Ethan's, staring down at the water, then ahead of us, and down at the water again. We inched along slowly, nothing like before, but it was something. And in the silence, the conversation we'd had played in my head. What Ethan had said about being complicated, about God.

He's right, I thought, *why do I think those things? It's just like Tuy kept saying, making things overly complicated, messy, hypothetical. Is there a god? Is there not a god? Calling on god, waiting on god, listening for a god.* "What a waste of time," I said aloud.

"Paddling's a waste of time?" Ethan said impatiently.

"No, no," I said. "Not this." I paused for a few strokes. "I was thinking about something else."

"Mmkay."

We kept going, slapping the water in sync, drawing it back, lifting the paddles, sliding them forward against the side of the boat.

"No, dude," I finally said emphatically, "this is definitely not a waste of time."

My arms were feeling it now, but I kept up the pace. After a while Ethan began counting, one, two, three, stroke, one, two, three, stroke. He began playing around with it, trying to entertain us. First in Spanish, then French, German, then making up Russian numbers.

"Oneski, vladski, Dostoevsky!"

I laughed. "Dostoevsky? Really?"

"Hey, I can't help it. The fucker's last name was three!" he said dryly.

"Oh, well, I'm sure!" I giggled.

Suddenly a pop came from the back of the boat, and the motor roared. Ethan and I turned around. "Well, holy shit!" Ethan said.

Hazim looked at us, smiling, and shrugged his shoulders.

"Thank . . . God!" I said mockingly at Hazim.

"Okay, how long was that?" Ethan said. "Forty minutes?"

Hazim looked at his phone. "Now it is 11:50."

Our excitement didn't last long. The motor made an odd whining sound and cut out. Hazim messed around with it for a minute before giving up.

"Damn," Ethan said.

Our paddles hit the water again. My arms were killing me, but I kept on. Ethan got back to his counting game, and I joined in. We played around with different languages, just making words up on the spot. Japanese, Italian, Portuguese, Greek. He'd make up one, repeat it a few times, and then I'd think of one and cut in. It helped pass the time. Hazim seemed amused. He was impressed with my pronunciation when we did the Arabic.

"Oh shit," Ethan said, "we forgot. Try the cell phone again."

Hazim checked his phone, and his face lit up. "It is working." I wanted to take a break from paddling, but Ethan got back to it, and I knew we should keep up the pace.

"Feel the burn!" he said, digging a deep stroke into the water. All I could do was expel a vocal breath of exhaustion.

Hazim reached someone and began talking excitedly in Arabic. He blurted out short questions and paused for the responses. I heard him say his cousin's name several times. Finally he said, "*Shukran,*" and hung up. This time we did stop paddling. We both turned around toward Hazim.

"Talk to us," Ethan said.

"Mohammed is left already, his wife says."

"Oh, okay," I said.

"She says he left his cell phone with her at home," Hazim said. "She is not sure why, saying he forgot it . . . because maybe he is late."

"Hmm, seems like he'd want his cell so he can call her, send her pics or whatever," Ethan said, looking at me.

"Why isn't she going?" I said. "Isn't her kid in the play?"

"She has baby," Hazim said, "but he will call her, and she calls us."

Ethan turned to Hazim. "I'm confused. Does her husband have *another* cell phone? Why can't he just call you back?"

"She says he has no cell, but he said to her, if he calls her, she answers his phone."

Ethan gave him a confused look, then said, "So *he* told her that if his cell rings, for her to answer it because it might be him calling her."

Hazim seemed iffy on following the sentence but nodded at the end. "Yes . . . yes, correct."

Ethan turned slowly toward the front of the boat again. "Mmkay," he said, putting the paddle in the water.

"Probably left it just so she'd have a phone with her," I said.

"I know, except she said he forgot it."

"Hmm, I don't know, maybe Hazim misunderstood . . . or she misspoke."

Ethan took a couple strokes, thinking. "No. 'Cause she also said her husband was in a hurry. People don't misspeak with that much detail."

"Hmm," I said, pausing for breath. "I guess you're right. So . . ." I pulled the paddle toward me. "So what's that mean?"

"Dunno," he said. We kept paddling. The river had made a sharp turn, and the bank on the left was lower and clear of reeds. In the distance, along the surface of the flat brown terrain, I could see minuscule dust plumes kicking up, following a thin line in one direction.

"Hey, there's a road over there," I said.

"Yeah, I see," Ethan said.

"It goes to Hamza," Hazim said.

I stopped for a moment, resting the paddle on my lap. Ethan kept going in a robotic, almost meditative pattern.

"Dude, you're a machine."

He didn't respond, just inhaled sharply and took the next stroke. I dipped the paddle in again and pulled it toward me. My back and shoulders were tight, burning. My knees were cramped up against the hull. My thighs were numb, just underneath where they pressed onto the edge of the seat. And my arms trembled and wandered off course as I struggled to direct their movements—lift, reach, dip, pull. Lift, reach, dip, pull.

And so it went, for the last part of our journey. Under the vast, open sky, inching up the river, silent, toiling. We stopped paddling only to take our shirts off, splash our faces with the muddy water, and get the time from Hazim.

"Late," was all he'd tell us. "Very close, though," he added, pointing. "Just there."

I looked up and saw them. Sand-yellow rooftops, just behind a row of palms on the far bank.

Hazim directed us toward the bank, lined with reeds. Cinnamon-colored rolling hills rose above the palms beside the clearing, which edged up to the river. My paddle began hitting sparse blades of grass sticking up from the shallow bottom.

We pulled up close, against the edge of the riverbank, and began throwing our gear onto the ground. "Hazim, just cover the laptop and gas can," I said, pushing the tarp toward him.

He seemed unsure about this. "We don't take everything?"

"Fuck no! Shit's heavy," I said. I looked up toward the town. "Well, how far is it?"

"Just over there."

I hesitated. Then Ethan made the decision for me.

"Fuck the laptop. Just take the DVD. Come on!" He stepped off onto the shore, sticking his arm out to me. I handed him the remaining gear. "That everything?"

"Yeah," I said, standing up in the boat.

Ethan separated our battle rattle and handed my stuff to me, and we put everything on. I took another look at our gear. "Dude, I hate to say it, but I think we should take the laptop."

"Whatever, it's all you then," Ethan said. I ejected the drive and popped the DVD back in. He bent down to grab the front of the boat. I stuffed the computer and power cord in the remaining bag, then stepped off, and Hazim followed. We lifted the boat up and onto the sand and muddy reeds.

"Where do we hide this bitch?" Ethan said.

"Do not hide it," Hazim said. Ethan and I looked at him for a second.

"Oh, right, that's smart. Just leave it in plain sight. Draws less attention," Ethan said.

We dropped the boat a couple of meters from the water and took off, Hazim in the lead. He looked at his watch. We double-timed it up a sandy path, over a hill or two that led to a palm grove. We followed along the edge, obscured from the road on the opposite side. The strap pulled on my shoulder, which was killing me. *Great*, I thought, *watch this be the thing that makes us late by like thirty seconds.* Ethan's boot caught on a rock in front of me. Hazim called out something from ahead of us, but our feet were shuffling through the loose soil.

"What?" I asked Ethan.

"He said right up here."

We rounded the corner of the palm grove, and Hazim stopped.

We put our hands on our knees, panting. "We go there"—Hazim pointed—"then left, then it is the school." I squinted in the sunlight, unable to recognize anything yet. But I was already starting to feel it, the realization that this was it, this was the moment. What I was about to see would confirm everything. The first real, physical thing I could touch and feel to say, yes, this is it; this is where I was before. We continued on, trotting along the edge of the grove up to the first house, then down the street, to the next corner, left, past a row of shops, then several blocks down.

There were few people, at least that I saw. But I imagined they were there, just hidden from view. *No doubt we look out of place*, I thought, *three dudes in US military garb running down the street carrying a bunch of gear.* My heart was already racing, and I was too exhausted to expend the energy to try to be alert and ready. *Fuck it, we just have to get there.*

At the next block Hazim paused again. He wiped his brow and bent over, his chest heaving. The street ran a couple of blocks and opened up to a traffic circle surrounded by buildings. Again, nothing I recognized. "The school is there," Hazim said. I looked where he was pointing.

To the right of the circle, people were walking down a short path that led to a gate. A wall meandered along the hill and around the structure, mostly hidden from view.

"Holy shit," I said, stepping into the street to cross, my eyes fixed on the gate.

"Dude!" Ethan said, pulling me back by my collar. A rusty white taxi blasted its horn at me and stopped.

"Fuck!" I said, giving the driver an apologetic hand. He drove in front of us, honking. I scooted across and ran along the shoulder toward the circle. Once past the shops, I could see better. And there it was, at the top of the hill. Just like it was in my head. The school. I had never seen it from that angle, so it was slightly unfamiliar. But it stood out above the surrounding area. Not towering, but prominent, like a local landmark.

"That's it!" I shouted at the guys, smiling. Now I was in a full run. There were people at the top of the hill, gathering at the theater entrance. Women in long abayas were navigating up the hill, kids following behind.

"Is it the same?" Ethan said from behind me, breathing heavily.

"Exactly," I said, "and no damage either . . . oh my God." I gasped for breath. We reached the gate, and I knocked it open. "I fucking told you! It's just like before the explosion." I started up the hill. A man and woman stopped and looked over at us, watching us scramble on all fours up the dirt path.

"Hold up!" Ethan said.

His comment barely registered with me. I don't know how I found the energy, but I topped the hill and ran full speed until I reached the crowd gathered at the entrance. Everyone turned to me; their faces seemed to reflect both intrusion and mild curiosity. I waved my hands, pointing to the theater, trying to signal alarm.

"Stop the play!" I blurted out, immediately thinking how goofy this sounded. I turned toward Ethan and Hazim, who hadn't gotten up the hill yet. "Come on!" I waved to them frantically.

A man with a long, thin face and a dark mustache like an upside-down V stepped toward me, his white dishdasha billowing around his frame. He barked something in Arabic, gesturing forcefully with his hands.

"*Intother!*" I said. "Wait."

I addressed the other people, realizing that was a good word to use: "*Raja'an intother!*" "Wait, please!" A darker, clean-cut guy with three kids around him paused at the theater entrance. Others who had stopped continued on inside. Ethan and Hazim walked up as the guy with the upside-down V mustache was blabbing something at me as if I were fluent.

"Hey," I said, turning to Hazim, "tell this guy we need to talk to the staff."

Hazim smiled momentarily but began explaining to the man in a serious tone what we were there for. I turned to Ethan, who was taking his bag off his shoulders, breathing heavily. "The DVD," I said.

"You have it," he said.

"Oh yeah," I said. I dropped my bag to the ground and started to open the flaps. The man with the mustache blurted something out, pointing at me. Hazim waved his hands at the guy, trying to calm him. I heard the word "DVD" as he explained further and pointed to the theater. I had my hands on the laptop but let go, looking up at the man. At this point a dozen or so men in dishdashas and checkered keffiyehs were outside watching us.

Hazim waved me over. "Show him the movie."

I opened the bag and pointed it toward the man. "It's just a laptop . . . computer, see?" I reached inside in slow motion. "I'm getting a DVD, that's all." Hazim translated. I pushed the eject button and took the disc out, holding it up for the guy. "Now, Hazim," I said in an overly calm voice, "tell this dude very kindly: go get the fucking school staff, and right fucking now!"

Hazim rattled off something and turned to the other men. He

seemed to be pleading. Finally the guy with the V mustache motioned to a younger man near the office door and said something.

"He's going," Hazim said to us.

"And tell them, evac the theater," I said, pointing to the entrance. I exaggerated my expression and waved my hands pleadingly. But the guy with the mustache had no reaction. He motioned to Hazim, and I heard him say, "Come."

We followed him up to the office, where an older man in a dark keffiyeh met us outside the door. I recognized him as one of the elders Jacobs had sat down with over tea. For a split second I expected him to react to seeing me. It occurred to me that I wasn't even sure if he had died before.

The man led us inside to the same room where Jacobs had met with the protesters. He tried to motion for us to have a seat. I'd already slid the laptop out of the bag and powered it up.

"No!" I said. "You have to get everyone out of this building." I looked at Hazim, who translated quickly. The old man gave us an odd-looking half smile and motioned again at the seats, saying something. I didn't wait to hear what.

"Please!" I shouted. "Something is about to happen." I pointed to the laptop and held up the DVD. "Sir, please watch this video."

Another guy appeared at the door. Must have been a school official. He said something to the old man, who replied, gesturing at us. The official looked sternly at us and began asking Hazim questions. I inserted the disc and advanced the video to the explosion. The battery indicator on the laptop was solid red.

"They are saying they do not know who we are," Hazim said.

I grabbed the power cord out of the bag and held up the plug. "Do you have an outlet? Electricity?" I asked the old man. I tapped the cord and gestured the motion of plugging it into a wall. The old man stood with that same expression and said something to Hazim.

"Goddamn it!" I shouted, pointing to the theater next door. The laptop almost toppled over in my left hand. I sandwiched it awkwardly against my side. "That theater is going to be blown up in a huge fucking explosion! Lots of kids—dead!"

Hazim cautiously translated. Before he could finish, the old man said something to the official. The two men moved up to us. The official held out his hand toward the door.

"*Intother!* Please!" I said, following Ethan outside. Hazim said something too. He seemed to be pleading with them, but the old man just walked him out, that same stupid half smile on his face.

"They asked us to go," Hazim said.

"Pfft. Wow. Really?" Ethan said.

Outside the door, more parents and kids had gathered at the theater entrance. A few of the younger men had suits on, and plaid shirts and solid ties with a big knot. Through the big window of the theater I could see people already seated, filling up the first few rows. I stood for a moment, watching as women in colorful hijabs shuffled inside with their children. Ethan looked at me. I looked at him and then at Hazim. He glanced at his watch. "The play is now," he said.

"Eleven minutes," Ethan said.

"What?" I asked.

"From the time the play starts, it's T minus eleven minutes. I timed it."

"Fuck!" I said. I looked around again.

"Hazim," I said, and pulled him over to the theater entrance. "Get one of these fuckers to watch this." I pushed play and held the laptop open so that it faced the line of people. A woman glanced at me but looked away quickly.

Hazim spoke loudly but maintained a friendly voice. I handed the laptop to him and waved at the next man to step over, first pointing to the screen and then to the theater. Hazim was busy explaining. Finally a couple and their daughter stopped to watch. They seemed perplexed, curious, but confused. Hazim tried to engage them.

Ethan tapped my shoulder. "Shit. Looks like the goons are walking over here." I looked back at the office and saw the man with the V mustache leading the school official and two others toward us. As I turned back around, I noticed a man walking behind the couple Hazim was talking to. He paid no attention to us, walking toward the theater entrance. He led a little girl by the hand. I saw a flash of red as her pants appeared briefly and disappeared behind the woman's dark abaya.

My body reacted immediately. I felt a surge of adrenaline wash over me. For a second my mind stalled; I wasn't sure. But it was her, the little flower girl. Dark, cropped hair, cotton shirt with the cute bear on the front, the little bubble pipe stuck in her mouth. She twisted her body around, staring at us momentarily, then turned away from us. I was just processing all of this: the men approaching from behind us; the computer battery now beeping, its last gasp of air; the little girl. Then it happened. She whipped her head around, pulling her father's arm. And she pointed straight at me. "*Yaba!*" she said. "*Hatha il jundi shifta bil helem!*" She kept repeating it. I looked at Hazim. He had heard her.

"That's her!" I shouted. "What'd she say? Translate!"

Hazim looked shocked. "She said, 'Daddy, that is the soldier from my dream.'"

It was overwhelming enough just seeing her. Finally having the little girl to show them, even show myself—proof, or at least evidence, that the world I'd been describing to them was *this one*, was one and the same with theirs, not just a psychotic delusion for me to live in alone. So that was enough. But then her actually pointing to me as if to say, "That guy! I know that guy!" was a complete shock. Yet that wasn't all. What she said sent my mind over the edge, triggering something in my brain so gripping and poignant, I went into a near panic. It was the word *dream*. Somehow even in Arabic it was hugely familiar to me. And it couldn't have been in my vocabulary. I'd never known it, never used such a word, and why would I? Yet I did. I'd memorized it. Maybe that wasn't it. Maybe I'd made a mistake. I turned frantically to Hazim. "Say it!" I blurted out. "Say what she said!"

"'That's the soldier from my dream'?"

"No! In Arabic!"

"*Hatha il jundi shifta bil helem.*" I listened closely, waiting for the familiar sound. It was at the end.

"There! That word *helem*. Is that the word for 'dream'?"

"Yes," Hazim said. I looked toward the theater. The man was already walking inside, Abeer in tow behind him, still staring back at me.

I held out my hands toward his face. "Listen carefully and translate this for me." I focused, straining to remember the lines. "*Isma'onee. Hathi il bent? . . . Is maha Abeer.*" I looked at Hazim. "What's that mean?"

"It means 'Listen, everyone,'" Hazim said, "'that girl there, her name is Abeer.'"

I closed my eyes, struggling to concentrate, trying hard to pronounce the words correctly even if they came out slowly and haltingly, like from a second grader.

"*Hathi il bent . . . kanat tehlam . . . li mudat isbuayn.*" I paused to remember the rest. "*Bi anni wagif . . . ala il masrah.*"

Hazim translated: "For two weeks this girl has dreamed of me standing here on the stage."

"Oh God!" I said, choked up, tears welling up in my eyes. "*Wa ana agul . . . ikhriju gabel . . . il infijar,*" I said, and stopped. That was it. I stared desperately into his eyes for the translation.

"Telling you all to get out before the explosion."

Boom. The words hit me like a drug surging through my veins. I called out to Ethan, my body turning before I could even register my movements.

"Ethan!" I yelled. I pointed to the men coming toward us. "Distract these fuckers, then you two get your asses down the hill." I began backing away from them.

"What? What are you doing?" Ethan said. I had squeezed through the line of people walking into the theater.

"I know what I have to do," I said, running toward the playground.

I heard Ethan behind me, struggling to react. "Hey!" he shouted. "Eight minutes!" But I was already running full sprint, past the slide and swing set, in front of the big glass window down the side of the building, heading toward the rear of the school. No way could anyone have caught me. It didn't even occur to me they might have tried to take me out. I was up and over the wall surrounding the playground before they could do shit.

Even I didn't have time to process it. All I saw was the top of the wall that in that split second seemed to tower over my head, then my right leg bent, my foot stuck out, pressing against the wall, and I was launched, elbow on the top and my legs swinging out to the side and over. For a moment I remembered that adrenaline sensation from when I was a kid running from the cops—jumping bushes, diving off roofs, landing and rolling. Intense fear yet hyper focus, allowing my body to do things it normally couldn't.

The landing was not great. My feet hit flat, but all the rotation sent me toppling over, stumbling on the gravel into a nasty face-plant. My shoulder took most of the fall, but I scraped the shit out of my cheek. I felt none of it. All that mattered was that I was able to keep going and that none of the surroundings had changed. And they hadn't. There was the aluminum ladder, just as I'd seen it before, running up the back of the theater to the roof. And there was the wooden access door and the crawl space. *Which one?* I thought, imagining the two routes in my head. "Shorter," I said aloud, crouching to pull on the door handle. I thought I heard voices to my right, on the other side of the wall. But it didn't matter. I was crawling inside and had shut the door.

I hadn't thought about one thing: once I shut the access panel, the crawl space went completely dark. A thin aura of light leaked out around the edges of the door, but beyond a few feet toward the stage, I could see nothing. "Shit," I said. I checked all my pockets. "Great," I said, after the fourth one, "three packs of smokes and no fucking matches." I ripped open Velcro straps and thrust my hands inside my vest. Nothing. I didn't have time to keep looking. I cracked the door open to see if it lit the way. The storage crates we'd seen before came dimly into view, but the space was mostly formless. I shut the door again and shuffled a few meters into the darkness, crouching as I went, hands stretched out in front of me. I lost perspective on where the walls were, which direction exactly, and I couldn't be sure where the beams were, either. I felt like I could scrape my head on a nail or something. I ended up crawling in the sandy soil, with one hand sweeping back and forth in front of me like a radar. I could hear feet scampering overhead, clomping on the floor, and the muffled tones of the kids giggling and screaming in excitement. *Good. Don't stop*, I thought. *If it gets quiet, that means the play has started.*

I glanced back at the access panel and saw I'd only gone maybe a fifth of the way underneath. I stopped, staring into the pitch black, remembering how the rows of boxes were scattered around, oriented in different directions. "Shit!" I said, vacillating, frozen for a moment. All the momentum I'd had, running full speed to make it all happen, I felt it sputtering, coughing, about to send me into a panic. "Fuck this," I said, and scrambled back to the door and slapped it open. *If they're outside, then fuck it*, I thought, worming my way out the opening. No time. No time for anything. Now it was down to seconds. I got to my feet and grabbed the first rungs of the ladder and began climbing. The ladder wobbled and slid away from its bracket at the top, but held.

I got high enough to see just over the top of the wall. Men had gathered in the playground, looking up at me, pointing. Two hands appeared on the top of the playground wall, and a head popped up; it was the man with the V mustache. He shouted something as he hoisted himself up, then dropped down as I reached the roof. My first instinct was to rush to the roof access, but I quickly doubled back. I sat down and grasped the bracket of the ladder, bracing my feet against the concrete of the roof edge. I felt the ladder pull as the guy began climbing. No way I could lift it at that point, so I kicked the bracket. Once, and it bent. Twice, and it folded over. The third time it broke completely off, and the ladder was free.

I heard the guy yell some shit as the bottom of the ladder dug into the gravel and crashed into the trees. I placed the tips of my fingers underneath the lip of the roof cover and heaved it up, sliding it away and onto the tar surface. The sound was horrendous. *Thank God it doesn't matter this time*, I thought.

The storage loft above the stage looked the same as before: cardboard props, boxes of costumes made of cheap clothing, stage pieces. Like a cluttered attic. Through the spaces between the rafters I could see children below, moving around backstage. I grasped the edge of the opening and lowered myself onto the wood flooring. I worked my way through the junk toward the rear, eyes peeled for some way to get down. But there wasn't any; no ladder or ropes, no pipes or anything on the cement wall so I could slide down. I could see the stage now; the dusty makeshift curtain was drawn. But the two sides weren't quite joined in the middle, and I saw the crowd in the front rows. And the kids, they were now lined up, stepping one by one into the big flower box.

Where is she? I thought, trying to remember which side she'd be standing on, narrating the play. Then the curtains began to open. There was no time. Zero. And there was no easy way to get down. With all the mounds of paraphernalia they'd stashed away at the edge of the floorboards, I couldn't climb over to hang from one of the rafters and drop down. At the other end of the loft, above the stage, ropes and metal rods crisscrossed everywhere. That didn't seem any better. The front edge of the floor was clear of debris but butted right up against the curtain. Suddenly it hit me what I had to do, and I almost laughed out loud. *Holy shit. Of course!* I stumbled over the cardboard and piles of clothes, scrambling toward the front, and squeezed between and underneath the ropes. I reached up to grasp the wooden rod that held up the curtain and pulled myself up on it, seeing if it would hold my weight. *Good.* I took a quick look below at the front of the stage. There she was, walking up the steps all prim and proper, holding the piece of paper she'd be reading from. The audience had now gone quiet.

In that split second a random thought popped into my head, ridiculous as it may have been: *Those scenes in the movies where the hero jabs a big knife into the curtain and slides all the way down like a zip line? Bullshit. You'd fall. Probably kill yourself too.* I grabbed a clump of the fabric and leaned into it. The rings slid over a few inches and caught, which made a short, high-pitched squeak. One kid looked up, right at me. I dangled my feet and began clawing my way down. I heard voices below, but I couldn't worry about it. I was too concerned with holding my grip, not falling. I let the fabric slip through my grasp, inch by inch, burning. Over my shoulder I saw everyone had taken notice. *Some sensational entrance*, I thought. I had to go ahead with it. "*Ghuf!*" I shouted. "Halt"—the only word I knew for "stop." "Please!" I slid the rest of the way down, burning the shit out of my fingers. I stuck them in my mouth and winced visibly in a lame attempt to show them I was not an aggressor since I'd fucked up and hurt myself. I positioned myself on stage, with Abeer to my left, and held out my hands to the audience. "Please! Listen . . . listen," I said in Arabic, and I recited my lines.

The room full of brown faces stared back at me, somber, almost uninterested. One of the men standing in the back folded his arms. But there were mostly women, and the ones with the niqabs were what I focused on—nothing but two eyes burning into me. But I'd already started, and I tried to go with the momentum.

"Listen, everyone, that girl there," I said, "her name is Abeer." Not knowing which words were what, I pointed to her only after I'd said her name. This no doubt looked awkward, but my Arabic must have been passable, because Abeer's eyes widened and she covered her mouth in shock. I continued slowly, "For two weeks . . ." I stammered, forgetting the words. "Two for weeks . . . she's been dreaming of me standing . . ." I paused again, distracted by the stirring in the audience. I held out my arms with my palms upward. "*Ghuf!*" I said. "Hold on!" I dropped my arms quickly, not wanting to look aggressive. "Please listen," I said calmly. I picked up again: "Dreaming of me standing here on the stage, telling you . . . to get out of here before the explosion." And I pointed to the window.

The effect of this was immediate. Voices erupted. Several people whipped their heads around and called out to others in the audience. A woman stood up, holding a little kid on her arm, and pushed her way to the end of the row toward the exit. A man on the very end in the front approached the stage and called out to Abeer. I saw it was her father. He asked her a question, and she answered a quick yes, nodding her head. The room got quiet. He asked her something else and pointed to me. His face looked incredulous. She answered again, this time more elaborately, in her precocious way. She motioned to me and said as much with her animation and adorable gestures as with words. Her father stood for a moment, baffled. The crowd was stirring feverishly, talking to each other, agitated. A million phrases raced through my head, but I couldn't use them. "Please," I said, signaling them toward the exit. It didn't seem to be working. All I could do was repeat my lines: "Listen, everyone, that girl there, her name is Abeer—" Someone shouted something at me, and I stopped. Abeer's father turned to the audience and waved to get their attention. He spoke loudly, gesturing to me, Abeer, and the door. He seemed to be making a deal with them. I recognized the words for "dream" and "explosion" in his explanation. Finally he turned to Abeer, and they waited for her answer.

"*Na'am*," she said—"yes"—nodding her head. "*Hatha sahih*," she added, whatever that meant. But that did it. Everyone stood up and began hurrying toward the door. I turned my focus to the kids in the flower box. Some of them were too young to understand. Abeer came over and said something to get them moving. I began pulling them out of the box and onto the stage, pointing to some of the women. "*Mama*," I said, "*urkuth mama!*"—trying to say, "Go run to your mommy." Abeer helped, instructing them as if she were suddenly ten years older, leading them toward the steps.

"Hurry," I said in English, waving my hands. I grabbed another kid, and his flower bonnet fell off. Absurdly, he reached down to recover it. "Jesus, kid!" I said. Moments seemed to be flying by uncontrollably. I glanced at the big window as if to make sure the missile wasn't already blasting through it. When the last few kids were clomping down the steps, a huddle of women were at the foot of the steps, arms outstretched to comfort their children.

"*Yella!*"—"Quick!"—I shouted, remembering another word to use. I waved my arms toward the exit. The ones in back were hurrying out the doors, but through the window I could see them gathering right outside the door. "No!" I said. Abeer looked at me. "Tell them *infi-*

jar! Explosion!" and I pointed. She glanced outside and back at me, moving erratically, confused. Finally she grabbed her dad's hand and pulled him through the crowd, yelling something repeatedly.

I noticed one elderly woman left in an empty middle row, trying to get up from her chair. I worked my way to the aisle opposite the window and ran to get her. I instinctively put my hands on her shoulder, which freaked her out. She blurted something out and pulled away. *Oh, that's right,* I thought, *physical contact.* I retracted my hands. "You need help?" I said, giving her the friendliest expression I could. She turned and began plodding toward the window, holding on to the wobbly chair backs. The room was almost empty now. I could see Abeer, who'd come back to the building again. She was just outside the window, facing away, waving her arms wildly at people. *Oh God, what are you doing?* I glanced toward the sky, clear and blue beyond the egg-shaped minaret. I inhaled sharply, turning back to the woman. She was taking baby steps in front of me. When the last few men in keffiyehs got to the door, waiting for people to clear out, one of them noticed us. He was older and had a gut but was otherwise stocky. He ran down to our row and over to us and bent down to grab the old woman's ankles. He said something to her which she didn't seem to like, but I got what he was doing. "Sorry, lady," I said, and shot my hands under her armpits. We carried her to the exit and were the last ones out.

I woke to the sound of Arabic. Someone was standing next to my bed, back turned, phone up to his ear. Then I heard English. Ethan's voice, coming from behind the guy. I sat up, peering around. Ethan was in a chair, looking up at the guy, then glancing at me. He stood up to walk over. I tried to get my bearings. Hospital room, my head bandaged up. I felt a weird sensation—extremely relaxed, mellow. I lay back down again, closing my eyes, then opened them, staring up at Ethan, thinking how fascinating it was that he was this organism that interacted with others in the species, using random sounds made with the lungs and lips and vocal cords. My eyelids closed on their own. I slipped away for a few seconds, but my dream was unsettling. I was getting pulled downstream, away from everyone; they were all busy constructing props for a musical, and I was supposed to be there.

"Hazim!" The voice woke me again. It was Ethan's. He was still over me but had his head turned to the guy. "Ask him. . . look, he's gotta be absolutely fucking sure. Ask him if he's driven across it, like very recently."

I sat up, trancelike, and scanned my surroundings: A metal tray on wheels above my legs. A window—sheer blue curtains with stitched yellow flowers—luminescing in sunlight. A woman in a bed, motionless, breathing through a tube. Arabic, written in black marker on the tile wall above her headboard . . . and mine, and above the other bed too, on the other side, where a kid was sitting up, his leg in a long cast.

The guy kept talking on the phone. Ethan had turned back to me.

"Fucking sure of driven across what?" I smiled, knowing my words had come out sounding weird.

The guy clicked the phone shut. "Okay, I go to get the car."

"What'd he say about the bridge?" Ethan asked.

"He is sure. It is open now."

"And he's actually seen it with his own eyes—"

"Yes. Yes. I did not know yesterday, but yes, it is open since a week."

"Okay, well, hurry. We gotta get the fuck back," Ethan said, and the guy left.

I just gazed at Ethan. It felt like slow motion. "Dude, what the fuck meds did they give me?" I said.

He laughed. "A little thing called dihydromorphinone! Pretty potent shit, like a Percocet hopped up on Vicodin."

"Awesome," I said, beaming. "You're cool, man." I held my hand out to give him a fist bump, but it was half open.

He raised his eyebrows skeptically, then shook his head. "Okay, Slater, so are you in any pain? Head? Chest? Anywhere?"

"No, I'm feeling like super fuckin' chill."

"Pfft! Why'd I even ask? Well, they said there were no signs of anything major."

I sat for a few seconds, blinking. I felt the back of my head. "But the explosion," I said. "What happened? I can't remember. I mean, some things, but . . ." I paused in thought.

Ethan gave a short burst of laughter. "Your ass was shot through the air like a cannon, that's what!"

I looked at him. "I was?"

Ethan got all animated. "Yeah, I saw it, dude. So Hazim and I were standing at the bottom of the hill—"

"That was Hazim, right?" I said, pointing at the door.

"Yep." He nodded. "He's coming back. We got some time."

I frowned for a second, confused.

"We'll explain when he gets back . . . So anyway, you had just walked out of the doors. You and some guy were carrying that lady. I see this big fucking blast inside the theater. Next thing I know, you come flying up over the heads of everybody, do a perfect somersault, and slide down the hill on your ass to a stop. It looked like some Cirque du Soleil stunt."

"Damn. I don't remember that. All I—"

"You are one lucky motherfucker, holmes!" he said. He looked past me toward the other beds. "I scrambled to the bottom of the slope where you were, and you were talking. First you sounded perfectly fine. I asked if you were okay, and you said yeah, and I asked if anything hurt. You said no. You started to get up, and I was about to—I wanted to help lift your head in case you had a neck injury, but . . . dude," he said, "the back of your head was just *drenched* in blood. My hand almost slipped off, it was so bad."

"Shit," I said.

The look on his face changed from amazed and giddy with relief to unnerved and shaken, which I'd never seen with him. "And I felt something with my fingers. I thought it was . . . it felt like brain matter. Totally freaked me the fuck out." He inhaled sharply through his nose. "It was just the laceration. Skin and blood."

"It's okay, man," I said. "*I'm* okay." He looked away, toward the other end of the ward. I felt like crying, seeing how it had affected him. I'd gone from super-mellow to weepy in a split second.

"Oh, thank Christ!" he said. "Here comes some hospital slop."

A man made his way over to us, placing Styrofoam boxes on each of the metal trays. Ethan sat in front of the window, scooping rice and chickpeas with a plastic spoon. They gave me a tall glass of chai. We sat for a few minutes and ate, and my head started getting clearer.

"I do remember carrying that woman," I said finally. "There was this sweet, warm smell emanating from her. Jasmine, I think. Soft. Exotic. Almost peppery. I remember looking down at the top of her head, the dark fabric that seemed like a thousand years old to me."

"Yeah, two thousand, probably. I'm not sure what happened to her. Right after the explosion, several of the men chipped in, helped carry people. We flagged down taxis and other cars and brought you and a few others here. It's the only hospital in the village. More like a local clinic, really."

I pushed my food aside and lay back, closing my eyes. A few disjointed images flashed in my mind: Shops passing by through a window. The overly cushy backseat. Someone holding a towel to the back of my head, and my boots pressed up against the window, making a red-tinted smudge down the glass. Arabic hip-hop blaring from the radio, then the person leaning over me turning to yell at someone in English, and the music stopping. *Go back further. Rewind.* Nothing.

I sat up suddenly, hit with a wave of emotion. "Is everyone okay?"

"Dunno, it was complete mayhem, plus I was focusing on you. I just got your ass into the taxi. I didn't go back up the hill."

"What about Abeer? Is she okay?"

"Dude," he said, "I'm sure everyone is okay, but like I said, I was not—"

"I have to see her," I said, my lips quivering.

"Well, maybe her dad will bring her here," he said.

I put my head in my hand, rubbing my forehead, and shook my head slowly. I could tell he was just making something up.

Ethan slid the plastic chair over, and I heard him plop down. "Get some rest," he said. "We'll worry about that later."

W ake up!" The voice came to me from somewhere. Nameless, then converging on familiar as I came out of deep sleep.

"Werrrk aaahp!" Ethan said in my ear, distorting the pitch to a low vocal register like a supernatural presence. "Come on, man. Hazim's back. Time to go."

My eyes fluttered open. They were standing above me.

"We check the bandage now?" Hazim said.

"Oh yeah," Ethan said, reaching for my head.

"What the hell?" I moved his arm away from me and started to sit up. My head lolled slightly to one side. More wooziness.

Ethan pulled the sheet down toward the foot of the bed. "Car's waiting, holmes. Gotta get back to the CSH. We're AWOL status, bro."

He grabbed my arm and helped me turn and sit on the edge of the bed. I was trying to put things together again in my head, to remember what Ethan had told me had happened. *Okay, carrying that woman, walking out the door . . . wait, before that. Abeer outside, waving her hands . . .* "Where is she?" I said.

Ethan turned around, grabbing my shirt off the arm of the chair. "Who? The little girl?" he said, motioning for me to put it on.

"Yeah, Abeer. We—"

"Can't worry about that now." He turned to Hazim. "You fill up the tank?"

"Yes."

I unbuttoned my gown. Hazim started messing with my bandage. I pulled away from him. "What the fuck, dude?" They both backed off as I put my arms through my sleeves. I looked down and began to button my shirt, but slowly.

"Look," Ethan said, "we need to get you checked out, and this clinic sucks. The CSH is like two hours—"

"My head's fine. Doesn't even hurt," I said.

"Okay good," he said, "but here's the deal. We're gonna show up at the CSH, the three of us, and say you went outside the wire and we had to go find you."

Hazim noticed my boots at the foot of the bed and handed them to me. I bent over to put them on. I noticed the red tint again. "Maybe . . ." I said, thinking about when I'd climbed out of the window at the hospital. "I guess Tuy would back that up."

"Yeah, other than the guards, no one else saw the three of us together."

I looked up at Hazim. "Aren't you in a shitload of trouble?"

"Today I work in the night. Jim, he is the other guard, remember? He is not working today."

I sat there for a second, thinking.

"It's the only way, dude," Ethan said. "Hell, they already think you're *loco en la cabeza*, and my story works 'cause they know I was responsible for bringing you back to the FOB."

I pointed to my head. "What if they ask about the bandage?"

"Well," he said, "we might wanna take it off when we get there. Just start complaining about pain or something."

I shook my head. "Fine, whatever," I said. None of it really mattered to me. *Who gives a shit about getting written up. A fucking missile just hit the school.* "Hazim, did you see the little girl?"

"No," he said. "Before the play, yes, but not after."

"We were at the bottom of the hill, dude," Ethan said, "dealing with you."

"Fuck," I said, rubbing my forehead.

"I'm sure they're fine. Hazim can give us a report." Ethan put his hand on my shoulder as I stood up. The backs of my thighs stung, but it was bearable. "You good?"

"Yeah," I said, and we walked out of the clinic.

A s we drove off, I twisted my neck around to look out the rear window. A gated wall surrounded the hospital entrance. A taxi stood running, its driver leaning on the hood, smoking. I tried to get my bearings. It seemed the school was behind us, but it was really just a feeling. We headed down a busy street, slowing as we passed a market. I looked out the windows, hoping I'd see someone familiar. Ethan was telling Hazim to try to avoid traffic. A few men in dishdashas stared at us as we inched along.

Hazim honked the horn and went around a man on a donkey cart, and I saw something ahead I thought I recognized: the traffic circle at the bottom of the hill. It looked like we were approaching it from a different direction.

"Hazim!" I said. "Is that the school coming up?"

"Amiriyah is ahead, yes."

I leaned into the front seat to get a better view. Ethan pointed in the distance, where the school stood out above the surrounding area. I stared intently through the glass. There was a crowd of people on the other side of the traffic circle walking toward us, dozens, dressed in regular clothing. No one carried signs or seemed to be protesting, but there were tons of them, filling the street. As we got up to the circle, Hazim veered to the right and stopped to merge. I kept looking ahead as they approached the intersection. Hazim moved into the circle, driving halfway around, then turned off to the right.

"What are you . . ." I said.

Ethan turned around to me. "Dude, it's fucking gridlock up there."

"Come on!" I said, rolling down the window. Hazim had pulled off to the side and stopped. I stuck my head out, able to see just around the shop on the corner. The crowd was about to cross into the traffic circle. The car behind us blared its horn, and Hazim yelled something in Arabic. I looked ahead and saw cars next to us, coming the other direction. The car blared its horn again. Hazim turned to look at me.

"Fuck!" I said, turning back around. The crowd had filled the traffic circle. People were everywhere. As we drove away, I stared through the glass. I was too far away to make out any faces. I looked for a little figure wearing red pants, but it was impossible.

I woke with a jolt as the C-17 touched down at Landstuhl. The whole expanse of the metal cargo hold made a violent percussive ringing sound as the wheels slammed the tarmac again. The engines whined in reverse thrust, and I listed sideways, gripping the support bar. Sitting across from me, in the opposite row of seats bolted along the wall of the aircraft, a couple of guys cheered and clapped. A drink carton tumbled off a stack of crates behind us and slid along the metal floorboard toward the front. A few minutes later the rear cargo door dropped down, and behind the crates I could see a half-dozen wounded being unloaded on stretchers. We waited for the go-ahead, then single-filed it out the side door and toward one of several Blue Bird buses parked on the runway. It was three in the morning. The chilled night air struck me as I stepped outside. I hadn't even thought about Germany being cold. Hadn't even occurred to me that there were other places besides fucking sweltering Iraq. As I waited in line, the hair stood up on my bare arms and I shivered, but I didn't care. No one else did either, I could tell. Right there in front of us, the stretchers with IV bags were being hoisted through the rear doors of the bus. I nodded at one of the soldiers with tubes in her mouth, and she lifted her fingers to wave. All of us standing there—we were the lucky ones. Not only had we escaped the shit, but we could actually walk away.

On the bus I cracked the window and breathed in, staring outside at the dimly lit pubs and Bavarian houses as we meandered through the narrow streets of town. In the seats in front of me, two big-ass linebacker types were talking about getting stateside as soon as they fuckin' could. One said he couldn't wait to see his mom: "I straight up admit it, son. I muhfuckin' cried, I missed her so much!" he said. They exploded in a short burst of laughter. For a moment I realized I hadn't thought of my family. I hadn't even thought about getting back home, really. All I could think of was Abeer.

I pictured her again, outside that big window at the school, waving frantically. I winced, imagining the glass showering her little body. I inhaled quickly to shake off the thought and stared out the window again. We slowed to a stop, and I noticed a civilian car at the cross street, waiting for us to continue. The guy had gotten out of the vehicle and stood saluting us as we passed. I don't know what it was; I just started tearing up. It felt like everything all at once—sorrow, relief, worry, loss, freedom, guilt, being alone, wanting no one—all coming in a mess. I just leaned my head against the glass and let tears roll down and blur my vision.

"Specialist, we're disembarking." A guy stood over me, shaking my shoulder. I didn't realize I'd fallen asleep. I grabbed my gear out of the overhead and followed him to the exit. The medical center was huge, modern. We stepped off the bus right at the main entrance, which was also the emergency entrance.

A white-haired chaplain greeted each one of us, saying, "Welcome to Germany." *Right*, I thought, giving the guy a half smile, *more like another extension of America.*

When I got to my room, the nurses didn't seem to want to leave. They took my vitals and asked me questions, obviously assessing my mental capability. "Really, I'm fine," I said. "I'm sure there are other soldiers who need your help." They smiled and switched the TV on to CNN: Wolf Blitzer talking to an Aussie reporter in Baghdad, who was explaining why the surge wasn't working.

"Hey," I blurted out to one of the nurses before he closed the door. "Could you turn that shit?"

"No problem," he said, reaching up to the buttons.

"Wait," I said.

He looked over his shoulder at me.

"It's okay," I said.

"You sure?"

"Yeah. Leave it on."

At six the doc came in, examined me, asked more questions. I asked how to make calls to the FOB. The guy set me up with a DSN laptop to Skype with. After a few tries I was able to reach our team, and Ethan called back at eight. The video kept freezing and cutting out, so I borrowed a SAT phone and called him back.

"You'd better have a stein of Löwenbräu in your hand right now," he said.

I chuckled. "No, sorry. What's going on, man? Great to hear your voice."

"Totally dead, dude. Sittin' around, waitin' for a mission."

"Good. Hope it stays boring."

"How you doing? They fix your head?" he said facetiously.

"Ha ha, they got a whole team of doctors on it. Completely stumped."

He laughed. "Yeah, Freud's like, 'Zerr is nussing vee can do. He is juss plain coo coo.'"

"Yeah," I said, "the dumbasses can just keep believing that too, fine with me."

"Sorry, man," he said, sounding guilty. "I feel bad the plan kinda backfired . . . the idea was never for you to pull a Corporal Klinger."

"Oh dude, I could give a shit. My discharge is a good thing. Just wish *you* could get out."

"Well, speaking of which, looks like I might be stateside soon."

A wave of relief swept over me. "Really? That is fucking awesome!"

"Yeah. R&R leave program. We'll get up to fifteen days."

"Cool. So we gotta hook up, definitely."

"Definitely. Hey, you got some snail mail. From your mom and your sisters."

"Oh, okay," I said.

"They signed the outside of the envelope with all sorts of zany crayon colors. Want me to open it up?"

I paused for a second. "Uh, sure, I guess." I heard the paper tearing.

"So did they say how long you're gonna be there?"

"No, they're just going to run some tests, check for symptoms of TBI."

"It totally freaked me out back in Hamza. All that blood . . ."

"Nah, it was really nothing. Couple stitches. Nowhere near my personal best."

He chuckled. "Okay, let's see here," he said. "So I'm looking here at a . . . decidedly patriotic greeting card. Kid's drawing on the front, a house with one side painted like an American flag. Big SUV parked in front, mommy and daddy, a little boy. All holding hands, smiling. Across the sky it says 'Thank you for protecting our homes and our freedom.'"

As he talked I had the phone to my ear, leaning back in the chair so I could watch people in the hallway. A dark, thin girl came out of an entrance a few doors down. The elegant way she walked was striking. "Hey, Ethan, sorry. Hang on for a second," I said. I stepped outside as she came close, holding the phone to my side. "Excuse me," I said, and made up something about where I could find some bottled water. She began to answer. "Are you Ethiopian?" I said, interrupting her midsentence.

She smiled, looking quietly at me with dark eyes. She seemed to know what I was doing. "I get that a lot, but no. I'm just American," she said.

"No, no! It's a great look. Very exotic." There was an awkward pause. I tried to play it off. "Okay, so there's a vending machine? Second right?"

"That's correct," she said, pursing her mouth briefly. Her upper lip protruded just barely over her bottom one.

I smiled. "Thank you sooo much. It was very nice meeting you." I realized immediately how dumb that was. We hadn't exchanged names.

"You too," she said politely.

I stepped back into the room, putting the phone back to my ear. "Ethan, you still there?"

"Ah, workin' it, I see."

I chuckled. "Dude, she is . . . so hot. Poised, elegant. Wish you could see her."

"Cool, well, get her name, son!" he said. "Glad to see you are back to normal."

"Yeah. God, she's beautiful. So . . . formal."

"So you want me to read this card, or what?" he said, mocking disapproval.

"Oh. Okay. Sorry, man. Go ahead."

"All right. So it looks like all your sisters signed it. They drew little hearts and smiley faces. Let's see . . . Maddie says, 'Hey, bro, miss you bunches. You are my hero. They say we're fighting them over there so we don't have to fight them over here. Well, it's not *we* who are fighting them, it's *you*.'" Ethan paused. I inhaled sharply, feeling my jaw tighten. "Oh, and she underlined *you* like a zillion times."

"Yeah, they always do that. Who else signed?" I said.

"Well, looks like Karen. Jesus! She wrote a novel here." He took a deep breath. "'Dear beloved brother, my heart runneth over, it just yearns and reaches out to you each and every day.' Boy, she really lays it on thick, eh? 'Whether you are in a mess hall (do they still have those? I'm still in the *M*A*S*H* era! Ha ha) or a foxhole, I take comfort knowing God will watch over you, keep you in his hand for all—'"

"Okay, I get the point," I said. "Did my mom write anything?"

"Hmm, let's see," Ethan said. "Yeah, here at the bottom: 'Dear son, as all mothers do, I look at you and still see the child—my child—the one I carried for nine months. But I look at you now, all grown-up. And brave? Oh, far beyond brave, son. Valiant. I want you to know how proud I am of you, son. But most of all, I don't want you to worry. You are in God's hands, and you are a survivor. Don't you forget that. A survivor.'" Ethan chuckled. "She underlined *survivor* like a gazillion times."

"Hey," I said.

"Yeah?"

"Any word from Hazim?"

"No, he hasn't called."

"You got his number from the CSH though, right?"

"Uh," he said, "well, they couldn't give it out. Didn't seem to know where he was assigned, either."

"Oh, fucking great," I said, pausing to think.

"I dunno, man. We just gotta wait."

Oh Jesus Christ, I thought, *you're gonna pull your fatalism shit, after all we just went through?* "Can you just . . ." I exhaled. "Just let me know. Keep an ear out for any comm from Hamza."

"Yeah, yeah, of course," he said. There was a brief pause. "Okay, so, keep reading?"

"No," I said. "I'm good."

"Okay. Well, I'll let ya know about my R&R, though. We'll hook up stateside."

"Sure. But I'm serious, Ethan. You hear any goddamned thing, you email, text, call. All of the above."

"Roger that."

New York, 2016

know at the beginning I said that I'd saved the world, that I'd prevented the next 9/11. But I was only able to say that because it was proven to me, and this proof came to me after a long, long time. Six weeks after Landstuhl Ethan got his R&R. I was living in New York City. I drove down to Chattanooga to hang with him for a weekend. We sat outside at Brewhaus and drank pitchers of Hoegaarden all night 'til one of us threw up on the wooden bench seat and we were asked to leave. Stumbling back to the car, we laughed at our server, who was all buxom and had the cliché golden locks and dirndl dress but had a southern drawl that could make a Bavarian's ears bleed. We slept in, grabbed some carryout Carolina barbecue, and played Rock Band for the rest of the day. I asked about the little girl again but knew Ethan didn't know any more. I'd been asking about her constantly.

We were halfway through a case of beer already, and I got upset. Ethan did his best to empathize. "Sorry, man, wish I had an answer for you," he said, tipping his beer back. "It's like Hazim just fell off the face of the earth."

It was one of the few times I ever lashed out at him. "Gee, how do you do it, man?" I said, wiping my face on my shirt. "You're like the fucking Zen master of apathy."

"It's not apathy, a-hole," he said. "It's called survival. You want to obsess over this shit? Or you wanna accept it?"

"Fuck!" I screamed. "I just want to know the results!" I looked at him, almost pleading with him. "All that shit we did . . . to save that little girl. All that just to *never* know what it was for?"

"Pfft." He chuckled. "Hey, man, that's war for ya. It's part of the deal. No one gets to know."

I sat with that for a moment. He picked up the controller and exited the game, started scrolling through his downloaded movies. I got up from the recliner and stepped into the kitchen. "Where's the goddamned twenty-four beers we bought?"

"That was the last one, dude."

"Well, I'm fucking buying more, then," I said, grabbing my keys off the hook. I stepped outside and slammed the door.

S oon after that, Ethan rotated back to Iraq. He was there for another fifteen months, mostly in and around Baghdad, a detail that I wished I hadn't known. Sectarian violence there had gotten even worse. I hung out in New York, working jobs here and there, not really engaged, dealing with typical combat trauma shit—staring through the windshield at roadside trash, getting extremely agitated in crowds, sitting on the couch doing absolutely nothing, or obsessively playing scenes in my head, like getting the dreaded big phone call: "Sorry to inform you, Specialist Coffelt has been blown up. We understand you knew him."

When I wasn't bonkers OCD thinking about that shit, I was bored. Empty, wanting to be back in the suck, be useful. Ethan and I kept in contact; we even got to video call a couple times. The technology had gotten way better. My family kept calling, saying they wanted to stay in touch. Of course, I had come to know this meant just *saying* it, not actually getting in the car and driving up to see me. But that was fine. The war had inserted a Grand Canyon–sized chasm between me and them, and I'd accepted it. They spoke "God" on their side, and I spoke "whatever" on mine. I didn't want people close to me, anyway. I was deep inside myself, in a holding pattern, waiting. Bracing myself, actually. Not just for the dreaded phone call, but for the moment I knew was coming, when I'd have to give up on everything I'd been through: the war, the things I'd experienced, the things I'd done to people. Even the things I'd done *for* them. I'd have to give up because it had been too long and resolution had not come to me, and resolution would *never* come to me, just like Ethan had said. For a good part of the year, I was bracing myself for that moment.

When Ethan finished his tour and came home, things changed, but not as much as I'd thought they would. Of course I was totally pumped at first; we partied our asses off, watched a ton of movies, went back to the Brewhaus, saw that dirndl girl again. We poked fun at her, saying we'd been all over Germany but, gosh, couldn't quite place her accent. Got kicked out again. At four in the morning I called my boss in New York, just about the time he'd be locking up the bar, and told him I'd need a few more weeks off. I was slurring every word and giggling to Ethan, saying, "Shut up, I'm talking to my illuuuustrious commander!"

"Boss, not commander," Ethan said, trying to help.

When I put the phone back to my ear, I was summarily told not to come back. "Just promise me you'll get your shit together," he said.

I spent the next few months crashing at Ethan's, helping him at his mom's, mowing the lawn or putting linoleum down, but mostly staying up all night smoking weed. I wasn't online, wasn't taking calls or even answering texts most of the time. I figured I was too fucked up for people to handle. *Vines*, I thought. *What the fuck would they know about vines, anyway.*

I moved on from Ethan's but stayed in the area. He hooked me up with a friend of his, who helped get me a job downtown. She was part of the theatre crowd, so she knew people at a lot of the restaurants, and she just happened to also need a roommate. So I moved into the apartment. She and her girlfriend were hardly ever there, which was perfect for me. I worked 'til two, came home to my little room with the cheap dresser and the mattress on the floor, and slept. On weekends I'd hang with Ethan or go to some party I'd heard about at work. Anything to distract or insulate, maintain just the right distance from everything. So of course, this meant drugs. Molly, mostly; it seemed like it was the big thing. Acid here and there, though none of the hard shit or getting totally out of control. But every few months I'd hear someone mention Iraq, and I'd just walk out, maybe miss work the next day, and they eventually had enough. I landed another restaurant job, which lasted a little longer, but the same thing happened, so I was on to the next one. I managed to not get fired, but after a year of having to filter and tune out, ignore things I thought I'd heard, I couldn't take any more. So I tried working retail at the mall, but there were little girls there—Middle Eastern, even, in fucking Chattanooga.

And it seemed like I would go on that way forever, until one day Ethan got a Facebook message from Tuy. He was back for good and had been trying to get in touch with me. Ethan and I drove to DC for a weekend to visit him. He was making a shitload of money working for Homeland Security, driving a cool-ass little English Mini Cooper, and throwing au pair parties every weekend. The night we showed up, his townhouse in Tysons was jam-packed with people. "I'm Awesome" blared out of Tuy's laptop speakers, reminding me of Stuart's party in Iraq. Except there were women. Tons of them. Belgian girls speaking French with Moroccans, Salvadorians yapping away in the kitchen, making some dish called ceviche, a Swiss couple laughing at Tuy losing his ass in a round of poker. At one point Tuy was messing with a gay couple, accusing one of them of staring at Tuy's chest. He had the first few buttons of his shirt undone and was clasping it shut. "Hey, I *do* have eyes, you know!" Late in the night, after I'd had countless vodka tonics, Ethan and I stepped out on the deck to smoke. For a moment it was quiet, just the two of us talking about why American parties were nothing but shitty beer, vapid conversation, and trying to get laid. The sliding glass door opened and Tuy came blasting through, yelling what sounded like an insult in Italian at some girl with blue leather pants, but she laughed and started to blurt out a retort. Tuy just slid the door shut and turned to us. "Those crazy Cosa Nostra girls," he said in classic Tuy disdain-in-cheek style. He snapped his fingers at Ethan. "Redneck! Gimme *una sigaretti!*"

"Tuy!" I scolded him.

Ethan wasn't bothered a bit. "I believe *sigaretta* is the correct term," he said in his best James Bond.

Tuy pursed his lips and nodded, mocking respect. "A dumb redneck with brains. I like-ah you-ah style!"

Ethan chuckled. "No, just watched a ton of Roberto Benigni movies."

We stood there for a few minutes, shooting the shit. A motorcycle pulled up to the garage below the deck and honked obnoxiously. Tuy leaned over the railing. "Jason," he yelled, "did you bring Spanish mackerel?" They bantered back and forth, then Tuy went inside to coordinate the cooking. Ethan and I looked at each other, shaking our heads.

A guy with a plate of lamb came out on the porch, introduced himself as Thai, and started firing up the grill. Ethan finished off his drink and put it down on the railing. "Yeah, that Tuy, he's one, ahem, special individual," he said.

"Yeah, or just too insane to know he was in a fucking war."

Ethan stepped toward the door. "Okay, time to show these foreigner types a thing or two about Texas hold'em," he said. I stood out there, smoking, watching groups of girls below walk toward the townhouse garage.

"You guys talking about Tuy?" the guy at the grill said. He had a slight Vietnamese accent.

I turned around. "Ha ha, yep, who else?"

He laughed. "I known him for a long time, went to school in Maryland with him. A lot of people think he's crazy. He's actually incredibly smart."

"Pfft, oh yeah, I'm sure he is!" I said.

"No, really. Tuy is basically . . ." He thought for a moment. "Tuy is like the Great Gatsby, sort of—but minus the green light. You remember the book *Great Gatsby*?"

I tipped my drink up. "Not really, dude. Read it in high school."

"Yeah, the green light? You don't remember? It represents the girl. He was all the time reaching out for a green light across the bay where she lived. He was living the good life, rich as hell, pop'lar—all that things—but it was all just to get the girl."

"Oh, really?" I said, smirking. "So Tuy is the Great Gatsby."

"Yeah, except no girl. I mean"—he chuckled, pointing toward the kitchen—"plenty of girls, as you can see, but no *obsession* for a girl.

That's the difference. No obsession. No wasting time on shit he can't have."

He took the spatula and flipped the lamb over in a quick motion. I stared at it for a moment, thinking about what he'd said.

"Try some lamb?" he asked.

"No, thanks. I'm on a liquid diet," I said, and stepped inside for a refill. Kanye's "Runaway" was blaring from the speakers, and everyone was dancing and singing along, raising their glasses when he sang the verse. *Let's all toast to the douchebags and assholes*, I thought, *that's about right. No-names like us go off to war or try to save a little girl, and get shit for it. Meanwhile, Mr. Egotistical writes some trite-ass song about how fame's turned him into a jerk, and he gets all the recognition. What a joke.* I mixed my drink and then walked into the crowd, arms raised in the air, bobbing my head. "Ah, fuck it!" I yelled.

My memory of the rest of the night is sketchy, but I do remember pounding back more vodka tonics, trying to kiss some Syrian girl, and peeing right next to the front stoop while a couple just happened to be coming in. I tried to be funny and put out my hand to the guy, cheesily introducing myself, but they avoided eye contact and swerved around me. "Nice chat," I said, giggling as the door closed. I fumbled around for where I'd set my glass down, then gave up at some point. Ethan told me later he saw me out back near the garage, then saw me top the stairs next to the living room. He said he'd come in from the deck to keep an eye on me, but just as he had, I'd grabbed a wine bottle and tapped it to get everyone's attention. I don't remember the speech, not a thing. But Ethan said it started out embarrassingly, somewhat rambling, me announcing to everyone that the three of us had been in Iraq together and had met a little girl from the future, or the past, and maybe we had saved people, maybe we had killed people, who fuckin' knew. He said he'd full-on braced himself, expecting the speech to go terribly wrong, but I apparently ended up making a fairly coherent toast to Tuy, raising the bottle, saying, "Here's to Tuy, who saved himself from the war by being immune. Not for *letting go* of things that happened to him, but for never holding on to them in the first place." According to Ethan, people clapped, and some German girl spoke up and said yes, why should I suffer, it was not me who committed the war crimes, they were the ones who should be at The Hague.

S o that was how things changed for me. After Tuy's party, life seemed more urgent. Like waking with a start, realizing you'd left the stove on. When we got back to Chattanooga, I packed up my stuff, gave Ethan a big bear hug, and drove straight through to New York. I enrolled in the GI Bill program at NYU, then landed a temp job pulling security for a warehouse downtown. It was boring as hell, but it was decent money and allowed me time for studying. And reading. I got into novels like crazy. I wanted to live every experience, study every subject at school, know everything. Meanwhile, as a security guard I could be somewhat in my element, dressing in uniform, carrying a weapon, ready for action yet hoping for things to stay boring. Boring was good.

Eventually I got a job at the campus library, working with this crazy guy, Steve, who wore Hawaiian shirts, listened to Philip Glass, and read Camus and Kierkegaard. Said he went by the name "Dudeski." He was extremely colorful. He had yellowish hair that stood up like Einstein's, wore stylish Japanese rimmed glasses, and told stories with such excitement, it was like he himself was experiencing them for the first time. He'd tell me about his days stationed at the DMZ and his Korean *yobos*—something like a live-in call girl-slash-servant-slash-cook, maid, courier, translator. He'd tell stories about meeting Mapplethorpe at a party, the year he got totally obsessed with Stanley Kubrick films, or what it was like doing X and the whole rave scene. "How did Hunter S. Thompson put it?" he said. "Life's journey is not to arrive safe and all pretty, it's to skid in sideways, totally spent . . . saying, what a fuckin' ride."

We'd roll the cart upstairs and take like two hours to reshelve the books because he'd remember another incredible story: "Back in the eighties I worked for the White House during the Iran-Contra scandal. I was like green as shit. One time they told me, 'You, take this cart, run it across the street to the records building. They'll give you—' I don't remember, it was like three or four of those clunky magnetic tapes. 'Those are email files, okay? Bring them right back here. Don't stop anywhere. Don't go anywhere, period.' Well, guess what?" He exploded in laughter. "Turns out they were Ollie fucking North's emails! Back then people thought, 'Oh, I can just delete my email, and it's gone.' They had no idea we had backups of all that shit. Un-fucking-believable!"

And he talked about Iraq too, something no one who had not been there ever would, except maybe rattling off some canned bullshit about "Thank you for your service" or making some useless and maudlin symbolic gesture. Dudeski actually knew the shit. He had read everything about it. And he knew what he was talking about. Wilson, Plame, the CIA leak, the infamous sixteen words. He knew exact timelines, names, events, like it was his Watergate story, and he was not afraid to be pissed. It was a made-up war, plain and simple, he said. "Americans tricked into a complete waste of money, and thousands—*thousands*—killed or injured, for what? No fucking reason. Bush and Cheney are war criminals, fucking war criminals." I wasn't offended. Not at all. It was the first time I'd actually met someone like that—someone with a pulse, who cared, someone not personally affected by Iraq who was, in fact, personally affected by Iraq.

"Remember the 'bad apples,' as Rumsfeld called 'em? Those assholes who tortured prisoners at Abu Ghraib?" he said. "I'm reading a book called *The Lucifer Effect*. There *are* no bad apples, there are only bad barrel makers. Bad barrels come from a factory. Who runs the factory?" he said, raising his eyebrows and nodding for emphasis. "Who runs the factory."

And I told him what happened in Hamza. Told him the entire story. He leaned on the book cart and listened, then stopped me to go grab coffee. He wanted to hear every single detail. He didn't bat an eyelash at the relativity stuff. Almost seemed to just take it at face value: I went back in time, changed the past. No biggie.

"There's a ton of shit science doesn't yet know," he said. "Centuries after Newton, and we don't know what gravity is. Einstein said the speed of light was *c*, now experiments contradict that. Photons are waves and particles at the same time? Come on." But he did make a big deal of me going on my journey—"choosing karma," as he put it, "staring into the abyss and saying, 'Fuck you. I will *not* become you.'" He said he was absolutely blown away, said he was inspired, even jealous, that I had made perhaps the most profound contribution to society I would ever make.

"Yeah, except," I said, "I'll never know, more than likely, if I ever saved the little girl, the woman, anyone, really."

He shook his head. "Oh, come on! Are you kidding me? I send money to Doctors Without Borders every month. Do I ever see how many lives it saves? Does my money even get there?" He chugged his espresso and tossed it at the trash can. "It's karma, man. Best-case scenario? You saved lives. Worst case?" He twitched his eyebrows at me again. "What's the worst case? No change! That's what. Everything stays exactly as it was going to. Chaos theory: Butterfly flaps its wings. Six weeks later comes the tropical storm." He got all animated. "But what you did, you stopped the butterfly, man. No missile *kaboom*, no bad guys getting blown up. No terrorist bellies splitting open, spilling out hundreds of thousands of little terrorist babies scurrying about." He waved his hands across the table, wiggling his fingers.

A nother thing I told you at the beginning was that this story was a repeat of what happened to me when I was thirteen. A "reprise," I think I called it. Well, it's true; my losing my mind after 9/11, going to Iraq, trying to save the world from evil, doing what God couldn't do, or refused to do, whatever, was nothing more than me reliving what had happened the summer in Brazil when I got that devastating letter from Mom. I had to join up. I was going to ride in valiantly on my steed and save the town; I would be like Iron Man with his high-tech shit and kill bin Laden; I would be the guy who clips the wires on the ticking time bomb. It's so stupid what we do, spending huge chunks of our lives acting out scenes from our past that were seared into our psyches for some random reason; we're like toy robots with

OCD hitting up against the wall over and over, flailing our arms in preset whirring motions. We fall in the mud one day and wash our hands a thousand times a day forever. We lose something as a kid, and fifty years later we're still searching.

But I wouldn't have told this story if this had been all there was. It was what happened next that did it, something I had never imagined as the conclusion, had no idea my actions could have brought about, and even in all my delusion had never thought of or attempted. But this time there was no repeat, no reprise of things before it, which is exactly why it changed everything.

A few months after I graduated, I got a text from Ethan. He said he'd had a major WTF moment and realized we'd seen each other like twice in the last four years. "I'm callin' in a FRAGO, a-hole. Driving to NYC this weekend and we gunna party."

I laughed and texted back, "Roger that." I told him, "Just have to work Fri but after that free all wknd." On Friday morning he called me and said he'd already left, and he might be in New York early enough to swing by the library and see if I was really employed.

"Just a routine check," he said dryly. "It's something we have to do, part of the job."

I chuckled. "I understand," I said, and gave him directions.

By the time he got into Manhattan, found parking, and called me, I was already off work, so I waited at Washington Square Park across the street. I took him on a quick tour of the library and suggested we grab some espresso at Third Rail. "It's a nice little hangout. I go there a lot after work," I said.

"Cool," he said. We walked down to Third and then west across Thompson. Ethan began recounting his driving adventure, replete with funny anecdotes like how Interstate 81 was a goddamned autobahn, and his poor Bronto—he lovingly referred to his Plymouth as the Brontosaurus—could barely make it up to sixty before entire fenders started rattling loose.

I laughed as we made our way down the sidewalk, squeezing between students with backpacks and people in suits and tennis shoes pushing bikes. We stopped at the crosswalk on Sullivan, and I pointed over toward the coffee shop. "We just need to cross here. It's down half a block," I said. The light turned, and we started across, facing a mob of students coming the other way. I sensed Ethan was caught up behind me. Just before I reached the curb, a slender young woman wearing a yellow hijab passed by. I didn't really notice; I saw Middle Eastern people at school all the time.

"Hey!" Ethan called out behind me.

I stopped on the curb and turned. The woman had passed him, but he was turned toward her. She had slowed down and had her head turned around toward Ethan too. He glanced at me, then looked back at her, and I realized she had now stopped and was letting people pass by her. I stepped back onto the street, trying to see who it was, then made my way toward them. I thought maybe it was Homa, a girl I'd helped a couple of times at the library, but she wouldn't have known Ethan. I weaved through the crowd and got up to them. They were in the middle of the street. We stood there for an awkward few seconds, us staring at her, her at us, a nervous but excited smile on her face. I was a fraction of a second from the lightbulb going off when she said, "I'm Abeer."

I stood there in shock, taking her features in. Light caramel skin, deep-brown eyes, tiny nose.

"Oh my God!" I said. "I couldn't tell. I can't see your wavy hair!"

She began to pull her hijab down, and a car blared its horn at us. We burst into laughter. Ethan motioned us toward the curb.

"How 'bout we not get run over?" he said sarcastically.

We walked quickly. I instinctively put my hand on Abeer's shoulder as we scooted out of the way of traffic and onto the curb.

Then I turned to her, smiling and shaking my head. "So . . . what are the chances? What are you doing in the US? Well, obviously NYU . . . and you speak English? That's just crazy!" I was not even sure how much she understood.

"Well, yes, I live here with my relatives. I will be studying fine art."

Her inflection was slightly off but wasn't bad at all. I looked at Ethan incredulously. "Frickin' fluent. Can you believe this?" She grinned. I stood there staring at her with a huge smile, but my eyes were full of tears. Instinctively I hugged her, then realized it might not be cool with her. But she seemed okay.

"Coffee?" Ethan said.

"Oh yeah," I said, "we were gonna grab espressos. You want some?"

"Of course. Yes!" she said.

"You sure? You're probably on your way somewhere."

She shook her head. "No, it is okay. I just am shopping . . . for food. I go later. No problem."

When we got inside Third Rail, I wasn't sure it would be the right place to talk. It was hip enough, with its brick and glass and its wooden plank flooring, but gobs of people were crowded at the gray industrial metal counter in the back, ordering, checking their cells, hanging out talking. I turned around to ask Ethan and Abeer what they thought, but Ethan was already at the corner table near the front window, where people had just gotten up to leave. He looked over at me and gave me his standard "I kick ass" look and plopped down, tossing his keys on the table.

Abeer seemed amused. "Ethan already has an occupation of the café."

I laughed. "Oooh. Good one! Hey, it's what we're good at, right?"

By the time we got our specialty espresso drinks and Abeer's chai, a lot of the students had gone outside. Abeer bounced onto the wooden bench and pulled her purse off her shoulder, her back to the front bay window.

"You want to sit here, where it's more comfortable?" I said. She shook her head politely, appearing momentarily puzzled.

Ethan jumped all over that. "Dude, she's not seven years old anymore!"

Abeer cracked up. I noticed a curl of dark hair peeking out from underneath her hijab, atop her long forehead. Ethan stared down at the fleur-de-lis pattern on the surface of his latte. "Oh, come on! Am I supposed to *drink* this? Looks like it belongs in frickin' MOMA or something!" Abeer and I laughed. *He's so brilliant in these situations*, I thought, *helping everyone relax and feel comfortable*. I realized how nervous I was, anticipating talking to Abeer. As we started talking, it immediately felt warm and natural, and I was so curious to hear things, but I was also scared.

She told us about her life growing up, how she'd done well in school after all, always wanting to come to America, studying English, even on her own, and her parents agreeing when she was fifteen to send her to New York. She seemed to hesitate slightly when she mentioned her parents, and I inhaled sharply, feeling immediately nauseated. So many years I had spent waiting. Hoping to hear from someone. Needing to know what had happened in Hamza. That everyone had survived the missile. Now I could find out. Finally. But maybe they hadn't, and that was something I didn't feel prepared to hear.

Abeer reached into her purse. "I really love New York, but sometimes I am so sad to not see my mum and my father. You want to see? I have pictures."

I leaned across the table. "Oh my God, yeah, I remember him. He was so cool." I felt my body relax a little.

She continued, talking about how she got into art—she had begun drawing when she was very young—how she was working on getting a studio and wanted one day to go to Paris. As she spoke I watched her vibrant expressions, her hypnotic brown eyes, and the way she pursed her lips for emphasis. And the black curl continued to dance above her forehead. I smiled, thinking of that adorable and precocious little girl in red pants making her speech in front of the elders. I immediately thought of all those other little girls. My stomach reacted. I tried to steer my mind away from it. Abeer paused to take a sip of her chai, which she brought to her mouth quickly with both hands.

"Oh!" she said, catching me staring at her forehead, "you can see my hair, of course, like when I was young?" And she untied her hijab and pulled it away from her, revealing a full head of pitch-black curls. She ran her fingers through in a quick, careless movement. "It's not many Iraqi girls who have this hair. Most are long and straight. I am weird."

Ethan and I laughed. "Okay, *now* you look exactly like I remember," Ethan said, immediately catching himself. "Except . . . I mean, above the neck, at least."

She laughed and looked at him with wide eyes, acting offended. "Well, I hope so!"

I shook my head. "I am terribly sorry for my colleague here, he has no couth."

"What is cooch?" she said to me. I could hear Ethan almost explode, covering his mouth and failing in his attempt to not let any air escape.

"Couth," I said, pronouncing the *th* to a ridiculous extreme. "It means, like, having manners."

She repeated it: "Okay, couth."

Ethan and I talked about ourselves and what we'd done since coming home after the war—me being messed up for a while, ending up in New York; Ethan living in Soddy so he could look after his mom and try to fix her house that was falling apart. As usual, Ethan was better at getting the chronology right, even for stuff that had happened to me, so I let him talk, mostly. I was anxious to get back to Abeer's story, even if parts of it scared the shit out of me. It's not like I had planned on ever seeing her, and I'd had no idea whatsoever what I'd say. *Just shut up, Ethan. Abeer has to tell us how many people died*, I thought. *How many little kids we failed to save.*

I felt a full-on stomachache as I rehearsed ways I could broach the subject with her. Ethan was talking about his sister Deb and how she left home when she was in tenth grade, came up here to New York to try to make it as a dancer at only fifteen. I glanced out the window. A guy standing next to a meter lit up his cigarette as formless figures walked in front of him along the sidewalk. It had gotten dark.

"Gotta run to the little boys' room. Back in a second," I said.

Abeer looked up at me as if about to say something.

"You guys keep talking. I've heard this part." In the small unisex bathroom I splashed water on my face, hoping it would help. I sat and tried to go for a few minutes, wet my face again, stared in the mirror.

Finally someone jiggled the door handle. I dried off with one of the soft white towels and left.

Now the café was empty except for the three of us. From the counter I got Ethan's attention. "Another round?"

"Sure," he said. Abeer nodded.

I ordered, paid, and then stood there to wait, but the girl behind the counter opened her big mouth and said she'd bring them to the table.

"Sure, well," I said, "I'm gonna go out for a smoke."

The dude who was there before had left, so I took his place at the curb, watching Ethan and Abeer inside. They seemed to be pretty comfortable. I went through three cigarettes waiting, and when the drinks arrived, Ethan rapped on the glass obnoxiously and waved at me to come in. I pointed to my cig and turned around, pacing back and forth. I smoked it down as much as I could, then finally went in. Ethan was in the middle of a story: "So anyway, because of the election parade, the bus was going like two miles an hour, so I just got off and had to walk the entire last mile or so to the metro."

"Oh, wow, so you missed the plane?" Abeer said.

"No, no, I made it . . . barely," Ethan said, "but only 'cause the cab driver went like Mach 10 through downtown Manhattan. I suspect he must have been waiting all month to just open her wide up, and soon as I said I was late for the flight, that gave him just the excuse he needed."

She laughed, seeming very amused by Ethan's story.

"I mean, the dude was flying! At one point he roared down half an entire block on the wrong side of the road, and got up to the light—which had just turned green, and cars were already starting to go—and he swerved at a forty-five-degree diagonal through the intersection, jumping in front of the cars going our direction, and at the same time barely avoiding head-on collisions with the ones coming at us. It was pretty insane."

At that point I recognized the story. "Oh, this was your trip up here to see Deb and Tony."

Ethan turned to me. "Yeah, the time I flew back two days before 9/11."

Abeer's eyes widened. "Wow, you must be so lucky you left before, because you could not after, I heard."

"Oh, I know. All flights were grounded for three days; JFK was a god-awful nightmare." Ethan motioned to me. "He and I actually came back up here right after. Drove, of course. And having a car in the city, oh my God. New York was just complete chaos." He turned to me. "Dude, you remember."

"Yeah, it was pretty bad," I said. I felt my body tense up. I didn't want to go there, and I think they sensed it. For a few moments we sat and sipped our drinks, turning to look out the window to at least do something. It felt awkward. I was hoping Ethan would save us with a witty remark, but it was Abeer who spoke first.

"I have to—I want, rather—to tell you something," she said, looking at each of us individually. *Oh no.*

"It is about Hamza, what happened."

"I'm not sure I am—not sure I can hear this," I blurted out.

Abeer stopped, and there was another lull.

I attempted to respond. "It's just that—"

"He's just nervous," Ethan interjected. "He's lost a lot of sleep over it, wondering how bad it was—the explosion, all that."

Abeer looked shocked, confused. "But you don't know?"

She had addressed the question to me, but I just stared at her, my brain racing one hundred miles an hour. I felt the muscles in my arms and face tremble.

"No," Ethan answered. "We left—we had to get back. And then . . ."

"We never heard from Hazim," I said.

"That is bad, very bad!" she said, shaking her head. "For all this time?"

"Yep," Ethan said. I nodded.

"You must know, then, that everyone is living!" She waved her hands excitedly in front of us. "Everyone. Every person that day. They are all okay! You have saved them. I am very upset because of all these years that you did not know."

I put my hand up to my lips. "So, are you saying that every person there survived?"

"Yes! Of course!"

"Not one person died. Not even the old man who got thrown into the air?"

Abeer nodded. "Yes, the shopkeeper. He has broken legs. He does not walk, but he is not died."

I laughed, not because of her English but because it felt like a pressure relief valve had been activated. "Jesus! That is awesome! I can't believe it!" I looked at Ethan.

"Yeah, pretty amazing. I saw some pretty gruesome stuff. I thought for sure five or so wouldn't make it."

"Well"—Abeer took a quick sip of her chai— "I was very young, so it is all what I have heard many times from people."

"You sure they didn't just *tell* you that? So you wouldn't be upset?"

Abeer laughed. "No, impossible! The whole town, they know this story very well. Every year is a big day; they cook food, tell the story, people from that day speak."

Ethan and I looked at each other. "Wow, like an anniversary celebration," I said.

Abeer nodded. "Yes. Do you understand? You have saved a lot of people. The whole town knows about you. You are famous."

I felt a chill hearing those words, yet I wasn't sure I believed them. She reached into her purse. "Let me show you something." She pulled her smartphone out and swiped through a few pics, then held it in front of us. "This is the day I left to come to New York." Ethan and I leaned in to see. Abeer and her parents stood in front of a large mural. Her father, dressed in a plaid shirt and sandals, smiled proudly, his head cocked slightly upward and his arm around Abeer's shoulders. Her mom stood close, wearing a turquoise hijab and glasses. Her arm hung by her side, clasping Abeer's hand.

"Oh, what a great picture!" I said. "That's your mom?"

"Yes, Shazia is her name." She let us look for a few seconds.

I sat back up in my chair. "They seem very nice," I said.

Abeer shook her head. "But look, do you see what we are in front of?" She zoomed the image with her fingers, showing the details of one part of the mural, then swiped to the right and back again. "Wait, it is hidden. Maybe I have a better one."

She looked around and showed us another shot, just of the mural. It was painted on the entire side of a building I recognized right away as the school in Hamza. And I was immediately blown away, not just by the size, but also by the complexity, so many things going on in it, and such elaborate detail. The style seemed like a mix of Dalí and one of those three-dimensional chalk drawings. I knew immediately it was her work. The entire background was painted in photo-realism, just like what she'd done with the colored pencils. There was a large window being shattered, and the nose of a humongous missile was piercing the glass, coming at us. Superimposed on that image, a number of characters, each frozen in time, reacted to the impact. One stood out from the others because it was clearly a depiction of me. I was in full ACU dress—helmet, vest, dark sunglasses, everything. I was diving away from the blast, my mouth stretched impossibly wide open, and my arm was reaching out as if in a sweeping motion.

My eyes moved around the image. There were ropes drifting in midair, coiled around people, pregnant women with transparent bellies, a suicide bomber with his chest exploding, little numbers and dates flying out of him. It was mind-boggling how much was going on.

"Jesus!" I said, scrolling and zooming in for more detail. "I am absolutely . . . completely amazed by this. Oh my God, is that Ethan?"

"Yes, he is with Hazim near the boat," she said.

"What is that in his hand? Looks like a—oh, it is a DVD, it's the DVD!"

I looked at Ethan. My eyes started to well up. But I was smiling, and overjoyed, and relieved and astonished and incredulous all at the same time.

"But the boat, the helo? How could you know—"

She smiled at me. "Oh, from my dreams. Even still I can remember. Everything."

Ethan took the phone. I sat back and wiped my eyes.

Abeer smiled. "It's okay. Some people who sees it cry."

"Oh my God!" Ethan said. "The bubble pipe. Is this you?" He rotated the phone around.

"Yes," she said, turning to me. "You are carrying me, see? That is my tiny butt."

I laughed, but at the same time tears came uncontrollably. I hadn't noticed before, but I was holding Abeer under my left arm, her legs flailing. She was wearing her red pants. Several bubbles with images in them floated up from the pipe she had clenched in her teeth.

"And you see?" Abeer said, pointing. "Here is the rope. It is tied around me and comes here and then around and connects to you!" Her voice was full of excitement.

"Right, just like in the helicopter."

I noticed the barista leaning over the counter toward us. "Hey guys, we're closing in ten minutes."

"Okay," I said.

Ethan motioned with his hands to get our attention. "Okay, hold on. Abeer, this is obviously symbolic—okay, earth-shatteringly symbolic—I get that, but nobody knows what this means, right?"

Abeer's eyes widened. "Oh, no! Everyone knows. Hazim and I told everyone the story." She waved her hand at the image. "This painting. Everyone knows the meaning."

I shook my head. "Holy shit." I smiled sheepishly at Abeer. "Sorry. But this is unbelievable." My swearing didn't seem to faze her. She took the phone again.

"So you must see. The rope? It is tied from me to you, but look." She slid the image to the right.

I saw the rope, coiled up, floating, but one end disappeared behind us into the distance and wrapped around a man being yanked backward, trying to hold a cell phone to his ear. His face was painted to look censored by pixilation.

"Okay," I said, "anonymous guy making a call?"

"The guy Hazim tried to call," Ethan said.

"Yes! But see Hazim? He is *not* on his phone this moment," Abeer said. I watched her explain, trying to take it all in. "And see the rope is around his cell? And then it travels to these men here being pulled back?"

I squinted. "Hmm, yeah, a bunch of them," I said, "and they each have only one leg."

"Not legs. They are also flowers," Abeer said.

"Shit, this is deep," Ethan said.

"Oh, so this is like the play!" I said.

"No, no! This *is* the play," she said. "It is the same story. Do you know what this is about?"

Ethan and I looked at her blankly.

"Well, just like the play," she said, "these men here, they are bad men, they are going to do something . . . something horrible."

"Terrorist attack?" Ethan said.

Abeer hesitated, looking at Ethan. She zoomed in on one of the faces of the men. It looked demonic, distorted, with eyes like black holes but bulging outward.

She addressed both of us. "This painting. It is not about what you did in Hamza only. It is what was *going* to happen." She paused for a moment.

Ethan raised his eyebrows. "But that was the drone strike, right? *That* was what was going to happen. That's what we stopped."

She nodded. "Yes, yes, but . . . the man with no face? With the cell? I cannot tell you who he is, and no one knows, almost. It is a secret. But he was Al-Qaida in Iraq. Very important person, very important. And the missile at the school was going to kill him."

Ethan's mouth dropped open. "Oh my God! He was the target!" he said, turning to me. "You remember on the river? Hazim tried to call? And the guy's wife answered, and he wasn't there?"

"Oh, he didn't want to use his own cell phone," I said.

"Yes. But then everything changed that day when you came. And when the sheikh and tribal elders saw what you did, they talked to him and told him not to do it, and it never happened."

I looked at Abeer. "I'm sorry. I'm gonna have to swear again; you have *got* to be shitting me!"

She shook her head. "No, it is not shitting! You can ask everyone."

We burst into laughter. "Abeer!" I said.

Ethan looked at me and made a *tsk* sound. "And *you* doubted the mission."

I rolled my eyes. "Hey, so maybe Hazim couldn't contact us."

"Right," Ethan said, tipping his cup back to finish off his drink. "Wanted to, but the sheikh put the kibosh on it? Who knows."

"Hold on," I said, turning to Abeer. "You said all this is the same as the play. I don't get that."

"Yeah, we never got to hear the story," Ethan said. "Hazim was supposed to tell us, but . . ."

"Yeah." I nodded. "All we know is that it was based on some kind of legend."

"Oh," she said, "I thought all this time you know the story. Well . . ." She took a deep breath. "Well, it is kind of long, and my English, I hope, is okay, but I can tell you."

"They're closing up, so I guess we should leave first," Ethan said.

Abeer stood up and wrapped her hijab around her head. I gathered the cups and set them in the bin on the counter. We walked out together. Ethan held the door for Abeer, and I said good night to the guys in the back. The little bell rang as the door closed behind us.

"So," Abeer began, "like you say in stories for children, once upon a time . . ."

The Killing Flower

In the ancient land once called Sumer, between the two great rivers, lived a rich and powerful king. His kingdom was vast, and all who lived there were blessed. The fields were filled with grain, the cows gave birth, and every tree they planted yielded fruit.

The king had three sons: Utu and Shukaletuda, who were the eldest, and Nergal, who was younger. And the king was very proud of them. He began to build magnificent hanging gardens filled with olive and gum trees, acacia and sage, and plants of all kinds. The birds made their nests in the branches; fish filled the ponds; and the walls were adorned with beautiful flowers. A day would come when one of his sons would become king, and he wanted them to see the great prosperity of the kingdom.

But just over the mountains there was another kingdom, much smaller and not powerful, but rich with wild plants and creatures of all sorts. And in this land, in certain spots along the banks of the river, grew the most beautiful flower on earth. Its color, which could not be found anywhere else, was so radiant it could be seen through skin, and its petals made sounds when anyone came close. The flower had great value to the people. Its leaves were dried and made into tea, its oils could be used for perfumes or fuel for lamps, and its roots were known to make wounds heal within hours.

Shukaletuda, who had taken great interest in overseeing the hanging gardens, came to the king one day. "Father, our kingdom must have this flower. We are great and powerful, and it would be wise to possess for trade."

The king was hesitant, looking upon his magnificent gardens. "Yes, I see you are ambitious. But we already have abundance and are wanting of nothing. This flower which you see in someone's hand, do not call it yours."

Shukaletuda, who was envious and bitter for not being very skilled at gardening, turned quickly toward the king. "You are wrong, Father. This flower was created for us. It has been told to me in a vision by Enlil himself."

The king looked at Shukaletuda, knowing to be cautious of his son's words. "Well, go if you must, but remember: like us they can choose their gods, and thus visions, to their liking."

Shukaletuda, despite knowing his father's meaning, crossed the mountains with a group of merchants, found the river, and gathered as many flowers as he could. They returned with a myriad of crates, which they stored in a locked room, and sold the plant in its many forms to the people of the kingdom.

But one night, after Shukaletuda had spent the whole day trading and selling and had made the last remaining flower into tea, there came a terrible thunder. In every house, in every garden, in every vase or window of the kingdom, the flowers all at once turned into a thousand savage lions, who roared across the land, killing multitudes in their path, until they returned over the mountains.

The next morning the king woke to find Shukaletuda dead, and was beside himself with grief. He stayed inside the fortress, weeping. Utu came to him and said, "Father, justice and vengeance are my calling. Send me across the mountains to kill the lions and punish the kingdom."

The king was hesitant, hearing the mourning of his people outside the window. "Utu, you must do what is lawful, but nothing else, for it could bring us more harm."

Utu argued, being arrogant and unforgiving. "No, Father, you are wrong. They must know our wrath, to never forget our dominion. Only this way will we be protected."

The king was troubled by these words but reluctantly agreed. "Go, do what you must, but remember: vengeance gives birth like no mother, because it is to herself."

Utu, despite knowing his father's meaning, gathered hunters

and warriors to cross the mountains and invade the land. First they speared the lions, which were sleeping soundly beneath the trees. Then they raided every village, slaughtering every sheep, every lamb, every calf the people used for sustenance. Finally Utu went to the riverbank and took a flower to keep as a symbol of the battle.

When he got back to the kingdom he placed it in a cage, to be careful. "Look, Father, this is to honor our loved ones, and now we will be safe."

But that night, when the kingdom was asleep, the flower turned into a roaring river of snakes, which spilled across the land and over the mountains, killing everyone in its path.

When the king woke the next morning, he found Utu dead, and was struck with horrible grief and anger. He ran to his youngest son. "Nergal, you are known for your rage and fury. Go without hesitation, take the army, every single soldier, cross the mountains, and burn the entire kingdom. Only this will save us."

But this time it was Nergal who was hesitant. For months he had had strange dreams of the flower, of him protecting it in order to save his father's kingdom. Finally he understood. "But Father, you are wrong!" he said.

"Are you not a warrior?" the king yelled. "Do as I command, or you will never be ruler!"

Nergal was unsure, but he agreed. He assembled the army and crossed the mountains. But when he reached the top he looked out on the small kingdom before him and looked behind him at his own, and said to himself, "These are the same." He ran ahead of the army and down to the river, and he gathered as many flowers as he could. Then he ran off in secret and found a cave in which to hide them. There Nergal planted the flowers and stayed, guarding the cave from the army and watering the soil. A few days later he brought them out of the cave and into the sun. He planted them near a stream at the foot of the mountain, climbed to the top, and built a house, and there he stayed, watching for danger from either direction.

Years passed, and the king finally died, and Nergal became ruler of the land. He forbade anyone by law to cross the mountains, and he traveled across many lands, telling the story of the killing flower. One day he woke to a strange sound and saw a radiant light shining through the walls of the fortress. He looked out the window toward the hanging gardens, and to his amazement, the colors of the flower were everywhere. A wide path of blooming flowers could be seen winding across the land and up and over the mountains. He gathered the people of the kingdom and declared a day of celebration of the killing flower, for all to make use of it as they wished, for every purpose.

"But forget my father's words," he warned them as he reached down and picked one, holding it out in front of him, "forget these words, all you merchants, warriors, leaders, and all you future kings, and we shall perish." And he opened up his palm and looked at the flower. "My kingdom, tell me! What are the words?"

And they all answered together: "This flower, which you see in someone's hand, do not call it yours."

Acknowledgments

Novels tend to be associated solely with authors, their creation attributed to whoever's name is on the cover. Having gone through the process, I realize what mythology this is. This book is the product of an entire team—those on the payroll and off, consultants, beta readers, coworkers, friends, and family. Without this awesome team *The Killing Flower* simply could not have been created.

First there was my girlfriend, Bonnie, who provided the safe environment to create in, but also knew not to let me escape: "Oh, no. This one you're going to finish."

There was my buddy Greg, who marked up the first drafts—dude, you are such a natural at this stuff it's annoying!

Steve, Sharon, and Derek, your consulting on all things military saved me from total embarrassment. Kay, my translator, you encouraged me to publish and shared your journey in creating *The Iraqi Cookbook*.

In no way can I take credit for the transformation of my story into an actual novel. Katherine and Christina, you have got to be the best editors any author would ever need. You adopted this story as you would your own, totally got what I was going for, coached and guided me, corrected me, and held my hand the entire way. I could write a book on just how invaluable this process and interaction has been.

Amber, your interior design was spot on from the beginning. Lori, you were a stickler and it paid off. And finally, Carl, what a brilliant piece of artwork you came up with for the cover—a simply awesome interpretation of this story. I am forever indebted to you.

I want to also thank my parents. Dad, your objective analysis just days after 9/11 was what got me thinking about the root causes of terrorism. Mom, you left this world a little better than when you got here; this was my inspiration.

W.K. Dwyer has written short stories and poetry for decades and was trained as a musician under J. D. Blair. Following the events of September 11, he stopped creating music to focus on writing and podcasting about the root causes of terrorism.

W.K. holds a bachelor's degree in aerospace engineering and has done post-graduate work in AI and cognitive science. He works as a government contractor, developing targeting systems for counterterrorism.

This is his first novel.

Twitter: wkdwyer
Email: dwyerwk@gmx.com